OKLAHOMA
Weddings

HARDWORKING MEN AND SOFTHEARTED WOMEN
MEET IN THREE NOVELS

CATHY MARIE HAKE
KELLY EILEEN HAKE
JENNIFER JOHNSON

BARBOUR
PUBLISHING

Published by Barbour Publishing, Inc., P.O. Box 719, Uhrichsville, Ohio 44683, www.barbourbooks.com

Our mission is to publish and distribute inspirational products offering exceptional value and biblical encouragement to the masses.

ecpa Member of the
Evangelical Christian
Publishers Association

Printed in the United States of America.

In His Will

Dedication

To my daddy—who has been a wonderful example
and a reflection of how deep and true
our heavenly Father's love can and will be.

Chapter 1

"The old man's gone to the Big Daddy in the sky."

Dylan Ward winced. The opening remark set the tone for a memorial service that turned into a full-fledged travesty. No respect. No reverence. No words of redemption. Their pastor from back home got sick, so the funeral home hastily plugged in a replacement. Though he didn't hold with judging another man's walk with the Lord, Dylan suspected this so-called preacher had gotten his degree from a matchbook cover. While leading them in the Lord's Prayer, he flubbed the recitation in several spots.

Following that debacle, Miller Quintain's relatives gave eulogies revolving around memories of his financial generosity. Their words became a can-you-top-this, he-loved-me-most competition.

Unwilling to let a good friend's life be summed up in such shallow terms, Dylan rose and buttoned his suit coat as he walked to the front of the chapel. Turning to face the small collection of people, he caught sight of a woman who must have slipped in late. She sat at the very back, alone. Over her black dress, she wore a blue-and-green-plaid flannel shirt. Everything about this funeral was surreal.

Dylan looked at the rose-decked casket and then faced the room. "When I was seven, Miller Quintain told me a man can live with gritty hands and muddy boots, but he's got to have a clean heart. . . ."

A short while later, Miller's relatives jockeyed for one of the four seats at the graveside. If last night's storm hadn't softened the hard-packed Oklahoma soil, their crocodile tears could. Dylan stood off to the side and understood why Miller specified the service was for family only. He'd been a simple man who didn't want a lot of fuss and wouldn't want the folks back home to witness a circus like this.

Things would get much worse before the day ended. After several years of open discussion, Dylan knew what Quintain's will would hold. Miller warned him to expect a nasty scene once these greedy relatives discovered they weren't inheriting his fortune.

The woman in the flannel shirt walked the long way around the cemetery and silently took a place a few feet from Dylan. High cheekbones and slightly slanted green eyes set her apart—she didn't look anything like Miller's relatives. She'd put her mahogany-red hair into a sophisticated bun at the top of her head and probably used half a can of hair spray today to keep it under control. Small wisps teased their way free and coiled into twirly, springy tendrils.

The way she clutched a bunch of wildflowers to her heart touched Dylan—not only because of her sorrow, but also because of the devotion it revealed. Instead of buying something, she must've gotten up early to gather the bouquet from the Oklahoma countryside Miller had loved. Silently she slipped forward, laid the offering by the head of the casket, and stepped back.

The substitute showed up and nervously rubbed his hands together. "You've already said your good-byes. It's an emotional time. Why don't we say the Twenty-second Psalm together in closing?" He looked at the redhead. "Do you know it? Would you like to start us off?"

She gave him a baffled look, seemed to think for a moment, and slowly nodded. "My God, my God, why have you forsaken me? Why are you so far from saving me, so far from the words of my groaning? O my God, I cry out by day, but you do not answer, by night, and am not silent."

"No, no. That's not it." The preacher's brows beetled.

Dylan looked at the woman, astonished she'd been able to remember that passage. "What about the Twenty-third Psalm?" They made eye contact, and she nodded. He started out, and she joined in. "The Lord is my shepherd...."

At least they could make this right.

⤸⊶⊷⤸

Sondra Thankful huddled in Kenny's old shirt. It offered little solace. Grief crashed over her. First her husband, then her dear friend, Miller. *God, why is it Your will for me to be alone?*

The minute the prayer ended, Miller's relatives started to bicker. Sondra backed away from the ugliness. She'd forgotten how her heels sank into the ground at Kenny's funeral until they did the same thing now.

"Careful." The tall man who'd recited the psalm braced her elbow for a moment. From what he said during the service, she knew who he was: Dylan, the neighbor Miller thought of as a son.

Sondra subtly took stock of him. His warmth and spicy aftershave filled her senses as his six-foot height and broad frame blocked the wind. Steady gray eyes seemed to search out details and file them away, and the shadow on his square jaw made it look as though he'd spent a less than restful night. The wind played havoc with his fine black hair, and his charcoal gray suit jacket gaped as he raised a hand to shove back a lock of it. He looked ill-at-ease in the suit, and freshly polished cowboy boots made it clear where he'd rather be.

"I'm Dylan Ward. Miller was my neighbor."

"I'm Sondra Thankful. Miller spoke very highly of you, Dylan."

"That means a lot—especially today." He studied her for a long moment. "He was pretty cryptic about you. All I know is that you're a teacher and volunteer at a children's group home here in Lawton. He used to loan you baby chicks."

"Mmm-hmm. I posted a note in several feed stores, asking if someone would let me borrow chicks for troubled children to hold. Only one rancher in the whole area responded—Miller Quintain."

"That's Miller," Dylan confirmed with a decisive nod. "The man had a knack for filling the empty places in other people's lives."

"He did." She turned to stare at the horizon.

"Why chicks?"

"They're teeny and light—quiet, too. Even the smallest child can cradle one. It's great therapy for kids who've gotten beaten up by life. When they feel completely out of control, it helps to have something soft and warm to hold on to."

Dylan's gaze dropped to her hand. Sondra hadn't realized she'd bunched the flannel shirttail in her palm until his eyes narrowed. Just as quickly, compassion softened his features.

"Excuse me." Overwhelmed by grief, Sondra barely choked out the words and turned away. Her heel sank in the grass as she buried her face in her hands and wept.

"Whoa. Easy there." Dylan gathered her closer to his side and cradled her head to his chest. He didn't shush her or even say anything more; he merely held her as she sobbed. When she started to calm down, he pressed a handkerchief into her hands. "Here."

"Thanks." She pulled away and dabbed at her eyes. "I'm going to miss him so much."

"So will I." Dylan's solemn voice carried the ache of deep loss. Sondra sensed his presence at her side as they walked across the cemetery.

A man in a custom-tailored suit who'd been on the fringes of the funeral stood at the curb. He raised his voice because of the wind. "Are you Sondra Thankful?"

"Yes."

"I'm Geoffrey Cheviot of Cheviot, Masters, and Associates. My apologies that I relied on my secretary to call you. You are coming back to the office?"

Sondra gave him a baffled look. "I don't belong."

"Mr. Quintain was an old-fashioned man. He specified his last will and testament was to be read following the service." The attorney's face reflected no emotion as he added, "Miller requested you be present."

"Who is she, anyway?" one woman wondered aloud. Miller Quintain's relatives all suddenly focused on her—but their interest carried more malevolence than curiosity.

Dylan gently curled his hand around Sondra's elbow. He kept his voice low. "Come—for Miller."

Put in that light, she didn't give it further consideration. "I'll be there."

The attorney smiled with unmistakable relief. "Good. I'll see you at the office."

Dylan kept hold of Sondra and headed toward the parking lot. She inched closer to him, both for warmth and protection. The wind carried a chill, but the stares of Miller's relatives were downright frigid. Dylan halted for a split second to allow the wind to buffet a crinkling sheet of newspaper across their path and then continued on. "Which car is yours?"

"My ride's just around the corner."

He leaned forward and looked past her. "The bus?" Incredulity filled his voice.

"My car's in the shop."

"I'll give you a ride." He nodded decisively. "We'll swap stories about Miller." He strode along until they made it to a well-kept, older pickup.

"I can take the bus. Really."

Dylan shook his head. "I'll put you in a cab. You can't wait in the cold and ride on a crowded bus."

She couldn't afford to pay for a cab. *Miller trusted him, and the lawyer knows I'm with him.* She gave him a sad smile. "I'm not very good company today."

"Neither am I. Here." He unlocked and opened the door.

Once in the truck, Sondra fell silent. They both stared out of the windshield. Yesterday's thunderstorm hadn't lost steam until early this morning, and the clouds hung low, like ominous, gray monoliths in the vast Oklahoma sky. Dreariness coated Lawton as Dylan drove through the streets.

He turned on the radio. A quartet sang "Rock of Ages" *a cappella.* "This okay with you?"

"Yes. Comforting, even."

Sondra's thoughts wandered aimlessly, and Dylan seemed equally content with the silence. The hymn ended, and another began. *I should ask him to tell me more about Miller. Hearing about Miller would—*

"How long did you know Miller?"

"Just about two years." She smiled at the memory. "The first time we met, I thought he looked like the man on the Luden's cough drop box."

Dylan chuckled. They spent the next fifteen minutes remembering their friend. Dylan pulled to the curb and announced, "Here we are."

"Thanks for the ride. Sharing memories like that has helped me."

"Me, too."

She shrugged. "I don't see why I'm here."

"Miller was a generous man. He may have left you a bit of money so you could keep taking the baby chicks to the kids."

"It'd be great. They really make a difference."

He nodded. "Yeah, I'll bet they do. Tell you what—I don't have a coop, but if Miller didn't arrange for you to keep getting chicks, I'll put one in, and you're welcome to come pick them up just like you did before."

Her lips parted in surprise. "Wow. Thanks!" As he shut his door, she took a couple of deep breaths and whispered, "Lord, I could really use Your help here. You know—courage and strength. . . ." As soon as she unlocked her door, Dylan helped her out.

Geoffrey Cheviot personally met them at the door of the building. "If you'll follow me. . ." He led them to the law offices and into a sizable corner meeting room. Plush, camel-colored carpeting muffled their steps, and the oppressive gray from the sky filtered through the wall-to-wall plate glass windows. Several chairs sat in a semicircle facing an oak wall unit. Gesturing toward a pair of chairs closest to the door, he invited, "Please be seated."

Sondra lowered herself into one of them and tucked her purse on the floor. Mr. Cheviot returned with the family members, and she shifted in her seat. *I don't belong here with the friends and family.*

The staid-looking attorney waited until everyone settled into the seats, then opened the center doors of the wall unit to reveal a large television screen. He pulled a CD from a nearby shelf. "Miller Quintain has a written testament. You will all receive copies, but he also recorded it. He wanted to express his wishes to you directly. I'll play it for you now."

The sight of Miller's sunbaked, laugh-wrinkled face made Sondra suck in a quick breath. Dylan must have heard that soft gasp, because he slid his big, rough hand over and gently patted her arm.

Miller stared into the camera and spoke as he always had—straight, to the point, and with a minimum of fuss. "Well, folks, this is it. My will is absolutely airtight. Settle for what I give you, or challenge my wishes and receive a single dollar for your gall. That being said, let me make it clear I just came from the doctor, and he's certified me as being completely of sound mind. This is what I want done with all that I've amassed."

"The old coot never did have any class," one relative muttered.

Miller rattled off the names of seven relatives then drawled, "You never much bothered with me while I was alive, so I'm not feeling it necessary to fret much over your welfare, either. Getting here for the funeral set you back a tad, so I'm leaving each of you three thousand dollars to cover expenses. Consider yourselves lucky to get that much out of me. It's a better return on those annual Christmas cards than you deserve."

The room erupted. Angry shouts, cries, and growls filled the air. "Silence, please!" Mr. Cheviot demanded.

Miller continued on. "Edwin, as my brother, you never did have it in you to completely forget me. I know my money interested you far more than my companionship, but I want you to have one last go at something, so I'm bequeathing you fifty grand."

"Fifty grand! Is that all?"

The image on the monitor spoke on. "Then I come to Dylan Ward. Dylan. . ." Miller paused. A kind smile creased his weather-beaten face, making him look just the way Sondra remembered him. It was eerie to see the fondness and compassionate quality looming there when they'd just buried him. His lips moved. "Dylan, I think of you as being the son I never had."

Dylan's hand slid away from her arm. For some inexplicable reason, she had an almost overwhelming urge to snatch it back.

"The antique gun collection is yours. My horse and saddle—you've admired them, and I want them to go to you. Oh—and the gray enamel coffeepot? You know where to find it. It's yours, Dylan.

"I hope you'll understand." Miller chuckled roughly. "Come to think of it, you probably won't understand for a while, but I trust you will someday. I'm not going along with my original plan.

"I'm leaving you the easternmost two hundred acres and thirty percent of the value of my livestock, all to be granted to you one year from today—under one condition: the Curly Q must achieve the same annual profit margin for this fiscal year as it has averaged in the past five. Mr. Cheviot has the parameters in a file for your reference."

Sondra couldn't tear her gaze from Miller's image. She heard the rough sound of Dylan clearing his throat. She didn't care what Miller and he had worked out. It wasn't any of her business. Miller had a right to do what he wanted, but she sensed something about this arrangement came as a huge blow.

"That brings me to Sondra Thankful."

Chapter 2

Everyone in the room turned and stared at her. Dylan was no exception.

"Sondra, sugar, you made these last years the happiest ones of my life. We were kindred spirits who weathered life's storms on our own terms. My only regret is that I'm not there to give you some help, but I'm trusting Dylan to fill in for me." He chuckled again in that odd, rasping way he'd had. "He'll be forced to, since I've saddled him with leaving the livestock on my land during the next year. You can rely on him. He has a sound head on his shoulders."

Sondra felt the blood seep from her face in slow degrees as Miller's voice droned on. "As for the balance of my estate, real and personal—home, ranch, and possessions, as well as the remaining livestock and balance of funds—I leave them all in total to Sondra Thankful with two provisions: She is to take immediate possession and live at the Curly Q for the next full year, and the ranch must reach the profit level I mentioned earlier. If those conditions aren't met, Mr. Cheviot will give Sondra fifteen thousand dollars and then accept the offer from Tuttlesworth Developers to turn the land into a housing subdivision."

A ruckus ensued. Dylan shot to his feet, scooped her purse from the floor, and shoved it in her numb hands. "Let's go."

"But—"

Dylan took hold of her arm, yanked her from the room, and steered her through the office. Mr. Cheviot scurried alongside them, blurting out two alternatives they'd not heard because of the ruckus. He'd just finished telling them Sondra could immediately opt out for fifteen grand, or "You and Mr. Ward can marry and have full, unconditional possession." He looked at Sondra expectantly.

Dylan growled, "Of course she's taking the ranch." Then he pulled her out of the office and stuffed her in his truck. After he slammed his own door, he let out a long, gusty breath and started the engine.

"I don't believe it."

His jaw clenched. "Neither do I."

"He didn't really. . ."

"He did. You got it." Dylan kept staring ahead. "What's your address?"

She stammered her cross streets. "You know I didn't—" She shook her head. "I don't understand. I didn't know."

Finally he shot her a sideways glance. The muscle in his cheek twitched, and his lips pressed together. Determination, grudging as it sounded, finally echoed in his curt words. "What's done is done. I'll pull you through for a year."

Sondra swallowed hard. She'd been a charity case all her life and struggled so hard to be self-sufficient. The depth of his upset was clear, even if he'd not voiced a word of it. "You expected more."

His long fingers tightened around the steering wheel. "No. Absolutely not. And yes. We didn't have it on paper. There was an understanding. I've already made arrangements for a loan; I planned to buy all of the Curly Q, and the money was to fund Miller's favorite charities."

"I see."

"No, you don't." He hit the turn signal indicator with notable force. The clicking sounded preternaturally loud until he made a right turn and it automatically shut off. Though clearly upset, he kept his voice so carefully modulated and low that it gave her the willies. "I need the land."

Shocked by the whole turn of events, Sondra stared out the windshield. Month by month, she barely eked by. In one incredibly generous gesture, Miller had rescued her. *A home. I'll have a home.* None of it seemed real. She cast a glance at Dylan. The set of his jaw and way his fingers curled in a near death grip around the steering wheel made it clear her windfall was his loss. "I'm sorry the will ruined your plans."

He slowly eased his hold and flexed long, callused fingers. "Not ruined. Delayed." He nodded resolutely, as if confirming something to himself, and kept his eyes trained on the road. "As soon as we're through this year, that acreage will be mine, but I may as well put my offer on the table here and now—I want first bidding rights to buy the rest off of you when we finish the contract year."

Her chin lifted. He'd stung her with that demand. By willing her that land, Miller gave her a home—the one thing she'd never had. "I'm not going to sell it."

"Don't get your dander up. The original agreement I reached with Miller stipulated the money would go to a charity. This way, you'll get it instead."

"So instead of *worthy* causes, *I've* turned out to be Miller's 'charity.'"

"It's none of my business. As I said, what's done is done. Like it or not, we're partners for the next year." A wry smile twisted his lips. "Actually, it's a little shy of a year. The Curly Q is set up so the fiscal year hits in mid-March. I reckon we can tolerate each other that long."

"Not necessarily. I can turn down the ranch and take the fifteen thousand dollars Mr. Cheviot mentioned."

He snorted. "That's as likely as us getting married."

"No kidding," she snapped.

"Okay, I'm sorry. I can't believe Miller even put that as an option. I've got more pride and sense than to marry a woman to get land. Judging from today, you're still reeling from your own loss."

"Maybe I should just hire a consultant."

Dylan pulled his truck to an abrupt stop next to her apartment building. He twisted to face her, his eyes alight with ire. "Not a chance, lady. You stick some idiot in there who messes things up, and the profit margin will be too low. You're not putting my future in someone else's hands."

"So you expect me to place my future in your hands?"

"You got that straight." He slid out of the truck and opened her door. Towering over her, he gritted, "Get it in your pretty little head right now: I'm running the show."

"Not unless I say so. I could take the money and let the developers cement in the whole place!" Sondra marched to her apartment, let herself in, and shut the door. A glance showed Dylan standing on the pavement, his hands on his hips and a scowl darkening his much-too-handsome features. If she accepted the conditions of the will and kept control of her life and affairs, she'd have an enemy for a neighbor.

Two hours later, Sondra looked around her cramped apartment. Her teacher's salary qualified as modest, and hefty college loans ate into her budget. Fifteen thousand dollars would barely get her out of debt. Financially she needed to work—and she'd be forced to leave the baby with a sitter all the time once it came. *On the ranch, I can be a full-time mother. Miller did that for you and me, sweetie.*

She slumped on the sofa and rested her hand over her slightly rounded tummy. Just last week, she'd started to wear maternity clothes. They weren't absolutely necessary, but some of her regular clothes felt binding. Three months of morning sickness had made her weight dip dangerously. Then, too, grieving didn't do much for her appetite. Most women looked noticeably pregnant by the beginning of their sixth month.

Lord, I don't know what to do. Guide me.

In the quiet, reality started to sink in. *Miller's friendship was such a blessing. When everything else fell apart, he cared and showed God's love to me. I've been praying for months now. I've asked God to show me His will. Could this be it?*

By taking the ranch, she'd have to work hard—but that was nothing new. With this, she'd be financially stable. She'd have a place all her own, a forever-ours home in which to rear her son, and they wouldn't have to scrimp from week to week. Of all the people Miller knew, all the lives he'd touched, he'd singled her out. Why? She'd never know, but she'd eternally be grateful.

What did she know about ranching? She was twenty-five and never once had ridden a horse. Cattle were cute, splotchy animals in picture books. Yes, she did a creditable *moo* sound. Other than that, ignorance abounded.

The simple fact of the matter hit hard—she needed to enlist some sound help. Miller planned on having her go to Dylan Ward for advice. She ought to abide by Miller's wishes—even though Dylan had gotten overbearing. Truth was, she needed him.

Regardless of his dissatisfaction with the will, Dylan needed to work with her. He had too much riding on it—thirty percent of the value of the livestock and an awesome chunk of land, to be precise. If he tried to take his anger out on her, he'd be cheating himself, too. Whether she liked Dylan or not, Miller trusted him. That was the best endorsement she could get. For whatever reason, Miller bound them together in the deal, and their futures hinged on cooperating to keep the Curly Q profitable. Her child's future depended on things working out, so she was going to have to set aside her ironclad rule of self-determination and control.

She splayed her fingers over her tummy and slowly rubbed a few circles. "Miller did this so I could be there for you all of the time. Maybe that's God's plan, too. For you, my little one, I'll do anything."

She took the business card the lawyer discreetly had slipped into her pocket, picked up the telephone, and dialed. "Mr. Cheviot? This is Sondra Thankful. I've decided to move to the Curly Q as soon as we take care of the arrangements."

Dylan dumped a bale of hay onto the barn floor. The wire snapped, just like his temper. How could Miller do this to him? He'd arranged long ago for the loan it would take to gain the greater portion of the land. He owned sufficient collateral and kept enough in the bank to swing the deal. No one knew the land better; no one loved it more. He didn't *want* a handout. Hadn't expected one. Accustomed to working hard for everything he ever got, Dylan never once presumed that Miller would simply hand over the ranch. Still, he'd said things over the years, which made it clear that he fully expected Dylan to own the land when he was gone.

The strange bequest came as such a shock. A nasty one, at that. Even worse, it went to a city-girl. She'd foul things up so badly the Curly Q wouldn't be worth a plugged nickel in a year. It would serve her right for him to let her flounder.

Then Dylan looked out of the open barn door. Land was too precious to be squandered, too dear to be misused. Livestock was certainly too valuable to be mistreated. . .and thirty percent of the value of that livestock waited for him at the end of the year. He couldn't let all that go to rack and ruin any more than he could chop off his right arm. Kicking the hay, he bitterly accepted Miller had counted on that very fact.

Even worse, the thought of the land being leveled, cemented, and turned into row upon row of cookie-cutter tract homes made his blood curdle. He loved standing in a field and seeing nothing but God's beautiful earth for almost as far as the eye could see. Marring this with noise, traffic, and houses—*never*. Sondra actually threatened yesterday that she could opt for the fifteen grand and let the land go to the developers. Whatever it took, Dylan vowed he'd make certain the land wasn't violated like that.

What it would take was honoring Miller's request. He'd call and reason with her. For the sake of a dead friend's last request, Dylan would do it.

"Okay. I bail her out for one stinking year," he muttered under his breath. "I'm not letting her hire someone to run the show, though. That's asking far too much."

⌒⌒⌒

Sondra carried in her suitcase, set it on the bed, and opened the window. Sunshine filtered through the dusty window, and a breeze made the brown paisley curtains sway. She looked around with a sense of awe.

She'd been in the house on several occasions, but most of the rooms were closed off. Taking a tentative tour, she decided to occupy the master bedroom and turn the adjacent bedroom into a nursery. The third bedroom looked to be a guest room, so it could be left alone. Miller had converted the fourth bedroom into an office, and she felt a spurt of relief at the neatly arranged books and files that would help guide her through the next year. The kitchen looked old but serviceable. Gouges in the walnut coffee table reminded her of Miller's habit of propping his feet up. This house felt lived-in and comfortable. *God, You've blessed me far beyond what I ever dreamed of.*

She traipsed down the stairs into the basement and noted with glee that the washer and dryer were in good condition. The far corner boasted an iron-reinforced, cement tornado shelter. Once, last spring, when the skies turned an ugly green and hail started falling, Miller had grabbed her and taken her there for safety. Yes, safety. This house was a monument to the security God was providing for her and the baby. Sondra came back upstairs, made a few quick phone calls, then went out into the yard.

Unsure of where to start, Sondra headed for the henhouse. She'd been there dozens of times, and it shouldn't be too hard to gather eggs. The hens seemed crazy, squawking and trying to get out of the door. Fifteen minutes later, her wrists pecked raw, Sondra reached into the last nest. She jerked back with a shriek as a snake slithered from the bits of hay.

Nothing, but nothing, could keep her there. Sondra rocketed out of the door, screaming bloody murder. She careened straight into none other than Dylan Ward.

Chapter 3

S nake!"

He braced her slender arms for a moment and drawled, "Are you calling me names, or is there a snake in the henhouse?"

Wide-eyed, she stood there.

Grit beneath his boots scraped loudly as Dylan set Sondra aside. He strode into the henhouse and came back out holding a squirming, twenty-inch reptile. Extending it toward her, he grinned. "This is a common milk snake. They've been known to eat eggs. They certainly don't eat people. If anything, the poor thing is terrified of you. You sure can kick up a powerful fuss."

Sondra made a strangled sound.

"Anytime you see a snake, just walk the other way or grab a hoe and chop off his head. Here by the stable, be sure to kill 'em, because they spook the horses." Taking his own advice, Dylan tossed down the snake, armed himself with a hoe, and beheaded it. He then picked up the body and hung it over the nearest fence rail where it continued to squirm.

Sondra barely made it around to the back of the barn before she lost her breakfast.

Dylan shoved a bandanna at her so she could wipe her face. "I suppose I ought to be glad you got that out of your system straight off. The rest of the day probably won't go any better."

"What are you doing here?"

"I came to show you around. I've already checked on the horses, and Joseph's mucking out the stable. You have plenty to do. Someone needs to clean out the water troughs. They're getting slimy."

Sondra closed her eyes and swayed a bit.

He felt a little sorry when she turned green after his last comment. After all, she'd just thrown up. Then again, he wasn't about to handle matters for her just because she felt queasy.

As if she dreaded asking, she gulped before asking, "What else?"

"Chickens—they aren't a profitable venture. Most ranches that run beef don't mess with poultry, but Miller was softhearted. He did it and donated the eggs to the food bank. A local man picks them up as a public service. It's a fair bit of work with no financial return. You could get a piddly sum if you sold off those hens and the incubator in the hatchery, but the coop and stuff would have to be trashed."

Without hesitation, she said, "I'm not selling. I want to continue with Miller's plan. We loved what we were doing with those chicks."

"Caring for them takes time."

She looked him in the eye. "I make time for what's important to me."

"Even if the chickens are a pittance, it's going to cost you money. You'll have to hire someone in to keep them for you. I've temporarily assigned my man, Luna, to cover for you since he grew up on a spread that kept laying hens."

"Thanks. I'll start learning right away so I can assume full responsibility. I expect to pay his wages in the meantime."

At least she's not shutting down a charity operation or asking for any more favors.

Sondra gave one of the yard dogs a pat on the head. He was an ugly mongrel with a naturally mean-looking sneer, but she didn't seem in the least bit afraid. Chickens and dogs. At least she wasn't afraid of every small creature—just snakes.

"I called the library, and they're setting aside books on cows for me."

He tried to quell the smile, but it wasn't possible. "You're going to read up on everything?"

"Yes, I am."

"Fine. Until you cuddle up with those books, schoolteacher, let me give you a glimpse at the real thing." He took her around the ranch. They didn't go far; she needed to get a feel for the major setup before he bogged her down with details, however important they might be.

"Instead of taking Pretty Boy to my stable, I'll leave him here. Times when I drive over and need a mount, he'll be available."

Sondra nodded. "When can you take the guns?"

"I brought my truck today."

"I'll leave the house unlocked. Were there other things you'd like—anything with sentimental value?"

He hooked his thumbs in his belt loops. "I got the coffeepot. I'm happy."

Patting another dog, she said, "Holler if you think of anything else." She straightened. "Back to business—when's payday for the hands?"

Dylan gave her an assessing look. "Know much about computers?"

"Enough to get by."

"Miller kept spreadsheets, feed records, supply lists, and the like computer-ized. I'll keep you informed so you can update them." He locked eyes with her to underscore the significance of what he said next. "Most important thing you'll do is payroll. Payday is every other Friday; you'll need to cut the men checks this week. Miller paid his men well, and they earn every cent of it."

She nodded. Funny how she wasn't overly talkative like most women he knew. Kind of kept to herself.

Dylan continued his instructions. "Most ranches end up with a fair percentage of drifters, but your crew is long-term and steady. Keep it that way. They'll manage nicely with supervision." *Mine*, he silently vowed. The minute he'd learned Sondra took up residence, Dylan had hightailed on over to reinforce his position. Resolved to fulfill Miller's directive, he wasn't about to let this city-gal plug someone else into a position of authority. Judging from how her men nodded or greeted him, they'd already accepted his presence.

"Dylan?"

"Yeah?"

She stared up at him somberly. "I don't like being dependent. I know it's not much, but I'd be happy to take on your spread's bookkeeping and payroll duties, too."

She took him by surprise with her offer, but he didn't want her dabbling in his business. "My sister, Teresa, handles all of that for me."

"Oh. I'd like to meet her."

"She's staying with a friend for a few days, shopping and stuff. I'm sure she'll come by when she gets back."

Dylan squinted at the horizon and watched a calf wobble around on unsteady legs. Kinda like this woman—so brand-spankin' new to the world that she didn't even have solid footing.

"Out here, we're tight-knit. The Merriweathers have the spread off to the west of you. You know my spread is yonder." He jabbed his thumb in the air toward the east. "Langstons are on the other side of me. Teresa's marrying Jeff Langston."

"She's really marrying the boy next door?"

"Mom would have been thrilled." He gestured toward a pasture and filled her in on the grazing rotation patterns then continued the tour.

At one point, Sondra turned around and gave him a quizzical look. "What?"

He'd been noticing her attire. Sondra wore that same bedraggled flannel shirt, but it managed to give her a get-down-to-business air. Her choice of footwear was another story. "You can't wear those shoes around here anymore. You need boots."

She blurted out, "I can't afford boots right now."

Dylan gave her a sardonic grin. "I'm sure Miller would want you to buy some for yourself, Sondra. *Nice* ones."

Her lips parted momentarily and then thinned. "I'll go see about the water troughs."

"I'm not finished showing you around."

She said nothing more and started walking off.

He scowled then let out a loud sigh. "You already running scared, city-girl?"

Sondra turned and folded her arms akimbo. "I understand you're upset about Miller's will—"

"There's an understatement." His eyes narrowed.

She stared straight back at him. "We have to make this work. It's not going to be easy. Since I know how to take care of the troughs, I'll stay busy while you take care of more pressing issues."

"You got that right." He said nothing more and strode off.

His tone left her steaming in the tennis shoes he disapproved of. By noon, she was a mess. It turned out they used sawdust instead of straw or hay in the stable. It supposedly absorbed better and needed changing less often—both strong points as far as she was concerned. Even then, being around as Joseph mucked out the stable nearly sent her running back out behind the barn again.

She'd scrubbed the cement water troughs herself. When she finished that chore, she slogged back to the house, shook off as much sawdust as she could, and toed out of her shoes before stepping over the threshold. Sondra hadn't engaged in anything half so strenuous in years. After indulging in a long shower, she stared at her reflection in the mirror and gave herself a much-needed pep talk. " 'I can do everything through him who gives me strength.' Yes, I can. With God's help, I can do this—even if Dylan's going to be a pain."

After hastily slapping together a peanut butter sandwich, she went back out to gather up the loose chickens and shove them back into the henhouse. One of the ranch hands, Edgar, came by and gave her a little help. He then mentioned, "Nickels is in the barn. You've got a late-calving Holstein. Things ain't goin' so good."

"Oh." She paused for a second, then decided, "I'll go check to see if he needs something."

Edgar waited until he thought she was out of range and then moaned, "Lord, help us all. A meddlin' city-gal in a birthin' shed."

His low opinion of her, though deserved, nettled Sondra. She'd stay up late, read everything she could, and work twice—no, three times—as hard as they expected to prove she had what it took.

Nickels greeted her with a silent bob of his head. Other than that, he completely ignored Sondra as he ran his weathered hand over the cow's bulging side. For a few minutes, Sondra looked at the cow. She was huge. Somehow a picture in a book made cattle look cute and of manageable size. Up close, they appeared more like odd-colored, spindle-legged fortresses. Especially pregnant, this one could pass for a small principality in Europe. Big, sad eyes rolled up at Sondra, and her heart melted. She carefully made her way across the pen and knelt by the cow's head. She petted her and murmured, "You'll be fine."

"Don't go tellin' her things are gonna be okay, ma'am. From the looks of it, they ain't," Nickels stated grimly. "Gonna have to call the vet."

"I'll do it." She went back to the house. Just as she located the vet's number, the phone rang. "Hello?"

"Mrs. Thankful, I—"

She interrupted, "Mr. Ward, I don't have time to waste listening to your innuendos and suppositions. If that's all this is, forget it."

"I figured we ought to talk."

She shifted in the chair. "Perhaps, but you've gotten me at a bad time. At the moment, I need to call the vet."

"Why?"

"A cow is having trouble calving."

"Why didn't you call me? I'm on my way. Don't bother trying to reach the vet. He's out of town." He hung up before she could say another word.

Dylan got there in just a few minutes. He took one look at the cow and started to unbutton his shirt. Nickels spouted off any number of salient facts and made a few suggestions. Sondra didn't understand half of what he said. It irked her that Nickels became so talkative with Dylan when he'd been silent with her.

"City-girl, this is going to get ugly," Dylan warned with a lopsided, mocking smile. "You'd best scamper on back inside unless you want to lose your supper."

"I guess it's fortunate I haven't eaten supper yet."

She fought the heated blush that zoomed clear up from her toes as Dylan took off his shirt. His shoulders looked even broader without the covering of a shirt. His skin matched the color of fire-glazed pottery—tanned to the point of redness.

Dylan gave her an impatient look. She stood there, feeling completely flummoxed. "Lady, you'll need to learn to pitch in if you plan to make it through the next year," he snapped. "So, if you're staying, make yourself useful."

"What do you want?"

"Bring in six buckets of water and some soap."

By the time she hauled in the sixth bucket of water, Sondra had gathered her wits enough to also bring a few towels. She watched as Dylan soaped all the way up to his shoulder. He grimaced, then knelt down at the business end of the cow.

Feeling sympathetic, Sondra went back by the cow's head, sat cross-legged in the thin layer of sawdust covering the floor, and took hold of the rope Nickels had tied around the cow's neck. "It's okay, girl. Take it easy. Easy." She winced as she watched Dylan.

"It's malpresentation, all right. Lateral. I'll see if I can't. . .nudge. . . Nickels, brace her. I'm going to have to get some pressure going here."

With obvious skill, patience, luck, and strength, Dylan managed to turn the calf. Weak as the cow was, he ended up pulling the calf out. As he washed the worst of the mess from himself, he and Nickels discussed what remained to be done.

"Any other late calves due?"

Nickels shrugged. "One that I know of."

"I'll have my men pull down the fence tomorrow. We'll have both herds summer together for now. I'll decide the rest later."

Sondra stewed silently. Even if she didn't know diddly-squat about ranching, he owed her the courtesy of informing her about these matters before he made announcements. She didn't expect a full-on consultation, but a brief word in advance was reasonable. To her dismay, Dylan Ward didn't seem like the reasonable sort at all.

Dylan turned and gave her that mocking smile again. "You kept your stomach, city-girl. I'm surprised."

"I'm sure you'll be surprised a few more times before our year is up."

He tilted his head at the calf. "So what do you think?"

"I think it was a miracle," she said in awe.

"Don't expect too many miracles." Dylan then rasped at Nickels, "I expect to be called any time there's a problem. Don't let me find one out by accident again."

"You got it, boss."

As much as it galled her, Sondra kept her mouth shut. She didn't dare alienate her ranch hands. Miller had known his business well, and he'd hired only the best. She shouldn't make matters so uncomfortable that they'd decide to leave.

Both men were looking at her. Sondra sensed that they wanted to be rid of her. They'd been working a long while and probably missed supper, but she didn't have much of a notion what was in her kitchen. Instead of offering to rustle up a quick meal, she excused herself and bade them a good night.

Bed never felt so good, and night never passed so quickly. Her muscles protested as much as her grainy eyes did, but Sondra dragged herself out of bed at first light and hastily prepared to meet the day. She headed for the stable and used a dolly to move the hay bales to help Joseph feed the horses.

Feeling quite proud of herself, she then went to the henhouse to meet Luna. In a soft drawl, he told her all about the coop, how he cleaned and packaged eggs, and how much to feed the chickens.

Dylan sauntered up. He looked cocky—just like the class troublemaker before he pulled a stunt. Sondra got suspicious.

"I have men taking down that section of fencing. Get in the Rover, and I'll take you to see what we're doing. I have the others retagging some of the stock we purchased at auction."

"I'd like that." After seeing more of the outlying area of the ranch, she felt breathless. How could Miller have given her all of this? It amazed her. Then again, it humbled her. She now knew she wouldn't ever be equal to the task of running it. She also knew precisely why Dylan insisted on this expanded tour—he wanted to drive that fact home.

Chapter 4

Sondra arrived back at the house just in time to have the Battered Women's Society take away a few pieces of the furniture. She and Kenny hadn't started out with much, but her own things were due the next day. Miller would have been glad the things she didn't need went to a good cause.

She couldn't believe how the place already felt like home. Cleaning each room, putting her things in the drawers, just angling a chair toward the window so it would catch the morning sun—each little thing made this her refuge, her haven.

Never before had a place seemed so right, so welcoming. Even her apartment with Kenny hadn't felt this way. She'd barely gotten her meager belongings in the door the week they got back from their honeymoon, and they'd been so wrapped up in each other that she didn't cull through everything until the last week before he died. Then she hated going home because it constantly reminded her of the emptiness in her heart.

This was different. It was home—good, pure, safe—hopefully, forever.

She put her Bible and the Bible study book she'd been working through on an end table and wrapped her arms about her ribs. *Lord, thank You for providing this home for my baby and me. Grant me wisdom so I can keep it and use it to Your glory, I pray. And, Father—about Dylan—help me deal with him.*

After doing some housekeeping, she drove into Lasso, stopped at the library, slipped in to see the doctor, and went through the grocery store. She located the community church and noticed Sunday morning worship started at half past eight.

Weary beyond her tolerance, she went to bed early, then barely managed to wake up in time to let the movers bring in her things. They didn't take long, but she directed them to place the furnishings exactly where she wanted them. Her tiny dinette set looked perky in the kitchen.

This was to be her son's home, and she wanted it perfect. Her child would never be passed around and suffer living without roots the way she had. He'd know the security of growing up in one house, loved. He'd have his very own bedroom, and he'd go to the same school year after year. It was a priceless gift, and Sondra could scarcely close her eyes at night, fearing she'd wake up and find it was all just a dream.

The last couple of days had been overcast, so she'd worn loose-fitting sweats. Since today's forecast boasted sun, she put on lightweight jeans and teamed them with an oversized pink T-shirt. Feeling encouraged with her progress all around, she skipped down the steps and off to check in over at the stable. Nickels was saddling up a mare. "I'll be in the coop," she mentioned.

He shot her an approving smile. "You're not letting weeds grow 'round your feet, are you?"

"Not at all. There's too much to do!"

He nodded sagely. "Yep. Always is."

Hens clucked a welcome to her, and Sondra stepped into the coop. Luna wasn't here yet, but she wanted a chance to start in on the chores so she wouldn't be relying on others. A short while later, feeling a presence, she looked up and gave her neighbor a nod. "Mr. Ward."

Finding her pitching in at barely past daybreak settled well with Dylan. "Luna's sick."

"That's too bad. Does he need anything?" She stood up and wiped the back of her wrist across her forehead. With her other hand, she cupped a little chick to her breastbone as if she'd never held anything quite so precious.

"You're already busy enough. His wife is taking care of him." Her concern threw him for a loop. Dylan liked seeing that she had some redeeming qualities. He silently reminded himself that she was a city-gal. A helpless one. The only real connection she claimed to the Curly Q was the chickens.

Swiping the chick she held and giving it a gentle buff with his knuckles, he wondered aloud, "Just how often do you take these little critters into town?" He watched as she bent over and nabbed another chick. Tenderness washed over her face as she fingered it. The look in her eyes made his heart beat a bit faster.

"Every other week. It's often enough to let the kids enjoy them, but stretched out just enough that they still think it's special. It lets them anticipate." She lifted the downy little ball and turned him so they were face-to-beak. Her voice went up half an octave. "And the kids just love you to pieces, don't they?"

The chick peeped on cue.

Sondra then cuddled it against her ribs and wet her lips. She looked Dylan in the eye and lifted her chin. The sweetness in her face disappeared, only to be replaced by cool resolve. "Since we're alone—about the boots—"

He lifted a hand to halt her. "I need to speak my piece first, if you don't mind."

The corners of her mouth tightened, and the tension he'd first felt when he entered the coop returned. Feeling rather silly to be fiddling with a handful of fluff when he planned to eat crow, Dylan passed the chick back to her. As she juggled both, he cleared his throat and remembered what he'd resolved last night as he lay awake and chafed at this whole arrangement. "I've been thinking. We've gotta make the best of things for a year. It's obvious we started off on the wrong foot."

"And started rubbing blisters," she added under her breath.

He raised his brows. This gal had gumption. "I gotta admit, you're turning out to be a bit of a surprise. You seem like a ready-to-work woman, and you're learning mighty fast."

She carefully set down the chicks, folded her arms across her ribs, and looked at him for a long count. She had to realize Miller trapped him into a heap of hard work since she didn't have much to offer in this so-called partnership. One year of work, and he'd drag her through...but he figured she'd realize she wasn't cut out for this life. Then he'd buy the place at a fair price. He could tolerate the wait.

He cleared his throat. "I think it would make things go a lot better if we try to keep them on a neighborly basis."

They were both tense as just-strung clothesline. Finally she nodded. "You've got a deal."

"Dandy." Relief flooded him. At least she didn't carry a grudge. Hardworking. Fast learning. Tenderhearted. Best he concentrate on those good qualities and show her a few of his own. "I thought maybe we could ride today. You need to see some of the rest of your land. There are parts that only have a rough fire road."

"I've never ridden before."

He groaned.

"Not to worry. I have a good sense of balance and a daredevil streak. If I'm on a calm mount, I'll manage."

"That remains to be seen." They left the coop and went to the stable. The gelding Miller left Dylan patiently waited outside. Dylan gave Pretty Boy an affectionate pat on the withers as they passed by him.

She stopped and visually measured the Standardbred. "That beast is huge!"

"Not particularly. He's sturdy and reliable, though."

She got up on her tiptoes and bravely gave his gelding her hand to take her scent, then petted his mane and neck. The sight of her appreciating the gelding instead of veering away gave him hope. Maybe she wouldn't be as antsy as most greenhorns. He stood back and took in how surely she moved her slender hands and wondered if she'd take umbrage if he suggested she wear some snug jeans instead of those baggy ones so she wouldn't get rubbed raw. No. He'd just get her in a saddle and take her a short distance today. They'd barely waded into peace; the last thing he needed to do was get personal.

She pivoted around and smiled.

Dylan chuckled at her enthusiasm. "We can put you on a calm little pony. Come on." He accompanied Sondra into the cool stable to choose a mount.

The condition of the stable impressed him. It smelled of fresh sawdust. "Joseph already mucked in here today?"

"Yep." She shot him a quicksilver smile. "I even helped. I figure I need to know everything from the ground up—literally."

"Betcha you're getting sore muscles, city-girl."

"I'm doing whatever I need to get done."

A grin lit his face. For a tenderfoot, she didn't slack in the least. "So let's see you saddle Crackers. Take that saddle blanket and toss it over him."

"You got it." She let Crackers catch her scent, too. Dylan tilted his head in silent query, so she volunteered, "I took my class to the petting zoo every year. Along the way, I learned domesticated animals like to get to know their human partners."

"Horses are smart. You respect them, and they'll give you their heart."

Sondra nodded, flipped the rough blanket over the horse, and patted it for good measure. "Okay."

"The saddle now—heft it onto him. The knoblike thing is called a pommel. It goes in the front."

After she shot him an insulted glare, Sondra grabbed hold of the saddle and yanked. It didn't move an inch. She rubbed her hands on her thighs to dry them off.

Dylan stood back and watched. *Nervous*, he assessed, *but willing to try. She's not a coward.*

She shifted her feet wider apart. After she sucked in a deep breath, she gripped the saddle and jerked with all her might. The saddle cleared the rail by a good four inches. Suddenly Dylan slammed it back down.

Sondra wheeled around. "Why did you do that?"

He glowered at her for a solid fifteen seconds, anger gusting out with every breath. He latched onto her arm and hauled her out of the stall, away from the horse.

Sondra pulled free and stared at him with wide, wary eyes.

"Hold it right there." Dylan gritted the words as he took a determined step and backed her against the gate of the next stall. He grabbed her tiny wrists and held them together in one hand while his other fleetingly slid over her belly to confirm what he'd just seen. He let go of her and jerked back as if he'd discovered bubonic plague.

They stared at each other in shock. His impulsive action left her speechless, and he felt as amazed at his behavior as she was. For a long moment, they stood almost a yard apart in taut silence. Then the whole place shook with his bellow. "You're pregnant!"

Chapter 5

Thanks for telling me. I hadn't noticed."

"Don't you have any sense at all? You can't ride!"

"You invited me to!"

"I didn't know you were in the family way!"

She scowled at him. "Of course you did. How could you possibly miss it?"

He impatiently flailed an arm in the air. "How could I tell? You always roam around in that dumb shirt."

Her eyes shot sparks.

He glowered right back. "Trying to heft that kind of weight when you're carrying a baby is insane!" Long moments passed in tense silence. His gaze slowly dropped to her middle as he wondered aloud, "When did your husband die, anyway?"

Sondra stared straight through him.

He sucked in a noisy breath. Everything went stock-still for a moment; then Dylan grated, "That's it, isn't it? You hardly even show, and your husband died months ago. Whose baby is it, Sondra? Miller's? Is that why he left you everything?" When she didn't answer, Dylan kicked a post and smacked his Stetson on his thigh in exasperation. Slamming it on his head, he stomped out without a backward glance.

❦

Sondra turned back to work. All her life, people held low opinions of her—after all, her own parents neglected her so badly that she'd been removed from their care. If her own family felt she was worthless, why should anyone else consider her of value? She'd learned to ignore the sly looks, whispers, and pity of others. Protesting usually didn't solve the problem; it often cemented the wrong notion in folks' minds.

None of that matters. It doesn't. Christ paid the ultimate price for me. I don't have to worry about what others think, because in His eyes, I'm priceless.

That night, Dylan Ward's voice seeped into her dreams and kept taunting her, *Whose baby is it? Whose?* By morning, she wanted to curl up into a tight ball, pull the covers over her head, and forget the world. She couldn't do that, though. Sondra Thankful was not a quitter. She'd do anything within her power to succeed—she had to, for her baby's sake.

It would be smart to hire a manager to help, though. Surely Miller would understand—especially after what happened yesterday. Until she found that elusive person, though, she would keep going. If she secured someone soon, he'd get a chance to find his stride with the men and get the feel of the ranch. Then when Dylan walked off with his share after the year was up, she wouldn't be left high and dry. With great resolve, she determined to see to the matter, then left the house to start her day as a know-nothing rancher.

She popped into the coop and swiftly filled the basket. The fear of finding another snake lurked in the back of her mind, but Sondra kept reminding herself that the hens were calm. When the snake was there, they'd been wild. Reassured with that observation, she finished the task and moved on to the stable.

Howie tipped his hat ever so slightly before resuming mucking the stalls.

Sondra tried hard to ignore the odor and turned to grab a spare shovel.

Howie swiped the shovel from her hands as his face puckered into a scowl. "You ain't got no call doin' that these days."

"I've been doing it!"

"Not anymore, you're not. Why didn't ya tell us you're in a delicate condition?"

Sondra looked down at her waist. "I can't for the life of me understand this. You're acting like I intentionally kept it a big secret, and I'm *showing*!"

"Not much. Not much at all. Coulda been that you needed to shed a few pounds."

"It's not a deadly disease. I'm a normal, healthy woman."

"Practicin' lullabies," he added hastily.

His choice of words amused her, but Sondra was careful not to hurt his feelings by laughing. "I'm not going to laze around. What can I do?"

"How 'bout"—He seemed a bit surprised she wanted to work, but he looked around to come up with something—"if I show you how to take care of the horses?"

"Great!"

"I've gotta finish up here first." *Plop.* A shovelful of muck punctuated his comment.

Sondra fought the impulse to step back a bit. The smell nearly overpowered her. "When do the eggs get picked up?"

"Couple or three times a week. To my reckonin', Chris Ratliff oughtta be by today."

"Fine." She smiled. "I'll go box up the eggs; then I'll be back to learn about the horses."

He paused and leaned on his shovel. "Think you're up to that?"

"Without a doubt."

Just as she finished readying the eggs, an old truck with By His Hand painted along the side pulled in to take her supply. Chris Ratliff gently set her aside and insisted on lifting the crates of eggs into the truck himself. He then surprised her by pressing a carton of milk into her arms.

"What is this for?"

"Ma'am." He gave her an assessing look, and his mouth crooked into a sheepish grin. "A mother-to-be needs to be drinking plenty of milk. Dylan asked me to bring by half a gallon twice a week. More often if you say so."

Sondra laughed and waved her hand toward the pasture. "I have hundreds of cows. Not to sound ungrateful, but isn't this like taking sand to the beach?"

"No, ma'am. You're not supposed to be drinking raw milk. Most city-folk don't care for the taste of it, but even if you did, it's not pasteurized." He shook his head. "Now you let me know if you need more milk. Got that?"

"Yes, and thank you. Let me go get my purse."

He frowned at her. "We're neighbors."

"Yes, but—"

"Ma'am, you'd best talk to Dylan so's you'll get the picture. We all chip in and help each other out. Our extras go to the By His Hand food bank, but we swap goods as a matter of course. Just makes sense."

She felt awkward. "I'm sorry if I offended you."

"Dylan'll fill you in. You didn't get a garden in this year, so my family'll send over tomatoes and squash and the like."

"That sounds wonderful. When we slaughter a steer, I'll be sure to send over some beef."

A smile lit his face. "Ma'am, you just might fit in." He glanced back at her belly and nodded as if to punctuate his opinion. "Things'll turn out just fine."

She held the milk carton and stared at the back of the truck as he left. Dylan Ward, for seeming like the quintessential cowboy-of-few-words, sure didn't waste a moment before spreading gossip about her.

The chill from the carton sent her into the kitchen for a moment. As she put the milk into her refrigerator, the abundance of all she'd been given hit her. Gratitude swelled. She went back out singing "For the Beauty of the Earth." Most often, it was a Thanksgiving hymn, but it fit her mood perfectly.

She spent the balance of the day in the stable, happily rubbing saddle soap into the leather until it shone and brushing a few of the geldings and one of the mares. She chided Crackers for whipping her with a swish of his tail and giggled at the way the beasts twitched their skin to get rid of flies.

Though far more important things needed to be done, she lacked the experience to accomplish them—or the men wouldn't allow her to. She determined to pitch in with whatever tasks they wouldn't fret about and help everywhere she could. If she could free a man up to put his hands to something more pressing, she'd be satisfied. She buffed a saddle horn and nodded to herself. Yes, she was going to learn as much as she could, jump in wherever possible. This had to work out. Her son's future was riding on it.

"Howie?"

"Hmm?"

"Why wouldn't Dylan let me ride? I thought it was okay."

"Not if you don't have a clue about what you're doing. A fall could cost you the babe you're carryin'."

She bit her lip and asked nothing more for a while. Howie whistled the same tune over and over as he repaired a harness until she finally gave him a sidelong glance. "What did Dylan tell you? About the baby and me?"

"Ward don't talk all that much. He's a closemouthed sorta man. Just said you're in a motherly way and we'd better look out for you because. . ." His voice died off.

Her cheeks tingled with heat. "Because?"

"Well, ma'am. . ." He paused uncomfortably then blurted, "Dylan said to look out for you because you ain't got enough sense to watch out after yourself!"

It should have been an insult, but considering the fact that she'd wondered if Dylan might have spread word that the baby was Miller's, she could only laugh.

After stopping by the coop to sneak a minute of cuddling a few chicks, she plodded back to the house. Her energy level needed a boost. Nuking and eating a frozen dinner would help. She felt too tired to do any cooking.

Sondra fussed around the house late that night. It took a lot of patience and concentration to make a place look just right. Too exhausted to stay up any longer, she eventually collapsed into bed, then regretted those late hours the next morning. Knowing she had no one to blame but herself for feeling weary, she had her morning devotions then started off on her chores.

Edgar checked in on her at the coop and gave her a thumbs-up gesture. Heartened by that small sign of approval, she gathered the eggs and filled the feeders as she tried to decide how best to hire a manager. Even after she had one, she planned to continue to take care of the chickens. She loved scooping up the chicks and cradling them in her palm, petting their downy bodies, and lifting them to brush their softness against her cheek. In those moments, she felt close to Miller again. He'd brought so much sunshine and laughter into her life with these balls of fluff.

The day had already started building into a scorcher, and Sondra thought about changing into a lighter blouse after finishing there. First, though, she needed to add oyster shells to the feed. Searching around the barn, she spotted a small bag leaning against the wall next to the chicken feed. Unsure how much to use, she sat on the floor and cocked her head to read the bag. Still tired, she momentarily rested her cheek against another sack as she decided what else needed to be done.

"Luna's still sick."

Her eyes shot open at the sound of Dylan's voice.

"I noticed you already took care of the chickens—any questions?"

"No, I'm just getting oyster shells. I was figuring out how much, but it's here on the label, so I'm set."

Dylan fought to keep from shuffling his boots like a naughty eight-year-old. "Ma'am, I owe you an apology."

He paused a moment when her face went a shade paler, but maybe after he cleared the air, she wouldn't look quite so. . .wary. "I don't hold with a man using his strength against a woman. The other day—well, I gave you ample cause to be scared. Not that I would ever do you any harm, but you don't know me well enough to trust me yet. I stepped way over the line, prying into your personal business, too. You can be sure from here on out I'll keep my hands to myself and my big mouth shut."

Her head dipped, and she mumbled something that sounded vaguely like, "Thanks." Dylan figured that was the best he'd get out of her—better than he deserved.

He headed out to give the men their daily orders. When he finished, he remembered he needed to tell Sondra about the feed bill. Dylan looked around and realized he hadn't seen her come back out of the barn. He found her exactly where he'd left her—sitting on the floor, her temple resting against a green-and-white-checkered feed sack. Sleepy-eyed, she stared at her hands in her lap.

She didn't even realize he'd come close enough to touch her, so he quietly hunkered down to keep from startling her. Apparently she'd lost track of the last twenty minutes. Dylan noted the dark circles under her eyes and her marked pallor.

He had stayed away all day yesterday in order for his temper to cool. At first, he could hardly fathom how a gent-down-to-the-sole-of-his-boots like Miller ever set aside his scruples enough to dally with a woman one-third his age. Then he admitted to himself that Sondra happened to be a stunning woman, and Miller probably didn't stand a chance against her feminine wiles. At least he now understood why Miller left the ranch to her. His child should inherit the land. The fact that he'd been generous enough to leave Dylan any land or livestock bespoke a deep level of personal regard.

Dylan used that time to face the cold, hard truth and came to accept the disappointment—after a year, he wasn't going to be able to buy the rest of the ranch. He owed it to the old man to help keep the place in prime condition until his child could take over. The years of commitment were staggering, but he'd do it for Miller.

Having arrived at that decision, getting along with Sondra ought to be easier. Certainly a working relationship between them needed to be forged. He'd offended Sondra. Now that he looked at her again, he revised his thinking. She seemed more like the lost-and-lonely variety. Presumably she had gravitated toward Miller in her grief, and things just kind of happened.

He felt guilty as a hound with a mouthful of chicken feathers. He'd spent the last thirty-six hours bitterly recriminating himself for how he'd treated her. He'd acted on sheer impulse and scared the daylights out of her. Dylan couldn't remember ever being so out of control, and it disgusted him that he'd frightened a small, pregnant woman. He'd never been more serious in his life than when he'd vowed he'd never do that again.

Watching her now, Dylan purposefully kept his voice low and mild. "Ma'am, if you're this miserable with morning sickness, why don't you stay in bed until a bit later?"

"I haven't had morning sickness for months," she muttered.

He shelved that piece of information to process later. For now, helping her seemed to be the priority. He'd been foolish enough to give her cause to loathe his contact. Limited to making a connection with speech, he ventured, "You're not sleeping worth a hoot, are you?"

Sondra gave him a helpless look, but she said nothing. Her defenseless expression cut him to the heart. The eloquent ache in her eyes transcended language. As if too exhausted to do or say a thing, she leaned back into the feed sack, and her eyes drifted shut.

Dylan eliminated the small space between them. "Bedtime, city-girl," he whispered in Sondra's fiery hair as he hitched her high against his chest. In just those few seconds, scorching heat burned through her shirt and his. Resting his jaw along her temple, he confirmed her fever. "Why didn't you tell me you're sick?"

Chapter 6

N ot sick," Sondra muttered, "just pregnant."

"You're hot as the devil's skillet." He strode toward the door. "Luna probably gave you whatever he has."

"Just hot." Being jostled seemed to awaken her a bit. "Need to change into a cooler blouse."

"Sondra, you're burning up."

"No time to be sick. I'll just get a drink of water and—"

"Go straight to bed," Dylan cut in. "If you want, I'll even bring you a baby chick to hold."

"Don't start being nice to me now," she whispered brokenly. "Don't you dare. I can't take it."

His heart twisted. The woman in his arms was weak and small as a freshly hatched chick, and—his thoughts stalled when her baby somersaulted. Dylan felt the movement clearly to the marrow of his bones. No matter what feelings he had about getting saddled with watching her ranch and missing the chance to purchase the land he craved, he still couldn't abandon his basic protective urge.

"Put me down. I can walk. I promise I'll take a nap in a little while."

"Shush. You'll take more than a nap. You're staying in bed 'til Doc gives you an all clear."

"The doctor in town won't take care of me."

He carried her across the barnyard, and Nickels hightailed it to intercept them. "What's up?"

"Nothing," Sondra whispered faintly.

"Nothing, my foot! She's taken sick." Dylan kept right on moving. He shouldered his way into her door. Suddenly, Sondra's fingers scrabbled across his chest as she weakly tried to push away. Dylan reflexively tightened his hold.

Sondra let out a garbled, frantic, "Sick!"

That one word turned out to be a very pale warning for how violently ill she got. She'd been weak before that episode; afterward the woman was positively helpless. Dylan carried Sondra to the master bedroom, laid her on the bed, and gritted his teeth at the sight of her. The woman was just plain too thin. Dylan turned her face back to his. "Where do you keep your nighties?"

"Don't fit anymore," she quavered. "I wear Kenny's T-shirts. Second drawer."

Dylan yanked open the drawer. A dead man's shirts lay there in two neatly folded stacks. *They're just shirts.* "Here."

"Thank you." Hotter than hot, she took the thin cotton garment from him.

Dylan left her some privacy; then he stalked back in the room only long enough to take her temperature and follow it up with a glass of water. Needing to put some space between them, he went back out to the living room and plopped down on the couch as he grabbed for the phone.

It wasn't until then he noticed the stacks of boxes with a moving company's name emblazoned across them. Here and there, she'd already set out a few things. The place smelled of fresh-baked bread and lemon furniture polish. Instead of the well-worn, slightly dusty-and-rumpled look, the living room now carried a tidy, welcoming air. The woman acted like a little hen, setting up her nest.

Dylan mentally kicked himself. He should have asked his sister to round up a few neighbors to come help Sondra settle in. As soon as she got well, he'd pass the word that the little gal needed a bit of company and a helping hand to finish sprucing up the place. In spite of her feisty streak, he sensed a shyness about her. He'd nudge Teresa to help Sondra move in and make friends. She wouldn't be well enough to go to church day after tomorrow, but he'd invite her to start going to worship once she recovered. The worn-looking Bible on the end table told him her heart was in the right place.

He sighed and dialed the doctor. "Michelle? Dylan Ward. Let me talk to Doc."

"You okay, Dylan?"

"I'm fine. Listen—Sondra Thankful is sick. Probably the flu, but I don't like the way she looks."

"Isn't she the pregnant woman who came in yesterday?"

He didn't know she'd already gotten hooked up with Doc. It showed common sense and caution. "Yeah, she's in the family way."

"Sorry, Dylan. I tried to explain it to her yesterday. Doc doesn't treat pregnant women. His malpractice insurance is too high if he does."

"I'm asking him for advice about the flu, not the baby."

"He can't advise you since the patient is pregnant."

They went round and round until Dylan hung up in disgust. Then he heard Sondra stumble into the bathroom and retch. She slumped against the side of the tub afterward. "I'm okay. You can go home."

"Not a chance." Dylan lifted her and slipped her back into bed. She'd started shivering, so he tucked the sheet back up to her neck. "Let me make a few phone calls. You need to see a doctor—have him give you a quick look-see."

He ended up driving her back to her old obstetrician over an hour away. Luckily the office was on the ground floor, because Sondra adamantly insisted upon walking in under her own steam. The receptionist jumped to her feet as soon as she spotted Sondra. "Come on in. I have an empty exam room."

Sondra shuffled toward the connecting door, and Dylan's hand shot out to twist the knob. He warned under his breath, "I'm coming back there with you. Don't you dare kick up a fuss."

Sondra's legs began to buckle. Wordlessly he scooped her up, strode forward, and laid her in the room. She'd grown even hotter during the ride, and her lethargy couldn't bode well. Bright red fever flags rode her cheeks, but otherwise, the woman was whiter than the paper on the exam table.

The doctor came in. His face puckered with concern. He peeked at something on her chart, set it aside, and drew closer to examine Sondra. Within mere minutes, he observed, "Mrs. Thankful, you've obviously contracted a nasty virus."

Sondra lay there, eyes closed, silent as a stone. Dylan wondered if she'd passed out.

The doctor continued, "You're badly dehydrated again."

Her eyes fluttered open. They were luminescent from tears and fever. "Please don't put me back in the hospital."

Back in the hospital? She'd been in the hospital already for something? Dylan scowled. This didn't sound good at all. Sondra didn't look any better than she sounded. Hopeless. That's how she looked. Her faint voice carried that tone, too.

The nurse gave her arm a compassionate stroke. "Sondra, at least there's someone at the hospital to take care of you."

Horrified by that justification, Dylan blurted out, "I'll take care of her."

Much later that evening, Dylan turned off the bedroom light. He'd never seen a more pathetic sight. From the nurse's comments while they waited for a bag of IV fluid to finish draining into Sondra, Dylan gleaned she'd reached her sixth month of pregnancy. Kenny had accompanied her to the doctor's office for her very first visit and impressed the nurse with how proud and attentive he'd been.

And I thought the kid was Miller's. She clings to a stupid flannel shirt—I was an idiot to ignore how deeply she loved her husband and make such an assumption. The thermometer registered her as too hot to wear one of those flannel jobs, but Dylan knew how much comfort she got from them, so he'd quietly tucked a shirt under the sheet with her when he'd gotten her back home.

She curled around it, smiled like she'd been given the key to heaven's pearly gates, and slipped right off to sleep.

On top of it all, Dylan felt a terrible sense of emptiness. He'd never once had a woman love him. Not like that. Not with all of her heart, the kind of love that went even beyond the grave. Sure, there had been girlfriends—but none of them ever came close to working out. Ken Thankful might be dead, but he'd been an incredibly lucky man to have received that kind of utter devotion.

Chapter 7

It had been a bad night. Sondra looked completely wiped out. Bless her heart, though, she'd never once complained. In fact, Dylan found her up twice and scolded her for not calling out to get help.

As the sun peeked through the window, Dylan brought her some juice and set a plate of crackers at the bedside. "Sondra, I've called my sister, Teresa. She's coming to stay with you. I think you'll like her."

She stared bleakly at the wall and nodded.

Worry speared through him. "Still feeling the baby move?"

"Yes."

"Good. Those kicks are a reminder of your husband's love."

She weakly rested a hand on her tummy. "This is all I have left. It's just him and me now."

Taking up a cool washrag, Dylan wiped her cheeks. Her skin was still hot as a branding iron. Lousy as she felt, she tried to valiantly spare him the tears filling her fever-glassy eyes. The woman deserved to bawl her eyes out. Instead, Sondra instinctively turned her face into the small comfort of the cloth and let out a shattered sigh.

Then the baby somersaulted.

The way her belly heaved and rolled beneath the sheets with the baby's actions shouldn't have amazed him. He saw pregnant animals all the time. It was a common enough sight. But on her, it looked intimate beyond telling.

"My last little part of Kenny's love," she told herself in a whisper.

He'd been surrounded by family all his life; she had no one. Sympathy and compassion welled up. "Can't think of a better gift of love than a baby."

"Thanks for saying that, Dylan. For your help, too."

He rubbed the back of his wrist against the bristles of his jaw. Instead of focusing on her loss, she concentrated on the positive. He admired that.

"I decided something."

He looked at her and waited. No telling what she was going to say.

"I'm not great at trusting people, but Miller loved and trusted you. There's no better recommendation. This ranch is a lot of work." The corners of her mouth tightened. "But you said you want to run it."

He nodded. "That's a fact."

"Then I'll rely on you instead of hiring a manager."

Her trust meant a lot. He curled his rough fingers around her small, soft hand and stroked the back of her fingers with his thumb. "We'll do it together."

Rustling in the doorway made him jump and turn loose of her hand.

"Help's arrived." Teresa bustled into the room. "Hi, Sondra. I'm Teresa."

"She's still running a fever and weak as a kitten," Dylan reported.

"So I see. We'll turn that around in a few days' time," Teresa decided crisply as she nudged him to the side and grabbed the glass of juice. "So is that a boy or a girl you're carrying, Sondra?"

"A boy."

"Isn't that nice?" Teresa's hand dove under Sondra's shoulders and lifted her head. "A ranch is the ideal place for children to grow up. When are you due?"

"September second." Sondra sipped the juice. "Thanks."

"September second," Teresa echoed.

Patting her tummy weakly, Sondra added, "This is Oklahoma, baby. Folks call us Sooners, and if you take a mind to come out sooner than September, I won't complain."

Dylan chuckled as he stretched. "I need to get going. The day's already half over."

"It sure is," Teresa teased. She glanced at the clock and declared, "It's already a quarter past six! The day's half done."

He playfully nudged his sister's hip with his own. "Just because you keep me from starving isn't an excuse to be sarcastic."

"I put a pan of cinnamon buns on the kitchen counter. Have a few."

"Nothing doing. I'm eating every last one of 'em."

"Impossible. Nickels and Joseph saw me bring them in. I already gave them each a pair. Bet you they take some out for Howie and Edgar, too."

"Then you're disowned."

"Teresa, I'll adopt you!"

Dylan shook his finger at Sondra. "You keep your paws off of my relatives!"

"You just disowned her!"

"He does that once or twice a week. I just don't listen." Teresa laughed. She urged Sondra to drink more then added, "He doesn't listen to me any better."

"Sounds like plenty of the brothers and sisters I know," Sondra quipped.

"Marriages, too," Teresa tacked on.

"I'm out of here!" Dylan boomed as he turned and fled.

Teresa went into gales of laughter. "My brother is marriage-shy. Nothing gets rid of him faster than bringing up the topic of matrimony."

Three days later, Sondra dragged herself out of bed. She took a shower and felt weak enough to whirl down the drain with the water.

"What are you doin' outta bed?" Nickels demanded as she passed by him out in the yard.

"I'm doing my chores. Did that last cow ever drop her calf?"

He avoided her gaze. "That's taken care of."

"Oh?"

His mouth pulled downward, and he scuffed a boot in the dirt. "Take my word for it, ma'am. It's all done."

"And mother and calf? How are they?"

His face twisted. "Ma'am, you don't want to ask 'bout this. Take my word for it."

She took a deep breath and let it out slowly. "All right. I'm going to gather the eggs."

"Dylan ain't gonna like that, ma'am. He said you're too sick to lift a finger. One glimpse of you backs up the notion, too."

"Nonsense."

The egg basket shouldn't be heavy, but it felt like a block of cement. The world tilted a bit each time Sondra got up and down, and she finally felt too dizzy to continue. Deciding a breath of fresh air would cure her, she went to the door of the coop and froze. Nickels and Dylan stood close by, holding a whispered conversation.

"Dylan, Sondra asked 'bout that last calving. I put her off."

"Good. Wait—what do you mean? Is she out of bed?"

"Yep," Nickels hissed, "and she looks plumb awful."

"One stillbirth is bad enough. The last thing she needs to do is have one herself. Stubborn woman!"

Stillbirth? The word made her reel.

Dylan's voice rose in volume, "Where is she? I'm going to tie her to the bedpost if I have to!"

"I saw her heading for the coop."

"If she isn't out cold on the floor, it'll be a miracle."

Sondra secretly smiled at his worried tone of voice. In spite of his disappointments and heavier workload, Dylan Ward cared about her. Dylan did precisely what Miller expected: He shouldered responsibilities and showed true cowboy gallantry.

Dear, sweet Miller willed her this place and provided help in the form of a black-haired, gruff-voiced, softhearted rancher—sort of an angel in bat-wing chaps.

It would be a mistake to walk out into the middle of their conversation, but she didn't dare stay in the henhouse and wait for Dylan to stomp in and chew her out. Sondra managed to give a fair rendition of a muffled cough and walked out into the sunlight. She manufactured a tentative smile. "My body's not quite as strong as my will. Could I trouble you to please finish crating up the eggs?"

"I'll get it," Nickels volunteered. He turned sideways and sidled past her, though he and another man could have walked abreast past her with room to spare.

Dylan hooked a thumb in a belt loop, scanned her up and down, and drawled, "Woman, you have a habit of biting off more than you can chew."

"Probably."

"You're still as pasty as a plucked chicken."

Sondra leaned against the doorjamb. "I'm a bit plumper."

"Not by much." He absently shook his head and twitched a self-conscious smile. "I probably ought to apologize. That sounded a mite bit personal."

Laughter colored her voice. "Don't bother. I've been plucked, so you can't ruffle my feathers!"

Dylan started to chuckle. The rich sound filled the barnyard and made something deep inside her glow. During those moments, he looked ten years younger. His loose, leggy stride brought him to her. Without a word, he slipped his arm around her waist and started back toward the house. "Feathers," he repeated, as if it were the best joke he'd heard in ages.

His strength seeped into her. She offered, "I know chickens don't drink soda, but this one happens to have a variety of them in the fridge. You're welcome anytime."

"I'll keep that in mind. At the moment, I'm more concerned with you staying hydrated."

"I'm a big girl. I can take care of myself."

"In a pig's eye." He crooked another of those smiles. "You may as well be warned: Everyone is going to boss you around unmercifully for the next few months."

"Aren't there other women for them to nag?"

"Can't rightly say. You already discovered that Doc won't take care of you. It's not just you, either. BobbyJo Lintz up and moved back to Galveston to stay with her folks until she has her baby. Greg sent her there, but he's climbing the walls. Other than her, you're the community's only mother-to-be."

"Is that your way of telling me that I've suddenly become community property?"

"Yes, ma'am, it means precisely that." His hold tightened as they mounted the porch steps.

Trying to ignore how much she needed his support, she asked, "How is it the citizens all want to have a say when the town doctor won't speak a word to me?"

"That's a good question." He leaned forward slightly and opened the door.

She stepped inside, looked at all the boxes, and grimaced. "This mess is awful."

"You're not doing a blessed thing other than to laze in bed. Do I need to phone Teresa and ask her to come sit on top of you?"

Teresa's voice sounded from the living room. "I'd crush the poor gal! I invited myself over because I thought Sondra might be going a little stir-crazy. I'm trying my best to fix this rip in the sofa. The movers must—"

"No!" Sondra tried to wrestle free from Dylan. "No! Don't!"

Dylan's hold tightened, and he rumbled, "Settle down."

"Don't let her do it!" She twisted from Dylan toward Teresa. "I don't want it fixed!"

Dylan strode around to Teresa's side and looked at a five-inch gash in the fabric. "Sondra, it needs stitching."

"No!"

Teresa frowned. "Why not?"

"Kenny did it." She knelt on the carpeting. Reaching out, she tentatively touched the slit. "His footrest had a rough spot."

Dylan and Teresa exchanged puzzled looks and echoed, "Footrest?"

"On his wheelchair."

Teresa crouched down and cocked her head. "I'll bet he'd want it to get fixed up."

"I know," Sondra whispered thickly. "But he did it right before he left our place. It was the last time I ever saw him, and I was so mad. . . ."

Dylan hunkered down on the other side of her and tilted her face to his. "No man worth his salt would want you punishing yourself like this, Sondra. So what if you had a spat? You would have made up, too. Let go of this. Patch it up, just like you would have patched up the fight."

"That's sound advice," Teresa concurred. "Do you want to sew it up, or do you want me to do it while you sit there?"

Dylan still hadn't let go of her. Sondra rasped, "I need to do it myself."

"Okay. Afterward, you go on in and take a nap."

"What about your soda?"

Dylan smiled softly. "I'll claim it some other time."

Chapter 8

Two days later, Dylan banged on the back door. When Sondra opened it, he dusted his hands off on the thighs of his jeans. "Is that offer for a soda still open?"

"Sure. Come on in."

"I'd rather sit out here, if you don't mind. I'm gritty as a gopher hole."

She opened the refrigerator, took out two cans, and went to the sink. A few seconds later, Sondra nudged him a bit so she could sit beside him on the porch steps. He tipped back his Stetson, rolled the can very slowly across his forehead, and sighed with the pleasure of that simple act. Sondra chortled softly as she handed him a wet dishcloth. "This is almost as cool."

"Mmm. Thanks."

While he swiped at his hands, face, and neck, she popped open the tab on his soda. He accepted it with a grateful nod. "Did you and Teresa have fun today?"

"Oh yes. Your sister is terrific with kids." He'd called her each evening to see how she fared, and he'd about had a fit last night when she let slip that she'd be going to the foster home today. Next thing she knew, Teresa invited herself to go along. They'd had a wonderful time.

"Yeah, well, she said the same thing about you." He took another gulp and swallowed it.

"If I were in a more stable situation, I'd be tempted to scoop up half a dozen of those kids and bring them home."

He gave her an alarmed look. "You wouldn't—"

She shook her head. "No. I'm already in over my head. Still, I love children. I sit them in a circle and let each one hold a chick. You should see how the kids respond. It's delightful."

He tilted the can at her. "It's delightful what it does for you."

His observation made her feel unaccountably shy. During the time she'd been sick, they'd crossed over from being unwilling partners to fledgling friends. He'd proven himself trustworthy. Since then, the aching loneliness she'd felt since Kenny's death seemed less intense.

Unaware of her musings, Dylan said, "Yep." He took another healthy swig. "It's easy to see why Miller kept the henhouse. You beam when you leave here with those chicks, and you come back aglow. Not many women find contentment with such simple pleasures."

40

She shrugged self-consciously. "I've never been like other gals." Uncomfortable, she quickly changed the subject. "I have hot dogs and corn on the cob in the house. Are you hungry?"

"Starving!"

He said it with such gusto she smiled. "What do you like on your dogs?"

"Ketchup, mustard, and pickle relish."

"No onions or cheese?"

He chugged down the soda and let out a long, slow, noisy breath of bliss. "You really do 'em up. No onions. Cheese, if you have it." He then hitched a shoulder. "Sondra, I'm sweaty, hot, and real hungry. Maybe you'd rather—"

"I left a few of Miller's shirts hanging in the guest room. You're welcome to go have a quick shower. As much time as you spend here, it'd probably be a good idea for you to bring over a change of clothing. I'll eat one hot dog, maybe two. The rest are going to go rotten before I eat them again, and the buns go stale in this heat. Feel free to polish off as many as you want."

"You don't know what you're asking for."

Sondra did know what she was asking for. She hadn't shared a meal with anyone in ages. If she wanted, she could attribute feeding him to good manners and basic gratitude; the truth of the matter was, she wanted company, and Dylan propped open the door of friendship by dropping in for a drink.

For the first time, they shared a meal. Sondra folded her hands in her lap and dipped her head for a quick, silent prayer. To her surprise, Dylan immediately started, "Heavenly Father, we give You thanks for Your grace and mercy, for Your bounty and care."

Afterward, he cleared his throat. "I guess I should have asked. It was presumptuous for me to dive in like that in your home."

"Oh no! It was lovely. I only wish I'd made a real meal instead—"

"Hold it right there." He gave her an outraged look. "Hot dogs are an all-American meal, and I'm dead serious when I give thanks for them."

Half an hour later, Sondra asked, "How does ice cream sound?"

Dylan's eyes lit up. "Only if you eat a whole bowl full. You're still too skinny."

Glancing down at her tummy, Sondra refuted, "I'm not skinny. I've probably put on an inch a week this last month!"

"What does the doctor say about that?"

Sondra waggled her finger at him. "I knew you put your sister up to that! She just happened to know where the doctor's office was, and they just happened to slip me in for a quick checkup so the chicks wouldn't overheat in the car."

"Hey, I'm not denying it. Since you were in town, it made sense for you to see the doc. So what did he say?"

"Believe it or not, even with being sick, I gained weight this time." She grinned. "Must have been the great care my neighbors gave me."

"You're like one of those women from olden days. I'll bet my hands could about span your waist."

"That's not saying much. You have huge hands. This baby isn't staying little, either."

Dylan strove to keep a casual pitch to his voice. "What did the doc say?"

"The obstetrician said he looks fine. Everything is right on schedule, including the fact that the baby is getting the hiccups."

"They really don't—do they?"

"Oh yes. The rascal bumps up and down like he's on a teeter-totter."

"I still don't believe it. If he does it when I'm around, you let me know."

Sondra gave him a wary look. "Why?"

A wave of awkwardness swelled. Dylan shifted and groused, "Because. . .aw, just forget it. Skip the ice cream. I need to get going."

"I love Rocky Road. That and Fudge Brownie. There's always one or the other in the freezer, and I'll keep soda in the fridge. You're welcome to help yourself anytime." She dipped her head and wondered what made her blurt that out. His quick wit and easygoing nature made him fun to be around. Though she'd surprised herself with that invitation, she meant every word of it.

Shuffling his weight from his left boot to his right, Dylan stood at the door, plunked his Stetson on, and rumbled, "You strike me as a woman who values her privacy. I don't imagine I'll claim those much."

She looked directly at him. "I'm not the type to make empty gestures. Some women are good at coy games and small talk. Me?" She flicked him a strained smile. "I got shuffled around in the system too much to ever get good at those social conventions. You can take whatever I say at face value, so don't feel shy about popping in the back door if you're thirsty."

"I'll keep that in mind." He left.

Sondra stared at the door and wondered what had gotten into her. The only other men she'd ever felt that way with were Kenny and Miller. That fact jarred her.

Still, she went to the refrigerator and rearranged things. . . just so the soda cans would be up front. After all, what were partners for?

She made it through her seventh month of pregnancy quite nicely. The hands wouldn't let her do much of anything. They gave her tummy assessing looks and nudged her out of the way. Gathering eggs, helping groom the horses, and feeding the dogs and cats were her chores. She quickly mastered the software on Miller's computer so she could keep track of orders, bills, and payroll. Every other Friday, she passed paychecks out to the hands and thanked them wholeheartedly for their labor.

Since they wouldn't hear of her doing many of the ranching chores, Sondra made it a practice to bake something a couple of times a week. The men cooked for themselves at the bunkhouse, but they definitely appreciated having her desserts. She soon learned Howie liked pie of any variety, Nickels shared her weakness for chocolate, and Frank didn't care what it was as long as it was sweet. Edgar liked apples in his things, while Joseph could eat an entire batch of cookies all by himself. With those preferences in mind, she tried to rotate her choices.

It wasn't long before she ran into one of the men from Dylan's spread at the grocery store. Scanning the flour and butter in her cart, he drawled, "Heard tell you make a mean apple pie."

Her lips parted in surprise. Folks in this small town were astonishingly friendly. Men and women she'd never met chatted with her at the store or on the sidewalk. They invariably asked about Dylan, too. She wasn't comfortable talking about herself, and she had no idea what to say about him other than to mention he was a hardworking man. That always garnered a nod of agreement.

Dylan's ranch hand grinned. "Edgar came over. He and Dylan planned tomorrow."

Sondra still didn't see the connection.

"Edgar told Dylan they'd save him a slice of your pie. Said you just put a couple in the bunkhouse."

"Oh." She wrinkled her nose. "What's happening tomorrow?"

"We're going to cull the herds and sell off some beef. Dylan has Teresa making barbecue afterward."

"Why hasn't Teresa called me?"

"Ma'am, I never pretended to be able to read a woman's mind."

She barely quelled her laugh. "Can you read a man's?"

"Every once in a while. Mostly when he's lookin' at a woman or something good to eat."

"That doesn't take much skill," Sondra decided with mock solemnity. "It's a good thing you're a decent cowboy."

He gave her a slow smile and shook his head. "You know, Dylan's right. That spunk of yours might get you through this."

Sondra smiled and pushed her cart down the next aisle. She cruised to the produce section again to pick up more apples.

The next day, Sondra called Teresa. At four thirty, she showed up at Dylan's ranch, the Laughingstock. Teresa helped her transfer five apple pies, a chocolate cake, potato salad, and six dozen homemade rolls from her car to the picnic tables. She made lemonade as Teresa filled her in on snippets of news.

The air was redolent with the heady aroma of roasting beef when the men sauntered over. Soon as Dylan asked grace, a solid dozen men attacked the table. "Hey! Sondra made pie!"

"That's dessert!" Teresa shouted. "You leatherhands leave it be 'til you've eaten everything else!"

"Whoa! Them rolls ain't store-bought."

"Pitch me a couple!"

Dylan paced up to Sondra. She turned away and fussed to keep napkins from blowing away. She didn't want to look at him. He made her breath hitch.

Due to being in a wheelchair, Kenny had boasted impressive chest and arm muscles. Dylan, though—on him, those corded muscles spoke of heavy labor and the ability to tackle any task. He walked with rugged assurance, and every inch of him shouted masculine confidence. He'd easily held and carried her—and that somehow suddenly seemed significant. *What am I doing even looking at him?*

Unaware of his effect on her, Dylan arrived at her side with a heaping plate of beef in his hands. He extended it to her. "You'd best elbow in and get some of that food, or these hogs'll inhale it all in five minutes flat."

Sondra shook her head. "I can't eat a fraction of this."

"That's nothing!"

"It's too much, seeing as I have a passenger on board. Plain and simple, there's just not enough room."

"That passenger needs good nutrition. How much milk are you drinking? What about fruits and vegetables?"

"Dylan, I'm a grown woman. I don't need you to hover."

"How much weight have you gained?"

Her jaw dropped.

"Well?"

"That's none of your business!"

He grabbed her arm. "Make way, guys. Sondra needs to eat up."

"Stop this!" she hissed.

"Give her a roll. They taste mighty fine."

"You knothead! She made 'em," Edgar announced.

Dylan paused for a second and looked at her. "You're supposed to be resting. You made the pies. What were you thinking, making rolls, too?"

"If you're going to give her the business, best you do it up right," the man behind her tattled. "She made that there potato salad and the chocolate cake, too." He then tugged on Sondra's maternity smock. "If he fires me, I expect a job on your spread."

"Are you kidding? You've just gotten the man so mad at me, I'm mincemeat! All I owe you is indigestion!" She set her plate down. "I already have a good enough case of it to last both of us!"

"It's no wonder. You push yourself too hard and don't eat right," Dylan snapped. "This kid is going to be a sickly little thing if you don't start filling up with decent grub. When's the last time you ate liver?"

Momentarily closing her eyes in horror, she shuddered. "Liver?"

"You heard me right. Liver. For iron."

"I take an iron tablet."

"Not good enough. You don't get all you need from a stinking, little artificial pill. Quit stalling. When's the last time you had liver? Last week? Two weeks ago?" When she shook her head, he growled threateningly, "Last month?"

"Kindergarten."

"That does it!" He raised his voice. "Teresa, where's the liver from this beast? Fix it up right quick. Sondra needs to eat it."

Sondra shook her head. "I won't."

"Yes, you will. Your son deserves it."

"What did he ever do to you?"

Dylan gave her a disapproving look.

Pressing her hand over her stomach, Sondra complained, "You're making my indigestion even worse, so stop scowling at me."

"We'll walk you."

She gave him an incredulous look. "Walk me?"

Nodding curtly, as if he'd come to some momentous decision and solved the entire problem, Dylan informed her, "Walking. Until your colic passes. It works great for horses."

Sondra turned away, and everyone glared at him. *Now what did I do wrong?* Suddenly his eyes widened. He stepped back, but the table stopped him. "Sond—" A perfectly good apple pie hit his face.

Chapter 9

Her phone jangled incessantly for the next hour. Sondra finally unplugged it. She curled up in bed and stewed. How dare Dylan treat her like that? *A horse!*

Mixed in with her anger was a dawning sense of embarrassment. She'd actually hit Dylan with a pie—took the tin and smeared the whole thing all over his face. He must be absolutely livid. She'd humiliated him in front of all his men.

He was clueless. I overreacted. She lay in the dark and winced. Apologizing to him wouldn't be easy, but she owed him that much. In fact, nothing would ever cancel the debt she owed him. Yes, he'd get land and livestock at the end of the year. . . but he'd earn it.

One thing for sure: Dylan needed the land. Wisely enough, he'd refrained from repeating his desire to have first bid at the remainder of the ranch after the year lapsed. He was doing the nearly impossible, running two ranches. She appreciated it, but at the same time, on nights like tonight, Sondra was reminded it wasn't an altruistic gesture. He helped her because of what he'd get in the end.

Doing the books let her plainly see what the value of the cattle would be, come reckoning time. Then, too, Mr. Cheviot had advised her to get the land appraised so she could adequately deduct it from the property tax when it came due. Dylan was putting in hard work—but in the end, he would walk away with a very handsome reward. If he failed, he was no worse off—but she'd lose her home, her dreams, and the future she wanted for her son.

From the day she moved in, she'd never considered that tract of land or portion of cattle hers. Miller dangled it in front of Dylan to ensure his capable assistance. Sondra wanted him to succeed—not only so she'd be able to stay, but also because Dylan worked with incredible diligence. He deserved what Miller bequeathed him.

But then why is he fretting over the baby?

The next morning, Sondra fumbled to open her car door. She needed to go apologize.

"Ain't gonna open unless you unlock it," Edgar drawled.

Sondra's face twisted in chagrin as she realized she'd locked her keys in the car. Her moan brought Edgar closer.

"Don't get yourself in a tizzy. It's no big deal." Edgar whistled and waved.

Chris Ratliff pulled up. "Perfect timing. The lady's locked herself out. How's about you helping her?"

"No problem." Chris pulled a metal strip from beneath the front seat of a battered-looking green work truck. Seconds later, he opened Sondra's door with a flourish.

"How'd you do that?" She gaped at him.

"I repair cars for a living. It would be too embarrassing to call up customers and tell them I locked myself out of their cars."

Sondra ventured, "If I made both of you your very own treat, would that suffice as hush money?"

"No need to," Chris said.

Grinning from ear to ear, Edgar shook his head. "Ma'am, if you'd offered that yesterday, I'd take you up on it in a hot second. I can't now."

Dread iced down her spine. "Just what do you mean?"

"I can't rightly say." He rubbed the back of his neck and looked guilty as sin.

Chris chuckled and drove toward Nickels to pick up the eggs.

"Edgar—"

Her steely tone seemed to amuse him. "You may as well be mad at me, but I'd rather suffer your wrath than Dylan's any day. 'Specially since I've tasted your pies."

"Argh!" she said theatrically. She may as well make fun of herself. "I have a sneaking suspicion I'm never going to live that down."

He thumbed his hat back a tad. "Now that's probably a fact."

Rats.

"Then again, good as I heard tell the other pies were, I suspect we're all gonna hold Dylan to blame for costing us one."

Sondra laughed at his hangdog expression. "Didn't you get a slice?"

"Mournful fact is I barely got a taste."

"I see. Give me a day or so, and I'll make it up to you."

His eyes locked in on her belly. "I'd be much obliged, but I'm not sure you ought to be going to such trouble."

"It's no trouble. I like being in a kitchen."

He shook his head. "Never did see me a woman who kept as busy as you do. Suspect it has to do with you being on the nest, so to speak. Between you peekin' and peckin' into everything 'round the ranch and Dylan gettin' antsy 'bout trying to tie you down, a body could be rightfully entertained."

"The show's over for today." She scooched behind the wheel and headed toward Dylan's spread—LAUGHINGSTOCK, proclaimed the sign over the gate. Sondra winced. *That's me, all right. I've managed to let go of my temper and make a fool of myself.*

One of Dylan's men said he wasn't there and he didn't know where to find him. Sondra thought about calling him, but she wanted to apologize in person. Driving on, she went to Lawton and parked at the first store she found. After a month and a half of poring over the computer and tending to bills, Sondra knew full well that her financial state might be characterized as exceedingly stable. As a matter of fact, she'd never imagined that Miller Quintain possessed such staggering wealth. Though she didn't particularly want anything for herself, she knew the time had come to buy things for the baby.

Accustomed to the sight of Sondra traipsing around with a couple of the hounds scrambling at her feet, Dylan missed seeing her that morning. Pressing business matters forced him away from the ranches until noon.

Last night, he'd tried to call her to apologize, but she wouldn't answer the phone. He'd gotten an earful from every man at the barbecue—they'd been ready to beat him to a bloody pulp. As if the men hadn't been voluble enough, his sister nearly smacked him. "What got in to you? The poor gal! A horse? Walk her like a horse?"

He clamped his big mouth shut.

"I can't believe you compared Sondra to a horse." She shook her head. "Go clean up. Afterward, you'd best crawl over there on your hands and knees and apologize!"

He barked defensively, "All I was trying to do was get her to eat better. How is a bachelor supposed to know what a pregnant widow does for indigestion?"

Howie piped up. "She's been keepin' a bottle of antacid tablets in the stable."

Dylan nearly exploded. "Anything you know about her comes directly to me, do you hear that? Anything! Miller put her in my care. The last thing I need is for the lot of you to go leavin' me in the dark about the particulars."

Someone grumbled, "She's an adult. She takes pretty good care of herself."

"You can't be serious! She hasn't had liver even once. Every fool knows she supposed to eat liver. And when she got sick—remember when she got sick?"

Nickels admitted, "She was pitiful."

Teresa rubbed her hands on a napkin. "Enough's been said. I doubt Sondra would appreciate being the topic of any further conversation. Just do your best by her."

Dylan held up a hand and added, "And each of you comes to me with anything—otherwise, you'll be looking for work elsewhere. Any questions?"

No one said a thing.

Still, his message got through. As soon as he showed up that afternoon, Edgar reported, "Miz Sondra locked herself out of her car today. Went shoppin', too. Brung back loads of baby stuff. She's up at the house."

Armed with a carton of Rocky Road ice cream as a peace offering, Dylan headed for her door. She didn't answer his knock. He wasn't sure whether she refused to speak to him or if she was in trouble. He knocked once more. With no response, he decided to take her at her word. Dylan opened the kitchen door. He strode into the kitchen, letting his boots scrape on the floor loudly in hopes she'd call out a howdy. She didn't.

He stuck the ice cream in her freezer, expecting she'd hear him and make an appearance. When she didn't, he peeked into the empty living room. Maybe in the basement—doing laundry perhaps? Nope. The light was off down there. Her bedroom was empty, too. His heart started to race.

A soft sound made him push open the last door. Dylan stood there and tilted his head to the side. His eyes narrowed. Asleep? In here? He drew closer and confirmed his suspicion. She looked vulnerable as she slept. Her lashes fanned across her cheekbones and fluttered a little. Her lips pouted. He winced at how kissable she looked.

Whoa. Where did that thought come from? For all of its surprise, the admission rang true.

She had no right to look so adorable. And cuddly. Peach and yellow flowers dotted the dress that draped her softer, fuller curves. Sondra had gained some weight—enough to fill in the hollows of her cheeks pleasantly, and the radiance of her skin brought to mind the cliché of how pregnant women glowed.

Oh, man. I'm getting lassoed by my own rope.

She favored some heady perfume—an exotic blend of subtle spices and a hint of flowers that left him inhaling deeply after she walked past. Just a whiff, and he'd hold his breath to appreciate the scent a moment longer. The intelligent sparkle in her eye captivated him. And the way she sometimes pursed her lips as she thought or absorbed something he told her—as if she were ready for a kiss.

Oh, he'd been appreciating the sight all along. Truth be told, she'd slowly been driving him crazy—but until this moment, he'd attributed it more to obligation and her quirky nature. Never once had he admitted his heart might be getting involved.

Through it all, he'd been sort of a neutral party. Exhibiting a polite modicum of concern and a proprietary interest were all that seemed appropriate. After all, they were partners of a sort. Miller had entrusted her into his care.

Besides, she was a widow. Carrying another man's baby. And he was a Christian brother. That certainly put him in a position of helping out.

Until now. Just as soon as Dylan admitted to himself that he'd fallen, and fallen hard, the sucker punch came. He could want her from now 'til the moon fell out of the sky, but wanting didn't matter when it was one-sided. Then, too, he didn't cotton to the notion that he would be last in line. Sondra's world revolved around the child she carried. That was admirable. . .but it also pointed out a glaring fact: That baby would always bind her heart to Kenny.

She cherished her memories of Kenny—and though that was well and good, he'd once been a mortal man—but Dylan knew he'd now be competing with saintly memories. That went over about as well as getting bucked off into a cactus patch. Nope. He shook his head. Partners. Brother and sister in Christ. That's all he and Sondra would ever be.

Other than when she had the flu, she'd been bouncing around and getting into everything. Indigestion might be a bit of a nuisance, but overall, she'd never complained or shied away from doing anything. Leave it to a sassy woman like her to carry a kid with confidence. She didn't want or need special considerations.

Just then, the baby moved, making the flowered fabric of her dress ripple in the most fascinating way. Dylan watched in silence. It was such an amazing sight. A little frog-catching, jackrabbit-chasing, cowlick-headed boy was inside of her. What a wonder!

Suddenly tension sang through every last inch of her. His eyes narrowed. "You're awake."

She let out a cry.

Chapter 10

ey, settle down," Dylan placated in a soft tone. "It's just me. Everything's okay. I brought some ice cream. Rocky Road."

Sondra wet her lips and nodded slowly. She sat on the far side of the bed, back pressed against the wall. Her eyes were huge.

Stuffing his hands in his pockets, Dylan realized aloud, "I spooked you. I'm sorry."

"'S okay."

"Not really. You look like you wanna scream. I'll go dish up ice cream. Okay?" He headed for the kitchen and decided to have a bowl, too. A relaxed time together was just the ticket—and no one could get het up while eating ice cream. He scooped out several hunks and created a mountain in each bowl.

"Dylan! What army is going to help me do that justice?"

He turned. "You're on your own." Grinning wasn't hard. She'd run a comb through her hair so it fell in a fiery, bouncy fall past her shoulders. Her flowered dress looked springy and cool.

Self-consciously smoothing out a few wrinkles over her tummy, Sondra said, "I should have changed."

"You look cuter than a bug's ear. Come sit down." Thumping the bowls onto the table, Dylan waggled his brows. "I brought your favorite."

She sat, took up her spoon, and let out a small sigh of pleasure as she swallowed her first bite. A moment later, she frowned at her hand. "My ring's getting tight."

"Better take it off."

She chewed on her lip and shrugged.

He wondered if it was already stuck. Forcing himself to not look at her hand took considerable self-control. He'd already blundered by giving his opinion about how she ought to take care of herself. A pregnant widow had every reason to want to keep on her wedding band. Still, she needed to be sensible. "When you're ready, a little butter might make it slip off a bit easier."

"I'll keep that in mind. I thought maybe bag balm would do the trick."

He shot her a quirky smile. "Ma'am, you said it; I didn't."

She wrinkled her nose. "Dylan, I owe you an apology. I let my hormones and temper get ahead of me last night—"

"I owe you an apology," he interrupted. He searched for the right words, "About the—"

"How about we both forget that unfortunate episode?"

He started to chuckle. "You're not hearing me complain. Your revenge was mighty sweet."

She smiled as she took a bite of ice cream.

He finally allowed himself to look at her left hand. "Ma'am, if your band gets much tighter, you'll be in trouble—but then again, I've proven myself to be wholly ignorant regarding maternity and women, in general. I'll have to beg your pardon if I get a mite jumpy about you. . . ." He waved his spoon toward her tummy. "And all of this."

"There's nothing to fret about. Overall, I've been very lucky. Six weeks to go, and I'm feeling fine." She looked pleased—though he wasn't sure whether her relief came from the fact that she was so close to the end of being in a family way or that they'd dropped the subject of her ring.

"When are you going to move into the city?"

Her spoon clattered to the table. "I'm not moving!"

"Oh, come on, Sondra! I wasn't talking about you leaving permanently."

"I'm staying right here."

"You have to be closer to medical care for when the baby comes. No one's gonna take that as abandonment. Other mothers-to-be do it. As a matter of fact, BobbyJo Lintz just came back home yesterday after having their kid."

"Really? What did she have?"

"A boy. Your youngster will have a pal on the school bus. Nice, eh?"

Sondra glowed. "Wonderful! I'll have to make her a few meals."

"Oh no, you don't! What you need to do is settle down and rest."

"I was lying down."

"After you went roaming all over creation. I saw all of those shopping bags."

"Those are a few essentials. I'm going to order the nursery furniture from Nielson's."

He nodded. Sondra showed good judgment, buying big-ticket items from a local family who also happened to worship at their church. She'd adjusted to small-town living like the proverbial duck to water. Rubbing his hand across his jaw, Dylan blurted out, "Are you sure the baby's healthy?"

"There aren't any guarantees, Dylan. So far, things look fine."

"Why was your husband in a wheelchair? I mean, was it because of a birth defect?"

"Motorcycle accident."

"Before or after you got married? Aw, forget I asked. It's none of my business."

Sondra licked a dot of chocolate off her lower lip and shook her head. "No one's asked me about Kenny since he died. It's spooky—like I'm supposed to pretend he never existed or anything. I loved him. I don't want to forget him."

"Makes sense." Dylan stared at the ice cream melting in his own bowl. The last thing he wanted to hear was how much she loved another man—even if Kenny was dead.

"Ken and I met at a coworker's birthday bash. He and I hit it off right away. I'd sprained my ankle and had to camp out on the couch. We ended up talking for hours."

"He must have had the time of his life."

"I sure did. I'm a sucker for a man in jeans and a flannel shirt."

"Hmm. You're in trouble." *And I'm in luck. I live in jeans and flannel shirts all winter.*

"Why am I in trouble?" Her brows rose. "Because the men around here wear them?"

When he nodded, she shrugged. "I don't think that'll be much of an issue. I'll be far too distracted to care about anyone who doesn't wear a diaper."

Dylan shifted uncomfortably. "Ah, Sondra?"

"Yes?"

"You're a pretty little gal. You've got a bunch of money and a fine ranch. I hope you'll be careful. Plenty of slick guys would be more than happy to slip in and get their hands on such a deal."

"Mr. Cheviot warned me of the same thing when I signed the papers. I'm not worried, Dylan. It's nice of you to be concerned, but I don't think I'm heart-whole enough to think about loving anyone again."

Some things can't be hurried. I'll give you time, honey.

She stared at the melting ice cream in her dish and his empty bowl. She made a ragged attempt to clear her throat. "I hate being a crybaby."

Dylan rose and stood by her. He skimmed his big hand up and down her back. "You're not being a crybaby. You're just a woman with too many responsibilities and a broken heart." He smoothed her hair as she took a few deep breaths to calm herself. "A man would be lucky to be loved the way you loved Ken."

"Don't you have someone, Dylan?"

"No. Miller must have eaten locoweed when he stuck that option in the will about us getting married. Bad enough he got that bee in his bonnet. Even worse, Teresa nearly drives me crazy with her matchmaking schemes. Our folks were one of those rare couples who were madly in love with each other. Teresa's engaged to Jeff Langston, and they're both disgustingly happy together. I couldn't be more pleased for them."

"With that kind of example, why haven't you taken the plunge?"

He shrugged. "I'm waiting on God's timing."

"The loneliness is awful, isn't it?"

"I'm not complaining." He intentionally kept his voice light. The last thing she needed was for him to underscore the emptiness of solitary nights and meals for one. He gave her a playful pat. "Eat the rest of your ice cream."

"I'm full."

"Want me to make you eat liver instead?"

***

Dylan finished putting the chicks back with the hens. Sondra still took them to the group home for foster kids every other week. He didn't cotton to her driving that far, but she always came back so happy that he couldn't very well discourage her. Instead he made it a habit to be there to help her gather them up. It was cute, seeing how she never just scooped them up and tucked them into the box. She always cradled them for a moment, rubbed them against her pleasure-flushed cheek, and temporarily lost all of her sadness. Usually she'd put them back, but at barely eleven o'clock, the day had already turned into a scorcher. He'd promised to take care of her little chicks if she'd go in and cut a few checks he vowed were urgently needed.

Dylan watched the Nielson's Furniture truck drive up and nonchalantly wandered over to get a gander. It was time he could ill-afford to waste. "That the stuff for the baby?"

"Yep." Jim Nielson jumped out of the delivery truck. "This is the biggest order we've gotten in a long time."

Dylan let out a low whistle when the kid opened the tailgate of the truck. "Need a hand getting all of this inside?"

"I'd be obliged. Dad promised her I'd set up everything. I may well still be in there clutching a screwdriver the day the kid comes home from the hospital!"

Dylan's smile faded. In fact, he gritted his teeth. Sondra was young. Pretty, too. Vulnerable. Some moon-eyed puppy like this could wriggle his way right into her heart if he did a few favors and acted understanding. Dylan half stomped up to the doorstep and pounded. "Sondra! Truck's here with the baby furniture!"

She opened the door and smiled at him. She didn't look at the truck—she looked at him! His heart did a genuine two-step. She was one fine-looking woman. He grinned right back like some nitwitted fool.

"Terrific!" She stepped back as Jimmy brought up the first load of boxes.

Steering her over to the couch, Dylan ordered, "You sit here and put your feet up. Did you want the baby to have the room next to the master bedroom?"

"Please."

Soon as they'd hauled the boxes inside, Sondra sat on the edge of the twin bed in the nursery and opened a box containing the swing. Dylan appreciated that about her—she was a dig-in-and-get-things-done kind of woman. She didn't expect everyone to fuss over her. Her attitude about getting on with life showed wisdom and strength.

She jutted her chin toward the far wall. "If you'd please put the crib over there, I'd appreciate it. It gets morning sun, but the baby won't be by the curtain's cord." She chewed on her lip. "I'm not sure about where to put the changing table."

Jabbing his thumb at the opposite wall, Dylan said, "There. When you're changing him and he sprouts a leak, the closet and curtains are both out of range."

Sondra blinked at him. "How did you know that?"

"Mom was a baby magnet. Folks knew she'd watch their kids anytime, for any reason. If someone was sick or needed a break or wanted to go off on a romantic getaway, they knew Mom would gladly take on their kids. I've changed more diapers than you could ever count," Dylan admitted gruffly.

She laughed then turned. "I'll bet you're thirsty, Jim. Can I get you some lemonade or soda?"

"Either would be nice, ma'am. Thanks."

Sondra went down the hall toward the kitchen. Dylan followed right behind her. When she opened the refrigerator, he reached and grabbed a soda. Dylan was careful not to touch her. Oh, he loomed as close as possible, but he didn't actually allow himself to make contact. He just might end up doing something stupid if he did. Like shaking her 'til her teeth rattled. *Or kissing her.*

Yeah, he wanted to spin her around and plant a kiss on her. He ached to hold her and stop pretending to be nothing more than a helpful neighbor or financial partner. A man couldn't be more warped than this—to want a woman carrying another man's child. His timing stank. She didn't want him; he'd undoubtedly drive himself insane, wanting her.

He tried to concentrate on the soda. Sondra had asked what brand he preferred and kept some on hand for him. He'd been flattered. Now that the soda was waiting, ice-cold, for him, he should have felt even better—but he didn't. He noticed she'd offered Jim a drink. Not him. Just Jim. He purposefully didn't straighten back up. His fingers flexed around the aluminum can as the cool air blasted out of the refrigerator.

"Please, Dylan, excuse me."

Something in her tone struck him as wrong. Mostly the way those last two words came out in a strained puff of air. He stepped back and wondered why she didn't uncurl. "Sondra?"

A long second passed. "Hmm?" Slowly, she straightened.

Scowling, he demanded, "What's going on?"

"Nothing."

"Baloney. You just shut the fridge and didn't get Jimmy-boy's drink."

Color tinged her cheeks. "Oh. I didn't, did I?" She opened the door again.

He slammed it shut. "Enough of this nonsense, woman. What just happened?"

"I had a little cramp is all."

His can was on the countertop in nothing flat. Dylan scooped her up and headed for the couch. "It's too soon! Why didn't you say something straight off?"

Chapter 11

Clutching his shoulders, she squeezed to stop his tirade. "Dylan, they're normal. The doctor calls them Braxton Hicks contractions. I can have four an hour without getting worried. It's simply a warm-up for the big event."

Stopping in the middle of the living room, he demanded, "Are you sure?"

"Yes."

His heart still thundered. "Just how many of those cramps have you been having?"

"Not that many."

He glanced at her belly. "Carrying a baby is normal, but you don't have to take it lightly. Cramps matter. Shouldn't you be counting them? We'll get a clock in here so you can keep track."

Her hand stayed stationary on his shoulder, but her thumbnail traced back and forth along the seam of his shirt. A bashful half smile flickered across her face. "Honest, Dylan, I'm doing fine. I just saw the doctor day before yesterday."

"What did he say?"

"I'm fine." She cast a look back toward the kitchen and gave his shoulder a pat. "Your cola's getting hot."

"Do you care?"

Her eyes widened and mouth fell open. "Why else do you think I keep it in the refrigerator?"

He slowly bent and put her feet back on the floor. As he completely turned loose of her, he let out a rude snort.

"What is that supposed to mean?"

"You asked Junior what he wanted." He knew he sounded like a jealous kid who got the skimpiest slice of cake. "Just forget it."

Her small hands both grabbed and clasped one of his. "Dylan, I knew what you'd want. I don't know Jim Nielson from Adam, so I was trying to be polite."

"Oh." He yanked away his hand and growled, "Great. You think you know me so well that you can read my mind? For your information, I wanted lemonade!"

She planted her hands in the region where her hips used to be. "And I suppose that's why you took out a soda?"

"Do you want to stand here all day jawing, or do you want that crib put together?"

She sidled past him. "I'll get your lemonade."

He captured her wrist. "I don't expect you to wait on me. I can get my own drink."

"You've never treated me like I'm a waitress, Dylan. I appreciate all you do, and you're going the extra mile—again, helping with this on top of everything else. I—"

Whatever she was going to say got lost in a thump and a yelp from the other room. Dylan muttered, "I'd better get back in there with Jimmy-boy before he kills himself."

Sondra supplied the men with lemonade and fixed chicken salad sandwiches for lunch. They all sat in the nursery and admired the way things began to take shape. After wolfing down one last bite, Jim dusted his hands. "I gotta go. I took the liberty of tucking the high chair in the far side of the closet. You won't need it for a long while. Those blankets in there are a real kick."

Sondra opened the closet door, took out a big stack, and set them on the dresser. "Did I show these to you, Dylan?"

He picked up one. She'd carefully cut Kenny's flannel shirts into neat squares, stitched them together, and made baby quilts. "Wanna put this in the crib now?"

"Please."

As Sondra walked Jimmy out, Dylan put the other blankets away. A teddy bear tumbled out. Dylan stooped to pick it up. It was dressed in a tiny flannel shirt. Suddenly Dylan felt completely out of place. He'd invaded her private domain. Just about the time he was feeling like his soda cans filled her fridge and he had a place in her home and life, he ran into the blatant reminder that in her heart, she still belonged to another man and was carrying his baby. Reality hit hard. He hurriedly stuffed the bear in place and strode to the front door. "I've got work to do. You rest up now."

"I don't do anything else." She paused and then said, "Dylan, I'm glad you were here to help me with the nursery. It made it easier. . . ."

He looked at her with a new tenderness. She gave her son special home-made blankets from a daddy he'd never know. Still, she appreciated Dylan's presence. That counted for a lot in his book. Unable to resist, he gently stroked his fingertips down her cheek. "Honey, you're gonna be a good mama."

"Thanks. Let me fix supper for you tomorrow night."

"You don't need to do that."

"I want to. I'm getting cabin fever, staying inside with nothing but the hum of the air conditioner. What would you like to have?"

"You have a knack in the kitchen. Do whatever sounds good to you." He worked like mad for the rest of the day to make up for the time he'd lost assembling the baby furniture.

The next day, Dylan got up early and pushed himself to get everything done. Teresa had given him a speculative look when he'd told her he already had plans and wouldn't be home for supper.

At ten 'til six, he shambled up to the back door and knocked. Sondra answered, looking fresh as a dewed wildflower. "Little lady, I'm as big a mess as a man ever was. I don't want to offend you, and I know you probably spent a lot of time fixin' a mighty fine meal, but I'll have to ask for a rain check."

Her gaze slid up and down him then concentrated on his left sleeve. Her dainty nose twitched. That particular smell was unmistakable. "You have a change of clothes here. Hop on in and take a shower."

"I don't think—"

She grabbed his other arm and gave it a tug. "The cool air is rushing out while you stand there trying to act as if I don't know what manure smells like. Last time I checked, this was a ranch. It isn't as if it's a totally foreign part of the package." She shoved him in the direction of the hall and then flooded the kitchen with a mouthwatering aroma as she opened the oven to check on the rolls.

"Mmm. I won't be long."

A red-and-white-checkered cloth graced the table when he padded into the kitchen in his stocking feet. Her smile suddenly melted.

"What's wrong?"

She wiggled a little and blushed. "I can't. . .seem to. . .untie. . . Oh! The apron strings are knotted."

"Come here." Dylan leaned against the counter and twirled her around. He deftly undid the small tangle. "What makes you wear an apron, anyhow? I thought those went out in the early sixties. Only time Teresa ever wears one is when she's basting half a cow for barbecue 'cause it's so messy."

"I drop everything down the front of me these days. I'm a first-class slob." She turned back around and let out a self-conscious laugh. "I guess I won't have any room to complain when the baby spills stuff all over his bibs and overalls."

"I've yet to hear you complain. Seems to me you've got cause to grouse a bit here and there."

For a minute, she couldn't seem to breathe. She closed her eyes. "I had to have the jeweler cut off my wedding band today."

"Aww." He pulled her into the shelter of his height as she steadied herself with a few deep breaths. "That's a pure pity. Why don't we get you a little something to wear so your finger doesn't feel so bare?"

"Nothing but Kenny's ring would feel right." She pushed away and forced a smile.

Dylan pulled her into his chest again and cupped her head to his shoulder. "How long has it been, sweetheart?"

"Seven months and three days."

She hadn't even had to think for a second before answering. He felt the waves of grief wash over her. He held her tightly, having to bow himself around her tummy. As if her grief wasn't enough, the baby kicked and squirmed between them—an ever-present and poignant reminder of a past she'd never leave behind. His lips barely grazed her temple as he quietly asked, "Want me to slip out of here?"

"No. Please, no!" Her fingers curled into the fabric of his chambray shirt. After taking another breath, she pushed away from him. "Supper's going to get cold. I hope you like Italian."

"The only thing I don't like is brussels sprouts. Other than that, I'm a human vacuum cleaner." He grinned at her and felt a flood of relief. The look of gratitude on her face made it clear he'd reacted the right way.

"Then you're in luck. In my opinion, they rate right up there with liver."

Wincing theatrically, Dylan held up both hands, as if to ward her off. "I know better than to touch that one!"

She'd made a marvelous meal. Manicotti, garlic bread, Caesar salad, and mixed vegetables should have been enough, but she even produced spumoni ice cream for dessert. "It's not chocolate, but I couldn't resist."

"You still could stand to put on a few pounds. I'm glad you didn't resist."

"Dylan, my weight isn't a topic of conversation."

"Then what about baby names? Are you going to name him after his dad?"

"Kenneth hated his name, so he made it clear from the get-go that he didn't want our son to be a Kenny Junior. I thought about naming him after Miller, but it's cruel to stick a kid with a name like that. Imagine going through life with the name *Thankful, Miller* on the classroom rosters."

Tearing off a chunk of garlic bread, Dylan agreed, "That's bad."

"I thought maybe I'd look in the big, old family Bible Miller had in the study. There are probably a couple of good names in it."

"I'll clear the table, Sondra. Go get it and let's see what's to be found." Dylan rose and grabbed a few dishes. Sondra took a few steps and suddenly skidded. All of the plates in his hands clattered to the floor as Dylan made a quick dive. Miraculously, he caught her before she landed. "Oh!" she gasped as she grabbed handfuls of his shirt.

"Are you all right?" He didn't like how pale she'd become. Quickly scooping her into his arms, Dylan carried her to the living room and laid her on the couch. "Sondra, honey, are you hurt?"

Her hands went to her tummy. His joined them. Four hands—two slender and white, the others larger, rough, and tanned—waited impatiently until the child somersaulted. Sondra burst into nervous laughter.

Dylan sat on the floor. He wanted to hold her. At least hold her hand. He settled for reaching up and gripping the back of the couch to keep her in the shelter of his arm, but she started to squirm. *She doesn't want me close.*

"Dylan? I need to turn onto my side. It's hard to breathe if I'm on my back."

"Here." He slipped her arm around his neck and took his sweet time helping her get readjusted. The baby tumbled again, rippling across his wide-open palm in a startling display of strength. "He's a mighty little cowhand, isn't he?"

She let out another small, tight laugh and nodded.

Tilting her face upward, Dylan demanded, "How 'bout you, sugar? Are you all right after that spill?"

She nodded and proceeded to huddle into him and start to shudder.

"Shaken up," he evaluated. He couldn't blame her at all. His hands were unsteady. After a long time, her shivers tapered off. She mumbled an apology.

"You're gonna be all right, little Sondra. You and that baby are just fine."

"Just fine," she agreed.

"That's right, honey." The swell of emotions he felt stunned him. Tenderness the likes of which he'd never known filled his heart. It wasn't pity, either. It was a deep kind of caring. Oh, he felt attracted in a purely masculine sense. She was feminine and soft and yielding. Even now, pregnant as could be, the way she moved mesmerized him. He grazed her temple with his fingertips.

She smiled. "Not a single bump, in case you're checking. Your reflexes are awesome. Thanks for the rescue."

Her gorgeous, fiery locks splayed across the throw pillow. He wanted to toy with them, but that wouldn't do. Dylan pushed to his feet. "You stay put."

"Why? I'm—"

"Going to drive me nuts," he interrupted. He strode to the kitchen and made sure to clean up the small spot of spaghetti sauce she'd slipped in. She shouldn't be living alone anymore. It was dangerous. What if she'd fallen and been all by herself?

He heard a sound and went back to the living room, but it was empty. "Sondra?"

Her voice drifted to him from the hallway. "Just a minute."

"Are you okay?"

She reappeared. "Sorry I was so clumsy."

"You oughtn't be all on your lonesome. Teresa can come stay a little while, or—"

"No!" She stepped back. "I'm not a child. It's humiliating enough to have to rely on everyone to do my work around here. I refuse to have someone lurking around the house, watching my every move."

"What's wrong with letting us help you out a bit?"

"I'm going to work up to the day I have this baby. There's no reason not to—I feel terrific. Besides, after I have him, I'll be out of commission for a couple of weeks."

"Six, minimum. More likely, eight or ten."

"Ten!"

"If you have a cesarean."

"I'm not having a cesarean!"

Noting how she glowered at him and still managed to protectively cover the undercurve of her tummy, Dylan knew he'd rattled her. "Sondra, even if you don't, the baby is going to need you nonstop."

"I'll carry him in one of those nifty slings, so he'll go wherever I go."

"Your back aches from carrying him on the inside. What makes you think carrying him on the outside will be any easier?"

"Who says my back hurts?"

He gave her an exasperated look. "You're rubbing it right now. Fact is, most anytime I see you, you've taken to bracing the small of your back with your hands."

"See? I told you I need some privacy!"

"Tough luck. If you won't let someone stay with you, then we're going to start checking in on you a couple of times a day."

"That's ridiculous. Heaven help me—"

Dylan cracked a laugh. "If you're referring to Miller looking down at you from heaven, you'd better start worrying."

"I meant the Lord, Dylan. Still, it's sweet to think Miller is walking the streets of gold with God and they can see how grateful I am."

"God's certainly watching over you, but I aim to help. As for Miller—I have news for you, Mother Hen: He was allergic to feathers. He put in that coop after he read your request for chicks."

"He never let on—"

He squeezed her arms. "Of course he didn't. That wasn't Miller's way. When I asked him about it, he told me he got so much joy out of your visits and stories about the children he'd have gladly built a coop ten times that size."

"He was a special man. I really miss him, Dylan."

He gave her hand a squeeze. "So do I."

"Thanks for coming over. I'm sorry I spoiled the evening."

"Hey, supper tasted terrific. You didn't spoil anything."

"I was clumsy as a cow."

Dylan forced himself to let go of her hand. He injected a mock sternness into his tone. "And here I thought you showed all of the potential to become a good rancher. Every cattleman knows cows are graceful as can be."

She turned him around and pushed him toward the front door. "And every cattle woman knows cowboys are full of beans."

Chapter 12

August arrived. Heat shimmered off the land. Chores not done early in the morning became almost impossible to accomplish until late afternoon because of the torturous conditions. Sondra was eternally grateful for the air-conditioning in her home. It took less than five minutes in the noonday sun for her to wilt.

A philanthropic organization operated a summer camp for foster kids, so she didn't visit the group home. She missed seeing the kids, but she decided to concentrate on getting ready for the baby. She put sheets on the crib, wallpapered the nursery, and read voluminously.

Teresa offered to come help with the housework before and after the baby was born. Sondra appreciated her kindness but didn't accept. "I'll be bored to tears if I don't have anything to do. By then, you'll be a newlywed and need to settle in."

Teresa shook her finger. "Don't you be too proud to go changing your mind."

"I'm okay. Really, I am. Housework keeps me busy. At least I'll be ready when the baby decides to make his appearance."

"Once you drop, you shouldn't be alone."

"You're as bad as Dylan! He's hovering. I'm just pregnant, not terminally ill."

"True enough. Still, if your water breaks, you'll need someone to drive you to the hospital lickety-split."

"I'm perfectly capable of driving myself."

Teresa gave her an appalled look. "You're not thinking clearly at all! Either you promise you'll call for help, or one of us is moving in with the other."

Dylan had come into the kitchen as her pronouncement was made. He sauntered over to the refrigerator, pulled out a can of soda, and popped the lid. "Guess you have things under control. Which way is the move going? Sondra to our place, or you comin' here?"

"Neither!" Sondra glowered at him. "The last thing I need is having everybody drive me crazy. It's natural to have a baby. Healthy. If you don't want to believe me, I have books by all sorts of experts—"

He raised his can in a toasting gesture. "Hats off to you. You've done the schoolteacher thing and read a heap and did a bunch of research to get ready. Just remember that there's a world of difference between all of the theory in your ivory-tower books and actual practice in real-life situations."

"I've also watched DVDs and births on cable!"

He nearly choked on his soda then shook his head. "Now why would a city-gal want to go do a thing like that?"

"City or country—what's the difference?"

"If you'd grown up out here, you would've seen animals give birth hundreds of times and figured it was. . .well, natural. I'll bet you've never even seen puppies born."

She lifted her chin. "I was there when you pulled that calf!"

Dylan winced at the memory. "If I'd have known you were expecting, I would've hustled you out of the birthing shed faster than a cricket can jump. Some things you just don't have to watch—like those movies. Are you trying to scare yourself half to death?"

"The women in the movies all manage just fine."

He stared at her in silence. Suddenly his face softened, as did his voice. His eyes glowed with compassion. "Yeah, Sondra, I'm sure they did, but they all had a husband to smooth things out and help them along. You haven't wanted or asked for any help. No one expects you to hang in there and take it all by yourself. No one's going to bat an eye when you have 'em give you a little something to take the edge off of the pain."

"The American Academy of Pediatrics says that if drugs are used in labor, the choice should be based on what has the least effect on the neonate."

Dylan grinned. "See? The least effect."

Sondra looked at him in disbelief. "I've done tons of reading, and it all boils down to the fact that the baby still gets some of the drug. That's why they say *if* drugs are used." She folded her arms across her chest and leaned back against the counter. She nodded resolutely. "I'm not about to subject my baby to any risk!"

"It seems to me you're putting him at risk by refusing to let anyone help you or stay with you." Dylan crushed the can in his hand then tossed it into the trash. "If something went wrong, it might be too late by the time any of us got here."

"What an awful thing to say!"

"Yes, it was," Teresa agreed softly. She then tacked on, "It takes a mighty good friend to point out something that touchy, though. Dylan did it because he cares about you and the baby. You can't fault him for being dead-straight honest."

"Excuse me." Sondra waddled out of the room and firmly shut her bedroom door. She had too much to worry about already. She didn't want to have them feed her any more concerns. Didn't they know how lonely she felt? How inept and overwhelmed? Didn't they understand she'd come here so her child would be well provided for and so she could stay with him?

It hadn't been easy in the least. The last thing she needed was for them to point out the obscure possibilities for complications. She stood at the crib and smoothed the sheet. A few moments later, she heard the kitchen door shut. Teresa's and Dylan's voices faded away. Letting out a shaky sigh, Sondra knew she was alone once again. She didn't know whether to be delighted or worried.

Dylan knew exactly how to feel: guilty. He'd up and scared the poor little widow-woman all over again. Often, when she wasn't watching, he checked her over really carefully, and her eyes managed to take on a desolate, haunted look.

Preoccupied, he rode Pretty Boy under a tree and whacked off his Stetson on a low-hanging branch. By noontime, Dylan had made a fair number of dumb blunders. Knowing full well he'd best go square matters away with Sondra or practically kill himself in an accident, he stopped at home and took out a half-gallon brick of Rocky Road. Just as Sondra kept his brand of soda at her place, he'd taken to storing her favorite flavors of ice cream at his.

She didn't answer his knock, and Dylan started feeling antsy. He tried again then walked on in. Tracking through the empty kitchen, he discovered the living room, bedrooms, and bathrooms were empty. Vexed, he walked back through the kitchen just in time to see the door to the basement open. Sondra stepped out.

She was wearing a gigantic, baby blue T-shirt. Singing loudly, she didn't realize he was there until she shut the door and took another step into the kitchen. As soon as she spied him, she let out a high-pitched shriek.

Dylan reached out to take the laundry basket from her.

"I'm so embarrassed!" An evasive move accompanied her wail.

Dylan kept hold of the basket. "For cryin' out loud, Sondra. You're covered up."

"Will you get out of here?"

"Nope." He glanced at the contents of the basket. As calm as you please, he plucked her pink, fluffy housecoat from the top of the laundry, shook it out, and slipped it around her shoulders. Curling his hands around the basket, he ordered, "Give this to me."

"Only if you promise to close your eyes and turn around."

Huffing, he complied. "Okay." He stood with his back to her, set the basket on the table, and decided to lessen the tension. "Remember those fluffy, round, pink lunch cakes?"

"Are you comparing me to one of those?"

"Yup. One of those pinky, dinky, sweet things."

She muttered, "As if there's anything dinky about me."

Dylan snagged the belt from the laundry basket. He turned around, pro-ceeded to slip it around her, and then tied it in a quick clove hitch. He patted the knot where it lay over the mound of her tummy and winked at her. "I defy you to look down and tell me you don't look just like—"

"Dylan?" she interrupted. "I'm not a violent woman, but I'm about to threaten grave, bodily harm if you don't hush."

"Didn't you ever learn about getting more flies with honey than vinegar? Instead of grousing, you should try to bribe me into silence by offering ice cream."

She gave him an exasperated look.

He held up his hands in a gesture of surrender. "I met you more than halfway—I brought the ice cream. Tell you what, you go sit on the sofa and I'll bring you some."

She slipped past him and headed for the hallway mumbling, "I don't want flies."

Dylan knew she hadn't gone to the living room, but he didn't chase after her. She was too embarrassed for him to push matters. He could hear her walking around in the master bedroom. If it made her feel better to pull on fifteen layers of clothes, he was going to let her—and he wouldn't say a word about it. After filling a pair of bowls, he went to the living room and ate several heaping bites while he waited.

Sondra reappeared wearing stretch slacks and a gauzy top the color of spring grass. She didn't meet his eyes when she finished easing herself into the corner of the couch.

Dylan pressed the bowl into her hands. "I changed my mind. The minute you turned your back and started walking down the hallway, I thought you looked like a polar bear with a sunburn."

"Well!" The affronted tone of voice was at direct odds with the smile on her face. "I'm offended. You could have said I looked like something cool and graceful—like, say. . .a flamingo."

"Nah. I'm not gonna encourage a nitwit notion like that. You might well take it in your mind to stand on one leg. You've managed to do just about everything else imaginable, but some things defy good sense."

She played with the spoon and ice cream. "I've been careful. I admit—it's driving me crazy not to do more around here, though. Holding back goes against my grain."

Dylan set down his ice cream. "You do plenty. It's not easy, adjusting to a new home. You're settling in and making friends. Keeping books and learning the ropes of a new business, too. Using your mind is every bit as valuable as using your muscles."

She swirled her spoon around and concentrated on the bowl as if she'd never seen anything half as intriguing. Her nonchalance was feigned, and poorly, at that.

Dylan leaned forward. "I confess, when we started out, I figured this was as lopsided as a partnership ever got. You've pitched in, dug deep, and have surprised everyone—me, most of all." She looked up at him. Her gaze locked with his, as if she needed to be certain he wasn't just giving her a pep talk. Dylan stared back at her, steady and sure. He wanted her to know she'd earned his admiration.

"You've been terrific about setting aside your plans and throwing yourself into this partnership. My role has been negligible. You'll never know how thankful I am."

He acknowledged her words with a dip of his head. "Mrs. Thankful, I do believe your name suits you fine."

She hitched her shoulder. "Other than the baby, it's about all I have to claim of Kenny's."

She didn't often say much about her husband. He wondered aloud, "How long were you together?"

"We dated for about four months."

Dylan picked up his ice cream again. "But how long were you together?"

"I thought you knew. I, um. . ." A virulent blush swept over her as her voice dropped shyly. "I got pregnant on our honeymoon. Kenny called it beginner's luck."

"But he died—," Dylan rasped. "You were married only two months?"

Her eyes filled with tears. "Six weeks and two days."

"Aww, baby." Dylan reached to pull her close.

She shoved her bowl into his hands instead. "I can't even eat that for solace!"

"Why not?"

A wry smile twisted her lips, even as her eyes swam with tears. "Because the baby has the hiccups!"

Dylan thumped the bowls down on the coffee table. "Really?"

She let out a watery laugh. "Look—you can see it."

His gaze locked on her tummy, and within a few seconds, his hands were there, too. Rhythmic knocking lifted and dropped her belly. Soon he couldn't feel it because her laughter made everything shake. "You ought to see the look on your face, Dylan!"

"That's wild!"

"It's rude. I'll have to teach this kid manners as soon as he makes an appearance."

"Don't ask me for any help. I'm the idiot who barged in on you today. I'm real sorry for that, you know."

Sondra patted his arm. The distraction of the baby's hiccups seemed to have bought her an opportunity to regain control of her emotions. "It was my fault. I invited you to come and go at will. The dress I wanted to wear today is down in the dryer. I just dashed down to get it, but it was still too damp to wear." She started to wallow.

"What are you doing?"

"I'm trying. . .to. . .get up!"

Dylan sprang to his feet. "Why didn't you just ask for help?"

"I'm. . .not. . .helpless." She let him haul her to her feet and excused herself.

Dylan knew she was heading for the bathroom. "I'll see you later. Oh— Sondra?"

She stopped.

"Teresa asked me to have you give her a call. Something about the wedding."

She gave him a winsome smile. "Okay." She watched his expression change. "What is it?"

"Something you said just passed through my mind."

"What?"

"You said it was a honeymoon baby."

"Yes."

Beginner's luck. She and Ken waited, just as God commands.

Sondra turned and started down the hallway. She called over her shoulder, "Thanks for the ice cream."

Dylan took his empty bowl and her melted mush into the kitchen. Rinsing them, he shook his head in utter astonishment. She'd had a single spoonful of ice cream, just as she'd had a single month of passion. However sweet a month of honeymooning had been, it couldn't make up for a lifetime of loneliness or the responsibilities of bearing and rearing a child. No wonder Sondra still clung to Kenny's shirts and wanted to save the rip in the sofa. She had hardly any memories and nothing else at all.

Chapter 13

Three days later, Dylan rapped on the back door. Sondra opened it, and he entered quickly so the hot air wouldn't rush in and heat up the house. "Need a drink?"

"Probably."

"Help yourself." She turned to leave the kitchen.

Dylan gently grabbed hold of what once had been her waist. "Hang on. Every time I get within ten yards of you, you drop out of sight like a prairie dog diving into the nearest hole. Why are you avoiding me?"

Sondra didn't bother to deny his assertion.

Dylan murmured, "You're still not looking me in the eye. Are you having a fit because I saw you in that big T-shirt, or are you embarrassed that I ferreted out that you were a virgin bride?"

Her cheeks tingled with heat. "I'm not ashamed of having waited for marriage."

"So you're being goosey because I saw you looking like one of the seven dwarfs?"

"Is that what you thought?"

"I think I'm ready for that drink now." He opened the refrigerator, got out a soda for himself, and handed her the milk. He gave her a wink and added, "You're getting a tad moody. Isn't that supposed to mean you're ready to have the little one?"

"Don't we just wish!"

"September second is eighteen days away. I counted on the calendar this morning."

"In eighteen days, I'm going to take out a full-page ad in the county newspaper, offering my services as a crop-dusting dirigible!"

His soda went down the wrong way, and he spluttered. Sondra whacked him on the back a few times then simpered, "Mr. Ward, I do believe that served you right after calling me moody."

"If the shoe fits. . ."

She made a face at him and grudgingly admitted, "I am grumpy today."

"So I see. Why?"

Heat and color flooded her face. "Never mind."

"Hmm. Must be something terrible. Something like stretch marks."

"I don't have those!" As soon as she reacted, she groaned and turned away.

"I'm not trying to offend you. I'm trying to help and listen. You're not making this easy at all!"

"Shouting at me doesn't make it any easier," she yelled back. "You can't possibly understand how humiliating it is to get so fat you can't fit behind the steering wheel!" As soon as the admission was made, she let out a shriek.

Dylan blocked her exit. "Where did you want to go?"

"Away from you!"

A grin twitched at the left corner of his lips. "I meant, where did you want to drive?"

She bowed her head and mumbled, "I had a doctor's appointment."

"Does it occur to you that if I have time to stop for a drink, I could take you?"

"Ten minutes for a soda is far different that an hour drive in each direction and the time in between at the office."

"Bravo. You can do math. I'll take you today. Nickels, Howie, or Teresa can take you next week. After that, there's no problem, because Junior will make his appearance."

"I don't need to go today."

His brow puckered. "You just said you had an appointment."

"It was at nine o'clock. I canceled it."

"What? That was the stupidest thing I've ever heard!"

She glowered at him. "If you think I enjoy having to depend on everyone around here, you can just guess again! I refuse to ask anyone to do anything more for me."

Dylan slammed his can down and bellowed, "Then you've got your priorities wrong, lady! Let the dumb ranch fail apart at the seams for all we care! Just take care of the poor baby!" He spun around, stomped out of the house, and slammed the door shut.

September second came and went. Sondra still hadn't had the baby. Her nerves were frayed, and she'd spent the last twenty days studiously avoiding Dylan Ward. She managed to be in the bathroom, on the phone, or somehow unavailable whenever he made an appearance. Church was the only place she couldn't avoid him, but because he kept busy as an usher, she didn't have to do more than merely greet him with a polite nod.

Half of the time, she was livid that Dylan dared to think she'd ever put anything above her baby's welfare. The other half of the time, she was embarrassed she'd given him so much latitude in her life that he felt free to speak to her that way.

If only he hadn't been such a good listener, so calm and undemanding, so kind and helpful. If only he hadn't let her weep on his shoulder and gently gotten her through her illness. Maybe then she would have kept a sense of perspective. But she hadn't. She'd opened her big mouth and spilled every intimate detail of her whole life. His rock-solid presence, understated ways, and quiet attentiveness all made it easy to keep company with him—but she could resist those qualities if she made a conscious effort. The truth of it was, he'd found her Achilles' heel. She found it impossible to resist a man who loved God and Rocky Road.

Dylan still saw to all of the ranching matters, and he'd taken to phoning her to transmit any information regarding bills or expenditures. She managed to be businesslike and polite, but an awkward distance stretched between them.

That distance left her feeling bereft. In many ways, it also made her feel crushingly guilty. Though she grieved for Kenny, she still thought of Dylan. He crossed her mind way too much, as a matter of fact. He'd somehow managed to fill in places in her life and heart that went far, far beyond a simple business partner's role.

She'd been stupid to let that happen. Now that it had, part of her wanted to shut down that connection; worse, part of her secretly wanted to tend the relationship and let it not only continue but deepen. What kind of widow leaned on a man when she'd lost her husband so recently and was pregnant with his child? Confused, lonely, and guilty, she kept to herself.

Sitting at the kitchen table, Sondra stared at a bowl of ice cream. She missed Dylan's impish smile, the rumble of his deep voice, the companionship they'd shared. She didn't understand the emptiness she felt. Twice during her courtship and once during their marriage, Kenny had to take a weeklong business trip. She'd missed him, but not like this. This odd ache took her by surprise. How had Dylan wormed his way into her life like this?

Dylan took a long, tepid drink from the garden hose. He'd far rather have a tall glass of sweet tea, but the welcome he'd once felt in Sondra's house was long gone. The contact he'd had with her had been the highlight of each day—a short interlude of laughter, planning, camaraderie, and mutual regard. That evaporated in this estrangement.

The distance between them puzzled him. He'd been blunt but honest—and she'd taken it badly. As he cranked off the faucet, a last bit of water drained from the hose and made a puddle of mud. Yeah, he'd made muck of everything.

He'd had enough of this strain. Playing games never suited him. Saturday was Teresa's wedding, and if he didn't do something quick, Sondra would probably concoct a flimsy excuse and not show up, just to avoid him. He'd been biding his time, but she needed a nudge. She needed folks' friendship and support, Teresa's feelings would be hurt if Sondra didn't come, and. . .well, he missed her company.

"Nickels," he called across the barnyard, "I need a word with you." After he arranged for Nickels to drive Sondra to the wedding, he whistled as he strode off. Things were going to fall into place.

꧁꧂

The photographer snapped portraits out on the church lawn, but Dylan left and strode over to the car. After he helped Sondra out, he whistled under his breath. "Aren't you pretty as can be?"

Sondra glanced at the striped canopy in the near distance, then looked down at her apple green and white maternity dress in utter dismay. She didn't manage to stifle her moan. "I match the tent we're going to be dining under!"

"No wonder you look good enough to eat," he shot back with a wink. He tucked her into a pew in the air-conditioned sanctuary and then rejoined the wedding party.

Sondra sat through the whole ceremony remembering her own wedding. It, too, had been small. Kenny had worn a white tux just like Jeff's. Some days, it was so hard to pretend that she was getting along well. This was one of them, yet she plastered a smile on her face. Teresa bent over backward to be a good friend. She deserved to have everyone celebrate her joy—not grow selfishly maudlin.

An intimate wedding, the bridal party consisted only of Teresa, Jeff, the matron of honor, and the best man. Dylan served as the best man, and Sondra couldn't help noticing how handsome he looked. He'd been kind to come walk her into the church. Had he sensed how hard today would be for her?

Sondra planned to sit toward the edge of the reception tent so she could duck away. To her amazement, Teresa tugged her to the bride's supper table. Dylan was her partner, and the matron of honor's husband partnered her. The whole arrangement felt horribly awkward.

The conversation stayed lively, thanks to Teresa's bubbly nature and Jeff's crazy sense of humor. Dylan glanced around and signaled the waiter with a suave motion. The waiter scuttled over, and Dylan quietly stated, "The lady and I would like sparkling cider in our toasting glasses."

Sondra slanted him a look. "You know I don't drink. Why are you playing Pregnancy Police?"

He simply chortled.

Jeff leaned forward. "What was so funny? What did I miss?"

"I told the waiter to get us sparkling cider so I could do the toast," Dylan tattled. "She's accusing me of being part of the Pregnancy Police."

Bride and groom both laughed; then Teresa smiled. "You've got a whole squadron of us."

Not wanting to put a damper on things, Sondra accepted the new glass then tilted it at Teresa. "Just you wait. One of these days, your turn is coming."

"I hope so!" She blushed.

"Yeah, me, too." Jeff waggled his brows.

Dylan stood and gave a witty, surprisingly sentimental toast. He was quite a man—more masculine than Adam on the day of creation, capable of running two ranches, and still tenderhearted toward his sister. . .*and good to me.*

That admission made the defenses Sondra tried to put up crumble. She'd been a fool to try to shut him out of her life. He'd let her withdraw, but he hadn't neglected his duties. Now he was including her as if nothing was wrong. . .*and it isn't,* a little voice whispered in her heart. Nothing was wrong. Dylan still cared for her.

"Sondra?" He cupped her elbow and gave the glass in her hand a puzzled look. She'd taken a sip, but everyone else started talking while she stood frozen in place. "Are you okay?"

She barely kept from scooting closer to him. As she set her glass down on the white linen tabletop, she whispered, "The heat must be getting to me."

"I'll take you home."

"No!" The last thing she wanted was for him to give up the only day he'd taken off for pure enjoyment since she'd taken possession of the Curly Q. Needing to signal their friendship was back on track, she stammered, "I'll have a seat and drink more cider. It's just that I need to leave before they cut the cake."

He pulled a bit closer. "Why?"

She waited a beat then started to laugh. "Remember what happens when you and I get near desserts?"

⁂

Dylan sat in his kitchen and dialed Sondra's number, but the line buzzed. *Busy. It's probably for the best. She gets under my skin too easily. I need to pay more attention to the ranches. One is more than enough to keep a man busy; two is far too much.*

He, Teresa, and Jeff had come to an agreement about leaving the Laughingstock Ranch undivided and splitting profits for the time being. With his livestock and Sondra's mingling in the pastures, it would be a disaster to take down or move fences at this point. Jeff and Teresa adamantly stated that the land and livestock he gained from Miller's bequest at the end of the year were Dylan's alone. They didn't expect a share of that windfall.

Dylan did a bit of figuring and estimated what the size of his herd would be once the dust settled. It would take a few years to build up his stock once Jeff and Teresa's half moved onto Langston property, but in the meantime, he'd grow less fodder—or continue production and sell the excess. He'd have to give some thought to letting the land lie fallow.

One thing for certain, land could be left unproductive for a season, but busy little Sondra probably wouldn't let grass grow under her feet. Silly woman didn't know the value of a field left unseeded or a moment left to leisure. He shook his head. How did his brain twist that direction?

She'd looked sweet as could be at the wedding—but she'd wilted all too fast at the reception. For the first time, she'd admitted she might be slowing down a bit. She valued her independence and got downright feisty whenever she figured anyone was trying to bulldoze her.

Self-reliance rated as a fine quality, and he respected the gutsy woman for charging ahead with life. She didn't wring her hands or bemoan her calamities; she took a deep breath and kept plowing ahead. Too bad she didn't understand that could be dangerous at times. She needed someone to temper her autonomy and moderate her drive. Sondra could easily misjudge her ability and get hurt—and that wasn't even taking into consideration her motherly condition. Heaven only knew how often he prayed for her safety and health. Yes, knowing Sondra certainly improved his prayer life!

She must be going stark raving mad, not having had the baby yet. What if she slipped in the kitchen or shower? And those stairs to the basement were steep. He didn't want to think about her carrying a laundry basket up and down them. No matter what image came to mind, each task was fraught with danger.

He tried to stay calm, but Dylan wanted to grab the phone and announce that he was moving in until the baby came. No, make it for a period including the first few weeks afterward when Sondra would need extra help. Miller asked him to look after her. He was the logical choice. After all, Teresa needed to take care of her own home and husband. None of the hands knew a thing about babies. Yes, Dylan knew he was the best man for the job. . .but Sondra wanted him in her home just about as much as she wanted whooping cough.

He could probably work around that. The clincher was the morality issue. Plenty of men and women shacked up without the benefit of marriage, but Dylan didn't approve. It went against his personal code to give anyone the slightest reason to question the morality of his actions. It made for a poor witness and opened a Christian to temptation. A man and a woman ought not live together without the benefit of marriage—well, unless some extreme situation dictated otherwise.

Try as he might, he couldn't stretch the facts that far. Sondra was one fine-looking woman. If he moved in, folks might well cook up some suspicions and gossip. *What kind of witness would that be?* A thought occurred to him. He picked up the phone and dialed. This time, it rang. And rang. And rang. By the fifth ring, he was ready to call paramedics to meet him at her place, but a breathless voice answered, "Hello?"

"Sondra? Are you all right?"

A short, mirthless laugh met his inquiry.

"What's so funny?"

"Absolutely nothing."

"Then why are you laughing?"

"Because I promised myself that if anyone else called me and asked if I'd had the baby yet, I'd do something rash."

"Oh." He paused then said in a level tone, "I guess it's a good thing I didn't ask."

"So what do you need?"

"Is Kenny's family coming to help you when the baby's born?"

"No!"

Dylan jerked at how harsh she sounded. "It was just a thought."

"They want nothing to do with the baby."

"What?"

"You heard me. I'm tired, Dylan. Did you need anything else?"

"It may not be my business, but an explanation would be nice."

She sighed. "It's a long story."

She'd said she was tired, but in an instant, she'd gone from sparky to sad; he didn't want to hang up without making sure she was okay. He'd hit a nerve, and it bothered him. He quietly invited, "Give me the Reader's Digest condensed version."

A long silence crackled over the line. Sondra sighed. "The Thankfuls equated Kenny's injury with complete disability. His parents presumed he wasn't capable of. . .being a complete husband. They want nothing to do with a baby they're sure isn't their son's, and they threatened to cut their daughter off without any college funds if she kept in contact with me."

"Oh, Sondra!" Dylan breathed in shocked sympathy.

"It doesn't matter. My son and I will get along just fine without them."

"Sure you will." *Comfort. How can I comfort her, Lord? Help me take away the sting of their rejection.* His gaze happened to land on the refrigerator, and inspiration struck. "I'm dying for some ice cream. What if I grab a carton and come over?"

"Sorry. I'm lousy company. I'm just going to go to bed."

"Okay. Sweet dreams, honey."

⟢⟝⟞⟣

Sondra hung up the phone, sat down, and cried. The weatherman took unholy glee in announcing the temperature hit an all-time record high for the fourth day in a row. She bet he wouldn't be half that perky if his wife were overdue and suffering from the heat.

Her attitude disintegrated even further over the next week. Twelve days overdue, she strained to be barely civil.

"Mornin', city-gal," a soft, teasing drawl sounded from beside her as she sat on the porch steps just past sunrise the next day.

Sondra jumped. "How'd you get here without me knowing it?"

Dylan gave her a lazy grin. "Because you're not all here, if you get my drift."

"If I were any more 'here,' my feet would grow roots."

"Ah. . .cabin fever. A terrible case of it, if I don't miss my guess." Dylan took a seat beside her, rested his forearms on his knees, and stared off at the horizon. "I need to tend to some things, but I'll come by tonight at seven. I'll take you to town, and we'll get an ice-cream cone."

"I'm pathetic, aren't I?"

Dylan gave consideration to her question, then pursed his lips as he turned to study her. A scampish grin tilted his mouth, and his wink warned her he was about to deliver one of his tongue-in-cheek zingers. "I don't think I'd tag you as pathetic. More pitiful, if you ask me."

"Oh, get out of here!"

"Are you talking to me or the baby?"

Dylan was going to have to hurry to be at Sondra's on time. A man had to be in sorry shape if all he could think about the whole livelong day was eating an ice-cream cone with a pregnant widow. Dylan glanced at a mirror and saw the sorriest-looking man he'd ever seen.

The phone rang, and he barked, "Hullo," as he clamped the receiver between his shoulder and ear so he'd have both hands free to yank on a sock.

"Dylan, there's been a change—"

"Oh no, there hasn't," he interrupted. "You have to get out a bit. What harm is there in a trip to Dairy Queen?"

"I changed my mind. . .or maybe I should say my mind was changed."

"So change it back."

"Dylan, I don't want you to argue with me."

Stubborn woman. "Do you even know what you want?"

She went quiet for a moment and then said in a strained voice, "I want you to take me to the hospital."

Chapter 14

The hospital!" He nearly dropped the phone and managed to jam his other sock painfully between his toes in his rattled state.

"Teresa's not home, and—"

"I'll be right over!"

"I think I'd better get moving. The contractions are getting strong—"

She went silent, and he barked, "You hang on. I'll be there in a jiffy." He hung up.

He didn't bother to button his shirt, drove like a maniac, and came to a screeching halt in front of her place.

Cool as a cucumber, she sauntered down the steps and opened the passenger door. "Thank you for coming."

He hopped out of the cab and hastily fastened his shirt as he went around to her side. In those brief seconds, she tucked a little suitcase into the cab. Her methodical actions didn't reassure him in the least. He'd learned when things were tough, Sondra got very subdued and businesslike. "How far apart are the contractions?"

She gave no answer. Instead, she started to pant softly. Her hand went to her tummy and brushed back and forth in cadence with her breathing. After a minute, she let out a sigh and gave him a wobbly grin. "I'm about as ready as I'm going to be."

"You were ready weeks ago." He grinned for her benefit. If she wanted to put an "I'm okay" veneer over this, he'd play along. "You're fretting like a hen 'bout ready to nest on her egg awhile. Guess we'd best get you to the hatchery—I mean, hospital."

Her lips bowed up in a smile. He knew he'd done the right thing. She needed him to be calm. *Yeah, that's me, all right. Mr. Easygoing. . . Relaxed as barbed wire and sedate as a charging bull. She'll never know, though. I'll play it mellow, act un-ruffled, and she'll stay composed.*

"Upsy-daisy." He gently cupped her middle and hoisted her into the truck, then pulled her seat belt out so it reached its fullest length. She snagged the buckle and snapped it into the holster. He'd have rather fastened it himself. It would have given him a good excuse to get close and kind of hug her. That realization made him mad at himself. He needed to get his head examined. He needed to get *her* examined.

She started panting once again.

"Just hang on!" He slammed her door shut, raced around, and vaulted into his seat. They were in motion before his door closed. He quickly buckled his seat belt and shot her a worried look. "How close together are the contractions?"

She didn't answer right away—a fact that made him antsy as could be. Finally she let out a deep sigh and whispered, "Six minutes or so."

"Six min—"

"Dylan?" She squeezed his arm. He cut off his impending tirade and waited for whatever she wanted to say. She smiled sweetly as her cheeks filled with color. "Could we still stop by Dairy Queen and get me an ice-cream cone to eat on the way?"

It should have been an hour-long drive to the hospital; they made it in thirty-nine minutes. Traffic had been light, and though he normally drove in a conservative manner, Dylan turned into a maniac behind the wheel. Sondra gave him a couple of worried glances and muffled more than a few gasps at the harrowing way he drove.

Each time she gasped, he moaned, "Another one? Already?"

She wasn't sure whether to say anything or not. The man looked downright sick. He looked like he needed medical attention more than she did! In fact, he acted as rattled as she felt. If she had any sense of humor left, she would have thought it was pretty funny that she was hurting and he was sweating bullets, but she'd forgotten how to laugh; a thousand fears and doubts assailed her.

For all of his panic, Dylan carried on with his trademark kindness. "Hang on, Sondra. I'll have you there real soon."

"I'm okay."

"Sure you are." His eyes accused her of lying, but he didn't challenge her. Instead, he wondered, "Why are you clutching that teddy bear so tight?"

"He's my focal point. I'm supposed to stare at him when I'm having a contraction."

"My staple gun's under the seat. Want me to stick him to the dash so you can relax a little?"

"What?"

"Forget it. That was a bad idea. I just thought maybe you'd like your hands free to rub your belly."

"I have two hands."

Dylan chuckled softly. "Once the baby's here, you're going to wish you had another pair. He's going to keep you mighty busy."

"It'll be a nice change. I've been bored to tears for weeks now."

"Have you missed taking the little chicks to the kids?"

She nodded. "Nickels volunteered to do it for a while so I can get the baby settled."

"That'd be real fine," he said. He tried to carry on a bit of conversation to distract her. It didn't work, but she appreciated the effort—as long as he kept his staple gun out of sight.

Relief flooded her when she saw the hospital. "You can drop me off at—"

"Drop you off? Are you out of your mind?"

Sondra dug her fingers into the teddy's plush, brown fur and began to pant once again. She'd done her best to keep from moaning, but the pains kept growing stronger. She didn't want Dylan to see her lose control. Having him think well of her mattered too much—more than she'd ever confess.

Early in life, she'd learned to keep some walls up to protect herself from being hurt. She'd let down the walls with Kenny—and now look what that got her. A heart full of grief and waves of gut-wrenching pain.

Dylan was already too adept at slipping past her defenses. When she realized she'd started into labor, she'd longed to call him—to have him drop everything and be with her. Instead she convinced herself to hold off then call Teresa. When Teresa failed to answer, she'd felt a flare of gladness that she had an excuse to lean on Dylan yet again. Though heading for heartache, she couldn't seem to stop herself.

The next contraction hit. *Lord, help me through this. I need Your strength. I can't do this on my own.* She made it through and let out another cleansing breath. She hoped it didn't sound weak and choppy to Dylan.

He parked and came around to help her out. His long, ropy arm went across her in an almost hug. He held it for a heartbeat before he unlatched her seat belt.

For an instant, Sondra nearly yielded to the temptation to lean into his warmth. *No. It's not right. He's a partner. Okay, he's a friend.* The temptation to depend on him was frightening. He'd made it so easy for her to rely on his wisdom and strength. There wasn't another soul on earth she'd ever counted on like this. Physically vulnerable and emotionally raw, she forced herself to lean back into the truck seat.

"Another one?"

She wet her lips and shook her head. Dylan must've figured she couldn't slide out without his support. He tempered his strength to pull her free and then set her on her feet. The movement triggered an unexpected contraction, and she cried out.

"It's all right, darlin'. Here—let me help you."

She'd knotted his shirt in her palms, but she shook her head. Her eyes swam with unshed tears, and her voice sounded thick as she quavered, "I'll manage. I'll call you—"

"What kind of man do you think I am, Sondra? How could I possibly leave you when you need so much help?" He tilted her face up to his. His steady, somber eyes read the emotion on her face, and he interpreted it aloud. "You've never had anyone to rely on. You're used to doing things for yourself."

She nodded.

"Not this time."

She ought to order him to go home. Deep in her heart, though, she wanted to throw her arms around him and hang on tight. Confusion and pain muddled her thinking.

"Here we go," he said softly as he slipped one arm around her and grabbed her suitcase with the other. "We'll make it through together."

Two hours later, she bit her lip, clenched her eyes shut, and gripped his wrist as the next pain hit. When it finally ended, Dylan straightened up.

Sondra grabbed for him. "No! I need *you*!"

Dylan went stock-still and looked down at her. No one had ever needed him. No one. Not once, ever. Oh, they'd needed his time, his knowledge, his strong back, a helping hand. . .but the truth was plain to see. Sondra needed *him*. All at once, something deep inside that had been so impossibly empty suddenly filled to overflowing.

The full truth finally hit him hard. He'd been praying for the right woman—here, now, he knew deep in his soul he'd finally found her. All along, he'd fought the truth, denying she was the one. He'd tried to chalk it up to feeling protective. To doing Miller a favor. Feeling sympathetic. Basic chemical attraction that clouded his thinking. He should have known. He'd been fighting the inevitable, but suddenly the last piece fell into place: She'd let him know the feelings weren't just one-sided.

The assurance nearly bowled him over, yet it filled him with a joy that he'd never dared hope would be his. It didn't matter that she was having Kenny's son. Dylan would love him every bit as much as if he were his own. She needed him. This woman who always tried to face storms all by herself was clinging to him for dear life. She wanted him here, now. At the most vulnerable time in her life, he was there to help her through it and share the miracle at the end. A man couldn't ask for more.

She shuddered with another pain and pled in a shaky voice, "Don't leave me."

He leaned close and promised, "I'm not going to leave you, Sondra." *Lord, please help her. She can't take much more.*

As rapidly as that panicky time started, it came to an abrupt halt. She curled forward, grabbed the rail, and gritted, "I've gotta push!"

The doctor had just come in. He finished snapping on a glove. "Let me check to see if it's time." A minute later, he ordered, "Hang on. Don't push. Blow."

Dylan looked from Sondra to the doctor. The doc grimaced as he finished the exam. He ordered over his shoulder, "Call anesthesiology."

Dylan's heart dropped to the toes of his boots. *Almighty Father, don't let anything go wrong.*

The doctor stripped off his glove and threw it away. He squeezed Sondra's arm. "We're going to have to do a cesarean."

Dylan grabbed Sondra's hand and held it tightly sandwiched between both of his. "Why?"

The doc shook his head. "Face presentation. The baby flexed his head so he's trying to come through face first. It's impossible. We'll have to section her."

⬥⬥⬥

"Nine pounds even," Dylan marveled as he finished buckling Matthew into the car seat.

"Congratulations, ma'am," the volunteer said. "You, too, sir. He's the spitting image of you."

Pain twisted Sondra's heart. How many times in the last few days had someone presumed Dylan was the baby's father? It was an understandable mistake. . . . But every time it happened, intense longing struck. She wanted her husband. Matthew deserved a daddy. God provided Dylan as a temporary fill-in, but that wasn't the same thing.

Dylan murmured, "Come on, Sondra. Get in the car."

She awkwardly lowered herself into the backseat so she could sit next to her son. Dylan pressed a tissue into her hand, buckled her seat belt, then winked. "Aren't you just the cutest little mama in three counties? I swear, your tummy and ankles are just about back to normal already!"

"Who cares?" she wailed. He said nothing, but his eyes narrowed and mouth tightened. "I'm sorry!"

"Hush. You'll wake up PeeWee. You both ought to nap on the trip home." He took one of the flannel-shirt blankets she'd made and draped it across her and the baby. "I'll run the air conditioner, so you'll probably want this as protection from the draft."

He remembered to bring Kenny's shirt blanket. I'm being a total shrew, and Dylan keeps being nice. Sondra choked out an apology, and he patted her hand. She tamped down her tears and leaned back against the upholstery. Within a few miles, her lids grew heavy. The next thing she knew, Matthew started crying. She peeled open her eyes and gently caressed the dark peach fuzz on his head. Dylan glanced back and smiled. "We'll be home in a jiffy."

"Dylan, thank you for all of the help. I don't know—"

"Don't go getting all flowery on me. What are friends for?"

"All I do is take. You've been on the giving end of this relationship since day one."

"Sharing the miracle of your son's birth was the most precious gift I've ever been given. You're plumb crazy if you think otherwise."

He stopped in front of her place and started to chuckle; she groaned. "Half the world is here."

"Nah. Just the folks from your spread and mine. Teresa arranged it. Otherwise, all of these curious men are going to slip up to the house and bother you at inopportune moments."

Matthew's cries turned into full-scale, outraged bellows. "Dylan, this *is* an inopportune moment!"

Teresa opened the door and crooned to the baby. "There, now. Don't you fret. It's lunchtime for everyone. Your mama will feed you while all of these big ol' cowboys chow down. They're dying to meet the littlest boss."

"Teresa, you carry in PeeWee; I'll take care of his mama." Dylan handed Matthew to his sister and smiled. "Careful. He's as loud as he is big!"

Sondra felt self-conscious about having Dylan haul her inside, but she wasn't sure she could manage to mount the steps under her own steam. He carried her easily and took her back to the master bedroom. "I'll bring in your suitcase. You'd best slip into a nightie before you get too tired to manage on your own."

"Oh no. I'm staying dressed!"

"Don't be knot-headed, Sondra."

Before she could argue anymore, Teresa interrupted, "This little fellow isn't going to wait much longer. Dylan, you get on outta here. Sondra, honey, if you don't change, Matthew isn't going to be able to get to the table, so to speak. That dress zips clear on up the back. Dylan's right. Put on a nightie, else these men'll think you're holding court and won't ever get back to work. Once they see your robe, they'll keep it short and sweet."

<hr/>

"Short and sweet, just like you," Dylan teased a little while later as the last of the hands left, the door shut, and the house fell silent. "Told you so."

Sondra patted Matthew and let her head fall back onto the sofa cushion. "Those have to be the three ugliest words in the English language."

" 'Go to bed' has to rate close to the top on the list of the best phrases."

"Far be it from me to put up a fuss." Sondra struggled to rise.

Teresa grinned. "I'm spending the night. What would you like for supper?"

"Sleep," Dylan answered.

"With a side order of peace and quiet," Teresa tacked on.

Matthew started to whimper. Dylan chuckled ruefully. "Fat chance."

"Don't mention that awful word! I'm never going to fit in my jeans again!"

"Sondra, bitty as you started out, I'll bet PeeWee could wear them when he turns five. There's nothing wrong with a woman carrying soft curves. Gives a man something to hold on to."

"Oh, so now you're admitting that I've gotten fat and I was too scrawny at first. There's just no pleasing some people!"

He waited until she sat on her bed then turned to his sister. "Teresa, talk some sense into her, will you? Oh, forget it!" Dylan stomped out of the house.

Chapter 15

Ranching—especially during the hot part of the year—demanded early morning work. Dylan had always been an early riser. The next day, he automatically woke up an hour earlier. He glanced over at the glowing numbers of his alarm clock and hopped out of bed. *If I hustle, I can have a bit of time with Sondra and PeeWee.*

He felt a bit self-conscious arriving at 5:00 a.m., but that initial wave of awkwardness disappeared when he heard the baby whimpering softly. A smile chased across his features. He wasn't going to be interrupting Sondra's precious sleep.

A blue diaper bag propped open her bedroom door. The white porcelain guardian angel night-light glowed from the dresser, casting a soft light on the bed. Sondra lay curled on her side, snuggled under a pale yellow sheet. Oddly, Matt's soft whimpers didn't seem to be coming from Sondra's bedroom. Dylan frowned, moseyed over to the bassinet, and wondered where the baby was.

Teresa came in with Matt snuggled over her shoulder. Her oversized Oklahoma State University T-shirt made Dylan grin. "With pj's like that, no wonder Jeff let you spend the night over here."

His sister laughed.

Dylan pointed at Matt. "Hey, I'm hoping you and Jeff don't wait long before you have one of those."

"Hmm," a sleep-husky voice whispered from the bed. "What's up?"

"Not what—who," Teresa said. "Your son started to wind up, so I changed him. Here you go."

Dylan nodded. "Breakfast of champions, huh?"

"Breakfast, lunch, dinner, midnight snack. . ." Sondra's voice sounded deep and slow. Waking up to that sultry purr would be the best alarm clock a man could ever have.

Teresa bumped him with her hip. "If you gather the eggs, I'll get breakfast going for us big people."

He wanted to protest that he'd come to see Sondra and the baby. . .but he stopped short. Even by the faint illumination of the night-light, he could see the flush on Sondra's cheeks. *It's me,* he wanted to say. *Just me. Go on ahead. . . .* But that wasn't right. He wasn't her husband. She had every reason and right to behave modestly. He spun around and headed for the coop.

As he put a third egg in the basket, Dylan tried to decide how to proceed with Sondra. She was his—she simply didn't know it yet—and he wanted her to make that realization. If not now, *soon.*

How did a man let his woman ignore a love that was meant to be? How long was he supposed to let her live in solitude? He'd given her time to grieve. Now she needed time to recover physically and adjust to motherhood. *But when will it be my turn, Lord?*

He finished collecting the eggs and took them into the kitchen. Coffee trickled through the auto-drip coffeemaker. Diced ham, tomatoes, mushrooms, and grated cheese on the cutting board let him know Teresa planned to make her killer omelets.

"Stop looking like you lost the 4-H roping," she teased.

"Huh?"

"Oh, don't play stupid with me," she whispered. "I saw the look on your face when you brought Sondra home yesterday. You've got it bad, and I couldn't be happier."

"The lady's not exactly husband hunting."

"Mom said something when I was in high school that made me realize how I felt about Jeff. I'll pass her wisdom to Sondra some day in the future: 'No need to search the world over for a stallion when you already have one in the stable next door.'"

Dylan raised his brows a notch. "Run it by Sondra and let me know how she reacts."

"Time, Dyl. Give her time. By the way, know how a hen gets pecky when she's on the nest with her first brood and how protective she is with the chicks? Expect Sondra to do the same thing. She's going to be feisty and particular. Don't take it personally."

"How'd you ever get so smart?"

She cracked an egg into a blue earthenware bowl. "I was always the smarter one. Since I'm so brilliant, I'll toss one last jewel of wisdom at your big old boots. The one thing a woman can't resist is a man who's crazy about her kid."

Dylan smiled. Little Matthew was hot stuff. While the doctors stitched Sondra back up, the pediatrician had put PeeWee in his arms. He'd lost his heart in that instant. For a selfish moment, he'd cuddled Matt before scooting closer to Sondra so she could nuzzle his little face and croon to him.

Unaware of his thoughts, his sister continued, "I'm not going to think badly of you if you can't love Matt as your own, but if that would be the deep-down truth, don't mess with Sondra's heart."

"Soon as I admitted to myself that she's my one and only, I knew Matt was part of the deal. I held him even before she did, and I swear on a stack of Bibles, in that instant, I claimed him as my own. He's a fine boy, and I'm gonna love being his daddy."

Teresa stood on tiptoe and kissed his cheek. "I was hoping you'd say that."

"So do me a favor. Don't offer to stick around after sunset. I'll take night shift."

"You got it."

Before Sondra had the baby, he couldn't possibly live here; now the situation had changed, and she needed round-the-clock help. It would be temporary, and folks could plainly see the necessity. No one in his right mind would question if any hanky-panky were going on.

Dylan widened his stance. "I'm going to work like crazy so this place turns even more of a profit than Miller required. I don't want Sondra thinking she had no choice but to marry a man who couldn't cut it, just so she could keep her home."

"Teresa?" Sondra's voice sounded from down the hall.

"Yeah?"

When Sondra didn't reply right away, Dylan went to see what she wanted. He got one look at her, clutching Matt and slumped against the wall over by the bedroom, and tamped down his alarm. He lengthened his stride. "Hey, there," he said softly, securely wrapping an arm around her waist and the other around the baby.

She sagged against him and confessed in a vague tone, "I'm a little dizzy."

Teresa slipped up behind him.

"Sondra, honey, give me the baby. I'll just ease him into Teresa's arms." To his relief, she cooperated. "Let's have you lie back down."

She didn't protest his plan. Her arm wound around his waist, and she shuffled a step. Her meek acquiescence bothered him. For her to yield without an argument went contrary to her nature. Dylan put her back to bed and quietly asked, "Are you having any other problems?"

"No." A hint of coloring started to suffuse her cheeks. Another few seconds passed, and though she didn't exactly look like her usual perky self, she revived a bit. "I just got up too quickly. I'm fine—I was worried that I might drop Matt."

Teresa laid the baby on the foot of the bed and sat next to him. "That could have been dangerous. I'll stay during the days for a week or two to help out."

Sondra took in a long, deep, choppy breath. Dylan watched as she blinked back tears. She nodded, though. "I'll keep Sondra company while you finish breakfast," he offered. "She needs some chow."

"I'm supposed to walk. I was going out to the kitchen."

Dylan scooted Matt across the bed and lifted him. Cradling him to his chest, he tried not to sound too bossy. If he started ordering Sondra from the get-go, she'd dig in her heels. "Walking's a good idea, but until you're not so shaky, Teresa or I will stay alongside you—like just now. Come Friday or so, you'll likely be able to tote PeeWee with you. Until then, what say you let us carry him, or you stick him in the bassinet and push it along like you did in the hospital? In a few weeks, you'll be a sassy ball of fire again."

"A few weeks!"

He toggled Matt back and forth a tiny bit. "Tell your mama to stop fussing."

For having ordered Sondra not to fuss about things, Dylan managed to do just that himself. He fretted all morning as he did his chores. There was a lot to occupy him, but he kept watch on the house. He normally wore a cell phone, and he'd checked the battery three times today, just to be sure it was fully charged. If Teresa needed help with Sondra or the baby, she could reach him in an instant.

He shook his head. Sondra likely felt hovered over. Still, the woman cherished the notion that she was capable enough to face everything on her own. Any reminders or hints to the contrary would get her back up.

Howie strode by and gave him a curt nod. Nickels leaned against a split rail fence, checking the frayed ends of a rope. He gave Dylan a cocky grin then drawled, "Gonna get a terminal case of whiplash, looking back at the house."

Why deny it? I'm head over heels for Sondra, and little Matt's the cuddliest baby a man ever hitched over his shoulder. He let out a self-conscious chuckle. "Caught red-handed."

"Some things are worth catching and holding."

Dylan bent over and plucked a weed from the ground with studied nonchalance. "Teresa's spending days with Sondra to help with the baby. I'll be taking night duty."

"Boss, ain't a man on the spread who's gonna bat an eye over that. She needs lookin' after. Onliest one who's gonna kick up a fuss is her." He chortled softly. "When she's upset, she tosses pies. I reckon that ain't much of a deterrent to your plans."

By midday, Dylan couldn't take it anymore. He used the excuse of being nearby to invite himself in for lunch. "What are you doing?" He gawked at Sondra as she sat on the couch, fully dressed except for shoes.

She looked at him with slumberous eyes. "I had lunch."

"Dressed in your work clothes?" He scowled at Teresa. "What got into her?"

Teresa sighed. "She took a notion that she was going to go out to the coop and make sure the chickens got enough feed and water."

"You've got to be kidding me!"

Teresa shrugged. "I promised I'd see to it and convinced her to take a pain pill, so she'll nap for a while. Tuck her in bed, Dylan. She's too tired to pester. I'll get the baby."

"Sondra." He leaned down and burrowed his hands beneath her.

She tilted her head and rested it on his shoulder. "Hmm?"

"Settle down," he demanded as he lifted her. "No more cockeyed plans to traipse outside to do chores."

She wrapped her arms around his neck and actually snuggled closer.

Dylan already had a secure hold of her, but he curled her closer to his heart. His concern for her mingled with astonishment—not that he minded in the least, but she'd always been circumspect. His surprise must have shown, because Teresa gave him a nudge to set him into motion.

Dylan put Sondra to bed. Loath to break contact with her, he traced a rough fingertip down her nose. "Aren't you going to tell me what's going on?"

She blinked slowly and wet her lips. "There's so much to do."

"There's no denying that, sweetheart—but all you need to do is sleep and feed PeeWee. I'll handle the rest for a while."

He'd started to tuck a wild strand of her hair behind her ear, and she turned to his touch. He froze for a moment at the feel of her soft cheek against the backs of his fingers, then rubbed his knuckles back and forth in a tender caress. She'd needed him during her labor; now she turned to him. The woman had a knack for finding his empty spots and filling them, for making him feel essential—not just for the chores he could shoulder, but because something about him made her feel safe and cared for.

Dangerous ground. Setting yourself up for a big letdown, cowboy. If she doesn't cross the bridge from her past to your future, you're going to get burned.

Chapter 16

Late that evening, Sondra gingerly eased herself down into the rocking chair. Dylan scowled at her. "Don't take this the wrong way, but you don't look so red-hot."

She slowly wiggled from side to side to ease her weight deeper into the chair. "It's going to take time." Just when she'd gotten settled, the baby whimpered.

Dylan hopped up and got the boy. He made a comical face. "Caution! Toxic waste on board. Detour to the changing table."

Sondra manufactured a watery smile. It was downright funny seeing how Dylan handled the baby. "You're in Oklahoma, boy. You'll love the OSU Cowboys. Soon as you start talkin', I'll teach you to holler for the orange and white." The patter went on, regardless of Matthew's increasingly loud cry. It stopped as he presented a squalling, flannel-wrapped bundle to Sondra and announced, "He's on empty. Fill up his tank."

She accepted her son. "Thank you for everything, Dylan. As soon as things settle down, I'll make you a nice supper."

"Sounds to me like you need to be making *him* supper."

"Uh-huh. Good night, Dylan."

He sat down and gave her a mutinous look. "Good night? You think you're dismissing me?" When she nodded, he shook his head. "Not a chance. I'm not budging. Whether you like it or not, I promised to help you for a year. That promise extends on to the baby. Teresa is spending days with you until you heal. I'm spending the nights."

Sondra was sure she hadn't heard him correctly. "You're spending the night? You can't do that!"

"Just watch me."

She looked down at her crying son and then back at him; then she blurted, "I don't want you to watch me!"

"Oh, stop fussing and feed the poor kid. You could've tossed a shawl or blanket over your shoulder and not shown a thing. It's not like I'm some kind of pervert or Peeping Tom." He heaved a long-suffering sigh and tromped out of the room.

Matthew snuggled close and nursed like a starving little piglet. He stopped crying, but Sondra started. She'd upset Dylan. She hurt. She was all alone, trying to rear a baby. Nothing was right. Tilting her head against the oak back of the rocker, she indulged in a fine fit of tears.

A week later, Sondra walked across the living room and eased herself down onto a chair. "Dylan, I can't tell you how much I've appreciated all of the help—"

"If this is your 'I'm fine now' speech, forget it. You're nowhere near ready to handle things on your lonesome."

"You can't mean to stay here for another week!"

He plopped down on the sofa, put both stocking feet up on the coffee table, and gave her a mutinous look. "You still move like a rusty oil derrick and need the help. Now hush a minute. I want to hear the weather forecast."

Hush? He was telling her to hush in her own home and putting his big feet up on the coffee table as if he were king of the castle. Sondra did a slow burn. She was just about ready to give him a piece of her mind, but Matthew started to snuffle in the bassinet. Before she could even lean forward to get up, Dylan shot to his feet. He hurried to the baby and picked him up. For such a large man, he showed astonishing gentleness with Matt. Her gaze went from the man to the infant on his shoulder, then back again.

Dylan's eyes were shadowed with weariness, but he'd never once complained. He worked far too much, minding both ranches. On top of that, he was babysitting the two of them and got up at least twice a night to help out.

At the moment, he wrinkled his nose and chortled softly. "You smell like a loaf of garlic bread. Your mama must have eaten the leftover lasagna for lunch!"

"I did," she confessed. "BobbyJo Lintz came over with her little boy. We shared it. Dylan, I can't believe it. Her baby is nearly five months old, and Matt is almost as big as he is!"

"Matt's gonna be a moose." Dylan laid the subject of their conversation on the couch and quickly changed his diaper.

The cable channel started showing grain, feed, and beef prices. Sondra had been absorbed with being overdue and with taking care of Matt. For the first time in two months, she stared at the figures on the television. "Dylan, look at those figures."

"I've been monitoring them."

She gave him a stricken look. "I'd better go review the books. Those are drastically different. If feed goes up higher and beef prices drop more, we won't turn enough of a profit!"

"Honey, the market fluctuates a lot. We'll ride it out."

"But this is Matt's home. We can't lose it."

"God and I'll get you through."

She gave him a pained look. "Dylan, I trust you to do your best. It's just that some things are beyond your control."

"That's why I gave God top billing. You're going to have to exercise your faith."

"Saying that is simple—doing it isn't!"

"Fretting won't change things." He yawned. "If all else fails, Miller gave us an escape hatch. We could always get married."

Sondra sucked in a sharp breath and stared down at Matt. By the time she gathered her scattered wits and found her voice, she rasped, "Dylan—"

She looked up and choked back a rueful laugh. Exhausted, Dylan had leaned back and fallen fast asleep.

Over the next three months, the market bounced and plummeted almost as often as Sondra's emotions. Dylan started spending the nights back at his own place, and she missed him terribly. Often she invited him to stay for supper—he accepted, but almost as soon as he finished eating, he'd leave.

She longed for those quiet evenings they'd shared right after Matt was born and wondered if she'd done something to offend Dylan, but Teresa and Howie both commented on how Dylan was working hard to keep both spreads going. Sondra felt selfish for wanting more from him when he already gave so much.

Every Sunday, Dylan showed up in his truck, complimented her, and buckled the baby into the car seat. He drove them to church in her car—a committed act of a brother in Christ who wanted to help out. "Exercising faith," he called it.

What should have been her first anniversary arrived the week before Thanksgiving. She sat at the graveside and nestled Matt to her bosom. Confusion filled her. She still missed Kenny and ached for the loss she and her son had suffered.

Still, there was a niggling guilt, because she longed to have someone. Her brief time with Kenny had opened her eyes to the wonders of love—not just the physical fulfillment, but the comfort of sharing the simple things of life.

Dylan's face flashed through her mind, but she shook her head. He'd already sacrificed too much for her. Oh, he did all the ranch work, but even more—he'd eased her life and heart in countless ways. When their one-year partnership was over, she knew she was going to be bereft. *Lord, what am I to do? How will I survive that loss, too?*

The holidays arrived. Sondra went shopping and bought a calendar for the next year. She counted months since the beginning of May. *I've been here for seven months now, Jesus. There's so much I don't know still, and I don't think I can learn it all fast enough. Please give me a chance, though. Let us do well enough this year so I can keep the ranch.*

When she got to the gate of the Curly Q, Dylan met her. "Looks like you're dressed warm enough. How 'bout PeeWee?"

"He's all bundled up. Why?"

" 'Cuz we're going to go get his first tree."

She and Kenny had tried to get a tree, but the smell of fresh pine made her so sick they'd gone back home. Kenny stopped along the way to buy a home pregnancy test. The next morning, they'd confirmed she was carrying a child.

Unaware of her memories, Dylan unlatched Matthew's car seat and transferred it to the jump seat of his pickup. "Do you have your heart set on anything particular?"

Sondra closed her eyes. "One that dusts the ceiling and is so wide it fills the whole corner opposite the fireplace. No lights. Just ornaments."

A rough finger tickled her cheek. "Sounds like you've been dreamin' on this."

She blinked and bobbed her head. "Twenty-five years. I've never bought a tree."

He studied her for a moment and didn't ask questions. She appreciated that to no end. Sondra didn't want pity, and she'd blurted out her fantasy before realizing it would tattle about holidays best left forgotten.

"I know just the right place."

Fifteen minutes later, Sondra sat in his truck and frowned. "The hardware store?"

"Just you wait. In fact, stay put with PeeWee. I'll only be a second."

For all the Christmases she'd spent as an unexpected and unwanted interloper in foster homes, Sondra determined to make Matt's holidays special. Having Dylan take them Christmas tree hunting meant the world to her. He insisted on carrying Matthew, brought along a camera, and snapped several photos. Instead of chopping down the tree, Dylan transplanted it into a huge pot he bought at the hardware store.

"Some things are meant to last," Dylan told her after finishing the task.

When they brought the tree back home, Dylan didn't leave. He stayed and helped her trim the tree with a box of beautiful, antique, handblown glass ornaments she'd unearthed in the attic. The newscaster started to discuss farm prices in the background, but Dylan switched off the TV and turned the radio on to a station playing carols.

Everyone seemed to be in the Christmas spirit. A sprig of mistletoe was mysteriously tacked in the doorway to the barn. No one admitted to putting it there. Sondra glanced at it and forced a tight laugh. She hadn't been kissed in ages. As she walked under it, her heart did a wicked little skip. Dear mercy. . . she wanted to be kissed. Not just kissed, *kissed*. And at that moment, she knew exactly by whom: Dylan.

The realization floored her. A few months ago, he'd flippantly mentioned the marriage clause in the will. She'd been so scared about losing the home she needed so desperately for her son that she'd actually swallowed her pride enough to tell Dylan she'd be willing to get married—but he'd fallen asleep, and the words never came out. That would have been a friendship kind of marriage.

What she wanted now was entirely different. *I've fallen in love with him!* A kiss wouldn't be near enough. An amiable partnership wouldn't suffice. What she wanted was a happily-ever-after, madly-in-love marriage with Dylan. That realization stopped her cold. *Dylan's a good man. Honest, kind, generous. If he ever detects even a hint of my feelings, he'll ignore them—unless push comes to shove. If ownership of the ranch is at stake, he'll probably rescue Matt and me. . . .* But she didn't want that. She wanted him to love her back with all of the intensity she now discovered she held for him.

"Hey, now, what's that you got there?"

Howie's words jolted her. Sondra wheeled around. "Pecan snowballs and molasses pinwheels." She shoved the plate of cookies into Howie's hands.

Nickels swiped a pinwheel, wolfed it down, and reached for another. "I vow, this place don't much smell like a ranch; it smells like a bakery. Not that I'm complaining, mind you." He popped the next one into his mouth.

Dylan strode up. He helped himself to a snowball, but instead of eating it, he popped it into Sondra's mouth. "You're spoiling your men." The corners of his mouth crinkled. "I thought that was above and beyond the call of duty, and I just found out today that you've buried the men in the Laughingstock bunkhouse under cinnamon rolls, strudels, cookies, and desserts, too."

She hastily swallowed the cookie. "We're—partners. Seemed fair to me. All of the men work hard. Matt and I want to show our appreciation."

Nickels pulled Howie back a few steps. Their boots crunched on the gritty soil. "Uhh, boss?" They shot a meaningful look upward at the mistletoe. "Showing appreciation sounds like a mighty fine plan. Don't you think, Howie?"

"Sure enough. We elect you to be our, um. . .whaddya call it?"

"Representative," Nickels filled in.

Sondra wished the ground would open up and swallow her. She felt a wave of heated embarrassment wash over her as Dylan studied the green sprigs dangling above them. He drew close, and she stopped breathing. He wrapped an arm around her. He smelled of soap and leather and man—a complex scent that enveloped her. Sondra's heart was about to pound out of her chest as his head dipped. . . . Then he ducked a bit more and pressed a kiss on Matt's downy head.

As he straightened, he stared into her wide eyes and ordered without looking behind him, "You men get back to work."

Sondra started to inch away, but his arm tightened. "I thought I was supposed to thank both of you."

If he kisses me, I'll never be able to face him again. He'll know. . . . He'll know. Dylan kept an arm around her and used the other hand to tilt her face up to his. Every shred of her wanted to run; every bit of her wanted to raise up on tiptoe and. . . She decided to play it safe. She popped up onto her tiptoes and gave him a hasty peck on the cheek.

His hold tightened, and his brows formed a stormy V. "Just what was that?"

"A—a holiday kiss."

"Not on your life. That pathetic excuse for a kiss was something a maidenly great-aunt might concoct." His voice deepened to a husky, predatory purr. "This is a kiss."

Once again, his head dipped. His mouth slanted across hers. For all the fire she'd seen in his eyes before she'd closed her own, he kept the contact tender. His lips brushed, teased, found a perfect fit. . .just as he shifted the baby between them slightly to the side, then cinched her so close he left her breathless and dizzy.

Matt wiggled and cooed, jarring her from her abandoned reaction. She jerked away and couldn't bear to look Dylan in the eye. She'd just done what she most feared—lost control completely. A man didn't need any emotional attachment to enjoy a woman. What was an intense, emotional connection for her had been mere biology for him. *I've made a fool of myself in front of him. . . .* She craned her head to the side. *I hope the hands didn't witness that!*

"Sondra—"

"Matt just soaked me," she lied.

<hr>

Dylan watched her scurry back into the house. In all honesty, he felt like he had a whole boxful of crickets jumping in his belly. He'd nearly gotten lost in the moment. After waiting forever to kiss her, he'd wanted to cast aside all self-control. Fighting that urge had to be the single hardest thing he'd ever done.

Good thing he did. For a glorious moment, she'd been with him. Then she jerked away like she couldn't stand his touch. Oh yeah, she said Matt had wet her; however, his own arm had been right beneath the little guy's bottom, and it was bone-dry. Never before had Sondra lied to him. She made a very poor fibber, too. Her cheeks went fiery, and she avoided looking him in the face.

He hadn't taken any liberties. The woman had no call to be embarrassed because she'd responded so naturally to him. . . . *Unless she's not embarrassed, but ashamed because she still loves Kenny.*

Dylan grabbed a bale of hay and heaved it into a stall. Once, he'd resented Miller for saddling him with a city girl and questioned God about why long-standing, charitable plans went awry. Now he understood Miller's matchmaking plans. . . . *But, Almighty Father, why are You allowing me to be tempted with a woman who's so stuck on her lost love that she doesn't want me?*

Chapter 17

All her life, Sondra made it through by hiding her feelings. No one knew when things bothered her, and she didn't let them know when she was hurt. Now, it strained her to the limit to keep her emotions hidden—at least where Dylan was concerned. She left her heart unguarded, and it counted as the most foolhardy thing she'd ever done. It took all her courage to face him and feign nonchalance.

Dylan showed up every single day. His dedication and faithfulness were unquestionable. Sondra tried to find comfort in the fact that his work would help her keep the ranch. In truth, the intensity he now showed accomplishing the chores about the place troubled her greatly. She'd been painfully obvious in her attraction. Now he was politely making it clear their partnership shouldn't have crossed the line. He was too much of a gentleman to say anything, but actions spoke louder than words. What good would it do if she kept the ranch but lost her friendship and partnership with her closest neighbor?

Another chilling thought occurred to her. Was she going to be able to keep the Curly Q? She pored over all Miller's old books, and the facts shook her to the core. The price of beef was lower than it had been in the past four years, and due to meager rainfall, feed prices kept creeping higher. Were the dark shadows in Dylan's eyes strictly due to overwork, or was worry causing them?

As she walked to the henhouse, Dylan rode off. Nickels beat his gloves against his thigh, creating a small cloud of dust. He squinted at Dylan's back. "That man couldn't get more work done if he was twins!"

Sondra nodded somberly. "What can I do to help?"

Nicholson shrugged. "Dylan's got us all organized just fine. Seems to me you already have your hands full with a little one."

Her arms automatically curled around a little baby carrier she wore. She gave Nickels a wry smile. "Matt keeps me busy, but I'm getting pretty good at reaching around him. I'm tired of not pulling my weight around here."

"Ma'am, far as I can see, you have no call to fret. Things go along at their own speed, and there's things on a ranch you can't change, hurry along, or make smell better."

After he strode off, Sondra shook her head. These men had seen the ups and downs of ranching. They were able to be more philosophical about the downturn in the market. Then again, even if the Curly Q didn't turn a profit, they could easily find a job elsewhere. She, on the other hand, stood to lose everything.

"I won't let that happen." She patted her baby on the back and vowed in an iron tone, "I'll do whatever it takes. We are not moving an inch."

⟨⟩

The kiss under the mistletoe had really done it. He knew they shared an explosive chemistry. Still, he didn't want Sondra thinking he chased after her for her land or livestock. If he got within three yards of her, he'd make a fool of himself because he'd likely grab her, kiss her silly, and confess his love.

Any fool could see she needed time yet. If he pressed her or started an obvious attempt at courtship, she'd bolt. One kiss, and she'd run away like a scalded cat. He ached for her, but for the sake of her peace of heart and his pride, he decided to back off. Day in, day out, he strove to keep some distance between them. He'd resolved to change that today. It seemed like a fair enough time to broach the topic of love and marriage, it being Valentine's Day and all.

Dylan planned each move. He'd pull out every stop, use every trick in the book, and turn a stellar profit. That way, marriage wouldn't be an escape hatch she resorted to out of desperation. Once Sondra held the deed, he'd propose—with an offer up front of a prenuptial. That would prove he wanted her, not what she finally owned. Today, though, he'd start doing the little things that made a woman feel courted. . .like giving her a card. Flowers would be coming on too strong. Just one thing at a time.

He popped the card into his shirt pocket, rode over, and pulled to an abrupt halt in her barnyard. The place was quiet—eerily quiet. Pink-and-red-iced doughnuts lay strewed and trampled on the ground.

⟨⟩

Sondra hit the automatic dial on the phone again. She twisted around and cranked the swing to keep Matt content, but with every ring and turn, her tension spiraled higher. "God, please help us."

"What's going on?"

She spun around. "Dylan! I've been trying to get you."

"What's going on?"

"Cows are down. Nickels said a dozen or more. South pasture."

He bolted out and vaulted onto Pretty Boy. Sondra ran to the door and called, "They already have the medical kit with them, and I called the vet."

After he'd gone, Sondra paced back and forth across the living room. Whatever it was, it was bad. She couldn't stay here when Matthew's future hung in the balance. She bundled Matthew up, strapped him into a car seat, and latched him into the jump seat of a pickup. They were halfway to the south pasture when her cell phone rang.

"Sondra, where are you?"

"By the old oak, turning toward the pasture. What do you need?"

"Rope and mineral oil."

"I have rope." In the distance, she saw him spin around and catch sight of her.

"You drove a trailer!" He hung up, and she wasn't sure whether he was glad or mad.

Dust swirled around the truck as she stopped. It didn't hide the appalling sight of cattle lying and staggering about. Sondra tore out of the cab. "What happened?"

"They ate mountain laurel." Dylan gestured toward clumps of shrubs and segments of branches along the fence and road. He didn't bother to hide the worry in his eyes or voice.

Not a day went by that Sondra didn't see Dylan and the men work hard, but never had she seen such grim determination or desperation. As they loaded several sick cows into the trailer, Dylan ordered, "Sondra, Milt came out in a jeep. Drive it to town and get as much mineral oil and lard as you can, then swing by the vet's. Once he's here, he'll call an order in to his assistant, and you can bring back everything."

After moving Matt to the jeep, Sondra called BobbyJo. "I need help. . . ."

By the time Sondra reached town, her new friend and Eva Nielson had two carts waiting outside the grocery store. "Here you go." BobbyJo tossed a box into the jeep. "I bought all their lard—seventeen buckets. Only nine bottles of mineral oil, though. Eva dashed to the drugstore and got two cases."

"Thank you both!"

"We're praying," Eva added.

"Please do. It looks bad." They loaded the jeep; then Sondra raced on to the vet's and back home.

❧

Dylan paced the length of the barn and back again. Thirteen cows had died. He shook his head. *Lord, if I were a superstitious man, that would spook me. You're in control of this, but I don't understand why this happened or how we'll get through.*

The vet had just left after staying round the clock. His assistant would be here for the next shift. From the looks of it, one or two more cows wouldn't pull through. The other eighteen would. Between the ones they lost and the medical cost of saving the others, the ranch had just suffered a nasty blow.

Lord, I'm grasping at straws here. You know how hard I've been working. You know how important it is to me to reach that goal so Sondra won't just marry me out of pressure. With the feed prices high and beef prices low, it was already tight. This—well, this is a disaster. Four weeks. There are only four weeks until the lawyer figures out the profit margin. What am I to do?

"Dylan."

He wheeled around. Sondra walked toward him. Over the past thirty-six hours, she'd brought mountains of food and gallons of good, strong coffee to the barn. Instead of getting underfoot and pestering the vet with a bunch of questions, she'd seen to the matters that didn't disappear just because an emergency cropped up. Sweet little Sondra didn't even make a big deal of it, either. Pitching in came naturally to her—a trait Dylan admired to no end.

Others noticed, too. Edgar wasn't a man to do a lot of extra talking, but he'd come to the barn this morning. Sondra had gotten up early and already mucked the horses' stalls in order to free him up to do something else. He'd slapped Dylan on the shoulder and murmured, "You better claim that gal soon, or I'm a-gonna."

Dylan folded his arms across his chest. "Over my dead body."

Edgar let out a rusty chuckle.

The moment of levity ended. More pressing issues were at hand. Dylan lowered his voice. "I want you to ride the fence. Keep close watch."

Solemnly nodding, Edgar rasped, "Gotcha."

Before Sondra arrived at the pasture yesterday, Dylan had ascertained the mountain laurel didn't end up in the pasture by accident. The sheer volume proved the wind couldn't have blown the heavy branches over the barbed wire fence. That was where it was, too—inside the pasture, not outside the wire blown against the fence. Someone had intentionally set the poison in the pasture.

The hands knew it, too. Plenty of hot words and suspicions flew—until Sondra arrived. Dylan barely had a chance to order the men to keep their conjecture to themselves before she'd gotten out of the truck. Since then, they'd been circumspect. No use scaring the poor widow half out of her wits.

Sabotage. But who had a motive? More importantly, how could Dylan protect Sondra and the ranch from any further danger? Oblivious, she crossed the floor as if it were freshly swept linoleum instead of ankle deep in cow patties. The tray she carried had several empty spots on it, telling him the men probably crowded around to grab sandwiches the minute she stepped foot out of the house. Even so, three big subs remained.

"I figured you must be starving."

As she drew closer, he squinted at the baby sling she used to carry PeeWee. It looked wrong.

"Chips and soda." She laughed weakly. "Teresa is at the house, watching Matt."

"Good." He took the tray from her and set it on a bale of hay.

"Middle one's roast beef and cheddar—your favorite."

Fishing into the roomy cloth sling, she pulled out a bag of barbecue chips and a soda.

"Mmm. Those are my favorites, too."

A smile sketched across her face. "I know."

She tilted her head toward the tray. "Roland, there's plenty more where this came from. Help yourself."

Nodding, the vet's assistant finished fiddling with an IV going to one of the cows. "Much obliged." He swiped a sandwich and soda and then cleared his throat. "They're doin' about the same. Mind if I go to the stables and look at the litter?"

"Go ahead." Sondra made a vague gesture. "The only one promised is the pup with white socks. You're welcome to any of the others."

"Thanks." He strode out.

Dylan took a bite. Her sandwiches always tasted great. This one might as well have been filled with sawdust. "Sondra, honey, I'm worried."

She motioned toward his sandwich. "Eat. Worrying won't change things."

He washed the bite down with soda.

She opened a soda and took a sip. "You're the one who's counseled me to exercise faith. I guess it's time for me to suggest it's your turn."

"Feeling sassy, are you?"

She lifted the can in a salute. "Probably. I'm a scrapper, you know."

"Yeah. It's an admirable quality. . .as long as you rein it in so you don't gallop straight into trouble."

"Trouble seems to find me enough. I'm not about to issue any invitations!"

Studying her, he forced a smile. "Does it go with the hair?"

She smoothed back a few stray, twirly wisps. "Probably. Kenny's mom said God painted me with red neon to warn men off."

His last gulp of soda didn't stay down. Dylan choked and crushed the can in his fist. "What did she know, anyway?"

Sondra shrugged, but Dylan knew her too well to be fooled by the nonchalant action. The words stung. He refused to let them remain unchallenged. Sauntering over, he tossed aside the can and stared at Sondra's hair. Her eyes dilated with surprise.

"Neon red? The woman's color-blind. It's mahogany. Rich, wonderful mahogany." He unfastened the barrette, threaded his hands through her hair, and growled, "Your hair doesn't warn a man off—it beckons him. Especially this man."

Her lips parted in surprise.

Dylan couldn't help himself. He'd longed to kiss her again, ever since that day under the mistletoe. Hands full of her hair, cradling her head, he lowered his head.

"Hey, boss!"

Sondra jerked away. His hands tangled in her hair, but she shook free, her cheeks scorched with color.

Nickels scuffled in. "Howie and me been think—oh!" He halted, and his gaze shifted from Dylan to Sondra and back. "I'll get back to you later."

"Don't let me keep you." Sondra sidled away. "I was just bringing food. There's a sandwich. Help yourself."

Once she was gone, Nickels smirked. "She's cuter 'n a bug's ear when she's all embarrassed like that. Voice goes up a whole octave, too."

Dylan didn't say a thing.

Nickels grinned unrepentantly. "Only other time I've seen her do that was when she hit you with that pie. I suspect you got something even sweeter this time."

"You're wrong." Dylan glowered.

"Sorry, my timing stunk. So anyway, Howie and me were talking. We wondered who had it in for you or Sondra. We've gotta puzzle out who's got motive."

Dylan turned to the side and gulped soda. "If you have any ideas, let me know."

"Can't think of anyone who's got a bone to pick with you. As for Miz Thankful, well, it stretches my mind to imagine anyone bein' upset with her."

"She's a good woman." Dylan changed the subject. He didn't want to say anything more, but he'd already called the sheriff. Dylan could think of several people with a grudge—Miller's relatives.

The vet's assistant returned. Weary to the bone, Dylan grabbed a blanket and headed toward the ladder to the loft. He'd ascended three rungs when his sister's voice stopped him. "Dylan, the guest bedroom is ready for you. I stopped by your place and brought fresh clothes, too."

He looked down at her. "No thanks. I'll catch a few winks here."

His sister gave him a searching look. "Okay. Gotcha. Best for you to sleep here. Definitely best."

He didn't reply. Once he settled into a bed of hay and covered himself with the blanket, weariness washed over him in waves. *Sondra couldn't face me after that almost-kiss.*

Chapter 18

The printouts from the computer formed tidy stacks on the table. Dylan and Sondra sat side by side as she looked at the bottom line. It showed a deficit of five thousand dollars. Five stinking thousand dollars. If they couldn't account for those monies, the ranch would fall below the guidelines listed in Miller's will.

"So if we sell some steers right now, it still won't boost the profit?"

"No. They'll register at the same value as the price you'd get for them."

"If we sell off most of the hay we have on hand, that could raise some money."

Dylan grimaced. "Not enough. I've already cut it close on ordering. With feed prices at this level, I'd hoped to skim by."

She chewed on the end of a pencil. "I thought you did that to reduce the chances for any other fires."

He didn't answer.

Sondra's eyes narrowed. "That big roll of hay didn't have any reason to catch fire, did it? It wasn't green, so it shouldn't have gotten hot. And there wasn't a thunderstorm, either. You still don't say anything about the fire."

Dylan shoved the calculator across the table. The last figure on the sheet still told the same tale: They couldn't wrangle an honest way of reaching the goal.

"What do you want me to say? It's a bad situation."

"This may sound paranoid, but I wondered if someone set it on fire." She sucked in a quick breath and added, "And as long as I'm sounding like a nutcase, I may as well confess that I suspect someone purposefully flung the branches into the pasture when the cattle got poisoned."

Dylan studied his knuckles. They'd gotten scraped yesterday. "What made you think that, and who'd do such a thing?"

"I don't know." She spread her hands wide. "You have to admit, it's pretty fishy that we've had two disasters in two weeks. There's not mountain laurel anywhere around that pasture, and that road's just a fire road that isn't on the map. It struck me odd at the time, but we were all so busy I didn't say anything. Then the hay roll caught fire. I don't think it's a coincidence that it just happened to be the one next to the tractor barn."

"Good thing Luna spotted the smoke. Replacing machinery is costly."

"Exactly my point. This is the only ranch in the whole county that seems to be running into trouble." She shoved back an errant curl. "Well, that's not true.

Compared to the Willards, I shouldn't complain at all. Those poor little kids lost their parents and home last week."

"That's not a good comparison. The tornado was a terrible tragedy, but at least we know what caused it. What's happened around here doesn't have an explanation. Who do you think would attempt to sabotage the Curly Q?"

She shrugged. "I don't have any enemies. And everyone in the community goes out of their way to sing your praises. The thing I keep coming back to is, if we don't turn enough of a profit, the ranch gets sold."

"But who benefits from that? None of Miller's relatives get a cent if we fail. A developer does."

"I told you you'd probably think I'm acting paranoid. I can't help it." She blinked madly. "My son's future is at risk."

He cupped her face and rubbed away the tears that began streaking down her cheeks. "It doesn't have to be, Sondra. Miller provided another way."

She smiled bravely. "You're right. Miller provided fifteen thousand in this eventuality. That'll help Matt and me get started."

"Don't be ridiculous. Fifteen won't cover rent and child care for the first year." His steady gaze held hers. "We'll get married."

"From the very start," she said unsteadily, "we agreed that wasn't an option."

"We were total strangers back then. We've had almost a year to get to know each other. We're far more compatible than either of us suspected."

She stayed silent.

"We just finished tallying it up again. I'm sorry I didn't pull you through."

"Dylan, I've never once doubted your commitment or generosity. No one else would have worked as tirelessly or diligently. It's not your fault."

"But I can make it right. Marry me, Sondra."

Matthew started crying. Sondra wanted to wail right along with him. She pushed away from the table. "We have one more week."

"Things won't be any different next Friday."

"Please excuse me." She hastened out of the room and headed for the nursery. Sondra stood in the shaft of moonlight flooding the nursery and swallowed back her tears as she changed Matt's diaper. A year and a half ago, she'd been planning her dream-come-true wedding to Kenny. Now, she was seriously contemplating pledging her hand to a man who never once mentioned love in his proposal. Her heart ached.

Was it grief for having lost Kenny? Was it sadness that Dylan didn't truly love her? She couldn't untangle the knotted threads of emotions. Having someone to help her rear Matt would be an answer to prayer. She was so afraid of being a single parent.

That's not a good enough reason to get married.

If she didn't marry him, she and Matt would lose their home and precious time together. She'd need to go back to work as a teacher and leave him with a babysitter each day. *That's a good enough reason for me to marry—but I'm just using Dylan. . .and that's wrong.*

She did care for him—deeply. She'd called it love, but that seemed impossible to believe. How could she have already opened her heart and soul to another man? *But I have.*

Matthew snuffled then let out a little squeak that quickly increased in pitch. A floorboard creaked as Dylan came in. "He thinks it's time for a snack, huh?"

"Actually, he's been sleeping through the night." She fastened up the snaps on the pale green sleeper and lifted Matt.

Dylan took the baby and surprised her by sitting on the ottoman in the moonlight. He patted the rocking chair in a silent invitation for her to join him. The soft, almost bluish light illuminated the patience on his weary face.

I want my son to have this man for his daddy. . .and I want him for myself, too. Sondra sat and rocked in pensive silence.

Matt snuggled into Dylan's arms, gave him a sleepy smile, and yawned. Dylan's callused hand smoothed errant baby curls. "Sondra, I'll be steady and true. We can build something good out of this. I don't want you thinking I'm doing this for the land or livestock, so I'll sign a prenuptial."

"No." She shook her head adamantly. "If we do this, it's because we plan to really make a go of it—not just to weather a bad turn in the market and a pair of ill-timed mishaps. Stability and commitment are too important. Signing papers like that presume the marriage will fail. If you have any notion that you'll want to divorce in the future, then I'm not going to even consider this far-fetched plan."

"It's not far-fetched, honey pie. It's real as real can be. A forever kind of deal."

"We still have a week, Dylan. You need to use the time to consider what you're proposing."

"I know exactly what I'm doing. It's the right thing, Sondra. Trust me."

The right thing. Why did something so right for her seem so wrong? *Because he's being gallant. He's offering me his hand, but his heart's not involved.* His scuffed work boots grew blurry. Sondra looked up and fought to paste on a smile as she blinked away the tears. He looked so earnest. *Lord, is this Your will? You've put the desire in my heart. With time, will You teach Dylan to love me?* They sat only two feet apart, but it felt like an unbridgeable gulf.

"Exercise faith." His words whispered across the distance.

Nothing he could ever say or do would have answered her troubled heart and mind better. Silence stretched as they studied each other in the muted light. "Do you mind if we get married in the pastor's study instead of city hall?"

"There's a pretty little prayer chapel tucked away behind the main sanctuary.

If it's all the same to you, I'd like to say our vows there."

A church wedding. Sort of. Well, it was fitting. God brought them together, and Sondra was taking a huge leap of faith in marrying Dylan. She desperately wanted the Lord's blessing on their union. "I'd like that."

"Do you want me to surprise you with a ring, or would you rather go shopping with me and choose something?"

"Dylan, we don't need to spend a lot of money on a ring. I—"

"Whoa." He held up a hand. "Hold it right there. This might not be one of those Valentine-y kind of high school romances, but some things aren't negotiable. This is one of them. You'll have a nice ring. Pretty, like you." He winked. "That's something I'll teach little Matt. Anything worth doin' is worth doin' right. No sliding by."

Not a romance. Her nails dug into the wooden arms of the chair as she leaned away from him. The rocking chair tilted back, then arced forward again—toward Dylan, then went back again. *Together, apart. Together, apart. Just like us.*

Dylan rose and tucked Matt into his crib with ease then turned to her. He took her hand and helped her from the rocking chair.

She fought the urge to lean into his strength. She'd done almost no dating at all until she met Kenny, and he'd been at an easy-to-reach level. Dylan was huge with brawny shoulders and arms from his heavy work. Long, toned legs gave him towering height, too. Dylan had a way of engulfing her with his presence and making her feel secure. Too secure.

His callused hand enveloped hers, wouldn't let go. His other hand slowly tilted her face to his, and his voice went as rough as his hand. "Let's seal it with a kiss."

Dylan strode up to the two-story clinic and would have taken the stairs, but a cordon across it warned WET VARNISH. The pungent smell of fresh varnish permeated the lobby as he wrinkled his nose and jammed the UP button on the elevator. He was alone in the stainless steel–lined car and did a quick check to make sure he didn't look too shabby. One glance at his reflection told him his hair needed taming in the worst way.

He got out of the elevator car, glanced about Doc's waiting room, and spotted Sondra in a mustard-colored plastic chair. She held the baby to her shoulder, and her head rested back against the wall. Her eyes were closed; her lips thinned.

"Here, Sondra, I'll take the little guy."

Her eyes flew open. "Dylan!"

He leaned forward and brushed a kiss on her cheek, then swiped Matthew from her. "Figured we'd make this a family trip."

"You're sick?"

Her concern warmed his heart. "No, honey. We need to have Doc do blood tests for the marriage license. I told Nickels to go on ahead. After we pick up the marriage license, I'll drive you home."

"Okay. Thanks."

Her face still looked strained. *She really doesn't want to marry me.*

The corner of her mouth twitched. "I hate this. Matt's going to get more shots today."

Relief flooded Dylan. *So at least it's not just the wedding; it's not just me.* He tickled her cheek. "You gonna cry more than he does?"

"Can't say I'm not tempted."

"Can't say I'll cope any better." Dylan winced theatrically and cuddled Matt closer. "Nothing worse than someone pickin' on a kid. You might have to hold me back so I don't grab the syringe and toss it out the window."

Sondra let out a small laugh. Her features finally eased, making the nonsensical conversation worthwhile. Dylan grinned. He knew he'd turned into a fool for love, and he didn't mind in the least.

A short while later, Dylan kept his left hand on the steering wheel and stuck out his right forearm. "You've kissed little PeeWee's boo-boo a hundred times or so. Don't I get a kiss for my boo-boo?"

"Boo-boo?"

The corner of his mouth kicked up. "What else do you call 'em?"

"Ouchies!"

Dylan chuckled. "I see. After you kiss my ouchie, it's plain we're going to have to have a serious talk."

"Dylan—"

"Kiss first," he ordered.

Her lips glanced off his arm—like a butterfly barely lighting before flitting away. A second later, she ripped off the tape and cotton ball.

"OUCH!"

"Told you it was an ouchie!"

He cocked a brow and muttered, "I'll give you that one."

Sondra took a deep breath and let it out. "Dylan, we do need to talk seriously."

"Uh-huh," he agreed gravely. "I wouldn't have it any other way, because I'm not about to have you teaching our boy sissy terms for things. As far as I'm concerned, it's nonnegotiable. He's going to learn the manly way of sayin' what needs to be said. . . . Take, well, say for instance, him needin' to go see a man about a horse. . . ."

Giggles spilled out of Sondra. "See a man about a horse?"

"No better way to say it." He punctuated his pronouncement with a definitive nod. "You get ouchie. I get that." His heart started to beat a million times a minute as he added, "There's something else I get. Kenny will always be his pa, and I won't challenge that one bit—but I'm the man who'll teach him to walk and ride, and I'm to be called his daddy."

He'd never risked so much, put his heart on the line like that. In one fell swoop, he'd managed to demand a place in Sondra's life—an official place as her husband and the daddy to her precious son. Never once had he dared to think of himself as lucky enough to find a woman to love with all his heart and soul. Now, with Sondra and little Matthew, he hungered so badly to have them be his very own that he risked grabbing for the future. She might think it was a business arrangement, but Sondra was a woman with a big heart. Given enough time, she'd come around. *Please, God, let it be true.*

His voice went rough as he pledged, "I'll be a good daddy to him. You have my word on it. I'll be firm but fair. I'll protect him and teach him."

Say something, Sondra. . . .

"If we ever have other children, little Matt will still be our firstborn and every bit as much mine—I wouldn't be the kind to shove him off to the side in favor of them."

Her hand squeezed his elbow. "You'd never show favorites, Dylan. I know that."

He shot her a quick look.

"I suffered that fate, and if I thought for one second you'd shortchange Matt, I'd walk away."

"Then take off your boots, honey, because you aren't going anyplace but home."

Chapter 19

Come on over here and sit down for a minute."

Dylan's invitation surprised her. Sondra figured the minute they got home he'd rush off. Instead he'd popped Matthew into the baby swing and taken a seat on the couch. She took a few steps closer. "What is it?"

He grinned. "Well, at least you followed half of my directions." He tugged her down beside him, reached over, and took her left hand in his. Slick as could be, he took a ring and slipped it onto her fourth finger. She hadn't gotten her wedding ring repaired yet, so the finger was bare. He adjusted it so the solitaire glittered.

"Dylan—"

His hand came up, lifted her chin, and his lips met hers in a soft, warm kiss. For this being a business agreement, it felt so good, so real. He cupped her cheek and wound his other arm around her shoulders so she was entirely in his keeping—and she could do nothing other than melt as Dylan continued to brush his lips gently across hers. He murmured something against her cheek, but her pulse thundered too much for her to distinguish the words.

Dylan whispered against her temple, "I'm ready for the two of you. You're a special woman, and I'm praying for God to bless us."

Click, clack, click, clack. . . Matthew's baby swing beat out a rhythm.

"I'm praying, too." What more could she say? *I'm asking the Lord for you to fall in love with me? I'm begging God that you won't feel this is a big mistake someday?*

"Do you want us to live here or over at the Laughingstock?"

Looking around, she fought a sense of dread. The last thing Sondra wanted to do was pack up and move again. But that was his home. He'd grown up there, and she'd been here just shy of a year. He was already making all the sacrifices. "Don't you want to live there?"

His arm tightened about her, and she rested her head on his shoulder. "If it's all the same to you, this place is bigger and you have it all fixed up the way you like. Teresa and Jeff are renting a dinky apartment. They'd probably jump at the chance to live over at the Laughingstock."

"I'm eavesdropping," Teresa sang from the other side of the screen door. "If you're really making the offer, we accept."

"Come on in." Sondra eased free from Dylan's hold.

"Dylan called from town and asked what size ring you wore," Teresa bubbled.

"I'm so excited for the two of you! I came by to help you plan everything."

Dylan stood. "I need to get back to work." Instead of just leaving, he tilted Sondra's face to his. One hard, quick kiss, and he was gone.

"Wow." Teresa laughed. "Let me see your ring."

After Teresa admired the engagement ring, she asked, "What are you wearing for the wedding?"

Sondra let out a yelp. "I don't have anything!"

Teresa laughed. "Of course not. You had a baby. Things change after that. Besides, you need a new dress for your wedding. I know just the thing, too." Teresa led her into the office and seated her at the computer. "Watch." Seconds later, she entered a Web site address.

"This is for bridal gowns!"

"That's exactly what you are." Teresa gave her a stern look. "You've done this before, but Dylan hasn't. He even took his suit to the dry cleaners."

"He hates wearing suits!"

"He did it so he'd look handsome for you. You need to look pretty for him." Teresa's fingers flitted over the keyboard. "You don't have to wear yards of white satin and lace, but look here."

"Those are too fancy."

"Wait a minute." Teresa continued to scroll down the page. She glanced up for a second. "It'll just be his hands and yours there. Probably thirty guests in all—not a huge gathering, but they're the men who owe their livelihoods to the both of you."

"I just thought it was going to be us and a couple of witnesses."

"Nonsense. Forget that old saw about the wedding being for the bride. It's for everybody, because they all want a chance to celebrate. You belong together—I've seen it from the day I walked into your bedroom and saw him cradlin' you on his lap like you were manna from heaven."

Had Dylan been attracted to her all this time? *No. Impossible. I was pregnant!*

Teresa squinted at the monitor. "What about maybe wearing something with a hint of apricot? With priority delivery, your wedding dress will be here tomorrow."

Sondra bumped her out of the way and found the perfect dress. *Maybe, if we really do this up right, Dylan will—*

"Here. Order by phone." Teresa nudged the phone closer. "See if they have it in a petite, or we'll need to order superhigh heels so the hem doesn't drag."

Placing the order, Sondra tried to tamp down the spurt of hope she felt. The years of shuffling from one home to the next taught her love didn't blossom just because people lived under the same roof. *But God can work miracles. . . .* She called a caterer and ordered a wedding supper, then called the florist.

Lord, I'm doing my part. I'll trust You to work on him.

Dylan's breath hitched. The last rays of sunlight spilled through the stained glass and gave a jubilant look to the church. Candles glowed. Two discreet flower arrangements dressed up the altar. Good thing the pastor's wife had insisted on them using the church instead of the little chapel. Folks sat squished together in the pews because word got around. Every last hand from both ranches, neighbors, the friends Sondra had made, and their church family all showed up.

Strains of the traditional "Wedding March" started, and the guests stood. For a moment, Dylan couldn't see Sondra at all. Nickels walked her down the center aisle, looking proud as could be. Dylan subtly rocked forward onto his toes to see his bride.

She looked beautiful. For a moment, he thought she'd come to him wearing white lace. As she drew closer, he realized the antique-looking dress was creamy, but she wore a peachy-colored slip underneath. It looked soft and feminine—not fussy and overblown, but just right. Bridal enough to let her look like she wanted to get married—not so fancy that he felt uncomfortable. She had a knack for doing things perfectly.

She'd woven a few sprigs of baby's breath into her fire-bright tresses. Teresa had clued him in about buying a bridal bouquet. The roses shook a bit as Nickels placed Sondra's hand in his.

Don't be scared, honey. I'll be a good husband to you.

At their request, the pastor kept things simple. Dylan warmed her cool hands in his as he said his vows. Her voice faltered slightly, but she kept her big, green eyes on his face the whole time. Once the words were said, she smiled. Dylan's tension drained away. *You're mine now.*

"You may kiss your bride."

He kissed her with a joy he'd never felt before. The scent of her roses and the glow of the candles faded away until Matthew cried.

"I'd like to present Mr. and Mrs. Dylan Ward."

Dylan motioned to Teresa. She came to the altar and gave him Matt. He kept one arm around Sondra and cradled Matt in his left arm as he tacked on, "And their son."

Everyone clapped. Music played, and he led her back down the aisle. As they stepped out the door into a small grass courtyard, he saw Miller's brother.

Edwin. He'd been skulking around. The sheriff suspected he'd been behind the sabotage. In fact, they'd discovered Edwin had invested his money in the Tuttlesworth developing company that stood to buy the land. Still, they couldn't find any concrete proof against him.

Dylan quickly turned so Sondra wouldn't catch sight of him. Anger surged. She and Matthew were his family, and he'd protect them and their land with everything he had in him. Nothing was going to ruin their wedding day. *"What God hath joined together, let no man put asunder. . . ."*

❧

Finally they were alone. Well, not exactly alone. Matt let out a happy squeal. Grateful for his interruption, Sondra let out a nervous laugh. "I hope you're used to his noise already. If anything, he's starting to make a lot more of it as the days pass."

Dylan chuckled as he pulled off his tie. "I'll get him. You probably want to change into something more comfortable."

She froze at that phrase. Did he mean. . . ?

"Um, scratch that. I mean, well, how about if we opt for jeans? I hate wearing a suit. Your dress is beautiful, but it can't be your first choice of something to lounge around in."

Her shoulders slid back down with the silent sigh of relief. Sondra sidled out of the room into the master bedroom. She shut the door very quietly and pressed her back to it. *This is so awkward.*

Matthew cooed loudly from his room next door. Dylan's deep chortle followed. "Hey, PeeWee, where are your jeans?" Drawers slid open and banged shut.

Sondra thought about calling out to tell him they were in the second dresser drawer. Instead, she headed toward her closet and grabbed a pair for herself. Baggy ones. Not that any of her jeans were tight, but she didn't want anything even vaguely formfitting. Unzipping her dress required gymnastic stretching and wiggling. Once it fell into a pool around her ankles, Sondra looked down at the frothy lace and peach satin. Dylan liked her wedding gown. She'd get it drycleaned and keep it special—maybe wear it on their first anniversary.

Ha. First anniversary. I'm thinking of twelve months from now, and I can't even imagine how I'm going to make it through the next twelve hours!

A daisy-printed T-shirt and jeans. Her hair clipped back into a bouncy ponytail. Sondra studied herself critically in the mirror. She looked. . .casual. Comfortable. At ease. Appearances certainly were deceiving. She felt all knotted up inside. The man she'd fallen in love with and married didn't love her. Without a heartfelt commitment, how could they share a wedding bed?

We should have discussed it before now. A three-day engagement definitely qualified as whirlwind, but they should have covered that important topic before now. Only they hadn't.

Sondra whispered a prayer for help then went in search of her husband.

"We're ready for you." Dylan plunked a bowl of ice cream on the table. "Matt and I decided the dinky slices of cake weren't enough to fill even a little cowhand like him."

"That bowl is big enough for Matt to swim in!"

"Yeah." Dylan pouted. "I looked for a bigger bowl, but I couldn't find one."

"It's the biggest I have!"

"You'd better buy a decent-sized one with one of the gift certificates we got."

"The only thing bigger would be a hot tub!"

"Good thinking." He pulled an aerosol can from the refrigerator, shook it, and squirted whipped cream atop what looked like an entire half gallon of Fudge Brownie ice cream.

Matt banged his palms on the plastic tray of his high chair and let out a stream of gibberish.

"Gotcha, PeeWee." Dylan pivoted and squirted a frothy pile of whipped cream onto the tray. "Snack time."

"Snack?" Sondra gasped. "That's the size of the iceberg that sank the Titanic!"

He added more. "Never let it be said that I skimp."

Sondra laughed in disbelief. Getting into the spirit of things, she sat down, swiped the big bowl, and gave Dylan a wink. "So where's *your* ice cream?"

He leaned against the counter and smirked. "Where's *your* spoon?"

"Oops." He blocked the silverware drawer.

"I think we have a standoff."

Easing back, Sondra gave him a "wanna bet?" smile. Swift as could be, she opened the dishwasher and pulled out a spoon. When she turned back around, the playful victory she felt turned into disbelief.

Dylan took advantage of the brief second while her back was turned to grab a big serving spoon from the ceramic jar by the stove. He'd scooped a big chunk from the bowl.

"Community property." He looked downright smug as he took a lick.

"Uh, Dylan?" She stared at the front of his shirt. "I don't want to rain on your parade, but you got the slotted spoon."

"Yah, yah, yah, yah!"

Dylan swiped a finger of ice cream and dabbed it on Matt's cream-covered chin. "You have no room to talk. Besides, we men have to stick together."

"With that mess, you're guaranteed to stick!"

The kitchen rang with his booming laughter. Sondra leaned back in her chair and let out a sigh of relief. At least for now, they'd gotten past the awkwardness. *Lord, please let everything else work out this easily!*

Chapter 20

Dylan stood by her side as she tucked the baby into his crib for the night. She covered Matthew with one of the blankets made from Kenny's shirts. *Well, that really puts me in my place. As if I needed any reminder that she still loves her late husband.*

He took a chance and slipped his arm around her waist. "What about bedtime prayers?"

She blinked up at him in surprise. "Really? This early? I mean, I pray for him, but well. . ." The corner of her mouth twitched nervously. "When I was a kid, no one ever said bedtime prayers. I sort of thought maybe you were supposed to start that when they could listen to a Bible story or something."

"One of my earliest memories is of my dad kneeling by my bed." Dylan kept his arm about her and reached over the rail to finger Matthew's soft baby curls. "As the years passed, I always loved having the security of him or Mom praying with me. Anything—big or small—got mentioned in those prayers. I have a distinct memory of Dad checking under the bed and Mom looking in the closet because I was so sure there were monsters. Even when they didn't find one, Dad prayed for God to set angels about me so I'd be safe. It's how I learned God cared and listened to all of my concerns."

"Oh, Dylan. I'd love to have Matt grow up with that assurance."

"Then let's start having bedtime prayers with him."

For all the times he'd heard Sondra say grace at a meal, Dylan was unprepared for her prayer over her son. Those brief, sweet moments gave him a glimpse of her heart. After she finished, he prayed, too.

Sondra left on the night-light. Dylan filed that detail away for future reference. Little things like that made a big difference to a kid. And to his mom. Especially to a mom like Sondra. She tried so hard to make everything perfect for her son—as if she had to make up for Kenny not being there and for her own poor childhood.

Well, he won't have Kenny, but he has me.

"That was so sweet, Dylan. Matthew's first bedtime prayer. I'll have to record it in the baby book."

"That baby book must weigh a ton by now."

"Haven't you seen it?"

"Nope."

Sondra scurried over to the cabinet. "You've got to see it. Really."

Dylan sat on the couch, figuring a groom ought to get to cuddle a bit with his bride on their wedding night. She carried a big, baby blue album over and sat close enough to have their elbows brush.

Dylan wrapped his arm around her and dragged her tight against his side. "There. Much better. Now we can lay it across our laps. That thing is huge. Lookie there." Dylan chuckled as he ran his fingertip around the border of baby-animal stickers she'd used to embellish the first page that held Matthew's birth certificate. "You got downright fancy on this page." The only thing that would have improved that page would be if his own name were listed as "father."

"Oh, you just wait." Sondra turned the page.

Pictures from the hospital filled the pair of pages. He'd taken those pictures himself, since she'd been so tired and weak. She'd filled in a little square with Matt's vital statistics. Dylan tapped it. "You thought he was so big, and he was just a tidbit."

"I know." She turned the next page. Dylan stared.

She'd blown up one photo to the full size of the page—it was nothing but Matt's little bitty hand resting in Dylan's. That photo now took on special significance.

Sondra shifted, and the caption she'd penned came into view. It was a line from a song they sometimes sang in church. *I am weak, but he is strong.* Below that, she'd written more. *God provides, Matt. He brought a kind, capable man into our lives who helped us through and cared.*

"It's true," she said in a shaky voice. "You've been wonderful, Dylan. I can't ever thank you enough or repay—"

He didn't want her gratitude; he wanted her love. Dylan shut the book and turned to her. She'd stopped speaking at his abrupt action, and her eyes widened in surprise. "Let's get something straight. Being married to you suits me just fine. I don't want to hear how thankful you are."

"Because I'm not Thankful anymore—I'm Ward, right?"

He nodded emphatically. "You got it." *Lord, I prayed that tonight would go well. You're coming through like gangbusters. Please give me the strength and ease us through this next topic.* Jutting his chin toward the suitcase by the door, he said, "I already carried my other suitcase into the spare bedroom. I know we touched on having kids some day, but well—" He paused, hoping she'd want him, want a real marriage, but she tensed and didn't say a word. Her eyes darkened and filled with tears. No way was he going to take her to bed unless she loved him.

"I—" He cleared his throat. "I—reckon the first one we have won't be another honeymoon baby."

Silently she nodded.

They gave each other a chaste hug in the hallway, then went to separate rooms. Dylan stared at the dinky twin bed as he unsnapped his shirt. He'd pledged himself to Christ and had waited all these years for his wedding night. So here it was. But he was alone, and the woman he loved couldn't bear the thought of sharing a bed with him.

They sat across the breakfast table in aching silence. The empty inches between them at the table might have just as well been miles. Sondra poked at the runny yolk of her egg, and Dylan gulped down scorching hot coffee. The idea of starting each day of the rest of her life awkwardly searching for something to say made her shudder.

"You okay?"

She forced a smile. "I, um. . .usually don't eat my eggs over easy. I wasn't paying attention."

"Listen, you don't need to get up this early to make breakfast."

Squaring her shoulders, Sondra said, "Hold it right there. As I recall, you're the one who recently said, 'Anything worth doin' is worth doin' right. No sliding by.'"

"Oh, ho. So you're tossin' my words back at me, are you?"

Her fork skidded through the egg and scraped on the plate. She couldn't bear to look at him as she mumbled, "This might not be one of those Valentine-y kind of marriages, but some things aren't negotiable. This is one of them."

"Fine." He rose from the table, stuck his plate in the sink, and popped a Cheerio into Matthew's mouth. Without another word, he left.

Sondra dumped her eggs down the sink and let out a shaky breath. *Lord, I don't know what to do. Give me strength and help me to become the wife Dylan needs.*

The next day, they barely spoke. Everything was ultrapolite. Only the most essential things were said, and the most necessary ones went left unsaid. They tucked Matt into his crib and prayed over him, then sat in the living room where the only sounds were the rustling of the newspaper and the tick of the clock. At bedtime, Dylan slept in the guest room again.

Over the following week, he was his usual, helpful self. Sondra pasted on a smile and tried to do as much as she could around the house. She paid bills, sewed buttons on Dylan's shirts, made nice meals, and set about trying to blend in some of the things from Dylan's house so this place would feel more like home.

More like home? This wouldn't ever be his home. He already regretted marrying her. She sat down to rock Matt and blinked back tears. Again.

The porch screen banged. "I brought over another box of Dylan's stuff," Teresa said. "I'll stick this on your bed."

"Just leave it there." Desperate to keep Teresa from knowing Dylan wasn't sharing her room, Sondra blurted out, "Dylan will carry it back later."

"Okay." *Thud.* The box landed on the floor. "I'm moving our stuff into the Laughingstock. If you need something, call and I'll see if I can find it. I'm telling you, Dylan was alone in that house for six months and everything's in the wrong place."

"New isn't wrong; it's just different."

"You tell her, honey," Dylan said from the doorway.

"Oh boy. You're just like Mom and Dad were—the united front, absolutely indivisible."

"Yup." Dylan jerked his thumb toward the box. "What's in that?"

"Stuff from the closet shelf. Jeff just dumped it all in there for me." Sondra gave her a mock look of outrage. "You have no room to talk about our teamwork. You and Jeff are quite a pair yourselves."

"I seem to remember you having a hand truck. Mind if I borrow it?"

"Help yourself. It's out in the barn." Sondra stood and slipped Matt into his playpen. "I've used it to move bales of hay, so you might want to hose it off."

"Okay. Why don't you come over tomorrow and take whatever you want? There's some stuff in the kitchen you might like that belonged to Mom or Grandma."

"Don't you want it?" Sondra couldn't hide the surprise in her voice.

"I took a few things that had sentimental value to me, but you're family, and the two of you ought to have some of it, too."

Dylan slid his arm around Sondra's waist. "Sure. You took Mom's china. Maybe we'll take Grandma's. There's this huge old turkey platter...."

"Oh boy. He's going to start drooling any minute." Laughing, Teresa gave them a quick hug. "I'm getting out of here. See you tomorrow!"

Dylan hefted the box and carried it off to the guest room. When he sauntered back in, he took one look at Sondra and silently grabbed the tissue box. Setting it closer to the rocking chair, he somberly looked into her brimming eyes. He sat down heavily on the coffee table, leaned forward so his forearms rested on his thighs, and let his hand dangle. "Guess we'd better talk."

Sondra slipped into the rocking chair. *If only he'd wrapped his arms around me or wanted to sit beside me on the couch.*

He waited a long second and then said very quietly, "I can't live like this."

Chapter 21

Sondra looked at him and tried to choke back a sob.

"I'm not good at this stuff," he rasped.

Before he could say more or she could respond, the phone rang. And rang. And rang. Neither of them moved. The answering machine clicked.

"Dylan? Sondra? This is Troy Upton. I need you to come down to the sheriff's office."

Dylan heaved a sigh and headed for the phone. Sondra listened as he spoke. The conversation was short and cryptic. When he hung up, he came back to her and rubbed his forehead. "Something's up, but I'm not sure what. We need to go there now."

Sondra threw a few essentials into a diaper bag while Dylan washed up. They didn't do much talking on the road. Sondra kept hearing his words echo in her mind. *I can't live like this....* She glanced at his profile then stared out the window. *God, what should I do? Love isn't supposed to hurt like this.*

As he pulled into a parking place, Dylan murmured, "I'll grab PeeWee."

Diaper bag slung over her shoulder, Sondra walked alongside Dylan down the sidewalk to the sheriff's office. Dylan held the heavy door, and Sondra slipped inside. He always minded those simple courtesies, and it made her feel like a queen. "Thank—" Her voice died out, and she froze in place.

Dylan slid his warm palm to the small of her back and stood beside her.

"What's he doing here?" Sondra inched closer to Dylan as she tried to focus anywhere other than on Miller's brother, who sat in a room off to the side.

"I have a feeling we're about to find out."

"Hi, Dylan," the receptionist said. "Y'all go on back to Troy's office."

Sondra looked around, and Dylan slipped his arm around her waist. "This way." He led her down a short hall and into an office. "What's up, Troy?"

"I need to ask you folks a few questions." As soon as they were seated, he asked, "Sondra, have you given away anything of Miller's?"

She gave him a surprised look. "Some of the furniture went to the Battered Women's Society." When he nodded and still looked as if he expected more, she continued, "His clothes and books went to the bunkhouse."

"Miller put his money into the ranch, not into things," Dylan said. "My wife was generous, though. She gave me that antique cavalry blanket—"

The sheriff whistled under his breath.

"—and Miller's favorite pocket knife. She made sure each of the hands got something special of Miller's, but why don't you tell us what this is all about?"

"What about Miller's rodeo buckles?"

"Oh." Sondra smiled. "Miller kept those in a case in the bottom drawer. They're beautiful. I thought maybe I'd have them framed."

"So you didn't give them away." The sheriff squinted at her.

"No. Why?"

"Those aren't just pretty, honey. They're valuable." Dylan and Troy exchanged a look.

"Anywhere from one hundred to five thousand dollars apiece." The sheriff bent down and put a box on his desk.

Sondra gaped at it. "That's Miller's!"

The sheriff opened the lid. "And the buckles?"

"Miller's," Dylan grated.

"I can confirm that by the event dates on some of them, but others are antiques and can't be traced. I needed you to confirm these were his and hadn't been given away."

"I've seen a file on the computer. I can e-mail it to you," Sondra said.

Tense as could be, Dylan demanded, "How did you get these?"

"The tire tracks we found by the fencing when the cattle were poisoned narrowed the make and model."

"So they were poisoned. It wasn't an accident." Sondra looked at Dylan.

He readjusted Matt in his arms. "I didn't have solid proof. Just a strong hunch."

"We've been following leads. When we searched the car, we found these and something else." The sheriff picked up a clear plastic envelope and laid it on the desk.

Sondra leaned forward and froze. The bag contained a pair of wedding bands. One was cut. *Kenny's and mine.*

❧

"Can you identify these?" Troy asked as Dylan watched his wife's reaction.

She nodded. "They're my wedding set—my old one."

"Are you sure?" the sheriff pressed.

"Yes." She turned to Dylan. "Someone has been in our house."

"Miller's brother," Dylan confirmed.

"But I wrote and asked if there was something he'd like to have. He made it clear he didn't want anything." Her voice shook. "He didn't have to sneak in and steal."

"Troy?" Someone from the doorway waved an envelope. "It's a match."

"Book him and add arson to the charges." Troy looked at Dylan. "Matched his footprint."

Dylan grimaced. "Why?"

"He invested his inheritance in that developing company."

Tears filled Sondra's eyes. "I would have given him the buckles."

But she's upset about Kenny's ring. That galled Dylan. No matter how much he loved her, her heart still belonged to another man.

"Thanks for coming in." Troy rose.

Dylan took the hint. They'd come and identified the stolen goods. There wouldn't be any more sabotage. He and Sondra stood. The rings on her left hand sparkled as she reached for the diaper bag. To his surprise, she didn't look back at the rings on the desk. She reached for Matt and snuggled him close.

"We already logged in this evidence. You're welcome to take it home."

"That would be nice." To Dylan's surprise, Sondra didn't sound desperately relieved. She looked up at him. "Maybe someday Matt would like those rings."

The sheriff nodded. "That's a fine idea. Speaking of rings, no one reckoned you'd slip a ring on Sondra's finger and secure the Curly Q at the last minute. Edwin's sabotage almost worked."

Dylan shook his head. "My plan was to make the Curly Q turn a stellar profit so Sondra would know I wanted her for herself—not for her land. The sabotage moved up the date is all. The provision in the will was just an excuse for me to wed this woman. I'd have done so in the months ahead."

Troy chuckled. "I guessed as much. Folks have had a high old time watching you fall for Sondra."

"I fell all right." Dylan looked into Sondra's eyes. He was taking a huge leap of faith here, but he'd been about to speak with her back home. God opened a door for him to tell Sondra how he felt, and he couldn't slam it shut. "What started out as a simple partnership between us because of Miller's will grew into something soul deep."

Tears glittered in her eyes. She dropped the diaper bag and slipped her hand into his.

He added, "What started out as accepting Miller's will turned into following God's will."

They headed toward home, but Sondra remained silent. Dylan couldn't take it anymore. "We've gotta talk."

Sondra leaned against the headrest and closed her eyes. "Last time we had a serious talk in the car, we agreed Matt would call you *Daddy*."

"Things there are settled. It's the you-me stuff that needs ironing out. I just announced that I love you, and you haven't said a thing."

She hitched her shoulder and looked out the window. "You didn't exactly say you love me. I understand. You said this wasn't a Valentine-y, romantic marriage. I know you do love me—as your Christian sister."

Dylan pulled over to the side of the road. In the end, it all boiled down to this. "Is that all I am to you? Just your brother in the Lord? Someone you married because you think this was God's will, even if it wasn't yours?"

Very slowly, she turned toward him. Her eyes opened and filled with tears. "No. You and Matt and Jesus—you're my whole world." Her voice broke. "But I understand that love can be one-sided. I haven't done anything to deserve your love."

"Honey pie, I'm wild about you. God taught us that love isn't earned. It's freely given. Believe me, I have a heart full of love to give you." He proved it, too, with a heated kiss. He pulled away and pressed his forehead to hers. "Believe me, I'm not feeling very brotherly right now. I'm crazy in love with you."

She tilted her head and kissed him then slowly pulled away. "Mmm. Then stay crazy, because I love you."

Dylan hastily buckled his seat belt and started the car. He pulled out onto the road and sped toward home.

"Dylan, what are you doing?"

"Speeding. I'd pay a million-dollar ticket without batting an eye."

"You would? Why?"

He gave her a long look, and his voice dropped to a rumble. "It's time to go home, city-girl."

⁓

Half an hour later, Sondra sat on the edge of the bed and pleated the satin of her nightgown between nervous fingers. Dylan came into the bedroom, gave her a searching look, and said, "We have a problem."

Her hand curled, smashing the satin into a ball. "We do?"

He surveyed the pillows and then lifted his chin. "Yup, we do." He didn't bat an eye or pause to take a breath. "You're on my side of the bed."

"I'm..."

"On my side of the bed. I'll try to be workable on lots of issues, but this is one time when I'm going to be stubborn."

"Oh." She hopped up, wound her arms around his waist, and laughed. "Now this is the way things are supposed to be."

Epilogue

Sondra's laughter shivered in the morning air. "Hey, Dylan!" She came out of the henhouse holding a squirming, twenty-inch reptile. Extending it toward him, she grinned playfully. "Proud of me? I'm not petrified this time."

Dylan felt everything inside of him lurch.

Completely oblivious to his reaction, she launched into a rendition of the speech he'd given her the last time she'd found a snake. "This is a common milk snake. They've been known to eat eggs. They certainly don't eat people. Stop spluttering, Dylan! I learned my lesson from you that first day. If anything, the poor thing is terrified of me. Can't say as I blame him, either. Talk about a bad-hair day!"

Dylan made a strangled sound and reached for his sheath knife. "Sondra, heave that snake away!"

"Oh, stop getting crazy. I'm not afraid of him." She turned her hands so she and the snake were facing one another. Playfully she stuck out her tongue a few times. "He's kind of cute, don't you think?"

"Now, Sondra—toss him!"

"I'm going to take him over closer to the fence so I can grab a hoe. You said I'm supposed to chop off his head, but the thought makes me a little sick to my stomach. Do you mind doing the honors?"

"Gladly! Just heave him as far away as you can."

"Boss—," Nickels's voice cut in. "I'll get him; you take care of her."

"You know," Sondra said as she twisted the snake to suit her will, "we talked about what to name the ranch. What do you think of—"

"Sondra!"

Sondra finally obeyed. She casually tossed the squirming reptile onto the ground just a few feet away. Dylan leaped and tackled her. They rolled over a few times and came to a stop with him lying fully on top of her.

"Wow, sweetheart," she whispered. "You really know how to knock a girl off her feet."

He forced a chuckle, then forked his fingers through her wild hair and kissed her until they were both breathless. "I'm never gonna get enough of you."

"You both okay, boss?"

"More than okay," Dylan said as he got to his feet and pulled Sondra upright. "Thanks for the coverage."

Nickels shook his head and pushed his hat back a bit. "Reckon you ought to teach that little city-gal wife of yours to be careful of copperheads."

"Oh, it wasn't a copperhead, Nickels—it was just a plain, old milk snake." Sondra's smile froze, then melted as she saw the look the men exchanged. She could feel the blood draining from her face. Unwilling to let them witness her embarrassing cowardice, she vaguely murmured, "We all have chores to do." Just a few more steps, and she could sit down on the bench Dylan put in her garden. . . .

"Whoa. Hey." Dylan caught her and chuckled. He got her to the bench and promptly tucked her head between her watery knees.

When she finally sat up again, he asked, "Better?"

"Yeah. Fine."

"Coulda fooled me. You know, the first time you saw a snake, you lost your breakfast. This time, you nigh unto fainted. Looks like I've saddled myself with a prissy little city-gal for a wife."

"Almost right." She rested her head on his shoulder. "I'm definitely your wife, but I'm not prissy, and it wasn't the snake."

"Oh? And what was it?"

"Morning sickness."

Dylan took a minute to digest that news. Once it sank in, he let out a loud whoop.

Nickels came running. "Boss?"

Dylan chortled and gave Sondra a big kiss. "Praise God! We're gonna have another baby!"

CATHY MARIE HAKE

Cathy lives in Anaheim, California, with her husband, daughter, and two big, noisy dogs. In addition to writing, she is an RN, teaches Lamaze and breast-feeding, and is currently changing the room her son vacated into an office, which she's decorating with Victorian antiques.

Through
His Grace

Dedication

For the wonderful people who helped create this story—
my family's support and the Barbour team's hard work were invaluable!
God blessed me through this project.

Prologue

*T*his is all your *fault!*" *She stopped packing for an instant, fury distorting her pretty face.*

"I only wanted to do what was right." *He fisted his hands against the pain tearing through his chest.*

"Too little, too late." *She grabbed a heap of clothes and shoved them into the open suitcase.*

"Baby—" *He broke off as the word dropped like a stone, deepening the chasm between them.*

"Don't look at me like that!" *She screamed at him, tears filling her eyes. In that moment, she looked so small and defeated; he moved closer. She put out her hand to stop him, and a glint of steel lit her gaze once more. "I did what had to be done."*

Eric Nichols drummed his fingers on the steering wheel as the memory ebbed. He let his breath out in a big *whoosh* before studying the sign across the street.

"LET'S MEET AT MY HOUSE BEFORE THE GAME"—GOD.

He idly wondered how long it had been since he'd watched a Sunday football game. But he had to admit it had been a lot longer since he'd set foot in a church. *Grandpa isn't expecting me to show up on his doorstep. I have no reason to pass up a sign that's inviting me in. Why not? What else do I possibly have to lose?* With this logic, he steered his car into the church lot and parked in the back before ambling toward the double oak doors. He slid in the back row as the choir finished a warbly hymn—just in time for the man next to him to pass along the collection plate.

Digging around in his pocket, Eric found two lonely nickels—the change from the last five dollars he'd spent on breakfast. He considered the practically worthless offering before plunking it into the plate. *It's fitting. I don't have much to offer anybody just now. Why pretend otherwise?*

"God cares for each and every one of us. We don't deserve it—we've all messed up. But He offers us grace and love." The pastor preached on about hope and faith, and during a reading of the Gospels, Eric thought it over and felt better than he had since. . .everything.

Everything I've tried has failed. I kept thinking if I worked hard enough, if I was successful enough, life would be good. The things I've put my faith in—my job, money, even human love—have let me down. Now I don't have any of those things. What better time to try a new approach?

125

He made the decision to keep coming to church—to learn more about God's grace. For the first time in a long time, he was sure he was traveling in the right direction. The pain and anger pressed him from the inside until he thought he'd explode from it all, but the prospect of change—hope for the future—made it seem less difficult to bear.

At the end of the service, he stood and made his way toward his car. He had barely made it past the door when the man who'd sat next to him touched him on his arm.

"Got a minute?" The stranger smiled.

"A lifetime full of 'em," Eric answered. *But maybe they won't be as bad as I thought.*

"How'd you like to put some of that time to use?" The man stuck out his hand. "Miller Quintain, owner of the Curly Q Ranch just up the road a ways. I've been praying for a strong new ranch hand, and it looks like God might've dropped the answer next to me in church."

"I can ride, but I don't know much else." Eric studied the stranger's lined, honest face and found himself hoping his inexperience didn't matter. A few weeks of good, hard work would help drive the memories from his dreams, and Grandpa's place was two cities over—away from the pastor whose words refreshed him like a glass of cool water on a hot summer's day and made him want to come back for more.

"Not a problem. We'll start you on a trial basis." Quintain slapped him on the back. "Now what's your name, son?"

"Eric Nichols, sir." He watched as a big grin spread across the older man's face.

"Now if that don't beat all—after I saw you slip two nickels into the offering plate. Reminded me of the widow with two mites." Quintain studied him for a minute before nodding. "Every ranch hand needs a nickname. I'll call you *Nickels.*"

Chapter 1

Five Years Later

"Nickels, would you mind taking the baby chicks over to the group home this morning?" Sondra Ward put her hands on the small of her back.

"Not at all." He finished rubbing oil into his saddle and hung it back up.

"While you're on your way, I'll tell Miss Chesterton to expect you. Thanks."

"Anytime." He nodded toward her. "Little one starting to make its presence known?"

"My back's a bit sore today," his boss's wife admitted. "But it could be from carrying Matt around. He's getting big."

"Sure is. Dylan's proud of that little tyke." Nickels didn't need to mention it. Dylan wasn't just Sondra's second husband—he was the boy's second father. Sondra's first husband had died soon after Matthew's conception. When Miller Quintain, Sondra's close friend, died just months after her husband, she'd inherited a controlling share of the Curly Q Ranch—and a disgruntled Dylan Ward. In one year, she'd pitched in around the place, taken over the house, and moved into Dylan's heart. "Never saw a man so over the moon about his boy."

"He has every right to be." Sondra rubbed her hand lovingly over her still-flat stomach, a motherly gesture that made him turn around.

"I'd better load 'em up and get 'em out there." He tromped over to where they kept the chicks and started scooting them into the carrying boxes. The little bits of soft yellow fluff cheeped and jostled gently as he closed the tops. He settled them in his pickup so as to make sure the airholes weren't blocked then headed out.

Not long after, he pulled up in front of the Lawton Group Home. A matronly woman bustled out the front door, followed by several children.

"You must be Eric Nichols. I'm Miss Chesterton." She dried her hands on her apron. "Sit down, children. This is Mr. Nichols, who's brought the chicks."

"Where's Miss Sondra?" Over twenty children were settling on the sparse grass in a wide circle. Each one stared expectantly at him.

"She's—" Nickels had been about to say she was home taking care of her son but realized that would be cruel to these children without families. He looked to Miss Chesterton for help.

"She's not going to be coming around for a while," the woman said. "Mr.

Nichols will be coming instead."

"Why?" the chorus resounded.

"She's having a baby."

"Again?"

"Why?"

Amid the hubbub, Nickels spotted a small boy, about six, whisper something to the girl next to him. He leaned over to listen as the older girl whispered back.

"I know you would've been part of Miss Sondra's family if she'd wanted more. I would, too." The girl pushed thick glasses farther up on her nose before hugging the boy. "But people want their own babies."

They're supposed to, Nickels thought angrily. *Not all of these children are orphans—their parents just didn't want them.*

He started pulling boxes out of the truck, making sure he was good and ready to face these lost little ones before turning back around.

"What's your name?" He squatted next to the chestnut-haired boy he'd overheard.

"Jake." He looked eagerly at the box Nickels held.

"Here you go, Jake." Nickels scooped a fluffy chick out of the box and nudged it into the little boy's cupped hands.

"Thanks, Mr. Nichols!" Jake cuddled the baby bird close to his chest, carefully stroking its soft fuzz.

Nickels gave the next one to the girl who had comforted the boy. He found out they were brother and sister and her name was Lizzie. He worked his way around the circle, getting each child's name and handing out smiles along with the chicks. The way the children lavished love and attention on these little critters clearly told him they didn't get enough of it themselves.

When it was time for lunch, a lot of the kids were reluctant to part with their downy friends. Jake lingered behind, nuzzling his cheek against his chick one last time before solemnly handing it back to Nickels.

"Will you bring them back, Mr. Nichols?"

"I wouldn't miss it," Nickels promised. "I'll see you next Saturday, all right, Jake?"

"Thanks, Mr. Nichols." Jake cast one last wistful look at the chicks as his sister herded him to the picnic tables.

Nickels promised himself right then and there, that come rain or shine, hail or high water, he would make sure Jake had a chick in his hands next Saturday.

Grace Willard hoisted her rucksack over her shoulder, grateful she'd packed light as she bypassed baggage claim. Soon she'd retrieved her green four-door compact car and was rolling home for the first time in almost three months. It felt strange to be driving again after ten weeks in Guatemala, where one walked everywhere and rarely left the area.

The air-conditioning seemed dry after the muggy heat of the jungles, so after she'd left Lawton and headed down the two-lane highway to Lasso, she rolled down the windows. It wouldn't be long before she pulled into her own driveway.

"Ooohklahoma..." Grace burst forth into song, her voice rising in joyful tribute to her home state. "O–K!"

When she saw her cream-colored, two-story town house with hunter green trimming, she grinned even wider. Nestled within lay the ultimate luxury after months with no electricity or running water: a hot shower. It beckoned so strongly that only years of conditioning kept her from abandoning her bag in the car, taking the stairs two at a time, and luxuriating in the glory of hot water. At least she'd been smart enough to tell everyone she'd be coming home tomorrow. She needed a little time to readjust before facing her friends and family, and knowing them, she'd have come home to a barbecue pitched in her honor, with Jim manning the grill while Lisa prodded him to flip the meat. This way she could settle in first.

Grace took the duffel with her for a brief stop at the trash can before she went in. She grabbed her laundry and plunked it in the garbage, squashing a wave of guilt. Four outfits seemed a luxury to the Guatemalan orphans, but almost three months of hard use had decorated everything with tears, loose threads, and stains. Even the tread on her sneakers had worn through in certain places. Grace shrugged, took off the shoes, spotted her big toe through the hole in her left sock and added her footwear to the bin.

No laundry for me! By the time she got inside, the only items left were her camera, the rolls of film she'd shot, and the necklace the little girls had woven for her. It took less than five minutes to unpack. *Shower time!* Grace headed for the stairs.

Forty minutes later, she emerged from the shower a new woman. She'd scrubbed, moisturized, washed, conditioned, and pumiced herself to a rosy pink glow. Every knot in her neck and back had unwound beneath the cascading heat, and now, wrapped in her fuzzy robe, Grace was ready to attack the mound of mail. *A surprising stack considering I only bought this place a month before I left for Guatemala...*

Grace caught sight of her reflection in the hall mirror, her skin tone three shades darker than when she'd left, her hair a good two inches longer. She fingered it, wondering when she could get into Cut and Dried for a trim. She'd set up an appointment tomorrow. The blinking light on her answering machine captured her attention. Why? She had told everyone she would be unreachable. She'd paid her bills in advance—who would have called? Had something happened to one of her kids? The students she counseled at Lawton High were priority number one. She hit the PLAY button.

"Honey, I've got some bad news. Yesterday, the day after you left for Guatemala, a tornado came through. Jake and Lizzie were at school and are fine, but Lisa and Jim were at home when it came. They. . .they didn't make it to the cellar in time. They were found three miles south—" The voice of her best friend, Mary, broke before she continued, "They didn't leave custody of the kids to anyone. . . no will at all, so Lizzie and Jake are going to live with their grandpa Carl. . . . I know how close you were. I'm sorry."

Grace stood before the machine, frozen. Her cousin Jim and his wife, Lisa? But they were so young. Thirty-one. . .and the kids—were Lizzie and Jake being counseled? Carl was getting on in years. Could he handle having an eight-year-old girl and a six-year-old boy on his hands? Thoughts whirled through her mind as the machine beeped out a second message.

"This message is for Miss Grace Willard. This is Kate McNarty calling from Child Placement Services." An icy grip tightened around Grace's heart as she listened. "Please call me back at. . ." She jotted down the number on a pad to call back immediately. Was this about one of her high school students or Lizzie and Jake?

The next three messages were from the same source. Something had to be terribly wrong.

After one offer for new windows, one for carpet cleaning, and three suggestions that she switch her long-distance carrier, Grace heard another familiar voice.

"Grace? Um. . .this is your uncle Carl." *Uncle Carl? This can't be good.* "I need your help. They've taken the kids away! I have to get them back. You're a school counselor. You have to convince these people. Lizzie and Jake need me! Call me back." *Beep.* The message ended before he gave her the number, and the next revealed the older man's voice once more.

"I think I might've forgotten to leave my number. It's 555-7778. Please call ASAP!" *Beep.*

"This is Carl again. I didn't think about how we've got different area codes. . . . No, wait. . .it's the same one. Okay. 'Bye."

The rest of the messages contained the same jumble of telemarketers, recorded updates about changes being implemented for the Lawton High staff, pleas from Uncle Carl, and increasingly urgent calls from Child Services, as Kate McNarty gave Grace her office number, cell phone number, and even home phone.

Grace stared at the numbers on her pad of paper in astonishment. Jim and Lisa. . .gone. Lizzie and Jake placed with Uncle Carl. Carl said they'd been taken away. Child Services was trying to reach her. Tears welled in her eyes at the loss, but she blinked them back. Later she would acknowledge her grief. For now she needed to find out where Lizzie and Jake were and how they were holding up.

She called Kate McNarty's office number, left a message on voice mail, then tried the cell phone. No luck. Taking a deep breath, Grace dialed her home number, praying as the phone rang that someone would pick up.

"Hello?" A pleasant voice answered.

"Hello, is this Kate McNarty?" Grace kept her voice as calm as possible.

"Yes, it is. With whom am I speaking?"

"This is Grace Willard. . . ."

Chapter 2

Grace Willard!" the woman exclaimed. "I've been trying to get in touch with you for over two months!"

"I've been out of the country, working with natives at a Guatemalan orphanage," Grace explained quickly. *When the people I love needed me right here at home.* Her heart constricted.

"That's a good reason—charitable work. Helping children. That, combined with your status as a counselor—"

"How are Lizzie and Jake?" Grace interrupted. "Where are they now?"

"We have a shortage of foster families right now, so they're at the Lawton Group Home," Kate began.

She had driven right past them earlier. Grace put her head in her hands.

"They haven't been placed yet. It's difficult to find a home for siblings. Jake is young enough that he'd have a better chance of finding a semipermanent family without Lizzie. Separating them would—"

"Be unacceptable," Grace cut in smoothly, tamping down the urge to yell over that last comment. She called upon every ounce of her past experience to maintain a professional tone.

"Of course, of course," Kate agreed quickly. "It hasn't come to that yet."

"I understand they were initially placed with their grandfather?" Grace prodded. "Carl Willard?"

"Yes. . .they've been removed from his custody."

"What happened?" Grace braced herself for the worst.

"As you know, the children were enrolled in a private school. Since their parents paid their tuition up front and we didn't want to change more of their daily lives than necessary, they continued attending. This school runs through June, so Mr. Willard was responsible for getting them to and from the campus each school day. Unfortunately, on several occasions, the children were not picked up." Kate kept going as images of Lizzie and Jake standing forlornly in front of their school flashed before Grace's eyes. "The long and short of the matter is, Mr. Willard is of an age where it is difficult to see after two children, and his forgetfulness makes him an unsuitable guardian."

"When were they taken to the group home?" Grace could hardly argue with their reasons for removing the children from Uncle Carl's care—or lack thereof.

"Six weeks ago. They're adjusting as well as can be expected after so much upheaval and loss. They don't cause trouble, are fairly polite. . .but Jake has withdrawn, and Lizzie refuses to leave him. They've had a few unpleasant scenes at bedtime when they're separated into the girls' and boys' quarters." Kate's words sank like stones.

"I don't blame them," Grace interjected quietly. "It's perfectly understandable. They've lost their parents, their home, been taken away from their grandfather. They only have each other to cling to. Until now."

Grace grabbed her keys. "I'm coming to the Lawton Group Home. You have the papers ready for releasing them to me. I'll be there in fifteen"—she glanced at herself in the hall mirror again, this time realizing she was in her bathrobe—"make that twenty-five minutes."

She was tempted to throw her hair into a ponytail, toss on jeans and a sweatshirt, and hit the door running. Instead she pulled her still-damp mahogany locks into a black barrette and donned a basic black day dress and low-heeled pumps. She knew that if she wanted to have the children released into her custody she'd have to look every inch the responsible adult. She grabbed her black bag from the closet, stuffed her wallet, keys, and a tube of lipstick inside, and was out the door in eight minutes.

She slicked on the lipstick at a stoplight in Lawton and still managed to knock on the door earlier than she'd expected. *Lord, please let them be okay. Give me the right words. Help me bring them home.* A slightly frazzled but pleasant-looking older woman opened the door.

"I'm Miss Chesterton. How can I help you?" She eyed Grace's attire judiciously, making her glad she'd spent the extra effort.

"I'm Grace Willard, and I'm looking for Lizzie and Jake." Grace issued a relieved sigh when the woman smiled and grabbed one of Grace's hands in her two.

"Praise God! Kate reached you."

Praise God. Grace seconded that. Miss Chesterton's first words gave her reassurance that God was with her.

"Lizzie!" the woman bellowed loudly over her shoulder, almost causing Grace's eyes to cross. "Jake!" She ushered Grace into the entryway. "Oh, they'll be so glad to see you."

"Yes, Miss Chesterton?" Lizzie appeared first, Jake holding her hand as he trotted to keep up with her faster pace.

Grace stepped away from Miss Chesterton and knelt, her arms open wide.

"Auntie Grace!" Jake caught sight of her first and plowed ahead like a steamroller, with Lizzie rushing behind him. They both hit her at the same time, nearly bowling her over.

"I'm here." Grace wrapped her arms around them, and they all clung together. When Lizzie began to cry softly, Grace let her own tears fall. "I'm so sorry

I wasn't here sooner."

"Why are you crying?" Jake scooched around to pat his sister's shoulder. "It's all right now." He beamed a brilliant smile. "Auntie Grace is here."

"It's okay to cry, Lizzie." Grace cupped the girl's cheek in her hand. "I understand." And she did. Lizzie had probably spent the past two and a half months suppressing her own grief as everything familiar was stripped away from her. First her parents, then her home, then her grandfather. Lizzie had no doubt poured all she had into being strong for Jake, and her relief at knowing her auntie Grace would take care of them had cracked through her fragile facade. But now wasn't the time to delve into all that. She'd have time to speak with Lizzie privately later.

A woman Grace presumed to be Kate McNarty sailed through the door. "I have the papers to release them into your custody temporarily." She stood alongside Miss Chesterton, who'd been watching their reunion with clasped hands.

"Auntie Grace needs to talk to Miss McNarty now so I can take you home with me." Grace gave the kids one last squeeze before standing up. Jake clung to her skirt with one hand, his other grasped in his sister's protective grip.

"Hi, Jake. Lizzie." Miss McNarty smiled encouragingly.

"Hello." Lizzie seemed to eye Kate McNarty with suspicion, apparently remembering her as the person who took her first from her home then from her grandfather's apartment. The little girl edged even closer to her brother.

"Lizzie." Grace moved so she could clasp Lizzie's free hand, creating a protective circle. When the little girl looked into her eyes, she smiled softly. "Auntie Grace needs you to get ready. Would you please help Jake pack?"

Lizzie darted another glance at Kate McNarty before refocusing on Grace, who held her gaze. A gleam of purpose seemed to light her hazel eyes as the little girl straightened her shoulders and tugged her brother down the hall.

Grace waited until they were out of sight—and earshot—before addressing Kate McNarty.

"There will be nothing temporary about this."

⎯⎯⎯⎯

"Mornin', little fellas," Nickels greeted the chicks the following Saturday, smiling when they cheerily cheeped back at him. A few even hopped toward him, tilting their heads curiously.

Nickels settled them into the cardboard travel boxes and started out, surprised by how much he looked forward to visiting the orphanage.

No, it's a group home. Not an orphanage, he reminded himself about what Sondra had told him. They were waiting to be put with foster families. Group homes were transition places, not meant to raise the kids long-term in most cases.

But if that were so, why had she asked about several of the children by name?

That indicated to him that the children had been in that "temporary" situation for quite a while.

The system is overburdened. There are more children than there are foster homes to put them in. Sondra had answered his question sadly, and Nickels belatedly remembered that she'd been a foster child herself. *That's part of the reason why it was so important to me that Miller kept chicks year-round before he left me the ranch—the kids need something to look forward to on a regular basis. They've already suffered too many disappointments.*

"No disappointments today." Nickels spoke aloud, giving voice to his determination to follow through on Sondra's efforts. He spent an enjoyable hour with the children, hearing all about what they'd done that week and answering questions about Miss Sondra. But something—or someone—was missing. As the kids gave their chicks one last snuggle, he approached Miss Chesterton.

"Where are Jake and Lizzie?" He'd made that little boy a promise, after all.

"Oh!" Miss Chesterton beamed, her hair a frizzy halo in the late-morning light. "Their aunt Grace—who's really their second cousin—came by and picked them up just yesterday. Isn't it wonderful?"

Nickels frowned, remembering Sondra mentioned something about their being at the group home all summer. Why had it taken her so long? Heat closed his throat.

"So she's their closest relative?"

"No. They were originally placed with their grandfather, but he wasn't up to raising two children." Miss Chesterton lowered her voice. "He was too forgetful, if you know what I mean. Jake and Lizzie will be better off with Grace Willard. Why do you ask?"

"I made a promise to Jake that he'd have a chick today," Nickels explained. "I know how important it is that they have stability."

"Absolutely," Miss Chesterton agreed. "But they'll be getting plenty of that now."

"Still"—he gave her a cajoling grin—"don't we need to show them how important it is to keep our word? Is there any way we can avoid letting them down?" *Again,* he tacked on silently.

"Well. . .they haven't even had two days to adjust to their new home." Miss Chesterton was hedging, but she hadn't said they lived too far away.

"So being denied something they looked forward to will contribute to their upheaval," Nickels put in.

"I'll tell you what," Miss Chesterton said. "I'll call Grace and ask what she wants to do. It's her decision, after all, and if you're kind enough to remember the children—hold on."

He considered waiting while she disappeared inside the building, but after assuring himself the group home workers had the kids well in hand, he followed.

"Hello, Miss Willard," Miss Chesterton began.

Miss? Nickels immediately envisioned a prickly old maid with a sharp voice and a well-honed pointing finger, an unpleasant woman who'd thought long and hard about taking in two unwanted orphans before determining she absolutely had to. Meanwhile, Lizzie and Jake had their lives put on hold and knew with each passing day just how unwanted they were.

"Well, I understand you have a lot of changes to make...." Miss Chesterton's voice stopped him.

Their aunt was apparently denying them a brief moment of joy *and* complaining about how much *her* life was changing. *Lord, forgive me if I'm not following Your will, but I feel I have to step in here. I pray this impulse is You directing me.*

"Hello?" He took the phone from Miss Chesterton's loose grasp and put it to his ear. "This is Eric Nichols. I don't think you're aware of it, but I made a promise to your new wards...."

Chapter 3

J ake especially looked forward to holding the chicks every weekend, and I told him man-to-man. . ."

Grace hunched her shoulder to keep the phone by her ear as the man's warm, deep voice explained about promises and stability and baby birds. She bent down to untangle Jake's shoelaces.

"So you want me to bring Jake and Lizzie back to the group home right now?" She mentally rescheduled an already full day. Jake and Lizzie needed so many things. A distressed squeak from the corner let Grace know Lizzie was behind her and had assumed the worst from her last statement. "Can you hold for a minute?"

She dropped the phone on the bed and scooped Jake in her arms, motioning for Lizzie to join them. "A Mr. Nichols wants to know if you want to stop by the group home to see the chicks. It's up to you guys."

"*Chickies!*" Jake bounced up and down, his motion making the waterbed dance, carrying Grace and Lizzie along on the waves of his enthusiasm.

"I—" Lizzie looked torn between wanting to give in to her brother and afraid they'd have to stay at the home again.

Grace waited while Lizzie bit her lip and Jake choroused, "Ohpleaseohpleaseohplease—can we?"

"Excuse me!" The muffled, tinny shout from the discarded phone grabbed her attention. She picked it up.

"Actually." The deep voice, this time with a slight edge after being left hanging for so long, proposed another option. "I need to leave the home and start getting back to the ranch. Miss Chesterton says you live along the way. How 'bout I just swing by?"

A stranger swinging by? But it was the perfect solution. Jake would see the chicks, and Lizzie wouldn't be afraid of being left at the home. Miss Chesterton vouched for him. . . . Reason warred with obligation for a moment before Grace assented and gave the man her address.

"Are we gonna go?" Jake danced anxiously around the room, almost tripping over his newly untangled but still untied shoelaces.

"Mr. Nichols is coming to us so you can see the chicks." Grace helped Jake tie his shoes and had both kids use the restroom one last time. She tossed some granola bars and hand sanitizer into her purse before ushering the children out the door. She wouldn't think about letting an unknown, grown man into her home—bearing chicks or not. The front porch swing would work just fine.

"Hi, Mr. Nichols!" Jake put his hands on the porch railing and hopped to get a better look at the tall man stepping out of a truck.

"Hi, Jake, Lizzie." The rumbling voice matched the tones she'd heard over the phone. The man, clad in worn jeans, scuffed boots, and a green T-shirt stretched over his broad shoulders, hit the porch in three easy strides. His tanned skin and sun-bleached hair bespoke a man who spent the bulk of his time in God's great outdoors. She recognized him as a man she'd spotted a few times at church, but only from afar. He stayed with a fairly centralized group of people Grace didn't know well, so they hadn't had much contact. She'd never seen him this close before.

"Nice to meet you." Grace snapped her attention away from his engaging grin and brown eyes to extend her hand in welcome.

"Pleasure's all mine." Instead of shaking it, he raised both hands to his chest—close to her eye level. Cupped in his large, work-worn palms sat four little blond balls of fluff. When he nudged her hand, she took the hint to scoop up one of the chicks for herself. She watched with fascination as Mr. Nichols squatted down to let the children each select one of the soft creatures, keeping one for himself.

Jake and Lizzie sat cross-legged on the porch, and since Mr. Nichols did so as well, Grace followed suit. She sat quietly, petting the mound of warm fluff in her hand, watching Jake and Lizzie.

The children cuddled, nuzzled, pet, stroked, and shifted their little friends with ease born of practice. Jake's face shone as his chick, apparently worn out, snuggled against his chest with closed eyes.

"Sweet, isn't it?" The low whisper startled her.

"Thank you for coming by," Grace whispered back as his gaze caught hers. Mr. Nichols had kind eyes and, apparently, the heart to match. She turned her attention to his bird. His chick was nestled atop his handkerchief, its little head peeking out of his T-shirt pocket.

"They like to be near a heartbeat," he explained, his hand brushing hers as he gently took her chick and tucked it in beside his. "It soothes them."

His proximity is anything but soothing, Grace thought. She stood up abruptly.

"All right, kids. The chicks seem to be done in, so while Mr. Nichols and I take them back to his truck, you wash your hands." She traded Lizzie the bottle of sanitizer for the other two chicks.

"Thanks, Mr. Nichols," the two chorused while the adults walked down the steps.

"Smart move," he inclined his head toward the children.

"I don't want them getting sick," Grace murmured, handing over the chicks.

"Naw. I meant keeping them on the porch." His wink made her breath hitch. "I'm glad to see you've enough sense not to invite strangers into your home." He stepped nearer, and his voice dropped a few octaves as he pulled a bit of fluff from her hair. "I hope I'm not a stranger anymore."

"You're welcome to come again next week, Mr. Nichols." Grace sucked in a breath before continuing. "I don't think the kids are ready to go back to the group home, even for a visit. They need to settle in here."

"Will do." He walked around to the driver's-side door but paused before getting in. "And, Miss Willard? You can call me Eric."

Spinster aunt, my boot. Nickels shook his head as he drove away from Grace Willard's well-kept home. He couldn't have been more off base if he'd tried to imagine her exact opposite. She wasn't sharp, bossy, self-centered, or anything remotely approaching an old maid. No, Miss Willard was none other than the pretty little lady he'd seen around the church. She hadn't been there in a while—which probably had something to do with how long the kids had been in the group home at Lawton.

He'd noticed her years ago, but she was always chatting with other people or leading little kids around. *I assumed she was married.* He shook his head ruefully. *I should've asked Miller or Dylan a long time ago—they are so much further along in their spiritual walks than I am now. Her name is Grace. Nothing could've fit her better.*

Even dressed in jeans and a light sweater today, with a few mahogany curls springing loose from her ponytail, she moved with an innate grace he hadn't seen often. Those hazel eyes of hers had enough colors and facets to captivate a man for hours. The warm honey of her gaze held a stardust spectrum of deeper brown and intriguing green flecks.

Her dainty hands made delicate motions, betraying when she felt flustered. *I made her flustered.* Nickels smiled as he remembered the surprised warmth he knew she'd felt, too, when he brushed her hand with his.

Lord, thank You for correcting my assumptions about this woman. For years he'd ignored the attraction. At first he wasn't ready to recognize it. Later he told himself she had to be taken. But no matter how hard he'd tried to bury it, it lay beneath the surface all along.

And I could be wrong now, but maybe I see Your hand in this unexpected introduction. Help me to discern, and help me not to let my assumptions of others replace seeing them.

Before he had even met her, he'd assumed the worst. But the way she watched Lizzie and Jake showed any onlooker how deeply she cared for them both. He thought she'd been complaining about having to "change" things, but when he'd been waiting, he'd heard her conversation with the kids. That, along with her whispered confidence that Lizzie wasn't ready to see the group home again yet, erased his idea that she'd been putting herself first.

Grace reminded him of a mother hen trying to see to the needs of her new brood. Her decisions showed forethought as well as love, and she'd make a good mama. Grace Willard was a woman recentering her life. Now he'd do his best to make sure she left a spot for him.

Nickels didn't know what was to come of his interest in the Willard family, but one thing was certain. He'd be sure to show up next Saturday. He grinned at the chicks next to him. Each one now seemed a golden ticket to a sweet new world.

~∞≫~

"Are you ready for a day full of shopping?" Grace adjusted her rearview mirror after checking to see that both children were safely belted in the back.

Thank You, Lord, that my car has lap and shoulder belts in the backseat. It's just one detail that makes a big difference in their safety and my peace of mind.

"Yeah!" Lizzie couldn't keep the excitement of a born shopper out of her voice.

"Shopping?" Jake's tone held an entirely different meaning.

"Yeah, Jake!" Lizzie answered before Grace even opened her mouth. "Remember? We're gonna go see Auntie Grace's friend Mary."

"Okay," Jake proclaimed his verdict. "But why shopping?"

Because your parents didn't leave a will, and under Oklahoma law, that means nothing passes on to you. Their savings, the house, the cars—all go to the state. Someone else lives in your house now, and you have only a few of your old toys and clothes you're rapidly outgrowing. The injustice of it made Grace grip the steering wheel so tightly her knuckles turned white. She'd wept last night, tears of loss and grief, regret and injustice, doubt and anger. . .but peace hadn't come until she'd prayed. Even so, she was still off-kilter by the staggering number of things to be done.

"We're shopping for you!" She put all the enthusiasm she didn't feel into her voice. "You're going to pick out the things for your new room."

"And I can have a race-car bed?" Jake demanded.

"If we find one," Grace said evasively. The answer must have satisfied him because he and his sister started talking about what they'd want in their rooms.

Beds, desks, chairs, clothes, shoes, toys, school supplies, groceries, books, toiletries, bathroom accessories, plug covers, cabinet locks. . . The list of things Grace needed to take care of went on and on. And those were only the items she knew she'd need! *Mary'll have way more to add to the list. I'll be so glad to see her.* They'd spoken last night, and Grace had filled her in on what was happening before enlisting her expertise for today's venture.

She'd briefly considered asking a friend to babysit while she went shopping. It would make things easier, but that wasn't the best option. Even if Lizzie and

Jake would let her out of their sight that long—something she had no evidence to suggest would happen since they'd all slept in her room last night—she wanted the kids to choose the things that would make them feel at home.

Chapter 4

Ten minutes later, Grace was glad she'd called ahead to let Mary know they were coming. Her friend welcomed them into her furniture shop with hugs, smiles, and juice boxes. No uncomfortable questions or long explanations needed, just loving support.

"Do you have a race-car bed?" Jake asked, getting them started right away.

"Boy, do I!" Mary led them to a beautiful display. A proud race-car bed in polished faux chrome more than satisfied the little boy. As Jake bounced up and down on the soft mattress, Mary whispered the specifics to Grace.

"The wheels and fenders come off," she elaborated, "so when he outgrows race cars, he won't need a new bed."

"I'll take it," Grace said. "Do you have a desk and dresser in the same shade of wood?"

"Absolutely." Mary led them over to a square desk with three drawers along one side and a matching hutch atop it. "It comes with a chair, and to the left is the dresser—Jake won't be able to reach the top drawer yet, but it's a pretty good size for the blue bedroom." Grace had told Mary which bedrooms the children had chosen. "There's even a matching toy chest. If you'd like, I have a wallpaper border with racing cars—you could put it on the walls and glue a strip across the box to carry out your theme."

"Perfect." Grace watched as Jake opened the toy box and sat inside. "Mary, you're a lifesaver."

"I'm not finished yet! Where's Lizzie?"

"She wandered that way." Grace, Mary, and Jake followed the sound of Lizzie's voice, finding her not too far away.

"Lizzie, Lizzie!" Jake rushed up to his sister. "I'm getting a race-car bed."

"That's great!" Lizzie grinned. "Now you can help me pick out stuff for my room."

"Okay." Jake looked around before pointing to a bunk bed. "How 'bout that one?"

"I only need one bed, silly." Lizzie peeked at a dainty, white, four-poster bed with a canopy.

"I like this one." Mary had apparently noticed Lizzie's glance, too.

"It's like a bed for a princess." Lizzie's eyes grew round.

"Yes, it is," Grace agreed, "and the roses on that canopy would look just right with the rose color of your room."

Lizzie ran her hand along one of the four posters before gingerly climbing onto the mattress. Jake clambered alongside her, and they both lay back on the bed.

"It's comfy," Jake announced, "but kinda"—he wrinkled his nose—"girly. Are you sure you don't wanna race car, Lizzie?"

"I'm sure." Lizzie didn't even slide off the bed before making her decision.

"This comes with it." Mary gestured to a desk/vanity with a mirror on top and two drawers below on either side and a high-backed chair in front of it.

"Oooh," Lizzie breathed, sitting before the mirror and opening the drawers in delight.

Grace looked at the tall dresser and spotted a white, cushioned bench beside it. She walked over and opened it to find a toy chest inside.

"We'll take the set," she told Mary.

"Wait a minute now," Mary said. "I think you'll need one more thing." She took Lizzie's hand and led her to a furniture grouping a few feet away. "What do you think of that bookcase?"

"It's like a dollhouse!" Lizzie rushed over to the white, house-shaped bookcase. It was cleverly made, with the shelves segmented in various places. The long sections would be for books, but the smaller areas formed "rooms." It would be a dollhouse and bookcase in one.

"This one's free." Mary stepped close to Grace. "The maker shipped it as a floor model before discontinuing the piece. I can't sell it so it's been in the back room for ages, just waiting for a little girl to love it."

"Thanks." Grace hugged her friend. She hadn't wanted to mention it, but the furniture price tags had caught her attention. She wasn't going to let that stop the kids from making their new home—well, home—but it was a concern.

"Come on. The kids can look around while we get squared away." Mary led her to the cash register.

Grace pulled out her checkbook, steeling herself for the total.

When Mary named the price, Grace glared at her friend. "What do you think you're doing?"

"Hush now." Mary folded her arms over her chest. "You think I'm going to make a profit off you?"

"You're already throwing in the bookcase and wallpaper border, Mary. This has to be. . .half off?"

"That's about right. Listen—my supplier pays the shipping for new pieces to replace these." Mary spoke in a rush. "I'm giving them to you wholesale—you pay back exactly what I paid to get them in the first place. I'm not losing a cent."

"You're a prize, you know that?" Grace hugged her friend.

"One daughter of the King, helping her sister in Christ." Mary hugged her back. "Now when do you want the items delivered?"

"Special delivery!" Nickels knocked on the Willard door at 11:00 the following Saturday, right after he'd left the group home. *They aren't waiting on the porch—I guess I'm not a stranger anymore.*

"Hello, Eric!" Grace ushered him in with a polite smile.

No one calls me Eric. What possessed me to tell her that instead of sticking with plain old Nickels? As if he didn't know. He wanted to hear his God-given name from her rosy lips. It sounded good, too.

"Good morning, Gr—" Nickels gave himself a mental kick. Just because he thought of her as Grace didn't mean he had the right to abandon his good manners. "Miss Willard."

"You had it right the first time." Grace's good-natured wink made him aware of how pretty she looked today. The hunter green of her blouse brought out the color of her eyes and a hint of burnished copper in her hair.

"Grace." He tested the word, drawing it out like a long, cool drink of water. Her eyebrows raised in a mute question he had no answer for just yet.

"Mr. Nichols!" Jake came barreling down the stairs, Lizzie right after him.

"Jake!" Grace's sharp tone brought the little boy to a skidding halt. "What do we know about running in the house—especially on the stairs?"

"Not to." Jake looked at his sneakers in penitence. "I'm sorry, Auntie Grace."

"I know you're excited. You'll do better next time." Grace stopped to give the boy a hug. "The rules are there so you don't get hurt." She drew Lizzie into the embrace. "You're both too precious to me, understand?"

They're not even her children, and she's a good mama. Nickels watched the tender moment with a lump in his throat. The boy's eyes weren't haunted by so much sorrow, and his sister no longer looked as though she shouldered the burdens of her small world. Just one week, and their aunt's loving heart had started to heal the wounds of the past.

"How 'bout we move these little fellas into the kitchen?" Nickels gestured to the box in his right hand.

"Good idea." Grace led him through the cool tones in the entryway, then into the warmer hues and furnishings of the living room, and finally into the kitchen.

The kitchen matched her smile—bright and welcoming. The light blue of her counters adorned shining white cabinets with glass knobs. He noted that the doors below the sink were constrained by a childproof lock. The areas beneath the counter had collected a swath of smudges—silent testimony to the presence of tiny fingers.

Over by the breakfast nook, she'd put a child-sized wooden table and chairs. Lizzie and Jake promptly sat down, though Jake swung his feet around, kicking the air in anticipation.

"Here you go, sir." Nickels scooped two chicks out of the box and delivered one to Jake.

"Thanks!" He cuddled the baby bird to his chest, completely focused on the ball of comfort in his hands.

"And one for you, milady." Nickels swept a slight bow and presented Lizzie with her chick. The little girl beamed at him before nodding regally.

From the corner of his eye, he saw Grace smiling at their little game. He swept a deeper bow and proffered another fluff ball. "Your Grace."

Her eyes danced with amusement as she took it from his hands, and he could tell she appreciated his little jest.

"No, Mr. Nichols." Jake scooted his chair back abruptly and stood by Lizzie, closer to Grace. "She's our auntie Grace."

"Of course." Nickels realized immediately how Jake had misunderstood. "It was kind of a joke. You see"—he squatted down to the boy's eye level—"in the past, a fine lady, like your aunt, could be a duchess. And when a person spoke to a duchess, he addressed her as 'Your Grace.' I was trying to tell all of you what a fine lady I think your aunt is." He looked over his shoulder and saw a faint blush tinge Grace's cheeks.

"Oh, that's nice." Lizzie smiled at him in approval. "That's how a gentleman should treat a lady."

"Okay." Jake trotted back to his seat after looking at Grace for confirmation.

Poor kids. They were afraid something would take their aunt Grace from them. He couldn't blame them. Nobody liked to have something precious snatched away.

He settled onto one of the tall stools by the breakfast nook beside Grace, enjoying his proximity to her but keeping his focus on the kids.

"Thanks." She leaned close to whisper, and he could smell the sweetness of mint on her breath. She didn't say more, making him wonder if she was thanking him for reassuring the kids or appreciating his compliment. He hoped it was both—it had been too long since he'd complimented a beautiful woman, and he liked to think he'd done it right.

"I meant every word." He held her gaze for a moment before reaching over and stroking the chick in her hands. It was the best reason he could think of to get a little closer. He'd thought about her all week.

"Oh." Her small gasp let him know she wasn't unaffected by his presence.

He was glad, because he intended to be around a lot more. He looked back at Lizzie and Jake and watched them trying to make their chicks race across the tabletop. *Jake's going to need a man in his life.* He sneaked another glance at Grace. *And I hope he's not the only one.*

Chapter 5

See you next week." Mr. Nichols—*Eric*, Grace reminded herself—made it a statement, not a question.

"We'll be here," she promised, hearing Lizzie and Jake slap their palms in a high five in the background.

"I look forward to it."

"So do I." Grace all but whispered this last, but he heard her. She could tell by the huge grin lighting his handsome face.

"Wait, Mr. Nichols!" Lizzie's voice stopped him as he was putting the chicks in his truck. "Auntie Grace, can't Mr. Nichols see our new rooms?"

"Yeah!" Jake put out his hands like a race-car driver and vroomed out to stand beside his sister.

"I'm sure Mr. Nichols has other things to do today," Grace said. It was one thing to have a handsome man in her kitchen—quite another to have that handsome man upstairs in her home. On the other hand, Lizzie and Jake were showing how proud they were. If they didn't feel it was their home, they wouldn't even ask. And, after all, they were the most important thing there. She pushed aside thoughts of the overflowing laundry hamper in the upstairs bathroom to glance at Eric. She'd take her cue from him. If he said yes, up they'd go. If he wanted to wait until next week, that would do, too.

He walked back. "I've got time." He looked at his wrist, but Grace noticed he didn't wear a watch.

"Pretty please?" Lizzie folded her hands behind her back and rocked up and down on her toes.

"I've got a race car in there!" Jake's fervor showed he found this to be the ultimate enticement.

"Well, I wouldn't want to miss that." Eric grinned. "I was about to put the chicks in the truck. Even with the windows rolled down, it's starting to get too hot to leave them there." He raised his eyebrow at Grace.

"Bring them in," she said, bowing to the inevitable. She was no math specialist, but three against one would clearly win her no points.

They left the boxes of chicks in the kitchen first. Jake rushed ahead of them at full gallop, heading for the stairs.

"Jake. . ." Grace used her warning tone, and the little boy pulled up short.

"Oh, right." He took the steps at a more reasonable pace.

When they reached the doorway, Eric let out a long whistle. "Now that's something!" Grace followed him into the room as he walked over to the bed, making quite a show of examining the wheels.

"I'm gonna be a race-car driver!" Jake proclaimed proudly, bouncing onto the still-unmade bed. "See?" He turned an imaginary wheel as though driving.

"And look at that," Eric said, spying the poster Grace had found at a discount store. "A long stretch of road straight ahead of you." He turned to Grace. "It looks like NASCAR came and did your room for you."

Grace looked around in satisfaction. The border on the walls showed race cars on a road, the poster on the wall above Jake's toy chest was a shot of the legendary Route 66, and a checkered flag hung above the bed. The shelves still needed books and toys, but it had been a busy week.

"Mine next!" Lizzie grabbed Eric by the hand and led him to the next room. Lizzie's walls, a shade of pale rose, showcased her oasis of girly frills to perfection.

"Wow!" Eric seemed a bit at a loss as his gaze traveled from the four-poster canopy bed to the dainty vanity.

"Isn't it beyootifull?" Lizzie spun around in the middle of the room.

"Fit for a princess," Eric agreed. He moved toward the empty bookcase/dollhouse and ran his hand along the sloping roofline. "Now this is awesome."

"Auntie Grace says it'll be a dollhouse, too," Lizzie added sagely before giving in to her excitement. "I get to decorate all the rooms!" She pointed to the smaller sections walled off in the bookshelf.

"It needs a garage," Jake pointed out.

"The house comes first." Lizzie shot Grace a look that clearly said, "Boys. Hmph."

At that moment, Grace caught a shared glance between Eric and Jake, which she took to mean, "Girls are so weird." *He should be able to share that type of look with his father.* The thought pierced her heart.

"What was that?" Lizzie's voice broke through Grace's reverie.

"It was Mr. Nichols!" Jake giggled.

"I'm afraid it was." Eric shrugged. "My stomach thinks it's lunchtime."

Grace glanced at her watch. "Your stomach is right. Would you like to stay for sandwiches?"

"Bologna?" Jake queried.

"Peanut butter!" Lizzie squealed.

"Bologna and peanut butter?" Eric made a face so the kids laughed. "Yuk."

"I was thinking more along the lines of grilled cheese with chicken soup," Grace said. "But"—she sneaked a look at Eric's face—"bologna and peanut butter sound awfully tempting."

"Yay!" Jake waved his hands in the air. "Can I help?"

"Can I eat something else?" Lizzie tugged on Grace's arm.

"How 'bout you help me make the grilled cheese instead?" Grace asked her.

"I'll take care of the soup," Eric offered. "No sense in children playing with fire."

I'm no child, Grace reminded herself. *All the same. . .I'd best be careful around Eric Nichols. There's a possibility I could get burned.*

❧

"C'mon, Brassy." Nickels nudged his mount to the left, where a steer ambled toward a patch of dandelions too far away. They were moving this herd to another pasture for good reason—if they didn't, there wouldn't be any grass left to seed and spring back later.

"Arf!" Skylar yipped happily at Brassy's side, jogging to keep up with the horse's trot.

"Hey, girl." Nickels kept an eye on the spunky cattle dog. Blue heelers were known for their incredible loyalty and herding ability, and Skylar was the best of the best. Her black-spotted, white barrel-shaped body jaunted along on four surprisingly dainty legs, her tail aloft as she headed for the errant cow. Nickels stayed beside her, glad for the presence of his trusted companions.

Brassy and Skylar might have four legs, but their willingness to follow his commands, coupled with their affectionate natures, made more like family than work animals. Now that they'd caught the stray, Nickels reined them in and looked beneath his dusty hat brim toward the horizon. Something was wrong, but he couldn't put his finger on it.

There. The western fence was missing a post. Nickels urged Brassy forward, and Skylar pranced back toward her charges. When he reached the area of the breach, he dismounted, letting his horse scrounge for whatever tasty tidbits the herd had left behind.

Two posts had bowed under considerable pressure. Bits of hide were snagged in the barbed wire.

Hank, another ranch hand, rode up to join him. "What'd you find?"

"Two posts down—pressed out from the inside." Nickels gestured. "Something spooked the steers."

"Wolf?"

"Or a coyote. Time to circle around—see if we can find tracks." It was late summer—too early in the year for wolves or coyotes to be eying such big animals as cows. "Pickings must be scarce for 'em."

"I reckon. Most land's fenced off now. A coyote's like to be shot as soon as looked at these days. I'll take a look around—you've been out all day."

"Thanks." Nickels stood up, clapping the dust from his gloves. "It'll give me a chance to repair these before the sun sets."

"When you go back for supplies, tell Rusty to check the herd." Hank shifted in the saddle. "There's some blood on this wire—we don't want infection."

"I know." Nickels nodded. "The blood is fresh, so the scratch happened recently. We can get to it before infection sets in."

With that, they set to their work. Nickels positioned the posts upright and banged them deeper with the mallet he kept in Brassy's saddlebag. Tomorrow he'd need to come back and restring the barbed wire—bent and slightly bloodied, it needed to be replaced so it didn't attract crows. If the wild dogs were that hungry, they'd come back for birds.

" 'Those living far away fear your wonders; where morning dawns and evening fades you call forth songs of joy.' " Nickels drank in another look at the pinks and oranges splashed across the clouds, citing a psalm as he marveled at the beauty God created.

The colors brought Grace to his mind. The curls that had escaped from her clip to frame her face had caught the light like this, reflecting hues of gold and red. He found himself thinking about the Willards a lot lately—Grace, in particular.

Lord, You know what—or should I say, who—is on my mind. Grace's lovely face is only the outward adornment of a loving heart and beautiful spirit. Lizzie's a regular little mother to Jake, always trying to guard her brother. And Jake. . . Nickels paused. *Well, he's like the son I never had.* He pushed aside his regret. *That little tyke has the courage and liveliness every young boy should, but he's still struggling. They all are.*

Father, I want to get closer. He wanted to support Grace, make sure there was a man in Jake's life and see that Lizzie didn't take so much upon herself. But he was just one step above a stranger, and they had a lot to deal with. They didn't need him pushing his way in—their fragile family needed time to stabilize.

Grace had risen to the challenge of taking on the kids—her welcoming nature and selfless decision made him admire her even more. But all three of them were grieving the loss of close family members—and their previous way of life. Things were confused enough for them. *I don't have any right to intrude, and I'm asking that You guide me on this.* He kept thinking of reasons why not to get involved—but he didn't want to listen to a single one.

149

Chapter 6

D on't go!" Jake sat on Grace's foot, wrapping both his feet and arms around her legs.

"I'll come back." She tried to maintain a soothing voice, but it was hard when she was limping along with a barnacle the size of a six-year-old boy attached to her leg. She stopped.

"Please." Jake's tearstained face nearly broke her heart.

"Come here." She leaned down and held out her arms. Like a baby koala, Jake untangled from her ankle and jumped into her embrace. Lizzie pressed up next to her, burying her face in Grace's hip.

Lord, give me strength. The three of them hadn't been apart since she'd picked them up from Lawton. The only time they were even in different rooms was nighttime. And then, more often than not, she would wake up to find Jake in Lizzie's room or vice versa. She knew today would be difficult. She had started preparing them days ago. She had told them she needed to go to work—that Mary would stay with them until she got home. How could she reassure them their lives wouldn't completely change again?

"Lizzie, do you remember what we talked about? How you're going to be Mary's special helper today? Jake, aren't you looking forward to the park?" Grace threw in one last enticement. "You'll have your favorite lunch."

"Hot dogs?" Jake scrutinized her carefully, obviously weighing the options.

"That's right. And when I get home, we'll play any game Lizzie chooses." Grace gave Lizzie a conspiratorial grin. She guessed Lizzie didn't want to show it, but she probably didn't want her aunt to go for a whole day either. By enlisting her "help" for the day, Grace hoped to offset the difficulty for her.

"Yeah." The little girl straightened up and pried Jake from his aunt's arms. "We'll have lots of fun, and we'll have tons to tell Auntie Grace when she gets home." Lizzie pasted on a brave smile.

"And I'll be home before you know it." Grace planted a kiss on each one's forehead. "I promise."

"All right now." Mary came out of the bathroom. "Let's get you into your sweaters and out to the park!"

Grace gave her a small wave and headed out the door before Jake and Lizzie could start worrying again. Mary could handle them. After all, it was only for a couple of days. They'd be off to school next week.

A different school. Grace sighed. When Jim and Lisa died without leaving a will, Lizzie and Jake were left without a thing except their parents' Social Security. Grace had tried to be a good steward. She'd saved up for her house, bought a sensible car, had a 401K and a retirement account. But she couldn't take care of Jake and Lizzie, pay the bills, and afford to send them back to the private academy. A wave of guilt crashed over her.

"Lord," she said aloud, "Lizzie and Jake lost their mother, their father, and their home in the course of one day. Shortly after, they were wrenched from their grandfather when he didn't care for them properly. Now they'll face a new school where they don't know anyone. Making friends in a new place is always tough." She knew first days at school were trials in general. Lizzie and Jake could barely handle her going to work. How would they all manage when the children were in school and she was working? Their schedules would be all right. She could drop them off and pick them up, but another transition would be difficult for them. She hadn't even gotten the list from their new teachers telling her what school supplies they would need. She sighed. "I'm in over my head here, Lord. Please help me!"

She pulled into the Lawton High staff parking lot. Today she and the other counselors would coordinate the school schedules of the students. Grace had the sophomores this year—the same kids she'd had last year as freshmen. They would be considering huge grids, class-size allotments, required instruction, special education needs, sports games, and requested electives. Creating the schedules of hundreds of students bore much in common with a giant, multifaceted, endlessly changing jigsaw puzzle.

And somehow it seems simple compared to how complicated my life has become.

❦

"Waffles," Nickels muttered as he swung his cart into the frozen-food section and scowled at the list in his hand. "Blueberry frozen waffles." Dylan had been out at a cattlemen's association meeting, so Sondra enlisted Nickels to fetch "a little something for her and the baby."

When I agreed to do this, I was thinking she wanted ice cream or something. Mmm. . . Nickels thought longingly of a mound of vanilla bean ice cream. *But no. She smiles and snookers me into saying yes before I ask what she wants.*

He glanced from the now-crumpled list to the contents of his cart. Not the basket he usually grabbed and carried when he set foot in a supermarket. She had added on a whole grocery list to boot! He made a face as he perused the items and fervently hoped he wouldn't be invited for dinner if she planned on combining any of them.

Orange juice, salsa, key lime yogurt, garlic bread, peach jam, bananas, pickles, and—he peered into the freezer case—*blueberry waffles.*

"That's quite a list you've got there." The voice behind made him realize he'd read it out loud.

"Well." He turned around, expecting to find a store associate who might be able to help him out. He pulled up short at the sight of—"Grace!"

"That's right." She gave a slightly tired smile. "Good to see you, Eric."

"This stuff isn't for me," he blurted out. "It's for Sondra. She's pregnant, and she has these weird cravings."

"Oh." Grace seemed taken aback.

"She's my boss's wife," Nickels added, gratified to have caught her looking at his ring-free left hand.

"And you didn't know what you were getting yourself into, eh?" Grace relaxed a bit. "I'm taking advantage of having my friend Mary watch Jake and Lizzie so I can pick up a few things. I went back to work today, but the kids don't start school until next week."

"You know, I never asked." Nickels leaned against one of the doors and shoved his hands into his jeans pockets. "What do you do?" What could have taken her away all summer? Did she travel a lot? He left these more personal questions unasked.

"I'm a counselor at Lawton High. That's good, because I have the same day schedule as the kids will, and I'm off on the same holidays so I won't need to find day care." Her smile showed how happy she was at the prospect.

"That's good." He ignored the memories of his past that threatened to revive. "The more time spent with family, the better."

"Yes." A shadow crossed Grace's lovely face. "I need to take Jake and Lizzie to visit their grandfather. Things have been so hectic that we haven't made the time yet."

Their grandfather. . . Nickels remembered Miss Chesterton saying he'd been too old and forgetful to take care of the children. "It's good of you to keep family members involved. He'll be glad to see them."

"I'm hoping it won't be awkward." She reached into the freezer and pulled out a carton of vanilla bean ice cream. "So have you. . ." Her voice trailed off as she caught his longing look.

"That's my favorite ice cream," he admitted. "To tell the truth"—he lowered his voice so he could lean in closer—"I had kinda hoped it would be on Sondra's list."

"Is it?" Grace peered at the paper in his left hand.

"Nope." He tried to look as hangdog as possible.

"All right, all right." Grace put up her hands in mock surrender. "Jake gets that same look. I'll tell you what—we'll be sure to have sundaes after lunch this Saturday."

"Great!" Nickels perked up. *I get to spend time with her and the kids and get an ice cream sundae! And am I crazy, or did she mention lunch, too?* "What can I bring?"

"Um. . ." Grace gave the contents of his cart a sideways glance. "Maybe you ought to leave the food to me. You just bring the chicks."

"You've got yourself a deal."

Did I just invite him to lunch? I don't invite hunky men anywhere. I don't even invite not-so-hunky men anywhere. Grace rubbed the bridge of her nose in bewilderment.

Lord, You know I've prayed about my singleness for a long time. I've striven mightily to come to peace with the idea that I'm not meant to have that kind of love in my life. It was why she had poured herself into her work. . .loving the students she worked with. When she turned twenty-nine without ever having a serious relationship, she gave her love life to God and accepted that the kids at the high school were the closest she'd come to having children of her own. It was so hard to admit that—a true test of faith that probably took her longer than it should have.

So when I gave up my hopes and dreams and devoted my summer to the orphans of Guatemala, why did You change everything? I know we didn't have any specifics laid out, but I thought we'd pretty much settled how things were going to be. She had come home to find she'd lost her cousin and his wife, who also happened to be two of her closest friends, and gained two children to raise as her own in their memory. In a few hours, her world had tilted on its axis, and she followed the Lord willingly. Abandoning Lizzie and Jake never even occurred to her. . . . She knew immediately that He intended her to take them.

As if that change weren't big enough, now it seemed He was bringing a God-fearing, thoughtful, intelligent, and attractive man to her door. A man whose smile brightened her day. How would she handle this? Her heart still grieved for Jim and Lisa. She prayed her weakness would not destroy her new family. *Can't we compromise, Lord? I'll do my best to care for Jake and Lizzie while You protect my heart. Please be close to me on Saturday!*

Grace looked at her own shopping list. The sheer volume of groceries she bought these days astounded her.

Orange juice, bananas, peanut butter, bread, apples, string cheese, spaghetti, granola bars, peas, applesauce. . . The list looked as if it could feed an army, but Grace had learned it was better to stock up now than come running back for a few things every other day. Finding healthy choices the kids would actually eat had proved something of a challenge. Pudding, cookies, potato chips, and ice cream were their favorite snacks, but growing children needed good nutrition. Grace picked up a bag of baked potato chips and the half gallon of ice cream.

Grace had too many charges at Lawton High whose eating habits and subsequent weight gain contributed to depression, diabetes, social awkwardness, and fatigue. She'd promised to be careful with Jake and Lizzie and make sure they didn't need to turn to empty calories for comfort. Striking a balance between favorite treats and health would be a continuous struggle.

That being said, she grabbed a bag of chocolates for herself before heading to the checkout. *Some things a woman just can't compromise on.*

Chapter 7

W ait just a sec!" Nickels rushed out of the kitchen when Grace pulled the ice cream from the freezer. He strode to his truck and picked up the bulging supermarket bag from the floor before returning to the house.

"What's that?" Grace eyed him.

"Yeah, what's in there?" Jake's query held significantly more enthusiasm.

"I brought a few things for the sundaes." He reached into the bag and pulled out a bunch of bright yellow bananas. "Ta-da!"

"May I have a banana split, Auntie Grace?" Lizzie begged with wide eyes.

"Of course you can." Grace winked at Nickels, and he felt about ten feet tall. "The more fruit, the better."

"I'm not finished yet." He plunged his arm back in the sack and came out with a jar of maraschino cherries.

"And I can have a cherry on top!" Jake chimed in.

"One more thing. . ." Nickels made a show of groping around, heightening the anticipation before emerging with—

"Chocolate syrup!" Grace grinned.

"I think we've found your auntie Grace's weakness," Nickels whispered loudly to Jake.

"Huh?" Jake didn't take his eyes from where Grace was dishing out ice cream.

"She likes things as sweet as she is." He grinned when he saw her stop short before finishing her task. *I'll be sure to bring chocolate regularly*, he told himself.

A few minutes later, the kids dug into their fantastic-looking, chocolate-and-cherry-covered banana splits. He stepped next to Grace, watching as she drizzled a thin ribbon of chocolate on top of her ice cream.

"I guess your hand must be tired from all that scooping." He raised his eyebrow. "You're not squeezing the bottle hard enough." He covered her hand with his own and added pressure. Her soft gasp as chocolate poured over the ice cream made him smile. He plunked a cherry on top at a rakish angle. "Now *that's* a sundae."

"No," she said as she dipped her spoon in the river of chocolate. "This"—she raised the bite to her lips and savored a taste—"is decadent. Mmm."

Finding his mouth inexplicably dry, Nickels took a heaping spoonful of ice cream. He barely tasted it but welcomed the cool sensation as it slid down his throat. It had become suddenly warm in the kitchen.

"Can we give some to the chickies?" Jake wanted to know, loudly slurping some of his melted dessert.

"Ice cream isn't meant for birds," Lizzie told him. "Right, Mr. Nichols?"

"Right." He nodded. "But it's perfect for humans on a Saturday afternoon. The chicks will get their treat when I have them back on the ranch."

"Okay." Jake smiled and finished his ice cream.

Such a thoughtful boy. Good with animals. He should have a pet of his own. He sneaked a glance at Grace. *I wonder. . .* But now wasn't the time to ask Grace about adding a furry friend to her burgeoning family. He could wait.

⁓⁓⁓

Grace couldn't wait until next Sunday. The babies in the nursery filled her heart with joy, but she needed the replenishment of the main service. It would be nice when this rotation was over and she'd be back with the adults. She loved the children dearly, but she could use some grown-up communion and conversation.

Grace finished changing the last diaper and gave the baby a quick tickle. When his mama came for him, she'd spray the place down with disinfectant and pick up Lizzie and Jake. She snuggled Matt for a moment, reluctant to put him down. He was already sitting up at six months, but he seemed so small. Besides, he was sweet and cuddly soft.

"It won't be long before you're crawling around, will it, baby?" She rubbed his back.

"About three months, at least—that's what the doctors say is typical." A tiny woman with glossy auburn hair and sparkling green eyes came through the child-locked gate and reached for the baby.

"Bye-bye, Matt," Grace whispered as she transferred him to his mother's arms. "I'll need your number."

"Here you go." The young woman looked at her name tag. "Grace." She waited a moment while Grace signed Matt out.

"All set." Grace handed her the baby's diaper bag.

"Your last name wouldn't happen to be Willard, would it?"

"Yes," Grace admitted hesitantly.

"I'm so glad to meet you! I'm Sondra Ward." Sondra grasped Grace's hand and shook it. "Nickels has told me so much about you!"

Sondra. . . She doesn't look pregnant. Grace remembered Eric's mentioning that Sondra was his boss's wife. Dylan Ward ran the Curly Q Ranch, but she didn't know Sondra.

"Not much to tell," Grace said. "I'm glad to meet you, too."

"Not much to tell?" Sondra rolled her eyes. "I heard about Jim and Lisa." Her tone lowered. "I'm so sorry about that. I hear they were good people. It's so good of you to take their children...Lizzie and Jake, is it?"

Grace nodded. *Eric really has told her a lot, and I don't know all that much about him.*

"Well, we're both new to raising children! What are your plans this afternoon?"

"I'll need to fix lunch for the kids," Grace began.

"No, you don't. Why don't you bring 'em on over to the Curly Q? I know Nickels'll be glad to see you."

Did she just wink at me? Surely she didn't just wink at me, Grace argued with herself.

"He's a fine man—it does him a world of good to focus on something other than cattle. Nickels stays pretty close to home." Sondra shifted Matt to her other hip. "That's why I had to find out what he was up to on Saturday afternoons."

No doubt about it. She definitely winked. This kind woman has the wrong idea entirely.

"I'd hate to impose," Grace said. *Do I want to spend two days in a row with this man, getting to know his friends and coworkers? Didn't we just discuss this, Lord?*

"Not at all. We have all the ranch hands, so there'll be plenty of food—baking is one of my passions. And, to tell the truth," Sondra said earnestly, "I could use some female company and conversation."

Hearing Sondra echo the same thought she'd had minutes ago clinched it. Grace gave in. *I'm slightly wary of where this is going, Lord, but I know when I'm beat.*

"We'll be there."

"Great!" Sondra gave her directions and a cheery wave before leaving.

Lord, I have every confidence that You know exactly what You're doing and where this is going. I just wish You'd let me in on the plan a bit more. As it was, she felt as if she were playing a precarious game of hopscotch, second-guessing every move she made as she jumped from one stage to the next. Creating a stable life for Lizzie and Jake had thrown her off balance. *I'll follow Your lead, Lord—help me have the faith to do it right!*

"Hey, you two!" Grace called to Lizzie and Jake as they played on the swings in the churchyard.

"Coming!" Lizzie pumped her legs one last time, soaring high into the air.

Grace's heart stopped as she watched the little girl let go of the chains and leap from her lofty perch, flailing her arms as she rushed to the ground. She ran to Lizzie when she hit the earth.

"Lizzie! Are you all right?" Grace ignored the wood chips snagging her pantyhose as she checked for broken ankles.

"I'm fine, Auntie Grace!" Lizzie giggled and stood up.

"That's dangerous!" Grace had difficulty catching her breath. "You could've been hurt!"

"Naw—it just looks cool. The trick is to jump off when you're close to the ground." Lizzie patted her on the back. "Everybody does it."

"I don't want *you* doing it!" Grace suddenly realized she had no idea how to get health coverage for Jake and Lizzie. Could they be covered under her insurance since she held custody? She would have to check on that first thing Monday morning.

"It's okay, Auntie Grace." Jake stroked her hair as if it were a puppy's fur, obviously trying to calm her down. "We're good."

"Yes." She took a deep breath and forced a smile. "You're both very good, but you can't scare Auntie Grace by doing things that could get you hurt."

"I'll do better," Lizzie promised. "Please don't be mad, Auntie Grace." The little girl was apparently afraid of upsetting her.

"I'm not mad. I just got upset because I love you so much." Grace hugged them both. "Now what do you say we go and get some lunch?"

"Yeah!" Jake patted his stomach. "Mr. Tummy is hungry."

"Let's go then." Grace held their hands and led them to the car, pushing away her doubts. "Miss Sondra's invited us to lunch on her ranch!"

"You invited who, where?" Nickels growled at the part owner of the Curly Q.

"Quit scowling, Nickels." Sondra patted him on the arm. "You look so much more handsome when you smile, and we both want you to look your best this afternoon."

"Why?" he managed to ask.

"Because I know you're friends with them, and it's the neighborly thing to do," Sondra explained.

"Don't you think you should have asked me first?" Nickels couldn't explain why he was so put out, but having Grace and the kids on the ranch while Sondra dragged them into every part of his life—it was too soon. *I was taking things slow!*

"Now why would I do a thing like that?" Sondra blinked up at him.

He sighed. "Because I might have preferred you not ask them."

"And that's just why I didn't ask." Sondra nodded pertly. "Sometimes men make cotton-headed decisions where pretty women are concerned." She shot him an appraising glance. "You never mentioned she was so pretty, Nickels."

"I—" Nickels bit his tongue before saying he hadn't noticed. *Of course I noticed. What red-blooded man wouldn't?* He squared his shoulders. "I don't want you doing something like this again."

"I think you're forgetting it's my ranch. I'll invite whomever I like into my home for a hospitable lunch." Steel underlined her words.

"I wasn't trying to get you riled, Sondra." Nickels knew she had a point.

Her voice softened. "And neither was I. Did you ever think that maybe I would enjoy having another woman around occasionally? Grace and I are both neighbors and have young ones. It's only right we share friendship and understanding."

"I wouldn't want to deny either of you something that important," he apologized. *I hadn't even thought about how selfish I was being, wanting to keep Grace and the kids to myself.*

"I knew you'd see things my way." Sondra flashed him a smile before heading toward Dylan.

I'm not sure, but I think she just got the better of me. He shook his head ruefully and caught sight of Grace leading the kids to the car. *Then again maybe I'll have cause to thank her before the day is done.*

Chapter 8

Hey, there." Nickels smiled and edged nearer the barbecue—and Grace.

"Hey, yourself." Grace shaded her eyes to look up at him. "I like your hat."

"Thank you kindly." He drew out the words in a slow drawl.

"Now you just need a six-shooter, and you'll be ready for a duel at high noon."

"You got someone who needs to learn a lesson?" He crossed his arms, playing along.

"Not really." She laughed. "Though everyone has some area that needs improvement."

"I'm not so sure about that." He reached around her for a paper napkin.

"Oh?" Her eyes held a question before she caught his meaningful gaze, and a becoming flush lit her features.

"I happen to have a very high opinion of myself," he said as she took a sip of lemonade, his grin stretching when she all but spit out her drink.

He handed her his napkin and stepped closer to reach for another one. "You ought to be more careful, Grace."

"That"—she dabbed at the corner of her mouth—"was all your fault, Eric Nichols."

"I wasn't talking about the way you drink your lemonade," he said. "But a reaction like that is liable to crush a man."

"Somehow I think you'll survive." With that, she wandered over to where Sondra sat with a heaping plate of food in her hands.

He waited and then took the seat on her other side.

"This looks wonderful, Sondra." Grace gestured toward where Jake and Lizzie were making a fine mess of their ribs.

"Dylan barbecues like nobody's business," Sondra said.

"I happen to know Grace thinks highly of your lemonade, Sondra." Nickels tossed her a wicked glance. "She's so eager to get to it that she practically breathed it in!" He ducked as a wadded-up napkin sailed his way.

"Now, Grace, I don't know how you do things at your house," Sondra teased, "but at the Curly Q, littering carries a severe penalty."

"I see I'll have to pay for my crimes." Grace hung her head in mock shame. "How much time will I have to serve?"

"This afternoon certainly won't cover it." Sondra turned to Nickels. "What do you think?"

"She'll have to come back next week." Nickels waggled his brows.

"Motion carried!" Sondra rapped on the picnic table with a barbecue fork. They all laughed before she became serious again. "Honestly, Grace—I love having another woman around. I'm just sure we're kindred spirits. Our hair color is even the same! We want you to know that you, Lizzie, and Jake are welcome anytime."

"I appreciate that, Sondra." Grace's carefree smile made the day complete.

I should never have doubted Sondra. She's reaching out in a good way. Everyone likes having Grace and the kids around. . . . I hope this will be the first of many happy afternoons.

Nevertheless he still had a score to settle. He reached behind his bench and groped around. *Now where's that napkin?*

<hr />

"I'm glad we stopped by home so the kids could change out of their church clothes," Grace observed after a lunch filled with as much good-natured ribbing as there were spareribs. "Lizzie's probably glad she's in her jeans instead of that dress."

"Looks as if the hands are having as good a time as the kids." Sondra pointed to where Eric and Hank, each with a child on his back, were racing toward the chicken coop. "Looks like Hank's got the lead."

"I wouldn't count Eric out just yet."

"Eric?" Sondra looked at her in surprise.

"That's what he told me to call him," Grace said. "Why?"

"I only know that's his name since I take care of the accounting for the Curly Q." Sondra squinted at him in the distance. "He's always just gone by Nickels, even though he spells it like the coins and not the same as his last name."

"It's not that unusual for a man to go by a nickname," Grace said. *But if he has everyone call him Nickels, why did he ask me to use Eric?*

"That's what I always thought." Sondra shot her a sideways glance. "I wonder why he changed his mind?"

Grace shrugged, grateful Sondra didn't delve into the matter further. No sense in overanalyzing something. *He probably goes by Nickels at the ranch, and that's all there is to it.*

"Auntie Grace, we won! We won!" Lizzie came running to the porch.

"That's great, sweetie!" She gave Jake an encouraging smile. "It was a close race."

"We'll get 'em next time, slugger." Eric clapped his hand on the boy's shoulder.

"That'll teach you to eat the last cookie!" Lizzie crowed.

"Now, Lizzie. Don't brag—it's not good sportsmanship."

"Sorry, Jake." Lizzie didn't look sorry for long, as she grabbed Grace's hand. "Come play with us! We're gonna try Blind Man's Bluff!"

Grace laughed. "I don't think so."

"I do." Eric's rumble instantly caught her attention.

"Oh?" She looked at him with wide-open eyes.

"If Auntie Grace doesn't play, nobody does." He put his hand on his hat brim. "Those're the rules, ma'am."

"He's got you there, Grace." Sondra gave her chair a nudge. "You'd better get going. You know these cowboys. . .they'll lasso you into anything!" She shared a smile with her husband, Dylan.

Grace couldn't help but grin at their good-natured relationship—a grin that got her into trouble.

"That means yes!" Jake proclaimed. "Mr. Nichols, how do we play?"

"First we take a blindfold." He whipped a bandanna out of his pocket and folded it lengthwise. "Like so. Then we put it on the 'blind man.'" He leaned over and demonstrated on Grace.

Deprived of her sight, Grace focused on her other senses. The scent of the man—leather, sawdust, and the earthy smell of cinnamon—enveloped her as he placed the folded cloth over her eyes. His roughened fingertips along her temples made her skin prickle as he brushed a few stray hairs away from the bandanna. She took a breath when he folded her hand in his warm grasp and led her off the porch.

"Now." His deep voice filled her ears as he finished instructing the children. "You stay in this clear area close by, but don't let her catch you." He spun her around, further disorienting her.

When he let go, the warm day took on a sudden chill. Reaching forward, her palms facing out, Grace took slow, questioning steps at first. As she heard the whisper of moving fabric, the patter of tiny feet, and the hushed giggles of the children trying not to give themselves away, she moved with more confidence. She chased after a loud breath, turning up nothing but air for her desperate lunge.

"I'll get you yet!" she threatened, giving a breathless chuckle of her own. *It would help if they were taller,* she thought and then remembered that a few of the ranch hands—including Eric—were playing, too. The heavy footfalls of their boots bore a marked contrast to Jake and Lizzie's lighter steps. *They'd make bigger targets, but I'm not aiming to catch a man—literally or figuratively.*

Just as she finished that thought, her arms closed around a big one.

ⁿ⁓⁓⁓

Nickels grinned to see Grace lost in the fun of the game. Her hair danced in the wind, framing cheeks rosy from exertion. Her disappointment when she caught nothing but air again and again swiftly gave way to laughter.

It'd be so easy to step behind her, a voice whispered inside him. *If you let her catch you, a moment in her arms will be more than reward enough.* But with Sondra watching, Nickels wasn't about to make any sudden moves.

But Danny didn't share his reservations. Nickels came to a dead stop and glowered as the muscular ranch hand, always ready to help out, edged closer to Grace. She had stooped over to try to grab Jake or Lizzie, but her arms closed around Danny's waist before she straightened.

Stable-mucking duty for the next week, Nickels told himself as he watched his so-called friend gently lift the blindfold from Grace's eyes. She blinked at the bright sunlight, smiling up at her catch. *No. Two weeks.*

"You caught me fair and square, miss." Grace's hands were no longer around his waist, but Danny hovered as close as possible.

"Bad luck for you." Grace shrugged, obviously comfortable with the man.

"I'll have to disagree with that." Danny stepped even closer and pulled a piece of nonexistent fluff from her hair.

And roadkill detail for a month. Nickels wouldn't watch another minute. He headed for the porch to get some lemonade. *I knew it was a bad idea for her to come to the ranch.*

"Now, now." Sondra wasn't put off by his baleful look. "You're a worse sport than Lizzie, huffing off like that!"

"I didn't huff," Nickels protested.

"You sure did," Dylan added, his thumbs hooked into his belt loops. "I'm kinda disappointed in you, Nickels."

"What for?" He glared into his cup.

"A strapping fellow like you should know better." Sondra grinned mischievously.

"What exactly"—he crumpled the now-empty paper cup in his fist—"should I know?"

"If you want to catch her—," Sondra began.

"You have to play the game," Dylan finished.

Chapter 9

I'm not going to argue with you, Uncle Carl." Grace kept her tone firm but not angry. She'd had a fine day at the Curly Q and was determined to resolve her issues with her uncle to top it off. "You hung up on me the night I brought Lizzie and Jake home and told you I had custody. You've had time to get used to the idea—weeks, in fact—and the time you waste being angry with me is time you could be spending with the children."

"You stole them from me." Uncle Carl's voice came through so loud Grace moved the receiver farther from her ear. "I asked for your help, and you took the kids for yourself!"

Lord, help me keep my patience. Her uncle's anger guided his choices. He hadn't visited the children at the group home, and he'd given her the silent treatment. She needed to remember how much he'd lost. His wife had passed on less than two years ago. His only son and daughter-in-law just died in a tornado. He had taken the children; she knew he'd done his best, but they were snatched away from him, too. Then he asked her for help.

"I did what I had to, to bring them home." Grace shot an anxious look upstairs where Lizzie and Jake were cleaning their rooms. She didn't want them to hear this conversation.

"Lasso is not home. Their home is in Buffalo Walk with me." The older man's voice broke on this last.

"Uncle Carl, I agree with you on some of that." Grace took a deep breath.

"You do?" Her words wiped the fight from his voice.

"Jake and Lizzie need all the family love and support they can get. That's why it's so important they see you regularly."

"But Lasso is a two-hour drive from Buffalo Walk," Uncle Carl complained. "That's a long way."

"You're right." Grace plunged ahead. "That's why I want you to think about moving in with us."

"What?" From his response, she couldn't tell if he was pleased or outraged by the invitation.

"I've been thinking about this a lot. Truth of the matter is, two small children are a handful for any one person," Grace admitted. "We could raise them together. I know Jake needs a man in his life."

"That he does." Uncle Carl spoke more calmly now. "Are there stairs at your place? They're hard on m' knees, you know."

"Yes, there are. I have a downstairs bedroom and a half bath. Right now I use it as my office, but it would be simple enough to move my desk into the den."

"And I can bring Queenie, of course?"

"Queenie?" *Oh, no.*

"She's my cat," Uncle Carl said. "And Lizzie and Jake are very fond of her."

Grace pinched the bridge of her nose. "I forgot you had a cat."

"She's a friendly thing," he began.

"I'm sure she is, Uncle Carl. Thing is, I'm very allergic to cats. And she's not an outdoor kitty, is she?"

"Absolutely not." He sounded affronted. "Well, that's a pickle. Queenie and I are a package deal, you see. Can't you just. . .I don't know. . .ask a doctor about it?"

"I have." Grace sighed. "Nothing helps. My eyelids swell shut, and I break out in hives."

"Then this isn't going to work." His disappointment came through loud and clear.

"Maybe we can meet in the middle." Grace's mind whirled as she tried to find a solution. "I'm sure we can find an apartment in Lawton, and then you'll be a lot closer."

"Moving is going to be a hassle," the older man hedged.

"I can help. And I have some friends who'll be glad to lend a hand." *Lord, thank You for today. I know Sondra meant it when she said to let her know of anything she could help with. Moving will be a snap with a ranch hand or two! I'll find some way to repay her. I'll babysit so she can have a romantic evening with Dylan.*

"I'll still be an hour away," Carl said. "That's not exactly spittin' distance." A long pause followed. "I don't have the car anymore."

"The bus goes from Lawton to Lasso." *It makes sense he's not allowed to drive; it's the reason he didn't visit the children at the group home.* Inspiration struck. "Besides, we can still move my desk to the den and put a bed in the spare room. That way you can spend the night and catch the bus again the next day. If need be, I can pick you up."

"That sounds like a good arrangement." He sounded pleased. "And I do want to be involved with the children. Jake and Lizzie. . .well, they're all I have left. And I thought I'd lost 'em." His voice grew gruff. "There aren't many times in a man's life when he gets a second chance."

"What do you say we meet in Lawton on Saturday for lunch with the kids and then find you an apartment? You'll stay the night and come to church with us the next morning."

"I wouldn't miss it for the world."

∞∞∞

"Scraper," Dylan stated in the tone of a surgeon requesting a scalpel.

"Here." Nickels passed it to his boss, who was cleaning the barbecue with near-clinical precision. He wandered off, stuffing napkins and paper plates into a garbage sack. They tidied up in silence for a while.

"I like her," Dylan said, breaking the calm.

"Don't let Sondra hear you talk like that." Nickels wanted to keep the conversation light.

"Sondra likes her, too." Dylan eyed him. "She's welcome anytime."

"Good thing. Sondra and I roped her into coming back next Sunday." Nickels sat down, stretching his legs out in front of him.

"So. . .what's the situation there?" Dylan took a chair next to him. "And I don't mean about her taking in the children."

"Are you sure?" Nickels adjusted his hat. "That one's easier to explain."

"You've been spending a lot of time over there lately. I haven't said anything since you never ask for time off, but I've noticed you've been scarce most Saturdays."

"Sondra has me taking the chicks by the group home," Nickels pointed out. "That's how I met Jake and Lizzie. Little tykes love them, and I promised to bring them back the next Saturday."

"But Jake and Lizzie weren't there anymore." Dylan filled in the blanks. "Or so Sondra told me."

"Yes, and a man's word is his bond. So I asked Miss Chesterton to call Grace and find out if I could swing by." He shifted a bit. "It's become a regular occurrence."

"I see." Dylan paused for a few minutes. "Judging by the way you glowered at Danny this afternoon, I'd say that's not the only thing occurring."

"You might have a point there."

"I've never seen you take such an interest in a woman, and it's only fair to warn you that Sondra's pretty keen on the idea."

"So I gathered." The two men shared a look that plainly said, "Women!" and laughed companionably.

"I've got a soft spot for her," Nickels ventured. "Thing is, it's not as simple as 'boy meets girl.'"

"First off, 'boy meets girl' is never simple." Dylan gave him a knowing look. "Second, I'd already figured that much out. . .*Eric.*"

Nickels glared at him.

"All right, all right!" Dylan held up his hands in mock surrender. "That glower of yours could scare the stripe off a skunk."

"Good." *It oughta work on Danny.*

"I'd hate to see you get moody, Nickels."

"All's fair in love and war," Nickels quipped.

"And which is this?"

"I'll have to get back to you on that." Nickels stood up and dusted his hands on his jeans. "I'm heading for the bunkhouse."

And a little peace and quiet. He gazed up at the stars. He hadn't sorted things out yet. No matter how good Dylan's intentions were, Nickels didn't like his boss putting him on the spot. Talking about Grace and the kids and how he figured into their lives was not something he was ready to discuss. He pushed open the door and headed for his bunk.

"Best afternoon I've spent in a while." Danny hung up his hat when he came in a few minutes later, stomping his feet to get the dirt off his boots.

Best one you're going to have for a longer while. Nickels slid him a sideways glance.

"That Grace Willard is a purty li'l thang," Hank agreed. "It's nice to have women on the ranch."

"Why is it we're only just meetin' her anyway?" Danny directed the question to Nickels.

"She just bought her house in Lasso." Nickels bent over to take off his boots. "Used to live in Lawton where she works."

"What's the deal with those kids—her niece and nephew?" Danny wasn't letting up.

"Parents died in the last tornado—she's taken 'em in as her own." He gave them the barest information he could.

"Should've known there'd be a catch." Hank rolled his eyes, and Nickels resisted the urge to jump from his bunk and let him have it.

"Lizzie and Jake are special—great kids."

"Grace is pretty special, too, taking 'em in like that." Danny rubbed the back of his neck. "I didn't see a ring on her finger."

"Watch yourself, Danny-boy," Nickels warned. "Grace is going through enough right now."

"Oh-ho!" Hank slapped his knee. "I think Nickels is staking his claim, Danny."

"No need to get hot under the collar, Nickels." Danny grinned. "Besides, it's up to the lady who she wants to spend time with when she's at the Curly Q."

"This is not a competition," he growled back. "She's not on the market, you hear me? Her close kin just died, and she's taken in two children all alone."

"She doesn't necessarily have to raise those kids alone," Danny pointed out. "Anyway I'm just talking about enjoying her company."

"Don't push this, Danny." Nickels crossed his arms menacingly.

"You may have seniority over me on the range, Nickels"—Danny set his jaw—"but you've got no authority on this matter."

"You're right, but remember this: A real man doesn't dally with a woman's affections, and he certainly doesn't drag two defenseless kids into it." Nickels stood up. "If you raise any expectations, you have to follow through. Lizzie and Jake have lost enough. Don't get involved unless you're willing to commit to all three."

"I don't know if I'm up for that." Danny gave him a measuring look. "Are you?"

Chapter 10

Yes, I am." Jake huddled under his race-car comforter, the top of his tousled brown hair sticking out.

"Oh no, you're not." Grace pulled the blanket off with one swift yank.

"Am so!" Jake's normally big, bright eyes narrowed to little more than slits as he glowered fiercely.

"Jake." Grace bit back a grin at the contrast between his glare and his wildly ridiculous hair. "I repeat—you are not staying here today. It's the first day of school!"

"What's wrong?" Lizzie appeared in her nightgown, rubbing her eyes.

Grace had decided to wake up Jake first, thinking Lizzie would follow suit when she saw her brother getting ready for school.

"I'm staying right here today." Jake stuck out his little chin defiantly.

"What?" Lizzie's sleepy eyes opened wide.

"Good morning, Lizzie. Now you can help me out." Grace smiled at her ally. "Tell your brother he can't stay here all alone."

"Auntie Grace is right. You can't stay here alone." Lizzie settled onto the bed beside Jake and wrapped her arms around him in a motherly fashion. Relief and pride swelled in Grace's chest at the sweet sight. "So I'll stay with you." She smiled innocently at her aunt.

Traitor! Grace barely refrained from burying her face in her hands. She'd known the first day of school would be a formidable challenge. New campus, new teachers, new schedules, and new faces. But she'd assumed the difficulties would start once she got them to Lawton Elementary.

"That won't work either." She stood up, taking advantage of her greater height. "I want both of you out of that bed this minute." *I'm in charge here,* she silently tacked on.

"No." Both children stared up at her—still on the bed.

I can't believe I'm being held hostage by two children! Grace cinched the belt of her bathrobe a bit tighter and squared her shoulders. She could show no weakness if she was going to break through their united front.

"This is not up for negotiation. You both have to go to school." She warned them of the impending consequences of their behavior. "If you disobey me again, you won't go to the ranch with me after church."

"You'd leave us behind?" Lizzie's hurt whisper almost broke through Grace's reserves.

"Mary would watch you while I went," she informed them. *It won't do to let them think I'd abandon them somewhere.*

"But. . ." Jake sniffled and clung to his sister. "We, we just want to stay h–h—" He took a hiccuplike breath and tried again. "We want to stay—"

Here. I know you want to stay here, but you can't. Grace formed her response before he finished.

"Home." A tear slid down his soft cheek, and that one drop dashed Grace's stern front.

Home. He called this home. *They aren't misbehaving because they're willful. Punishing them is the wrong approach.* Grace sat down on the bed next to them. *I was listening with my head, not my heart. They're simply children afraid of yet another change.*

"Home will still be here when you get back." Grace gave them each a hug.

"How do you know?" Lizzie's voice sounded tiny and far away, a dim echo of the loss she'd suffered.

What do I tell them, Lord? They know firsthand that bad things happen to good people. Lizzie and Jake were part of a happy family one morning, went off to school, and didn't have a home or family to go back to. One tornado whirled away the only life they'd ever known, and their world hasn't stopped spinning yet.

"Truth of the matter is, I don't." Grace refused to deceive them, though her gut wrenched as they gasped and huddled closer. "But here's what I do know. First of all, we have each other, and that's not going to change. Second, even if something happens to the house, I don't work at home. I'll be in Lawton with you. That's part of why it's so important you go to school—I'll be nearby." She gave them a reassuring squeeze. "But first, we all need to get ready!"

Miraculously her words had calmed the children. The next half hour was filled with cereal, outfits, missing shoes. Finally they settled into the car.

"Contact!" Grace clicked her seat belt into the holder.

"Contact!" Lizzie's clicked back, and she reached over to help Jake.

"Contact!"

"Then we're ready for a great new day at school?" Grace turned and smiled at the kids. A long pause stretched while she waited for them to smile back.

"What if"—Lizzie was wringing her hands—"what if we don't feel ready at all?"

"You pray." Grace knew the answer to that one. She stretched her arms so they held hands, forming a circle. "When you think you can't do something on your own, when you need to remember God is always with you, helping you be strong, you pray. Go ahead."

"Dear God," Lizzie began, "I don't want to go to a new school, but Auntie

Grace says it's important. Jake will be there with me since he's old enough now. Please keep us safe—and Auntie Grace, too." Her voice grew stronger. "And bless Mommy and Daddy in heaven. Amen."

"Amen." Grace continued holding their hands for another moment. "That was beautiful, Lizzie."

"Okay." The little girl sat up straight. "I think I'm ready now."

The smell of fried chicken filled the cab of Nickels's truck as he drove. Thursday nights were his time to visit his grandpa. At seventy-two, Aaron Nichols had a spring in his step untouched by his many years. Nickels watched him walk to the driveway.

"Lookin' good, Gramps." Nickels swung his door open and grabbed the bucket of chicken.

"Smellin' good, Eric." Gramps sniffed appreciatively.

"I thought so." Nickels grinned. "What do you say we sit on the porch and eat like kings?" They climbed the three short steps to the porch and settled into a pair of rocking chairs, their smooth surfaces attesting to many fine nights such as this.

"I'd say pass the bucket." Gramps accepted the drumstick—his favorite piece—and they ate in contented silence for a while.

"Stars are out in force," Nickels noted. "Seem even brighter than usual."

"Oh?" Gramps lifted his brow.

"What?"

"Stars don't often change their outlook, son." The older man observed his grandson intently. "But we do. What's got you seein' things in a whole new light?"

"Good company and a full belly make the world a brighter place." Nickels hoped to distract his grandpa with flattery. No sense delving into things better left alone.

"So who've you been keepin' company with?" Gramps saw right through him.

"Lasso's a small town, Gramps." Nickels knew he was being evasive, but Gramps had been on him for years about how it was—

"High time you found yourself the wife God planned for you. Man wasn't meant to walk this earth alone." He cast a glance toward the copse of trees to the east. "My Rosie Lou made my days brighter and my faith sweeter, and she fills my future with the anticipation of bein' at her side again."

"She was an incredible woman." Nickels put his hands behind his head. "You were blessed to find her."

"Funny thing about finding things, Eric." Gramps rocked forward, planting his feet on the porch and fixing his grandson with a steady stare. "It's hard to keep your eyes open when your heart's closed."

Nickels sucked in a slow breath. "My heart's not closed, Gramps." Things'd be easier if it were.

"Too closed for my comfort." Gramps clapped his hands on his knees. "Every woman out there isn't like Cassandra."

"I know." Nickels rolled his shoulders to ease the tension her very name caused inside him. How could she? Over five years had passed, and he still didn't understand.

Lord, why? Are the lives of others worth so little that she could destroy mine without a single regret for possibilities denied?

"I know the subject touches a nerve for you, but I'm gonna have to ask. After half a decade, you've yet to move on. Does she still carry part of you?"

"No." Nickels swallowed his bitterness. "The memories remain, though."

"That's the nature of memories, m'boy. They remain. The question is, do they fester?"

"Time heals all wounds." Nickels felt his jaw clench.

"Ah, but there's the problem. You're putting your faith in the wrong place."

"I'm a believer now," Nickels reminded his grandfather.

"And by now, you should've figured out the truth. Time doesn't heal an aching heart, Eric. Only one thing can manage that miracle."

"And what is it?" *I've prayed. Worked hard. Lived right. And I've waited for—*

"Love. Love is the heart's healer, Eric. And all pure and beautiful things come from God Himself."

"I love," he said. *What kind of monster does my own grandpa think I am?* "I love God. I also care for you. . .and Dylan and Sondra. . ." *and Grace, Lizzie, and Jake.*

"I know that, Eric. Still, love goes both ways. You love, yes—but do you let yourself be loved?"

"I—" Nickels bit back his hasty response and mulled it over. He took his time while his grandpa rocked quietly, patiently. "I never thought about the difference." When the admission came, it seemed as though he'd found something he hadn't realized he'd lost.

"I guess it's high time you got to thinkin' on it then." Gramps gave him an approving nod. "Between now and then, I'll keep on prayin'."

"Thanks." His voice sounded gruff to his own ears, and he wondered if Gramps heard the wealth of appreciation behind that simple word.

"Always." Gramps's own voice echoed the powerful emotion, and Nickels smiled at him before looking back at the sky.

"Stars seem brighter than ever."

Chapter 11

"You two wash up while I help Mr. Nichols take his chicks back to the truck." Grace made sure the kids were headed toward the restroom before catching up with him outside.

"Long time, no see." Humor tinged his words when she met him in the driveway.

"I know." Grace grinned at him. "But I wanted to ask you something."

"Shoot." He leaned against the hood, his long legs crossed.

"You know the kids and I are meeting their grandfather for lunch today and looking over apartments so he'll be close by." She waited for his nod before she plunged ahead. "He'll be spending the night with us and coming to church tomorrow morning...and it's all right either way, but—"

"Sondra and Dylan would welcome him over for lunch, too." He gently touched her arm. "So would I."

Warmth raced up her arm. "Thanks. We'll look forward to it."

"As do I." He plunked his hat on his head and swung the truck door open. "You might want to try Briarwood—I was at Chris's the other day for an oil change, and he mentioned someone's movin' out."

"We will." Grace waved as he backed out of the drive. That tip made three possibilities to check out this afternoon.

Lord, let one of them be right for Uncle Carl. Not only is it important for the kids to have him near, but I think it'll do him a world of good.

"Ready?" She grabbed Windbreaker jackets for herself and the kids, just in case it got chilly later. There was no telling when they'd find the right place.

"Uh-huh!" Lizzie and Jake rushed out the door to the car.

Grace knew they were eager to see their grandpa. They'd had a talk the night before about how much he wanted to be a part of their lives, even if they couldn't live with him. She'd explained that he loved them so much he was leaving his home to be closer. After leaving three homes in as many months, before finally settling in with their auntie Grace, Jake and Lizzie set great store in their grandpa's determination to move.

"Do you have your pictures?" Grace checked before turning on the engine.

"Yeah!" Lizzie handed them to her.

"These are wonderful—I know Grampa will love them." Grace popped in a children's CD, and they passed the hour-long drive singing along to favorite songs.

"Jesus loves me; this I know. . . ." They were all warbling enthusiastically, if off-key, when Grace pulled up to Danielle's Diner.

"Grampa!" Jake spotted him first, dashing over and all but tackling him at the knees.

"Easy there, buddy!" Uncle Carl had to take a step back to steady himself, but Grace could tell how pleased he was at Jake's welcome.

"We love you, Grampa." Lizzie's hug, though more sedate, matched Jake's in warmth.

"I love you, too, Lizzie-girl." He planted a kiss atop her brown hair. "What do you say we get a bite to eat?"

Before their hamburgers and sandwiches arrived at the table, Lizzie and Jake presented him with their pictures.

"It's you and me and Jake and Auntie Grace." Lizzie pointed to the figures she'd drawn. "And here in the clouds are Mommy and Daddy, smiling at us from heaven."

"I bet they're smiling right now." Uncle Carl beamed at his granddaughter.

Now this is the way it should be. Grace sat quietly, content to watch the reunion.

"It's Queenie!" Uncle Carl chortled at the lopsided orange ball—complete with tail—in the picture Jake proudly passed down the table.

"Yep." The little boy swung his feet as he sat in the booster seat, connecting with Grace's shin. She winced but let the accident go without comment.

"She misses you two." Uncle Carl grabbed a napkin and blew his nose. "So have I."

"That's why you're moving!" Lizzie broke in excitedly. "These pictures are for your new house!"

"I'll hang them up before I do anything else," Uncle Carl promised. "Just as soon as we find the place."

Finding the place proved to be more difficult than Grace anticipated as they walked into the first apartment.

"It's already furnished." The landlady unlocked the door. "Let me know when you're finished looking." With that, she stomped up the stairs and banged on another door.

"It's. . ." Words failed her. *Awful* was the closest she could manage.

"Cozy." Carl was obviously determined to make this work.

"Stinky." Jake wrinkled his nose. He had a point; the place smelled like an ashtray.

A quick tour revealed a brown kitchenette without a dishwasher, a dingy bathroom with a leaky shower, and a bedroom with a musty bed pressed along one wall, and nothing else in sight.

"We'll have a look at the other places before we make any decisions," Grace informed the owner after she rattled off a grossly inflated rent rate. "We'll let you know."

"You do that." The woman smirked. "Aren't too many places available. You'll be back before long."

"We'll see." Grace ushered everyone back to the car.

"I didn't like it," Lizzie announced with a child's bluntness.

"Me neither," Jake seconded.

"I'll make it work if I have to," Carl maintained.

The second choice was an upstairs apartment with no elevator.

"I'll make. . .it work. . .if. . .I have. . .to." Carl wheezed as he made his way up the stairs.

I don't think so. Grace kept the thought to herself. "Let's try Briarwood."

The manager of the grounds led them to a single-story building, made to look much like a cottage.

"There are two units in this building. This one's just become available." He looked a bit surprised. "Haven't even listed it yet. Keep in mind it'll be cleaned before the new resident moves in."

Cream walls brightened the place, making the most of the light let in by well-placed windows. The tan carpet seemed practically new, and the wood-toned kitchen boasted an oven, a dishwasher, and a microwave. Vertical blinds were already installed in every room.

"Thank You, Lord!" Grace said aloud.

"I like it." Lizzie twirled around in the middle of the living room.

"Me, too." Jake grabbed her hands, and they danced around in a wide circle.

"Are cats okay?" Uncle Carl seemed suspicious of the perfect setup.

"No more than two per unit." The manager shoved his hands in his pockets.

"That's fine. I've only got the one." Uncle Carl opened and shut the blinds on the nearest window before looking at Grace. "I can make this work." His comment lacked the "if I have to" brought forth by the other places.

"There's a jungle gym right this way." The manager indicated the play area. "That's the window to my office so you can watch them."

Grace left Jake and Lizzie happily climbing around while she and Carl went to finish the business at hand.

"Two bedrooms, one bath, kitchen, living room. Gas and utilities are included in the rent. It comes with air-conditioning, and the community pool is over by the laundry room."

Lord, please let it be in the right price range, Grace prayed fervently. When he came to the price, she almost hugged him. But instead she kept her cool.

"I believe we can work out something," she said. And, while Jake and Lizzie played on the tire swing, they did.

"You can move in anytime next week."

"Whooee. I am stuffed." Carl leaned back and patted his well-satisfied stomach. "Those were some mighty fine tacos, Mrs. Ward."

"Call me Sondra." She topped off his iced tea and passed it back. "And I'm glad you liked them."

"You won't be so glad when you have to call a tow truck to get me unwedged from this seat." He chuckled.

"You're welcome to stay as long as you like." Dylan spread his arms wide. "We'll just toss a tarp over you, come rainy season."

Carl guffawed. He clearly enjoyed being the center of attention.

"Come on, Grampa!" Jake tugged one of his hands. "We wanna show you the chicks!"

"You'll have to pull a lot harder than that, Jake!" Carl stayed settled until Lizzie grabbed his other arm, and brother and sister tugged in tandem.

"All right, all right." He stood. "Now where are these birds?"

When Grace followed, Nickels doubled his stride to catch up to her.

"Hold up a second." He cupped her elbow to get her attention.

"Oh, Eric!" Her smile shone in her eyes, beckoning him closer. "I wanted to thank you again for mentioning Briarwood to me. It's just perfect. Honestly, I don't know what we would have done."

"Happy to help." He didn't take his hand from her arm, liking the feel of her soft skin against his palm. "There's something I've been thinking about for a while, and I wanted to mention it."

"What is it?" She leaned slightly closer, making his breath hitch.

"I've been coming over with the chicks for a month now," he began.

"And Jake and Lizzie just love it." She looked down for a moment before meeting his gaze again. "I enjoy Saturday mornings, too."

"They're the high point of my week." He grinned back at her. "But I was thinking maybe there was something we could do for Jake and Lizzie. They love holding the chicks and taking care of them. What if they could keep that feeling all week long?"

"Do you mean—" Grace's brows came together as she thought it over. "You want them to raise one? Eric, I'm sorry, but I don't want a full-grown chicken running around the house. The only reason it works is that the Curly Q raises chicks year-round."

Nickels tilted his head back and laughed. When he composed himself, he agreed, "Chickens don't make the best houseguests."

"So what are you getting at?"

"Every kid needs a pet. I was just thinking more along the lines of friendly and furry." He put the proposition out there.

"I'm allergic to cats," Grace responded quickly, "and I don't have the time

175

to train a puppy. Lizzie and Jake can't care for something that needs so much attention."

"Agreed." Nickels pushed his hat back on his head. "So what if we took 'em to the pet store and found something else? Rabbits are cute but can scratch a kid something awful. How 'bout a hamster?"

"A hamster." He could almost see the wheels turning in Grace's head. "We could probably handle that. It would give them something to focus their attention on."

"And nothing teaches responsibility like caring for another living thing." He spoke straight from the heart. "You know that firsthand."

"Eric, I think you might be on to something."

Chapter 12

T hat'll be Mr. Nichols," Grace told the kids, hastily shutting the lid on the huge cooler she'd bought for this day. She hurried to open the door, finding Eric, Dylan, and Danny on her front porch.

"Thank you all!" She gave them each a hug and then gestured toward the kitchen. "I packed a cooler."

"That makes two." Dylan jerked his thumb toward his truck. "Sondra sent one along, too."

"She's so sweet. It's best to have plenty. And it's kind of her to watch Lizzie and Jake."

"I'll drop 'em off at the ranch and catch up to you in Buffalo Walk. Sondra plans on taking the chicks to Lawton later this morning."

"Thank you, Dylan. And Lizzie and Jake are rarin' to go. Your wife called last night." She stooped for a hug and a kiss good-bye. "I'll see you two later."

" 'Bye, Auntie Grace!"

"Get Grampa good and settled." Lizzie gave her last instruction before hopping into the backseat of Dylan's spacious cab.

"Well, you heard the lady." Eric grabbed Grace's hand and held his truck door open for her. "We'll meet you two there."

They kept the windows rolled down, enjoying the fresh air as they drove to Uncle Carl's old apartment. The local country station kept her fingers drumming on the windowsill as the miles passed.

As they drew close, Grace rolled up the window.

"Thank you so much for talking to Dylan. It'll make the move much easier to have friends helping out."

"Hmph," Eric grunted. "Here I was, hoping you'd asked me for my manly strength. Turns out I was almost the only one you could talk into helping."

Grace laughed at his teasing. "Your muscles are very much appreciated." She reached over and patted his bicep without thinking. She could feel his strength seep through the fabric of his T-shirt—and a warm flush spread into her own face.

"Now"—his voice deepened—"that's more like it."

"Next left." She quickly pointed to their destination. "We're here."

She kept a safe distance for the rest of the day, thankful to have so much to do. The men took the big pieces of furniture out, packing the trucks with overstuffed chairs, the couch, a coffee table, nightstand, and Uncle Carl's bed. While they made the first trip to Lawton, Grace packaged books, kitchen utensils, and knickknacks.

"Lunch break!" Danny said after they returned. He pulled the lid off each cooler and sat down at the dining table.

"What would you like?" Grace asked, digging around in the coolers. "Ham or turkey?" She held up one of each.

"Ham!" Danny exclaimed.

"Turkey," Carl said.

"One of each!" Dylan said as he stepped into the room.

"Eric?" Grace arched her brow after passing the requested lunch items along, offering another pair of sandwiches.

"Whatever you have left and don't want for yourself." He smiled. "I'm easy to please."

Grace handed him the ham, keeping the turkey for herself. Before she took a seat, she passed around some bananas and bottles of sports drinks.

"How're you holding up, Grace?" Uncle Carl peered at her intently.

"Fine." Grace averted her eyes, hoping Uncle Carl didn't ask anything about her and Nickels.

"I did everything I could," he continued anxiously. "Queenie's been at a neighbor's place most of this week. I hired a maid to come in yesterday to clean. Even sprayed some of that fancy fabric refresher you gave me on everything!"

"And it's worked." Grace smiled at him, hoping he didn't notice her red-rimmed eyes. She'd been sneezing a little, but the antihistamines and eyedrops had things pretty well under control. She hated to think what state she'd be in if Queenie were still in residence and the apartment hadn't been cleaned from top to bottom. When she'd unearthed an air purifier, she'd turned it on and hauled the thing around from room to room as a further precaution.

"Good thinking." Eric aimed his comment at Carl, but Grace saw him looking at the purifier humming in the corner. "Is there anything else that triggers your allergies—besides cats?" He helped himself to an apple.

"Not nearly so badly," Grace evaded. *We're talking about things that make my nose run and my eyes turn red. How do I change the topic?*

"My cousin couldn't eat peanuts," Danny added. "And I knew a gal once who couldn't have anything with milk in it."

"Jake can't eat eggs." Uncle Carl peeled the label off his sports drink. "I made egg salad sandwiches the first day the kids were here, and Jake wouldn't eat 'em. I thought he was just upset. . . ." His brown eyes grew misty. "We all were. But Lizzie told me his throat closes if he eats eggs. She's a good girl. Watches out for her brother." He cleared his throat and took a swig of his drink.

"Makes sense to me." Eric broke the heavy silence. "He loves the chicks too much to be able to eat eggs. Just isn't in his nature."

"Never thought of it that way." Uncle Carl nodded. "He sure did have a way with Queenie. Old girl doesn't take much to most folks, but she and Jake got along like peas and carrots."

"Animals can tell," Danny agreed. "If a ranch hand comes on the farm and the horses won't work with him, we know he's got to go."

"Skylar has a nose for character, too." Eric smiled at her. "Trailed Grace around like a lovesick pup all last Sunday."

"She wasn't the only one." Danny's whisper to Dylan carried across the room, and Grace pretended not to hear. She smiled at the table. When she looked up, she saw Carl gazing from her to Eric and back again. *Don't say anything*, she begged. She could feel her cheeks growing hot. She was thankful Uncle Carl popped the last bite of his sandwich in his mouth instead of pursuing Danny's ill-timed remark. When she saw Eric glaring at Danny, she hid her confusion by cleaning off the table.

"Let's get back to work."

⚬⚬⚬

"What do you have ready for us?" Nickels followed Grace from the table, shooting Danny a look that promised reckoning. "We can move the table."

"No, I need the flat surface for sorting. Let me see." She planted her hands on her hips and surveyed the apartment for the next load. "I've emptied those bookshelves." She gestured to the far wall.

"They look as if they're part of the apartment." Nickels strode over to have a look.

"Yeah." She came alongside him and stroked her hand down the side of one of the bookcases. "Jim made these for his dad, and they installed them together." Sadness filled her eyes at the memory. "Lisa and I watched the kids while they worked."

"Well made." Nickels felt the joints. "They'll be heavy but should hold up in the move."

"Thanks." Her soft smile tugged at his heart. "I know it'll mean a lot to Uncle Carl. I measured the new place. They should fit in the living room."

"I'll take care of it," he promised. "What else?"

"I've emptied his dresser in the bedroom. And I cleaned out the fridge, so that'll be ready. If you have more room in this load, you could roll up this rug." She pointed at their feet. "Though I would like to see it vacuumed first."

"Sure. This stuff will fill both trucks." Nickels visually measured what he was dealing with. "How much more are we moving?" The place looked pretty bare to him, save for the dining table and the boxes piled in the entryway.

"The table and the boxes." She ran a hand over her hair, smoothing back her springy curls. "While you're gone, I need to pack up the kitchen dishes and everything in his closets. I'm so glad we decided he'll spend the night at my place, since

179

it'll take all of tomorrow afternoon to get him settled in."

"But we'll have all of his things moved, except for the cat." He reached over and rubbed her shoulders.

"Oh." She tensed then let out a sigh. "You'd better stop that, or I'll be so relaxed I won't be able to finish packing." She pulled away.

"You work on the closets. The guys and I will get cracking on the other things." The next hour flew by as he, Dylan, and Danny loaded up the trucks again. Carl vacuumed the carpet where the furniture had covered it. It wasn't until late afternoon before he had the opportunity to catch Danny alone.

"Watch it," Nickels warned as he and Danny carried the dining table to the bed of his truck.

"I've got it." Danny readjusted his handhold as they lifted in tandem.

"I wasn't talking about the table." Nickels stared him down.

"Hey, I haven't made a move on her. You were right in what you said—I'm only here 'cuz Dylan asked me."

"I know." Nickels stayed tense. "That remark at lunch was out of line, Danny."

"I didn't mean for it to carry." His version of an apology seemed sincere.

"Whether you meant it to be heard or not, you had no business sayin' it." A muscle in his jaw twitched. "I don't appreciate being likened to a lovesick pup—especially when Grace's uncle, who's dealing with enough change as it is, can hear you."

"I see." Danny shot him a knowing look.

"I'm thinking you don't." Nickels slammed the gate of his pickup shut.

"You're riding that horse backward." Danny leaned against the truck. "I've been watching you with her, and I've listened as you spoke your piece."

"Then you won't be so foolish again." He turned to leave.

"I'm many things, Nickels, but a fool ain't one of 'em. See—you said you don't like being called a lovesick pup." Danny's grin spread from ear to ear. "But you didn't say I was wrong."

Wrong again." Grace herded the children toward the car. "You might as well quit guessing."

"Are we going to the zoo?" Jake asked.

"No." Nickels chuckled. "Your aunt is right not to tell you where we're going. It would ruin the surprise."

"We wanna know *now!*" Lizzie all but stomped her foot in her excitement.

"Patience is a virtue," Grace admonished as they stepped into the car.

"Have it if you can." Nickels shot her a grin before continuing the rhyme. "Seldom in a woman, but never in a man." His effort was rewarded when she burst out laughing.

"Is it such a difficult fruit to nourish?" Grace asked.

"Patience isn't a fruit," Lizzie said. Nickels could hear the frown in her voice.

"It's a fruit of the spirit, Lizzie," Grace clarified. "Do you remember them from Sunday school?"

"I do!" Jake began reciting: "Love, joy, peace—" He ground to a halt.

"Patience," Grace cut in.

"Do you know any more, Lizzie?" Nickels turned to look at the little girl, who bit her lip and thought for a while before nodding.

"Kindness, goodness. . ." Her voice trailed off, her brow wrinkling.

"Faithfulness, gentleness." Grace smiled at the kids in the rearview mirror. When she glanced at him, it was all Nickels could do not to plant a kiss on her rosy cheek.

"And self-control," he finished.

⌒⌒⌒⌒⌒

"Grampa's!" Lizzie squealed as they turned down the road leading to his apartment.

Grace angled into a slim parking spot. The kids hadn't seen their grandfather's place since the day they found it.

"Come on in." Uncle Carl ushered Lizzie and Jake inside and motioned for Grace and Eric to follow.

"You go on ahead." Grace inclined her head. "I'll just enjoy the fresh air." *I'm already going to a pet shop later—best not to set foot in Queenie's home. I might be frightfully allergic to cats, but that doesn't mean I can resist petting them.* If she touched Queenie, she'd be in awful shape for the rest of the day.

"I'll stick around out here." Eric surprised her by stepping away from the door and closer to her side. "I've seen it already—great place, too." He shared a manly nod with Uncle Carl. "You show the kids while Grace walks me around. I hear a pool and a playground are somewhere around here."

Uncle Carl gave them a measuring look, and Grace suddenly found the elm tree next to them absolutely fascinating. A dull thud from inside the apartment pulled Uncle Carl away before he'd opened his mouth.

"Which way?" Eric put his hand on her elbow and waited for her to point in the right direction before continuing. "Pity you can't go in, after you fixed it up so posh."

"Posh?" She laughed. "I just helped him settle in."

"You did more than unpack." He shot her a look that told her not to deny it. "It's practically a custom-designed palace now."

"So I brought some curtains." She shrugged off his compliment.

"And a whole bathroom set." Eric shook his head. "I couldn't believe the difference new towels and a bath mat made."

Grace envisioned her uncle's new home in her mind's eye, remembering the loving care she'd put into it. The living room boasted a fireplace on one wall, with the sofa and overstuffed chairs sitting on the rug before it. The bookcases Carl and Jim made covered the back wall of the room, filled with a lifetime's worth of memories and favorite books. If it weren't for the television set, the cozy room could almost pass for a library.

They'd set the dining table in the alcove near the kitchen, which Grace stocked with enough food for an army. She'd also gone to a Lawton discount store for curtains, blue dish towels, and the bathroom set Eric had noticed. She idly wondered if Queenie liked the scratching post and catnip mouse she'd found in the pet department while buying a hamster cage.

"Amazing, isn't it?" She watched a butterfly flutter around some fragrant jasmine. "How tiny things make a big difference."

"Agreed." He stopped to watch the delicate creature's progress. "You're a tiny thing." He shifted closer, as if to emphasize his words, making her aware of how tall and strong he stood. "And you make a very big difference in the lives of those fortunate enough to know you."

"Thank you." Now it seemed as though her heartbeat were competing with the beat of the butterfly's wings. "I do what I can, no less than you." She looked up into his velvety brown eyes. "You're always thinking of ways to help me with Lizzie and Jake. I don't think I've told you how much I appreciate that."

"My pleasure." He moved a step closer. "Grace—"

"There you are!" Lizzie was panting. "Grampa sent me to get you. I like this apartment better than the last one. It's bigger and cleaner, and he has juice boxes here." The little girl kept up a steady stream of chatter about the apartment before finishing breathlessly, "He says we're going to the mall!"

Eric took the little girl's hand, but his gaze stayed on Grace's face as he said, "That's only the beginning."

⁓⁓

"Hold up." Nickels crawled into the middle of the backseat, slapping on the lap belt. "Okay, kids."

Grace raised her eyebrows at him as Lizzie and Jake clambered in on either side. He smiled in return.

I must make quite a sight. His knees poked into the backs of the front seats. He scrunched down so his hat wouldn't be flattened beyond repair. Jake and Lizzie needed the shoulder straps of the door seats, and Carl could get in and out easier from the front. Besides, if he leaned forward—he tested this as Grace slid into the front seat—he was so close he could smell the fresh, sweet scent of her hair. He wished she would let her curls out of that clip. He itched to feel their silken texture.

"Nickels!" Jake tugged on his shirt, so he leaned back a bit.

"Yeess?" He drew out the word.

"Can I wear your hat?" The little boy looked at him with big, round eyes.

"Whoa, there, Jake," Grace interrupted. "A cowboy's hat is very important."

"Sure is, partner." Nickels plunked it on top of Jake's chestnut head. "I can't trust it with very many people. You keep it safe for me, okay?" *At least this way, it won't be crushed by the ceiling of the car.*

"Yee-haw!" Jake bounced up and down, pretending to ride a horse. "Look, Lizzie! I'm a cowboy!"

"You've never even ridden a horse," Lizzie pointed out.

"Neither have you!" Jake retorted.

"We'll have to fix that," Nickels commented. He saw Grace's expression in the rearview mirror. "Someday," he added hastily, relieved when she nodded at him.

"We're here." Carl broke in as they pulled into the mall parking lot. It was packed this Saturday, and they had to hike over the asphalt before they made it inside.

"Can I have an ice cream?" Lizzie was flapping her shirt to cool off.

"That's not why we're here," Grace answered, heading past the ice cream stand toward the escalator.

"Please?" Carl stopped in front of the case, looking longingly at the freezer.

"My treat." Nickels knew Grace was exhausted and pulled out his wallet before she could say a word. "Single scoop, Vanilla Bean, for me. And you?" He turned to Carl.

"Single scoop, Cookie Dough." The older man beamed at him with approval.

"I want Bubble Gum!" Lizzie jabbed her finger at the glass case.

"Rainbow Sherbet, please!" Jake grabbed the countertop and tried to peer over it.

"With a scoop of Double Fudge Brownie for the lady." Nickels winked at Grace as the teenager diligently scooped the icy treats into paper-wrapped cones and passed them to his customers.

"I think we owe Eric a big thank-you." Grace pulled a handful of napkins from the holder.

"Thanks!" Jake and Lizzie chorused as he handed them their cones.

He laid down the cash and found a table nearby. In the next ten minutes, he and Carl were finished. Grace was chewing on a brownie chunk, her eyes closed in bliss. Nickels took advantage of the opportunity, since Lizzie and Jake were happily chomping on their sugar cones, their cheeks smeared with streaks of ice cream, to grab some napkins and begin wiping their faces.

"All set?" Grace took one last bite and tossed what little was left of hers into the trash can.

"Yeah!"

"Where are we going?" Lizzie was at it again.

"You'll see. Let's all stick together." Grace grabbed the little girl's hand, and Nickels saw to Jake while Carl brought up the rear.

"I think it's time we told you why we're here." Grace stopped in front of a clothing store.

"Clothes?" Jake's voice sank with disappointment.

"No, not today." Nickels laughed.

"Today," Grace said, "we're going to get you and Lizzie"—she looked at Carl and Nickels, taking a deep breath before they chorused—"a hamster!"

"Really?" Lizzie sounded for all the world as if someone had told her she was being given a pony.

"Really," Grace confirmed. "Pet Palooza is next door, and you and Jake get to pick him out. But remember—you have to help take care of your pet, and you have to behave while in the store. Understood?"

The children nodded mutely, their eyes big as they looked at the Pet Palooza sign up ahead. Once in the store, they pressed their noses against the Plexiglas cases holding the bunnies, whistled at the birds in their cages, and tapped the glass on the fish tanks until an associate asked them not to. Jake looked longingly at the puppies frolicking together amid newspaper shavings, but Lizzie pulled him along.

Nickels hung back with Grace while Carl hustled the children over to the hamster cages. "They're excited," he observed needlessly.

"It was a good idea," she said as the kids came up to them.

"We've found him!" Jake announced.

"Come and see!" Lizzie grabbed Grace's hand and led her over to the cage.

Jake followed close on her heels, Nickels in tow. He gestured for an associate to follow.

"That one." Together they stopped in front of the hamsters, and Jake pointed to a brown-and-white teddy bear hamster, snacking on something up near the glass. The clerk opened the display and pulled him out. Lizzie let Jake hold him first.

"What're you going to name him?" Nickels asked as Jake generously passed their furry friend to his sister.

"That's the best part." Lizzie nestled the ball of fur close to her chest and shared a conspiratorial look with her brother. "We're gonna call him"—she waited for Jake to join in—"Nibbles."

Chapter 14

"Miss Willard, good to see you again." Lizzie's teacher shook her hand enthusiastically. "Why don't you come over to my desk area while Lizzie relaxes in the reading corner?" Miss Byerly smiled at Lizzie. "Your favorite beanbag is open."

"Goody!" Lizzie zoomed toward the corner, grabbing a paperback book and settling in to read to Jake.

Grace followed the teacher over to the far corner and took the chair she indicated.

"I'm so glad we could meet before the other parents got here. Back-to-School Night is usually a hard time for private conversation," Miss Byerly said.

"How is Lizzie adjusting in the classroom?" Grace asked.

"She's doing beautifully, for the most part." The woman smiled encouragingly. "Much better than I would have expected, given our first conversation about how much she and her brother have been through."

"I'm glad to hear it." Grace relaxed. "And I can't tell you how much I appreciate the special care you're taking with her."

"Of course. Shall we go into the details?" Miss Byerly pulled out a folder with Lizzie's name on it. "She does all her work. . .tells me you've made a homework area in the house for her and Jake to use."

"Yes. Atmosphere is an important part of learning." Grace looked admiringly at the colorful posters and bulletin boards around the room. "I can see you're of the same mind."

"Yes, I am." Miss Byerly smiled. "Lizzie's a bright girl, and she's making friends and participating in class. But I've noticed some things." She looked at Grace before moving on. "Lizzie's drawings for art time are fairly typical—self-portraits, a cat, you, Jake, and her grandpa. More recently there's been a hamster." Miss Byerly laid examples on the table. "Most hold something in common—her parents are somewhere in the picture."

Grace picked up a drawing of her own living room, spotting Lizzie's rendition of Jim and Lisa in a photo prominently displayed on one wall. A crayon-colored outline of the house showed Jake and Lizzie playing soccer outside, with her parents watching them from the small attic window. Pictures of clouds with Jim and Lisa waving were common, too. Lizzie's "family portrait" had their faces next to what Grace assumed were hers and Uncle Carl's.

"I see." Grace handed the artwork back.

"After showing them to you, I have to ask: In your opinion, do you think it's healthy that she's expressing her parents as still being such a part of her life?" Miss Byerly shut the file. "I'm wondering if it's a sign that she's in denial."

"It's not out of the question," Grace admitted. "But I don't believe that's the case. I would ask you a few questions if I may."

"Go ahead."

"What has Lizzie told the other children about her parents?"

"I've heard her tell them a tornado took them up to heaven."

"Does she say she does things with them?" Grace pressed forward. "Any stories about them taking her to the circus or coming home for a visit soon?"

"No." The teacher leaned back in relief, obviously seeing where Grace was headed.

"In that case," Grace concluded, "I would see these pictures as healthy—a way for Lizzie to express that, even though she misses her parents' physical presence, she still feels their love. Their memory will always be a part of her life."

"That makes sense to me." She stood. "Why don't we show you what Lizzie's been learning?"

"Sounds great." Grace pushed back her chair, only to have Miss Byerly stop.

"Oh, there was one more thing I wanted to ask you about, while you're here."

"Yes?"

"Who is this man Lizzie mentions all the time? She says he's not a relative, but I gather you're fairly close. I believe his name is Mr. Nichols?"

"Eric Nichols is a friend of the family," Grace answered.

"I was certain Mr. Nichols was all but part of the family, to hear Lizzie talk. Stories about chicks and how he helped her grandpa move and was with you all when she got her hamster. . ." Miss Byerly's voice trailed off.

"He works at the Curly Q Ranch in Lasso, for Sondra and Dylan Ward. The kids and I go there after church most Sundays. He's been great with the kids—very kind." *He's also God-fearing, generous, hardworking, and handsome,* she tacked on silently. *And I don't know exactly what role he plays in our lives, but it's about time I found out.*

⸎

"What's wrong?" Nickels walked over to where Grace was squinting at her car.

"Tire's flat." She gestured to the driver's-side rear. "I ran over a nail."

"Sure did." He scratched the back of his neck. "I can put the spare on."

When Grace didn't answer, he shifted his attention. The sun was setting; she and the kids had stayed late this Sunday—through dinner even. They'd been celebrating the fact that Matt started crawling on his own. Right now Jake was buckled in and snoozing in the backseat. Lizzie's eyelids were heavy as she peered at them through the window.

"Thanks." She headed for the trunk, accepting the inevitable.

"Wait a minute." He stopped her with his hand on her arm. "Why don't I drive you and the kids back home tonight? Looks as if they're beat. I'll put on the spare in the morning and return your car."

"I don't know." She caught the edge of her lower lip between her teeth. "Tomorrow is Columbus Day, so we don't have school. . . . Would you mind?"

"Not a bit," he assured her. "Let me go grab my keys." When he came back out, he found Grace and the drowsy children waiting by his truck. He bundled them all inside, driving the short distance in silence.

"Thanks," Grace whispered as she helped Lizzie out of the car and reached over as though to awaken Jake.

"I've got him." Nickels slid the sleeping boy into his arms and followed the girls up the porch steps. "Where do you want me to put him?"

"On his bed—he's tuckered out, and usually he'd be in bed about now," Grace told him. "I'll get Lizzie ready to sleep then wrestle him into his pj's."

"Need any help?"

"No, but thanks for offering." She hesitated. "There is something I've been meaning to talk with you about, though. Would you mind hanging around?"

"Sure." *What can it be?* He lowered himself onto the top step while Grace got Lizzie ready for bed.

"This one?" Grace's whisper carried.

"No, the one with the flowers," Lizzie responded, probably picking out her nightgown.

"All right. Go brush your teeth while I take care of your brother."

What does she want to talk about? The refrain repeated in his mind. *In my experience, it's never a good thing when a woman says we need to talk. It definitely didn't sound like she wanted to ask what kind of tires to buy.* Nickels heard water running and the sound of a toothbrush being used and suddenly wished he'd taken the time to brush his teeth after dinner. *Oh, well. It's a good reason to keep my distance.*

"Dear God, thank You for today. We had fun." Jake's voice, slurred with sleep, floated down the hall before Lizzie finished the prayer with, "And please bless Auntie Grace and Grampa and Mr. Nichols and the Wards here in Lasso and Mommy and Daddy in heaven. Oh, and please heal our car tonight. Amen."

"Amen," Grace echoed. The rustle of sheets being pulled up made Nickels remember his own childhood. "Good night, Jake." He assumed the boy was already sleeping again when Grace took Lizzie to her room.

"Sweet dreams, Lizzie." The last upstairs light was turned off.

"I love you, Auntie Grace." He could hear what sounded like a yawn from the little girl.

"I love you, too, honey." Grace tiptoed down the hall, stopping for a minute when she saw him. She put her finger to her lips and gestured for him to go downstairs while she followed.

At the end of the stairs, she flicked on the porch light and led him to the swing. He settled in next to her, his discomfort growing by the minute.

"What's on your mind?" he asked after a few minutes of tense silence.

"That's kind of what I wanted to ask you." Grace turned to face him.

"What do you mean?" *Lord, help me out here. I'm as lost as a poodle in a tiger's cage.*

"Before I go on, I want to tell you again how much I appreciate all the things you've done for Lizzie and Jake. . .for me." She offered a faint smile. "I've no doubt God sent you to make the transition easier on all of us."

"I've enjoyed every minute." He gathered her hand in his.

"I was talking with Lizzie's teacher at Back-to-School Night." She was staring at their joined hands, but he didn't feel a bit like letting go. "Lizzie talks about you a lot. I tried to explain that you're a close family friend. . . ." Her voice trailed off uncertainly.

"Yes," he encouraged.

"But she had the impression there was. . .more to it." Grace swallowed and plunged ahead. "I wouldn't mind if it was just a friendship, if it was just me. But with Lizzie and Jake, I have to be more discerning." She squared her shoulders. "Right now the kids and I see you multiple times per week. They're used to having you around as an almost daily part of their lives. They see you as much or more than they see their grandfather."

"That's fine by me." He rubbed his thumb across the sensitive skin on the back of her hand.

"It's not fine with me." She pulled her hand away. "Lizzie and Jake have lost too many loved ones. It's not fair to them to have you be such an integral part of their day-to-day lives if you won't always be there."

"What makes you think I won't be?" He reached for her hand again, but she moved away.

"There it is—the real question." She turned toward him. "Why are you spending all of your free time with a single woman raising two children?"

"I care for you." *They seem like such little words to cover such a big feeling.*

"Lizzie and Jake need a man in their lives."

"So do you." He moved closer and cupped her face with his palm.

"I need to know. . . . Do you intend to be that man?" Tears sparkled in her eyes. "It's a lot of pressure to put on you, but for the kids, I have to know if you'll always be there for them."

"I. . ." *want to say yes, but I don't know if I've truly given my past to God so that I'm able to make a commitment.* Regret welled inside his chest as he told her the truth. "I can't make any promises, Grace."

189

"I understand." She swiped at the tears. "From now on, I think it's best if we just see each other at church or the Curly Q. Good night, Eric." With that, she slipped into the house.

Away from him.

Chapter 15

Grace sagged onto her couch, longing to pray out the anguish she felt.
Lord, I think I'm following Your will on this, but it's so hard. Why?
Why—when she had accepted that a husband was not in His plan for her and that Lizzie and Jake would be her family—did it seem the Lord had changed her perception? He apparently brought Eric to the very door she had just closed on him. She'd tried not to, but she had begun to care for him as more than a friend—surely he felt it, too. If she were the only one involved, she would take things slowly and rejoice in it. Must she give up her chance at love to protect the precious children God had entrusted her with?

The tears came again, in full this time. Her home was filled with people she loved—why did she feel so alone? Grace wrapped her arms around her knees and let them fall. What started as hurt over Eric unleashed the tears she hadn't shed since she had come home and discovered the world had changed.

Jim, her favorite cousin. He'd hide in closets, jump out to scare her, then tickle her fears away. Her friend Mary had had a crush on him forever, and for the longest time, Grace had hoped he'd see Mary the same way. But it wasn't in God's plan. Lisa moved to town—Grace had met her at Bible study. Her warm smile and sugary popcorn balls had healed a world of minor hurts as she became like family. Grace had introduced her to Jim and saw firsthand how deep their connection became. She was maid of honor at their wedding and smiled as they pledged themselves to each other in love until the day of their deaths.

She bit her knuckle to stifle her sobs, not wanting to wake the children.

Death came so soon for them, she continued in her prayerful talk with God. *Too soon for the ones they left behind. Jim and Lisa didn't part from one another, and it comforts me that they're together with You. But for the rest of us—Uncle Carl, Jake, Lizzie, me—we're left with a Jim-and-Lisa-shaped hole in our lives and hearts. They gave so much while they were with us; I can't help but wonder how much more they could have accomplished for You here on earth before You took them home.* She missed them. When she said good-bye before she left for Guatemala, she'd had no idea it would be the last time she would ever see them. If only she'd known—she hadn't even been there for the funeral.

She groped for the tissues on her coffee table and blew her nose.

She hadn't been there for Lizzie and Jake. If she could have done one thing to honor their memory and care for their legacy, it would have been helping their children through that difficult time. And Uncle Carl. . .she'd heard it said that outliving one's child was the most difficult grief to come to terms with. Jim's passing had come not so long after that of his mother. Uncle Carl had had no time to reckon with the stages of grief before he took Lizzie and Jake to care for them. She knew his loss had been compounded when the children were taken away. It devastated all of them, and only now, months later, were the tattered remains of this family knitting together.

Grace rocked back and forth, praying through the anger, despair, and helplessness she'd kept at bay for months. And when she thought she'd spent all her tears, she remembered the regret traced on Eric's face as he gave her the only thing he could—honesty—and she'd returned it in full measure.

After the way Eric gentled this transition, helped me find my place in the community, and supported Lizzie and Jake more than I had any right to expect. . .this seems so abrupt. Lord, why does protecting my fledgling family against future heartbreak make me more vulnerable to the same?

Ending her prayer, Grace felt she needed the warmth of a friend and confidante. She picked up the telephone and dialed Mary's number.

"Hello?" Her friend's cheerful greeting raised Grace's spirits.

"Mary? It's Grace. Would you mind coming over tonight? I need to talk out some things."

"I'll be there in less than an hour." Mary paused. "Do I need to bring chocolate?"

"Your advice is what I'm after," Grace responded. "But it couldn't hurt."

"Gotcha. You put on some tea, and I'll be there before you know it."

"Thanks, Mary. See you soon." After she hung up, Grace went to splash cold water on her puffy face.

I look as awful as I feel, she observed in the mirror. *And Eric—how must he feel? Mary will listen to me, pray with me, and remind me of Your love. But men don't deal with things the same way we do. Eric made his decision, but I don't think it was easy for him either. Lord, please be with him now.*

<hr />

Nickels slammed the door to his truck and paced around it, jamming his hands in his pockets.

Lord, help me! I drove away. What more could he do? After talking with his grandfather and praying about it, he knew he wasn't ready for a full-fledged relationship with a woman like Grace, no matter how tempting the idea was. A man didn't fool around with a heart like hers. . . . She was the marryin' kind. The look on her face when she'd pulled away from him—it was like an icy knife had been plunged into his chest. She was right to ask him where it was heading. But he didn't even know—

"Where're you goin'?" Dylan's voice cut through his musings.

192

"What?" Nickels pulled up short.

"I asked if you had a particular place where you were goin'." Dylan's grin was measured with a hint of solemnity.

"Unfortunately"—he sighed—"no."

"Then what say we go for a walk?" Dylan clapped his hand on Nickels's shoulder and led him westward. They walked in silence, each wrapped in a blanket of his own thoughts, until Dylan broke the quiet. "Now Sondra would say men aren't perceptive enough, but it seems to me something's weighing on your mind."

And soul, Nickels agreed but simply nodded.

"Let's sit down and see if we can't lighten the load." Dylan headed for an old truck sitting near a fence.

They each took a seat in the now-doorless cab, peering through the dusty windshield at the sky. Nickels could barely make out any stars, the grime obscuring his vision.

"I could sit here all night waiting for you to spill your guts." Dylan slapped his hand on the dashboard for emphasis. "Instead I'm going to get this goin'. Grace kept her distance from you today. I know you drove her and the kids home, and when you got back here, you started pacing like the devil was on your back. Now, perceptive as I'm not, even I can see something happened with her." Having said his piece, Dylan gazed at him.

"Yep." Nickels ran his fingers along the cracked steering wheel. *I don't know when I've felt further from the driver's seat,* he mused without humor. Dylan's earnest stare made him shift uncomfortably. "She asked me to hang around while she put the kids to bed. We sat out on the porch swing." He waited for his friend's nod. "Said she'd gone to the kids' Back-to-School Night or somethin' like that. Lizzie's teacher asked who I was—seems as if she and Jake mention me a lot."

"That's a good thing." Dylan put his hands behind his head, leaning back a bit. "You're a part of their lives now, and it's right that they're comfortable with it."

"I thought so, too." Nickels ran his hand through his hair in frustration. "But it got Grace thinking about how much time we all spend together, and that made her edgy. She told me outright that she was worried for the children. Said they'd lost too many loved ones and it wasn't fair to them for me to hang around so much if I wouldn't always be there."

"Whew." Dylan sucked in a sharp breath. "What'd you say to that?"

"I asked her who said I wouldn't be?" Nickels banged his palm on the steering column. "And she admitted Jake and Lizzie needed a man in their lives. She said she knew it was a lot of pressure, but she needed to know if I intended to be that man."

"Seems like a fair question." Dylan's comment took him by surprise. "I've wondered the same thing myself."

"You—" Nickels stared at him for a moment. "I—"

"Kinda figured that was about as far as you'd thought it through." Dylan grinned. "You sound like I felt when I met Sondra. Grasping for sanity."

"That's about the long and short of it," he agreed, letting out a gust of a sigh.

"So what'd you tell her?"

"The truth." He swallowed hard at the memory. "I couldn't promise anything just yet."

"Honest—but I'm guessing she didn't take it so well."

"You might say that," Nickels admitted. "She told me it'd be best if she and the children only saw me in church or at the ranch. Then she slipped inside." He made no mention of the tears glimmering on her lashes before she'd made her escape. It was too personal.

"And now you're trying to work through it all." Dylan rubbed his jaw, thinking. "Between you and me—and I think I already know the answer, even if you're not certain—do you want to be the man in their lives?"

"Yes." Now wasn't the time for pussyfooting around the issue.

"Then what's holding you back?" Dylan waited while the silence stretched between them, and Nickels wrestled with the question. "Look, Nickels. Prying isn't in my nature. You've been a good friend for close to six years now, and I want to see you happy. Being with Grace makes you happier than I've ever seen you."

"I know." He put his hand to his temple. "Thing is, I don't deserve her."

Dylan's chuckle made Nickels jerk his head up.

"What's so funny?"

"Let me tell you something, Nickels. If amazing, God-fearing women like Sondra and Grace don't quibble about the fact we're unworthy of all they offer, we shouldn't stew on it." Dylan clapped him on the shoulder again. "Just thank the good Lord and move forward."

"It's not that simple." Nickels turned to look his friend in the eye. "There are things you don't know about my past, Dylan."

"No," his friend agreed, "I don't know everything. But I know all I need to. You're a man who tries to follow the Lord's will, a hardworking ranch hand, a good friend, and a bright spot in the lives of Jake and Lizzie."

"And that'd be enough for a boss and friend," Nickels said. "But not for Grace."

"All right." His words wiped the grin off Dylan's face. "What do you need to tell her, Nickels?"

"It has to do with what led me to Lawton the day I met Miller Quintain," he began. "You already know I was heading toward my grandpa's place when I stopped by the church in Lawton. What you don't know is what brought me there."

Chapter 16

Did Miller ever tell you why he called me 'Nickels'?"

"I always assumed it was a play on your last name—Nichols." Dylan rubbed a crick in his neck. "There's more to it?"

"You could say that." Nickels grinned. "Before that day, I wasn't a believer. But that Sunday, I was a man who'd hit rock bottom—and knew it. It was time to change my approach to life, and the preacher was talking about how God offered us grace." He stopped for a moment at the coincidence of how God's grace had led him to Grace Willard. "So I decided to take Him up on it. When the collection plate came around, I gave all the cash I had in my pocket. It was precious little: two nickels."

"And Miller spotted you," Dylan guessed.

"He'd sat next to me and caught up with me after the service. He told me I reminded him of the widow with two mites and offered me a trial run as his ranch hand."

"Sounds just like something Miller Quintain would've done." Dylan grinned. "I'll bet he was tickled pink when you told him your last name."

"Yep." Nickels smiled at the memory. "I stayed in Lasso, kept going to church in Lawton, and, with Miller's guidance and your example, became a full-fledged son of Christ. I owe the pair of you more than you'll ever know."

"I can't speak for Miller, but I'm always happy to help another brother in Christ." Dylan rubbed his hands together briskly. "So what brought you to that church?"

"The easy answer is the sign out front. You know—the one that says—"

" 'LET'S MEET AT MY HOUSE BEFORE THE GAME'—GOD."

"That's the one." Nickels blew out a deep breath. "The more complicated answer is the reason I'm floundering now."

"And that would be. . ."

"Keep in mind, I wasn't saved when this happened." He didn't look at Dylan's reaction to the warning. He'd never told anyone before and didn't want to lose his nerve.

"I worked for a large company at the time—I was a CEO, as a matter of fact. Cassandra was a secretary. Despite the taboo, we began dating. The relationship lasted quite awhile—we even moved in together." Nickels saw Dylan wince out of the corner of his eye but kept going.

"Then she told me she was pregnant. I had no doubts the baby was mine. I cared for Cassandra, we were living together, and she was expecting my child. It seemed so natural that we get married—I proposed that night." He paused to fortify himself. Dylan's expression gave nothing away—his friend sat still as a stone.

"She refused in the next instant, told me she didn't want to have our baby. She was on the fast track to success, and new mothers didn't get promotions after all. She needed to save up more money so she could pursue her dream of becoming an actress. Cassandra 'didn't have the time to waste,' as she put it."

"No." Dylan barely breathed the word.

"Exactly my reaction. I told her I would take care of the child and help support her while she tried to break into show business. I begged her not to abort my baby. She agreed—on the condition that I would buy her a house in Los Angeles so she'd have an investment and a home while she followed her dreams." He ran his hand over his face. "I agreed. It took most of my savings—the real estate prices in Southern California were staggering—but I bought the deed to a modest condo."

"You have a child you never see?" Dylan's voice was filled with wonder and a hint of anger.

"No." Nickels spat out the word bitterly. "The day after I closed on the condo, Cassandra went ahead with the abortion. She packed her things, blamed the whole mess on me, and walked out of my life. I tried to resell the condo, but her name was on the deed, too. When she found out, she wrote a letter to my superiors, alleging sexual harassment. She accused me of paying her off for her silence—sent a copy of the deed with my name on it. My company sacked me, and no other reputable business would hire me after an incident like that. That's why I was going to my grandfather's house." He finished the confession of his past and hung his head in shame, waiting for Dylan to denounce him.

"Do you blame Cassandra for it all?" His friend's voice sounded thoughtful, not condemning.

"For a long time," Nickels admitted. "I still hold her accountable in part, but mostly I know it's my fault."

"She made her own choices, same as you," Dylan said. "Have you forgiven her?"

"It's been a long process, but, yes. When I was able to pray for her, I thought I'd given up my past sins to God and could move on. I ran across her picture in the newspaper—she'd managed to be a supporting character on a popular sitcom. I learned then that she'd gotten caught up in the drug scene and overdosed. I mourned her passing all the more because I didn't think she was saved before her death."

"You've come a long way," Dylan said. "Have you forgiven yourself?" His question cut to the heart of what was bothering Nickels.

"No." His lips thinned. "How could I?"

"God has," Dylan pointed out. "Why do you still blame yourself?"

"I should never have dated her in the first place, never have lived in sin." Nickels choked out the words. "I should have drawn up a contract—she'd get the house after the delivery of my child, not before. The responsibility lies on my own shoulders. I was more aware of that than ever when I accepted Christ."

"As your *Savior*, Nickels." Dylan stressed the word. "You're saved, forgiven by God's grace. That's the gift you accepted when you became a believer."

"I don't deserve that, same as I'm not worthy of grace."

"None of us does, my friend. That's the miracle of Christ." Dylan closed his eyes. "Let me tell you something Miller once explained to me. The more righteous a man becomes, the fewer sins he commits. You know that's supposed to be the way of it." He waited until Nickels nodded morosely. "But the thing is, he's more aware of them. Miller had a point when he told me that the more a man walks in God's grace, the more he becomes aware of how little he deserves it."

"So the fact that I know what a low-down, rotten person I was is supposed to be a good thing?"

"In a way, yes. If you don't feel the depth of your transgressions, Christ's forgiveness doesn't mean as much to you."

"I understand what you're getting at."

"Then you know you have to forgive yourself to fully accept God's love for you. And when you're able to do that, nothing will stand between you and grace."

"The principle of faith or the woman?" Nickels wondered aloud.

"Either."

~

Grace sprang to her feet as a pair of headlights flashed in her driveway. She hurried to the door and opened it to find Mary poised to knock.

"Come on in." She ushered her friend inside and led her to the living room.

"First things first." Mary held out her arms for a comforting bear hug. "God'll see you through, Grace."

"Thanks for being here." Grace patted her friend on the back.

"Pah." Mary waved her gratitude away. "That's what friends are for. Besides, it's been too long since we had a good heart-to-heart."

"You're right." A fresh wave of guilt washed over Grace. "I've neglected you recently, and I'm sorry."

"Oh no, you don't." Mary glared at her. "I know that if I'd picked up the phone you would've invited me over no matter what the hour, so we'll hear no more about it." She thrust a bag toward Grace. "Chocolate?"

"Please." Grace grabbed a piece, unwrapped it, and sank into its sweet richness. "Mmm."

"Yum." Mary took a bite of another one, leaned back, and licked her fingers with satisfaction. "So either you've finally admitted you need to grieve like every other person on the planet when they lose someone they love or something's happened since Back-to-School Night. Which is it?"

"A bit of both," Grace murmured, swiping another sweet.

"Do tell." Mary pulled her feet—decked out in orange, fuzzy slippers—onto the couch and made herself comfortable. "Does it have anything to do with that tall, blond drink of water who keeps looking at you in church when he thinks no one's watching?" She laughed at Grace's thunderstruck look. "Don't pretend you didn't know he wasn't just coming around for the kids."

"Yes, it has to do with him—you can quit smiling now," Grace admonished her friend. "Lizzie's teacher told me she mentions Eric all the time. She got the impression. . ."

Mary nodded. "The same impression I did. Nothing wrong with that."

"Yes, there is." Grace fidgeted with the folds in the blanket slung over the back of the couch. "It made me realize just how much time the children are spending with him. I can't expect him to keep seeing us several times a week forever."

"I think I see where you're going with this." Mary frowned.

"Lizzie and Jake have lost too many people they care about. I hadn't realized how much Eric had become a part of our lives until Miss Byerly pointed it out. I can't afford to let Lizzie and Jake depend on him if I'm not positive he'll always follow through." She hoped her friend would understand.

"I understand your reasoning," Mary said, "but you can't put that kind of pressure on a new relationship. It's not as if you can just walk up and ask him if he'll always be the man in your lives." Her eyes widened at Grace's look of misery. "Oh, Grace, you didn't!"

"Oh yes, I did." She looked down at her lap. "Honesty is the only policy, and I can't beat around the bush when it comes to what's best for the children."

"What did he say?" Mary snatched another chocolate and held the bag out for Grace. "Tell me everything."

Grace retold their whole conversation and waited for the verdict. While Mary thought it over, Grace rubbed at the ache in her abdomen that had appeared a few days ago and wouldn't let up. *Stress,* she reasoned. *And the last thing I need is an ulcer.* When Mary began to speak, she snapped to attention. She had more important—and immediate—matters at hand.

"That didn't go nearly as badly as it could have." Mary paused. "He obviously cares for you and the kids—and he's got that honesty thing down pat." She winked at Grace. "He can't make any promises about forever—and, really, what were you expecting? But he didn't scream at the idea and run for the car. I think you're emotionally exhausted, Gracie. I could see the instant I walked in that you'd had a good cry. Long overdue, if you ask me. We'll say a prayer for your Mr. Nichols and let you have a good long rest. After all, tomorrow is—"

"Another day," Grace added.

"I was going to say 'Columbus Day,' so you can sleep in or take a nap, but yours sounds more dramatic." Mary stood up, her eyes sparkling with good humor. "But I have faith that, either way, you'll prevail."

Chapter 17

Hey, Nickels!" Chris walked toward him, wiping his hands on an oil rag. "That's not yours." He squinted at Grace's sedan. "Doesn't that belong to Grace Willard? She just had her oil changed and tires rotated here about a month ago."

"Yeah. She drove over a nail at the Curly Q yesterday. I know it's a holiday, but I had a suspicion you'd be around here anyway." He cast an admiring gaze over Chris's auto repair shop. "She has custody of her cousins and can't be driving around on this spare."

"I heard about that. Lemme have a look." Chris tucked the rag into his back pocket and squatted for a closer inspection. "You've got two options, Nickels. I can do a patch job on it until she can get in and have it replaced, or I can go ahead and replace it on your word that it'll be taken care of."

"Go ahead and replace it today, Chris. I'll take care of it."

"So that's the way the wind's blowin', eh?" The mechanic shot him a cheeky grin.

"Not yet," Nickels responded. *But soon enough, if the Lord is willing.*

"This won't take too long." Chris held out his hand for the keys.

"I'll keep you company. Been awhile since I've seen you."

"Keepin' busy." Chris shrugged. "There's always something that needs fixing. You?"

"I could say the same." Nickels grinned. He grabbed a pop from the nearby ice chest and passed it to his friend. "I don't suppose you want to come to the Curly Q for lunch?"

"Sounds good to me." He rolled over a new tire. "I need to bring Sondra some pasteurized milk."

"She'll appreciate that. It's good of you to take care of her and the baby while you're picking up the eggs for the food bank. Would you mind if I hitched a ride with you back to the Curly Q from the Willards'?" *Best if I give Grace some space for now—honor her wishes.*

"No problem," Chris said, hefting the tire into place.

Not a single problem at all, if I have my way.

~

"Wake up, Auntie Grace!" A small hand pushed at her shoulder.

"Five more minutes," she pleaded, the pain in her abdomen unrelenting. *Oh,*

Mary, if you only knew I tried to sleep in today!

"You wouldn't let us stay in bed on the first day of school." Lizzie reminded her that turnabout was fair play and seized her blankets with the ruthlessness of an invading army.

"All right, I'm up." Grace swung her legs over the side of the bed and looked at the kids, eyes bleary. Despite having cried herself to exhaustion last night, she hadn't slept well. The thudding pressure she'd dealt with for the past week had focused to a sharp spot of pain yesterday morning before church and then switched back to a generalized ache after lunch. The discomfort hadn't let up since then.

Lord, I don't know what this feeling is. I'd thought maybe I was so anxious over talking things out with Eric that I was having physical symptoms, but that theory doesn't work anymore. I'd call the doctor, but she'll be out of the office today—like everyone else.

"Get dressed, Auntie Grace!" Lizzie pulled open her closet door.

"I'm going to get you guys some breakfast then take a quick shower while you eat it," Grace decided aloud. She rubbed at her right side, which felt a little worse than the left, and made her way downstairs. Jake and Lizzie danced around her as she poured some cereal and milk and started peeling a banana for each of them.

"I won't be long. Lizzie, you know what to do." Grace headed back toward the stairs. Lizzie knew to watch Jake, not open the door to any strangers, let the answering machine get any phone calls, and call 911 if she or Jake were hurt. They'd been through the routine dozens of times to make absolutely sure.

Why is it so hot in here? she wondered, stepping to the thermostat. *Seventy-eight degrees? That can't be right.* She turned on the air conditioner, making a mental note to have a repairman come out. Winter wasn't that far away, and a heater on the fritz certainly wouldn't do.

The short shower made her feel slightly better. She tugged on a blue jean skirt and button-down top before seeing about some breakfast for herself. *Maybe having something in my stomach will make me feel better.*

She was finishing some oatmeal while the kids watched cartoons when she began thinking about the day. *Maybe I'll drop off the kids with Uncle Carl and take Mary's advice to relax awhile.* It was a good plan except for one thing—her car had a flat down at the Curly Q.

Eric said he'd put on the spare and bring it back, but he hasn't stopped by yet. I'll have to get that fixed today so we aren't driving around unsafely. So much for resting up. A wry grin painted her features. After the way she had all but shut the door in his face last night, she had no right to expect him to do anything for her. She'd have to call the Curly Q.

She pulled out her phone file and flipped through it until she came to the entry simply titled "Eric." The phone wasn't on its charger. Grace was hunting it down when the doorbell rang. She changed directions so she could answer the door but was brought up short by a streak of pain in her midsection that almost doubled her over. When it passed, she straightened up. *That does it. Tomorrow I make an appointment to see the doctor,* she told herself as she opened the door.

"Hello. . ." Her voice trailed off when she found no one standing there. Her car sat in the driveway, with a good tire replacing the flat from the previous evening.

He came back. Her heart sank. He came back, and she hadn't answered the door. What a selfish, snooty woman he must think she was, skulking around inside rather than facing him. And he'd already gone.

Now the pain in her abdomen seemed a mere echo of the ache in her heart. She would have to call him to explain. But explain what? That she'd had a tummy ache? Grace shook her head and closed the door. *Well, at least now I can call Uncle Carl and get that break. Now where did I find that phone?*

"Auntie Grace, it's cold in here." Jake came into the hall, his arms wrapped around himself.

"Are you sick, honey?" How could he be cold when the place was practically a furnace? Grace stooped to feel his temperature with her hand. His forehead did feel cool against her touch. Yet another reason to call the doctor. She straightened up, determined to get Jake a jacket. The move was too sudden. Pain streaked through her midsection.

Oh, Lord, she prayed as she clutched the door frame. *What's happening to me?* She took a step toward the phone, the pain intensifying until she was doubled over, gasping for breath.

"Auntie Grace! Are you okay?" Jake shook her shoulder. "*Lizzie!*" he hollered, taking off down the hall as fast as his little legs could carry him.

"Call for help," Grace barely whispered. It was her last thought before the blackness closed in.

<hr/>

She must be even more upset than I realized. Nickels stood on her doorstep, waiting for her to open the door and smile at him. Slowly he came to terms with the fact that when she said she and the kids would only see him on Sundays she meant it. Bewildered and frustrated, he dropped the key through her mail slot and went back to Chris's car.

Lord, I've botched things a bit, but it's nothing beyond Your ability to fix. I think it's best to abide by Grace's decision for a while—not push her. Please work in her heart so she'll be ready for me when the time is right.

Chris didn't say a word as he got in, just drove straight back to the Curly Q. Sometimes anyone could understand there was nothing to say. Nickels gave Chris a curt "Thanks" and headed for the bunkhouse. He needed time alone with the scriptures and his thoughts. He pulled out the now-worn Bible that Miller had given him so many years ago and prayed.

God, bless my time of study to grant me peace and understanding. I know I need to rely on Your plan and purpose for me. How do I make Grace see that she needs me as much as I need her?

In the midst of his meditation, his cell phone rang. His first inclination was to switch it off, but he noticed the identity of the caller. *Grace.* He immediately answered the call.

"Hello?"

"Mr. Nichols?" Lizzie's voice, reed-thin and shrill, piped into his eardrum.

"Yes, Lizzie." He tamped down his irritation. "What is it?"

"We don't know what to do. It's Auntie Grace. She fell down by the door and won't wake up. We need you."

Chapter 18

I'm coming, Lizzie. You stay by your auntie Grace, all right?" Nickels tore out of the bunkhouse like a man aflame. "I'm going to hang up now so I can call an ambulance."

"Okay," Lizzie promised before hanging up.

Nickels yanked his seat belt on and dialed 911 simultaneously.

"9-1-1. What's your emergency?" The dispatcher sounded far away—too far away for Nickels's peace of mind as he sped down the road.

"Grace Willard has collapsed and lost consciousness. I need a paramedic right away!" He rattled off her address.

"Dispatching immediately. They should be there within half an hour."

"Half an *hour!*" He nearly spat into the phone.

"We're based in Lawton," the dispatcher reminded him. "Sir, you need to stay calm. Now tell me—is her breathing labored? Does she have a steady pulse?"

"I don't know. I'm on my way over there right now. Her ward called me." He put more pressure on the gas pedal.

"How close are you?"

"I can see the driveway right now." He pulled a wide turn that would have done the Dukes of Hazzard proud.

"When you get inside, check on her pulse and breathing patterns." The cool voice boasted all the calm that had fled from Nickels the minute Lizzie told him what was wrong.

He hit the brake and jumped out of the truck, pounding on the door. "It's Nickels. Let me in, Lizzie!"

When the door swung open, he spotted Grace, still lying on the floor. He knelt beside her, feeling under her jaw for her pulse. *Lord, please let her be all right.*

"Her pulse is rapid, breathing quick and shallow." He felt her forehead. "She's burning up."

"Loosen any clothing that might constrict her airways," the dispatcher directed.

"What else?" Nickels unbuttoned the top two buttons near Grace's collar.

"You'll need to elevate her feet to help her from going into shock."

"Lizzie." Nickels cradled the phone to his shoulder. "Help is on the way. Right now I need you to go get me a pillow. Can you do that?"

"Yes!" Lizzie raced down the hallway. She brought back a throw pillow from the couch, and Nickels put it under Grace's feet.

"Now what?" He struggled to look as though he were calm, for Lizzie and Jake. In truth, he wanted to crawl into the phone and drag a paramedic back through with him.

"You said she's hot." He heard rapid typing over the phone. "Run cool water over some towels and try to bring down her temperature."

Again Lizzie and Jake were eager to help. While they went to get some wet towels, Nickels asked, "What's wrong with her? Will she be all right?"

"I can't say, sir." The man sounded apologetic. "The paramedics will do all they can and take her to the hospital. According to our contact, they're about five minutes away now."

Those five minutes passed with agonizing slowness as he knelt with Jake and Lizzie by Grace's prone form, all of them praying for her.

When the ambulance arrived, the scene changed rapidly. Nickels took Lizzie and Jake to the steps and sat down, making sure the paramedics had space to work.

One lifted Grace's eyelids, peering at her pupils. "Responsive," he noted. "She's definitely running a fever."

Another took her blood pressure. "Ninety over fifty-two. Low."

"What happened?" A third, holding a clipboard, blocked Nickels's view and peppered them with questions about Grace. Questions that, for the most part, none of them knew the answers to.

"She fell down and wouldn't wake up." Jake's lower lip trembled, and he began to cry.

"Does she have any health conditions we need to know about?" the man asked Nickels.

"She's allergic to cats." His knowledge seemed pathetically useless as they loaded Grace onto a gurney, wheeling her out to the ambulance.

"Okay. We're taking her to the ER. You can follow."

"What's wrong with her?" Lizzie's voice, full of fear, stopped the paramedic as he turned around.

"We're not sure, but we'll find out."

Nickels ushered the kids out to his truck. He made sure they were belted in before pulling out. He forced himself to obey the speed limits, hating every second it kept him from her side, but refusing to put the children at risk.

"Mr. Nichols." Jake's sobs tore at his heart. "Is Auntie Grace gonna go live with our parents now?"

Nickels swallowed past the lump in his throat. "Not if I can help it."

<hr/>

"Excuse me." With Lizzie and Jake in tow, he rushed up to the ER registration desk. "They just brought in a woman named Grace Willard," he told the nurse.

"May I get an update?"

"Are you her spouse?" The nurse checked a chart.

"No."

"Next of kin?"

"These children are." Nickels raised his hands, still clasped over theirs, for her view.

"I'm afraid I'll need a close adult relation. She's given clearance to one Carl Willard. I can also accept the emergency contact listed—one Mary Fellows."

"Look—this is an emergency. I'm a close family friend—" He was wasting his breath. The nurse gave him a sympathetic smile but kept stonewalling.

"I don't know this Mary, so we're going to go get Grampa Carl." They headed for the car.

Lord, thank You that Carl moved to Lawton. He's just down the street from the hospital! Please don't let anything be wrong with Grace. Let her be all right, Jesus. Please.

He repeated the prayer over and over until he reached the door of Carl's new apartment and pounded on it. Finally a light turned on.

"What—" The old man glared at him while an orange cat wound round his ankles.

"Auntie Grace is in the ho'pital!" Jake choked out the words between sobs.

"What's wrong?" Carl grabbed his wallet and a coat, threw it on over his pajamas, and locked the door behind him.

"We don't know. They won't tell anyone but her nearest adult relative or her emergency contact—Mary something or other," Nickels explained while he herded them all toward the truck.

Carl jumped into the front seat. "Let's go!"

At the emergency room, they stood in front of the same nurse.

"Here. This is Carl Willard, Grace's next of kin." Nickels pushed him forward.

"ID?" The medical assistant inspected Carl's expired driver's license. "Relation to the patient?"

"I'm her uncle," he declared. "Where is she?"

The assistant buzzed him in and several minutes later let Carl come back out.

"What's going on?" Nickels took heart that Carl didn't look as shaken as he felt.

"She's regained consciousness. They're taking a CT scan right now. Looks like appendicitis."

"What's that?" Lizzie cried.

"When can we see her?" Nickels asked the nurse.

"Mr. Willard may see her when the doctor allows." The nurse pointed toward some seats in the corner. "You may wait there until then."

Nickels sank into one chair, and Jake crawled onto his lap. Lizzie pressed close between him and Carl on another.

"What's a–pen–bite–us?" Jake asked.

"Appendicitis is when your appendix is swollen," Carl told his grandson. "Grace will be all right."

"What's your a–pen–bics?" Lizzie sounded out.

"A little part inside you that doctors can take out," Nickels tried to explain.

"Why is it hurting my auntie Grace?" Jake's fear changed to anger. "Let's get it out!" He was ready to go to war.

"That's the doctor's job," Carl told him.

"What do we do?" Lizzie jumped up, walking around in a small circle.

"We pray and remember to show your aunt how much we love her, so she'll get better." Nickels ignored the glance Carl shot him at the word *love*. "Don't we, Grampa Carl?"

"Yes." Carl reached for Lizzie. "That's exactly what we do now."

<hr/>

"We were right." Dr. Rutgers came into her room after the anesthesia from the emergency surgery had worn off. "Acute appendicitis with peritonitis."

"I can't believe it." Grace leaned back against the pillow.

"Believe it." He peered at her over the top of his glasses. "You say you'd been having intermittent abdominal pain for a few weeks?"

"Yes, but I thought maybe it was stress or something." That sounded feeble even to her own ears.

"If treated with antibiotics in the early stages, it probably would have healed on its own."

"Would have?" Grace echoed, not liking the sound of the phrase. *I've had the surgery. Won't the antibiotics help it heal quickly now?*

"When you felt the sharp pain on your right side, it indicated the inflammation had spread to the lining of your abdomen."

"What does that mean?" She plucked nervously at the bedsheet, shifting her weight to her left side to try to alleviate the discomfort on her right.

"That was your body's clearest sign that something was wrong with your appendix." He gave her a pointed look. "Your entire lower abdomen hurts now because your appendix had ruptured and the infection was spreading. We've taken out the appendix and cleared out a lot of the leakage."

"I feel much better now." Grace sat up, refusing to accept that anything was seriously wrong. *Much better, but still hurting.* She gritted her teeth against the ugly reality.

"I see you're still hurting, though. I'll prescribe some pain medication for you—but you should know they'll make you groggy."

He made an attempt at a smile. "The pain medication should prevent too much discomfort, and the IV will hydrate you. If you need help, call for a nurse tonight. I'll check on you during my rounds tomorrow."

"And I can go home after that?" *Thank You, Lord, that Uncle Carl and Eric are with the children. But they need me, and I have to get out of here!*

"Typically we send the patient home after one or two days," Dr. Rutgers said. "But in your case, since the organ had ruptured, it will more likely be between four and seven days before you're well enough to be released."

"A whole week?" Grace let out a deep sigh. *Lizzie and Jake will be taken back to the group home. I can't put them through that.*

"There must be some other way."

"I'm afraid not."

Chapter 19

Nickels shifted anxiously as he waited for Carl and the kids to come back. They were her kin. They had every right to go in first. He tried to see reason. But still! Why couldn't they bend the rules a little? He'd been waiting hours since they'd brought her in—during the tests and the operation. He needed to see with his own two eyes that she was awake and going to be okay.

"Nickels!" Sondra's voice brought him to his feet, and he received her anxious hug. "How is she? Where's Carl? Lizzie, Jake?"

"Hold on, honey." Dylan put a calming hand on her shoulder. "He can answer only one question at a time."

"She's had the surgery and regained consciousness. Carl and the kids are seeing her now." Nickels shook his head as though to clear it. "I thought I told you two not to come." He knew love was a crazy and powerful thing, but he didn't think it would make him lose his mind!

"You did." Dylan shot him a wry glance.

"As if we'd listen!" Sondra scowled at him in reproach for even thinking she'd stay away from her friend. "We've called Miss McNarty—Jake and Lizzie need to be taken care of while Grace recovers."

"You don't mean—" An icy chill shot down Nickels's spine. "They won't go back to the group home? We can't put them through that!" Grace had worked so hard to give them a stable home. If it was yanked away now, the kids would never feel safe.

"The state won't put them back in Carl's custody after they've been removed once," Sondra said. "And it's up to the doctors how long Grace will be here."

"I'll stay with Lizzie and Jake so long as they let me." Nickels set his jaw.

"They won't." A new voice joined the conversation as a rail-thin woman with cat's-eye glasses bustled up. "Unless you're Max Rockheart? The uncle I could never reach?" At Nickels's look of astonishment, she shook her head. "I thought not."

"Miss McNarty, I presume." Sondra shook the woman's hand. "Sondra Ward."

"Ah, the Wards." Miss McNarty eyed her and Nickels for a moment.

"Yes." Dylan placed a proprietary arm around his wife's shoulders.

"Oh." She seemed taken aback. "You're still working on your clearance to be officially sanctioned as foster parents, aren't you?"

"Yes." Sondra nodded.

"Hmm." Miss McNarty hesitated. "And what is your connection to Miss Willard?"

"Family friends," Sondra put in. She glanced at Dylan, and Nickels saw them exchange a slight nod. "Is there any way we would be allowed to watch Lizzie and Jake while Grace recuperates?"

"If Miss Willard is agreeable, I'll see what I can push through." Miss McNarty seemed willing to help but noncommittal. "It would be best if Lizzie and Jake could maintain as much of their day-to-day schedule as possible. Moving them back to the home, even for a short period of time, could prove traumatic after so much upheaval."

"Exactly," Nickels agreed. At Sondra's warning glance, he shut his mouth. He wasn't the one who'd be officially watching Lizzie and Jake. *I'm not qualified to be any kind of honorary parent.*

"We live just down the street. We could pick up their clothes, whatever they need. We know Jake is allergic to eggs. We can get them to school during the week and their church on Sunday," Dylan said, listing some of the benefits.

"As I said, Miss Willard must approve. Your home has already met inspection requirements so, provided you understand I'll visit to see how the children are, it should be doable."

"Miss Sondra!" Lizzie ran down the hall and flung herself at the woman.

"Hey, baby." Sondra hugged the little girl. "How's Auntie Grace?"

"Better." Jake kept a tight hold on Carl's hand. "She's awake now. But they stuck tubes and stuff on her."

"That's all to help her get better." Nickels stooped to console the child. "And they'll take them out when she is."

"Okay." Jake nodded.

"You can go in now," Carl told Nickels. He looked at Sondra and Dylan, refusing even to glance at Miss McNarty. It was obvious the older man still bore ill will toward the woman who'd taken Lizzie and Jake from him and placed them in the group home. "Three at a time."

Miss McNarty looked at Sondra and Dylan. "We need to get this straightened out."

"I'll wait." Nickels forced the words out. Making sure Lizzie and Jake were taken care of was the most important thing. They said she was getting better. He would have to trust that for a little while longer. But that didn't mean it didn't take every shred of self-control he possessed not to storm through those doors and hunt down Grace's room.

❧

"Thank the Lord," Grace said after Kate McNarty explained how the Wards had offered to take Lizzie and Jake. Even better, they would be allowed to do so. "And thank you," she told Sondra and Dylan.

Lord, You've sent me such precious friends. Thank You for taking care of Jake and Lizzie. I almost think they'll be less anxious this week than I will!

"I take that to mean you approve?"

"Absolutely," Grace affirmed.

After they worked out the details, Grace pushed the button to adjust her hospital bed. It didn't make a difference; she couldn't get comfortable. She made a vain attempt to smooth out her hair.

Isn't he going to check on me? She knew he was there. If he didn't, though, she shouldn't be upset. She had no one to blame but herself. She'd told him to stay away. But he hadn't. Lizzie called him, and he came running to take care of her. . . to take care of them.

She nibbled on her lip. *So where is he now?*

"Here you are!" Eric strode into the room, his face hidden behind a gigantic bouquet of slightly smooshed flowers. He put them on the nightstand and smiled at her.

Suddenly the stress of the day hit her—and hard. So long as she'd focused on the pain or the surgery or Lizzie and Jake or the arrangements to be made, she'd been able to keep going. But then he walked in with a smile that made her feel as if she'd just won a beauty pageant, and she couldn't keep it all under control.

"Don't cry!" Eric fumbled for the tiny box of tissues and thrust it at her. "I'll take them back!" He snatched up the bouquet and started looking around for a place to stash it.

"D–don't you dare, Eric," she gasped. "I love them."

"Then what's wrong?" He cautiously set down the glass vase and stepped closer.

"I—I—" Grace cried some more.

"You've had a rough day." He patted her hand gently.

"It's not just that." *My right side feels achy and throbbing. I'm in a hospital gown with messy hair. I have tubes in my arms and a runny nose. I'm crying like a nincompoop in front of the man I care for but sent away. . . .* The list made her cry harder.

"And you were worried about Lizzie and Jake," he said. "But now you're relieved."

"Yeah, but. . ." *How do I tell him I feel ugly and clumsy and stupid when he's giving me credit for caring about more important things? Maybe if I didn't hurt, I'd be in better control. I'm so glad the nurse is on her way.*

"You don't want to stay in the hospital." He rubbed his thumb across the back of her hand. "Nobody does, but it's to make sure you're okay. And that's the important thing."

"Oooh." She let out a breath, wiping her face with a tissue.

"And I'll bring Jake and Lizzie and even Carl over to visit you so you won't be lonely," he promised.

"Just stop it!" She ordered as she threw the tissue at the trash can—and missed.

"Stop what?" His brows knit in confusion.

"Stop being so. . .so. . ." She gulped air as she searched for the word.

"I'm sorry." He looked nothing short of crestfallen as he dropped her hand. "You said you didn't want me around. I shouldn't have—" He ran his hand through his dark blond hair. "Here I am, being—"

"Wonderful!" she cried. "Here you are, trying to comfort me about my health and the kids and even bringing me flowers." The words came out in a rush. "And no one's ever given me flowers except my parents. I just can't deal with it right now! You have to stop being so perfect." She glared at him.

He didn't help the situation when he threw back his head and laughed. "I was going to say selfish. You're not feeling your best, and you've told me to stay away." He grasped her hand again. "But I had to see you."

"You're being wonderful again," she mumbled.

"Well." He pulled over an uncomfortable-looking chair from across the room. "I'll just stick around until we fix that."

"Hello?" The nurse entered the room, took one look at Grace's tear-streaked face, and double-timed it toward the bed. "I have your medicine. You'll be feeling better in no time, Miss Willard."

"But they'll make me loopy." Grace frowned. *I don't want Eric to see me that way.*

"Groggy, more like." The nurse gave her the meds.

"Go on." Eric patted her hand. "I'll stay here until you fall asleep."

⟡

"She's sleeping soundly," the nurse said when she came in to check on Grace. "I think it'd be best if you left now."

Nickels yawned and stretched. Grace wasn't the only one who'd drifted off.

"Visiting hours are from eight to six, standard," the nurse informed him. "But she's doing well so she'll probably be moved from intensive care in the morning."

"Thanks." He gave the nurse a smile. "Have a good night." After she nodded and left, Nickels smoothed Grace's curls from her brow. "Lord," he prayed quietly, "keep pain at bay and let her heal. She's taken a lot on herself these past months, and it's not only her body that craves rest. Watch over her for me, as I'll watch over Lizzie and Jake. Thank You for safeguarding her this far." He leaned over to plant a soft kiss on her forehead and whispered, "Sleep well, honey. I'll be back later."

He couldn't be sure whether she heard him, but a contented smile tilted the corners of her lips as she inclined her head toward him. Unwilling to jolt her awake, he tiptoed out of the room.

When he slid into the driver's seat, he rolled his shoulders to ease the stiffness. The chair he'd fallen asleep in had been none too comfortable—but the twinge between his shoulder blades was a small price to pay for the balm to his heart.

When she started to cry, I was afraid she'd send me away. I misjudged her. He should have known something was wrong when she didn't answer the door. His Grace wouldn't do that to anyone. She seemed so small and fragile, almost as white as the sheets on her bed. It would have nearly killed him to leave her, but he would've done it to spare her any more pain.

He shook his head in amazement at the thought. *But I was wrong again. She wasn't upset that I'd dared to show my face—she felt embarrassed by how happy she was to see me.* He could feel the smug grin spread across his features.

"Lord, I've been carrying around so much anger at myself. It took the unselfish love of a woman to help me break down the barriers I'd raised to get by each day. And to think, tonight it was my small token of affection that crumbled her walls. She's stayed strong for Lizzie and Jake and even Carl, making it through the daily challenges with her own force of will and her belief that You'd see her through. Tonight she showed the same vulnerability I had to own up to." Nickels remembered the conversations with his grandpa and Dylan. "Thank You for the strong faith of the people You've brought close to me. When Grace is well again, I ask Your blessing to move forward with our life together."

They had weathered awkward introductions, self-doubt, and a breakup before they'd even started in earnest. Nothing could stop them now.

Chapter 20

Stop!" Lizzie shrieked and tried to wiggle away, elbowing Eric in the chest. "Stop it, and I mean it!" She slid to the floor, giggling long after he quit tickling her.

Grace couldn't help but giggle along, though it hurt to do so. The brief time in the afternoon when Eric brought the children by after picking them up from school was her favorite part of the day.

"My turn!" Jake launched himself onto Eric's lap.

"Are you sure you can handle it?" He gave the little boy an appraising look.

"No." Jake resolutely planted himself. "But it looks like fun."

"All right." Eric began tickling the boy until Jake, too, collapsed in a noodley heap of laughter.

"You did ask for it," Grace reminded him as they gasped for breath.

"Let's get her, Mr. Nichols!" Lizzie grabbed the bed rail as if she would vault onto her.

"Oh no!" Grace put out her arms to protect her sensitive abdomen, but Eric scooped up the little girl in his arms and set her back down.

"We have to be careful with Auntie Grace, remember?" he cautioned. "Now what do you say we head to the cafeteria and get some of that famous hospital gelatin salad?" Eric was so good about realizing when she'd hit her limit and needed a rest.

"Yeah!" Jake bolted for the door. "I want 'lello."

"I like the orange!" Lizzie joined him.

"What about you?" Eric patted the end of the bed.

"Strawberry, please." She'd been living on popsicles and broth for the past four and a half days. Gelatin salad was her favorite treat.

"We'll be back." With that, he took Lizzie and Jake out of the room.

Grace leaned back against the pillows and closed her eyes for a quick nap. She awoke from her doze when the door opened.

"Back already?" She struggled to sit up.

"Well, I do come by about this time every day." Dr. Rutgers gave her a wry smile.

"Oh." Grace pasted a smile on her lips as she answered his questions and let him poke and prod her. When he stood back, she mustered a hopeful question. "Does it look like I'll be back home tomorrow?"

"Hmm." A long silence stretched between them as he perused her chart. "You're still tender and not on solid food. You're using more painkillers than I'd like to see before we send you on your way, too."

"So. . .another day?" She tried to remain positive.

"At least." His blunt answer squashed her remaining hope. His steely gray gaze pierced her like a bug on a pin. "Even after you're feeling stronger, I would only release you on the condition that you'd be resting more often than not, with a relative taking care of you."

He paused as the sound of Jake's and Lizzie's laughter floated down the hall then hastily finished, "As is, you'd be expected to look after two children. Absolutely unacceptable, Miss Willard. You've already shown poor judgment in seeking medical treatment when needed."

Dr. Rutgers's scold brought a flush of color to Grace's cheeks, but she still pointed out, "I have friends to help me, and Lizzie and Jake's grandpa will be more than happy to lend a hand."

He opened his mouth to respond but merely shook his head as Eric and the children burst through the door. The good—if stern—doctor gave her a pointed glance. "I'll be back to see you tomorrow. Good day."

Eric glanced from her to the doctor. "Kids, why don't you go down the hall to the small lobby for a minute and bring back a magazine for Auntie Grace? And no running."

"Yes, Mr. Nichols." Jake, who'd already begun to jog, slowed down to a more sedate pace.

"What's going on?" Eric shut the door behind them.

"Miss Willard is disappointed that she'll be staying with us for a time more," Dr. Rutgers said, shaking his head.

"How much longer?" As he cut straight to the heart of the matter, Grace realized how nice it was to have someone back her up.

"That depends upon how she fares over the next few days. As I explained to her, her living situation is not conducive to recuperation, and that must be taken into account."

"You mean, because she lives alone with Jake and Lizzie?" Eric asked.

Grace saw his hands clench. *So he has the same reaction I did. I'm being penalized for raising children on my own. It bothers him, too.*

"Yes." The doctor seemed to realize he was treading on shaky ground because he added, "She needs rest."

"I'm right here, Doctor." Grace wouldn't let him continue speaking about her as though she were incapable of making an informed decision.

He turned to her. "I'm sure you agree that your health comes first. The fact that there is no one capable of giving aid should you need it must be taken into account."

"He's right." Eric came to stand by the side of her bed. "I resented every minute it took for me to get to you after Lizzie called. That can't happen again."

The warm flutter in her stomach had nothing to do with her recent appendectomy. *His eyes show how much he cares.*

"I don't want to put Lizzie and Jake through any more," she confessed.

"What if she had help, though?" Eric asked the doctor.

"That would mean a more timely release," he admitted, looking from her to Eric with raised brows.

Ooh. Grace felt her face flame. *For a man so schooled in reading clinical data, he jumps to his own conclusions far too quickly. How dare he think Eric is anything but the incredible gentleman he is!* She was squaring her shoulders to say so when Eric stopped her with a warning glance.

"I'm going to take Lizzie and Jake back to the ranch. I'll call you later." Eric squeezed her hand and headed for the door. "Thanks, Doc."

"Anytime." Dr. Rutgers watched his abrupt departure in apparent confusion.

Grace wondered at it, too, and what he might be up to.

⌒⌒⌒

"Sondra, I need a woman's perspective." Nickels walked over to where she was petting the dogs.

"I'll do my best," Sondra promised.

"The doctor won't let Grace go home while she's the only adult watching two children." He scratched Skylar's ears. "Carl could stay a little, but he doesn't want to leave Queenie alone for more than a night. And he doesn't know anyone in Lawton he trusts enough to care for his cat."

"I see."

"Well, I'm an adult. I can help with the kids and make sure Grace doesn't have another emergency while she's alone at the house. But she'll worry about small-town talk and propriety. How do I convince her to go ahead and accept my help?"

"You can't offer to stay at her place, Nickels." Sondra grinned at him. "I know you're an honorable man with good intentions, but we both know better than to pretend it's a workable option."

"What do I do?" He crossed his arms.

"I already thought this might be an issue. Dylan and I talked it over. We'd be fine with having Grace convalesce here. We can keep an eye on her, and she'd be with Lizzie and Jake and"—she shuddered—"out of the hospital."

"You're amazing, you know that?" If his boss's wife weren't pregnant, he would have picked her up and twirled her around. Instead he chucked her under the chin.

"I don't know about that." Sondra blushed. "Tell you what, I'll drop off the kids tomorrow and swing by the hospital to make arrangements."

"Thanks." He'd thought he would miss being alone with Grace and the kids, but now he realized he would see her even more if she stayed at the Curly Q. They'd come a long way, but he was waiting for her to be at full steam before declaring his intentions.

He had wasted enough time already. She needed to know he planned to be there for her, Lizzie, and Jake—forever. He had known her only a few months, but he knew what he needed to. God had used His grace to heal him of the past. Since he was starting fresh, he didn't want to make any more mistakes. Soon Grace would know he intended to court her in earnest.

"Well, don't just stand there." Sondra braced her back as she walked inside. "We've got work to do."

"Comin'." He hurried after her. "What do you need?"

"We need to move the crib and changing station into Dylan's and my room first." She walked into the nursery. "Then set up trundle beds for Lizzie and Jake in here."

"So Grace will be in the guest room?"

"Exactly." Sondra clapped her hands. "Let's get this done while the kids are watching cartoons." Under her direction, Nickels hefted the furniture to temporary new homes.

"Now we'll need to change the sheets in the guest bedroom and make up the beds." She handed him two sets. "You get the ones in the nursery; I'll take care of the guest room."

"Sondra," he called.

"Yes?" She stopped, her hand on the doorjamb.

"Thanks again. It'll really help us out."

"Us?" She quirked her brow.

"I meant what I said." Nickels shifted the linen to his other hand.

"And you said what you meant? I believe you." She winked. "One hundred percent."

Chapter 21

W hat?" Grace sat up at the doctor's words. "But yesterday you said I'd be here for. . ." Her voice trailed off as Sondra stepped into the room.

"This young woman has apprised me of the situation." The doctor's stiff manner unbent only a little as he spoke. "So I'm releasing you on the understanding that you remain at the Curly Q until fit to return to the workforce."

"The Curly Q—" Her brow knit. "But—"

"It'll be great." Sondra stood by her bed. "Carl already let me into your house, and I grabbed some clothes and such. The kids are moved to the nursery for now." She kept talking as the doctor conferred with a nurse in the corner. "We'll just get you packed up and out of here in no time." She finally stopped when Dr. Rutgers left the room.

"Take a deep breath," Grace instructed. Her good-hearted friend couldn't have inhaled enough air during that speech. "Now am I to understand you've conspired to have me released from the hospital early?"

"Exactly." Sondra beamed. "And I couldn't have you acting confused in front of the doctor. Between you and me, Nickels doesn't seem to like him too much."

"You could've spoken with me first." Grace swung her legs over the side of the bed.

"I meant to." Sondra held up Grace's slippers and slid them on her feet. "I ran into him in the hallway and seized the opportunity. How could I have known he was on his way here at the time?"

"Good point." Grace looked at her slippers. "So you're taking me to the ranch? I hate to burden you any more than I already have." Nor did she want to take advantage of the Wards' good natures.

"Fiddle-dee-dee." Sondra didn't look up from emptying the nightstand drawers—not that much was in them. "I'll be glad of the company. And you'll be able to help keep an eye on the kids—we just won't let you overdo it, that's all."

"What did Dylan tell me about your working like a ranch hand while six months' pregnant with Matthew?" Grace wondered aloud.

"That's different. Besides"—she straightened before finishing—"Nickels wants you close by."

Grace refused to comment on Sondra's last revelation.

"He said something about the hospital not technically being permitted, but the Curly Q was safe ground?" Sondra couldn't hide her curiosity.

From now on, I think it's best if we just see each other at church or the Curly Q. The memory, which should have made her cringe at her own foolishness, now made her smile. She'd set up boundaries, and he was playing to the letter of the law.

"Now that's a matter of opinion," she said, giving Sondra a mysterious smile.

"Are you in pain, Grace?" Sondra rushed to her side.

So much for my Mona Lisa wiles.

"I was just wondering. . .did you happen to bring anything from my house with you today?"

"What, like"—Sondra rummaged around in her tote bag then held up her hands—"jeans? And a red top?"

"Have I told you how wonderful you are?" Grace said as she began changing out of her hospital gown.

"Or possibly your travel makeup case?" Sondra produced the purple-zippered bag with a flourish.

After dabbing on some mascara and lip gloss, Grace almost felt ready to face Eric—or the mound of paperwork the nurse brought in. She clicked her pen with resolution.

"Take your time." Sondra cozied up in the chair by the bed. "Dylan is keeping an eye on Matt back home, and the kids don't need to be picked up for hours."

"You might not be in a hurry to get out of here"—Grace flipped to the next page as she spoke—"but I sure am."

❦

"Nibbles wants to see Auntie Grace." Lizzie tugged on Nickels's arm.

"I'll bet he does," Nickels answered. *So do I.* "But she's taking a nap right now, so we'll wait until she wakes up." Grace had arrived at the Curly Q earlier in the morning—while he was riding fences. By the time he'd come back to grab a late lunch, she'd settled in and dozed off.

"Do you want to help me?" Lizzie looked up at him expectantly, and Nickels belatedly realized she'd still been talking.

"I'll always help you when I can."

"You run water in the sink—make sure it's warm." With those cryptic instructions, Lizzie rushed off.

"Wha—" He gave up and went to run warm water in the bathroom sink.

Lizzie joined him, her tiny hands dwarfed by Sondra's yellow gloves for housework. "Here!" She thrust a bottle of bubble bath at him.

"Lizzie—," he started but stopped. It was so sweet that she wanted to help clean up so Grace was comfortable. The sink was already spotless, but if it made her happy, he'd go along with her on this.

"Just half a capful," she directed, rooting around in the other pocket of her sweatshirt. She had him drain the water a bit before taking out a round, brown scrubby. Lizzie plunked it in the water and began swishing it around in the shallow water. "He's going to be so soft!"

"He?" Nickels looked at the sink in horror. Surely that wasn't—

"Nibbles. He was kinda dirty," Lizzie explained. She carefully lathered the little hamster as Nickels watched in morbid fascination. "He wants to look good for Auntie Grace."

"I understand that." Nickels held Nibbles while Lizzie drained the soapy water and ran fresh into the basin. "But I didn't know you could give a hamster a bath."

"Why not?" Lizzie deposited the poor creature back in Nickels's hands, picked up a washcloth, and began to towel it dry. Nibbles didn't budge an inch.

"Have you ever given him a bath?" Nickels wondered if a hamster could go into shock.

"Tons of times." Lizzie squeezed out the cloth. "This is his favorite part." She gently set the damp hamster on the closed toilet lid and plugged in a hair dryer.

"You're not going to use that on the poor fella?" Nickels burst out when she switched the setting to low.

"Well, we can't very well leave him wet." Lizzie rolled her eyes. "He could catch cold." With that, she expertly blow-dried Nibbles to sartorial splendor and then handed him back to Nickels.

"All done?" Nickels couldn't believe how tolerant the pet was. How many hamsters in the world would sit calmly through a bubble bath?

"Just about." Lizzie produced a small pink comb and carefully brushed her hamster's hair with it.

"Do they sell those at the pet store?" Nickels marveled at the things people would buy these days.

"No. This belongs to my doll," Lizzie explained. She squinted at the hamster, stepped back, smoothed a little section of fur, and proclaimed, "Finished!" She clasped her hands and looked at Nickels. "Doesn't he look wonderful?"

"Incredible." He handed the hamster back to Lizzie, who fed it a pellet before taking it back to its cage. He dried the sink and went to check on Grace. After slowly cracking open the door, he poked his head through.

"Hi." Grace smiled at him even though he probably looked like the world's least successful cat burglar.

"Hi, yourself." He widened the opening and stepped into the room. "Did you know that Lizzie gives Nibbles baths?"

"Yes." Grace giggled. "Did she blow-dry him, too?"

"Sure did." Nickels chuckled. "I was a little worried, to tell you the truth."

"So was I the first time she showed me." Grace's hazel eyes sparkled. "He hardly moved the whole time."

"Still as a stone. But he seems just fine."

"He always does." Grace shook her head. "You ought to see Lizzie put him in her doll's sports car and drive him around the house."

"What?"

"You heard me." Grace shrugged. "He'll go along with whatever she's got planned."

"He's no fool. Spa treatment, drives a sports car? That hamster's living the high life!"

"Nibbles seems content—for the most part."

"For the most part?"

"Well, occasionally he'll plan to make a break for it," Grace admitted.

"The incredible adventures of Nibbles the hamster." Nickels figured she was weaving a story and decided to play along. *I'll go along with just about anything she says—as long as she wants me nearby.*

"No, really—he plans it!" Grace's eyes widened. "I can tell because he'll be sitting there, same as ever, but his cheeks are bulging with all the food he's packed in!"

He couldn't hold the laughter in anymore as Grace puffed out her own cheeks in demonstration.

"Shh." She put a finger to her lips. "You can't tell Lizzie or Jake. It'd break their hearts."

"Your secret is safe with me," Nickels pledged. "Cross my heart."

⸻

"Mmm." Grace savored a chocolate-chip cookie straight from the oven, loving the way the warm chocolate flooded her taste buds.

"I take that to mean you officially approve of this batch?" Sondra laughed.

"Further testing required." Grace snagged another cookie.

Sondra pulled a carton of milk out of the fridge. "You want some?"

"Sure," Grace mumbled around a mouthful of cookie. "Pasteurized?"

"Has to be for the baby." Sondra patted her tummy. "Chris is kind enough to bring me some when he picks up the eggs for By His Hand."

"Chris is the mechanic, right?" Grace tried to make the connection between a mechanic and pasteurized milk.

"Mm-hm." Sondra took a sip of the milk. "He volunteers for By His Hand—bringing food to the less fortunate. The Curly Q donates eggs, and when he comes to pick them up, he usually brings me the milk."

"Gotcha." Grace wiped her lips with a napkin. "Sounds like a worthy cause."

"We try to keep busy around this town." Sondra slid another sheet of cookies into the oven.

"No fooling." Grace grinned. "You bake more than anyone I've ever known."

"I know—but I've got enough men around the place to dispose of the evidence." Sondra piled a plate high. "Speaking of hungry men, why don't you take these out to Nickels and the kids?"

Matt was napping, but Lizzie and Jake were gallivanting around the ranch under Eric's close watch. Grace picked up the platter and nudged the screen door open with her hip. Placing her hand over her eyes, she scanned the horizon for a clue as to where everybody was.

A giggle floated on the warm breeze, and Grace headed around the barn to find everyone clustered at a corral.

"Cookie break!" She passed the platter to Danny, the nearest cowhand. "What're we watching?" Grace looked to where he pointed, since his mouth was full.

About twenty yards away, Eric led a chestnut mare at a sedate walk. Jake perched atop a small saddle, clinging to the pommel and grinning.

"Look, Auntie Grace!" He waved to her with one hand but swiftly clutched the horn again. "I'm a real cowboy!"

"Seems like it," she agreed. "Do real cowboys eat cookies?"

"I hope so!" Jake responded enthusiastically as Eric led him over to the fence, hitched the mare, and hefted Jake out of the saddle. "Yum!"

"Is it my turn, Mr. Nichols?" Lizzie straddled the lowest rung of the fence.

"Sure is." Eric lifted her into the saddle, carefully placing her tiny hands on the pommel. "Now I'm going to tell you the same thing I told Jake: Keep ahold of the pommel, grip your horse with your legs, and move along with her. Got it?"

"Almost." Lizzie looked down. "What happens if I fall?"

"I'll be right here," he assured her. "But I have a feeling you're going to do just fine." With that, he loosened the mare's reins and began leading Lizzie around the paddock.

Grace watched, admiring his easy rapport with the children and his broad shoulders as he kept firm control of the horse. *He'd make a good daddy,* she thought. *Kids love him. He's a natural.*

"A natural, don't you think?"

It took Grace a moment to realize Dylan was talking about Lizzie's riding skills. She drank in the sight of Eric helping the little girl dismount.

"Absolutely."

Chapter 22

"How about a walk?" Grace asked Eric when she found him in the barn.

"Sounds good." He gave Brassy one last pat and followed her out of the barn. "Look at that sky."

"Beautiful," Grace agreed. The setting sun streaked the clouds with glowing shades of rose and amber. They stopped for a moment to appreciate the sight. "I can't believe another day is gone."

"I can't believe you're taking Lizzie and Jake back home tomorrow." He started walking again, and Grace hurried to match his stride.

"Hold up." She put her hand on his forearm to slow him down. *Strange how I never really noticed how much he adjusts his pace to fit mine—until he doesn't do it.*

"Grace—" He stopped at the pressure of her hand, turning to look at her with an intensity that took her breath away.

He's going to kiss me, she realized. *And I want him to.* She forced herself to look away. *But not until we straighten out a few things.*

"To tell you the truth, we need to talk about a few things." Eric rubbed the back of his neck. "It's been a strange time, what with the hospital and you staying here, but—"

"Neither of us has forgotten our last conversation before my appendix ruptured," Grace finished for him.

"A lot has passed between us since that day," Eric pointed out.

"Yes," she agreed. "And I wanted to tell you I've known for a while that I was wrong." She held her breath, waiting for his response.

"No, you weren't."

How could three words tear a hole in her heart? She had just admitted she'd been wrong about staying away from him. . .and he took the opposite side. Had the time they'd spent over the past weeks deepened her affection and lessened his? She looked at him mutely.

"Protecting Jake and Lizzie is always the right thing to do, and I respect the fact that you were strong enough to stick to your priorities." He stepped closer. "It's one of the many things I admire about you, Grace."

"But I shouldn't have put you in that position," she whispered.

"I put myself in that position," he countered. "You made me face some things I'd been avoiding. I've sought wise counsel, prayed, and searched my heart. That day, I couldn't commit to you because I wasn't spiritually prepared." He slipped his arm around her waist and pulled her closer. "Now I am." He rested his forehead against hers, his warmth encompassing her. "Let me make myself clear, Grace. Friendship is only part of what I'm asking of you. With me it's all or nothin'. What do you say?"

⁓⁓

Nickels nestled her in his arms, loath to let her go. *Here's where I should probably give her some space and time to think it over,* he acknowledged. *But I've waited too long to get her in my arms.*

When Grace shook her head the barest amount, his heart froze.

"Here I was, trying to tell you I didn't need you to make any promises." Her words floated to his ears, a soft caress. "You've always been there for us. You don't have to prove anything or make a final decision, Eric."

"I know I don't have to." He cupped her cheek. "I want to."

"Oh." She sucked in a sharp breath as he drew closer.

"Now I'm giving you fair warning," Nickels rumbled. "I've been waiting to kiss you for months, and I need you to know that once I do there's no going back." He slowly lowered his mouth to hers, giving her time to pull away if she chose to.

Instead she raised her lips to meet his in a kiss sweeter than he'd ever imagined. He reveled in the feeling of holding her in his arms as she wrapped her arms around his neck.

"No going back now," he murmured triumphantly as she laid her head on his chest and snuggled closer.

"Who would want to?"

⁓⁓

"Welcome home!" Carl threw open the front door as they got out of the car.

"Good to see you, too." Grace hugged him, never mind the fact she'd seen him the day before.

Nickels grabbed luggage out of the bed of his truck to bring inside. He couldn't blame Carl. Grace's hugs were addictive. He set the suitcases on the floor in the hall and came back out.

"We're home!" Lizzie sped past him.

"Slow down," he warned.

"Sorry, Mr. Nichols." She stopped to look at him, excitement shining in her eyes. "I can't wait to put our furniture in my dollhouse."

"After we get you unpacked, I'll help you." Nickels grinned. Over the two weeks Lizzie'd spent on the Curly Q, they'd created a miniature store's worth of doll furniture.

"And then we'll show Auntie Grace the surprise!" They'd kept it secret, waiting until they'd finished. Only Sondra knew, and that was because she'd helped by sewing the pillows and cushions.

"Grace, could you make us some iced tea while I help Lizzie unpack?" Nickels tossed Lizzie a conspiratorial wink.

"Sure. Jake, why don't you help me in here?" she called.

"Okay!" Jake followed her into the kitchen. "Can we have some 'nilla wafers, too?"

"I'll take your suitcase up to your room." Carl grasped the handle and tugged it along, bumping the bottom on each stair.

It took hardly any time at all to help Lizzie unpack. Jake's room was easy—clothes in the hamper, shoes in the closet, and electric car on the desk hutch. They repeated the five-minute process in Lizzie's room, setting her doll on her bed and shelving a few books before getting down to serious matters.

"Ready?" Nickels withdrew the box of tiny furniture replicas.

"Oh, yes," Lizzie breathed as she opened the lid. "Which room first?"

"Maybe we should put down the rugs first," Nickels suggested. Sondra had given them velvet and wool scraps for carpeting. He used his pocket knife to slice off any long edges as Lizzie chose tan wool for the bedroom, light green felt for the living room, and deep blue velvet for the dining room.

"It already looks more like a home!" Lizzie clapped her hands excitedly. "Now the couch."

He'd made what was little more than a wooden bench, but Sondra's pink cushions turned the piece into a sofa. Lizzie tucked the matching coffee table in front of it.

The replica of Lizzie's own four-poster bed—complete with comforter, courtesy of Sondra's skill and enthusiasm—went in the bedroom, along with a minute facsimile of her vanity. Lizzie had glued a shiny bubble gum wrapper onto the frame for a mirror. The dining table took up most of its designated area—then it was time for the chairs. Of all the things he'd cobbled together, the chairs had been the most challenging. He watched with satisfaction as she carefully arranged the four pieces around the table and situated one of the figures so it was sitting down.

Another doll relaxed on the sofa before Lizzie sat back. "Perfect."

"You did a great job," Nickels praised her. "Anyone would want to live here."

"*We* did a great job," Lizzie corrected. "Now we can show Auntie Grace!"

"Wait. I have one more thing." Nickels pulled a wrapped bundle from his jacket pocket and handed it to her. He waited while she unwound the cotton batting he'd wrapped around his pièce de résistance.

"It's a rocking chair!" Lizzie looked at it in awe. "It's beautiful." She sat it down perpendicular to the couch and tested it by pressing gently on the seat. "And it really rocks!"

"I should hope so." Nickels grinned. "It wouldn't be a proper rocking chair otherwise."

"Thanks, Mr. Nichols!" Lizzie tackled him in a bear hug. "It's important for everyone to have a real home."

"You're right, Lizzie." He stroked her hair, his chest aching at the solemnity behind her words.

"Now can we show Auntie Grace?"

"I think so." Nickels put his finger to his lips when Lizzie opened her mouth wide as though to shout down the stairs. "Let's get her and bring her up, okay?"

"Okay!" She held his hand and headed down the stairs.

"Auntie Grace! You should come see. . ." Her voice trailed off as she looked from Grace to the strangers at the door. Further down the hallway, Jake stood clutching Carl's hand.

"Ah, Lizzie." Grace's smile was strained. "Come and meet your aunt Celine and her husband, Max. They've come a long way to see you."

Chapter 23

We've come for the children." Celine Rockheart's proclamation made Grace gasp.

"Of course you have." Nickels stood behind her, his hands bracing her arms. "We're all here for the children, aren't we, Carl?"

"That's what family's for," Uncle Carl added. "And Lizzie and Jake just got home from the ranch." Celine grimaced at his words, but he continued, "So they'll need to freshen up and change." With that, he herded the children up the stairs.

Grace caught Lizzie's worried glance and managed a smile. *Are they truly here for the children, Lord? They can't just waltz in here and take Jake and Lizzie!*

She waited until the children were upstairs before inviting the Rockhearts into the living room.

Max settled into the overstuffed armchair with a decided air of authority, while Celine perched delicately on the edge of the sofa.

Eric's hand on the small of her back steered her to the love seat, where he sat down beside her.

"You are Grace Willard?" Celine pursed her lips while she awaited the answer. "Relation to Jim Willard?"

"Yes," Grace confirmed. "And, pardon me, but what were you saying about the children?"

"We've come for them." Max looked at her as though she'd gone daft. "Lisa was Celine's sister, and naturally we're willing to take them on."

"Provide a proper home," Celine added in a tone that stirred Grace's anger.

"Their home is here." Eric placed a comforting hand on her shoulder.

"And who might you be?" Max raised a superior brow.

"Eric Nichols. A friend of the family."

"You have no jurisdiction in this matter." Celine sniffed. "We were on an anniversary cruise in Europe—unreachable. When we arrived home, we had several messages from a Miss McNarty regarding my niece and nephew. Naturally we came here at once."

"I appreciate your concern and am glad to hear you want to be a part of Lizzie's and Jake's lives." Grace tried to remain calm. "But this is their home."

"Temporarily." Celine waved her hand. "And you will, of course, be reimbursed for your trouble."

"That's not necessary." Grace gritted her teeth to keep her anger from spilling out. "I love having them."

"And I'm sure they've enjoyed their adventure in this. . .quaint little town." Max flashed a superwhite smile her way. "But with us, Elizabeth and Jacob will have every advantage."

"Lizzie and Jake," Grace said firmly, "have endured far too much upheaval in the past five months to even consider taking them from our home."

"Children are resilient," Celine informed her. "And they're all I have left of my sister."

"Lizzie and Jake are human beings." Grace saw the muscle work in Eric's jaw as he spoke. "Not possessions."

"Of course." Max looked surprised. "And we'll see to their every need."

"They need stability," Grace countered.

"They'll have it once they've moved to Maine," Celine said. "With us."

"No." Grace stood. It was time to end this dispute. "Here, in Oklahoma, where I have custody."

"*Temporary* custody," Celine corrected with a gleam in her eyes. "You've not been designated their legal guardian."

What with settling the children in, school starting, helping Uncle Carl move, and dealing with the appendectomy, I haven't had time for that yet. This couldn't cost me my family, could it, Lord?

"It's only a matter of time," Grace faltered.

"No, I'm afraid it isn't." Max Rockheart stood. "We gathered from Miss McNarty that you might prove difficult. We've retained a lawyer specializing in family law."

"A lawyer!" Eric's angry exclamation chorused with Grace's.

"If you refuse to see reason"—Celine gestured widely—"then we have no other recourse."

"There is nothing reasonable," Eric growled, "about dragging to court the woman who's made a home for Lizzie and Jake!"

"Well, that's just it, isn't it?" Celine smirked. "Grace is a woman. A single woman, trying to raise two orphans all alone and on a limited salary."

"I'll manage," Grace said.

"You'll manage, will you?" Max dusted a speck of nonexistent dirt from his well-tailored sleeve. "Lawyers' fees and court costs add up quickly, Grace." He handed her a business card. "Please call if you reconsider. Otherwise. . ." His voice drifted off as he walked past her toward the door.

"Our lawyer will be in touch." Celine breezed by them, closing the front door with a bang.

"No," Grace whispered. "Please, God, don't let this happen." She leaned into Eric's strong embrace. "How am I going to tell Lizzie and Jake?" The last word barely squeaked out as tears stung her eyes.

"We'll figure it out, honey." He held her tight. "One way or another, we'll get through this."

⌒⌒⌒⌒

"They're asleep." Grace came downstairs that night, looking defeated.

"Good." Nickels held her hand in his.

"Time for a family meeting." Carl jerked his thumb toward the dining room. Grace hesitated for an instant, and the old man chuckled.

"That meant both of you." He cast a meaningful glance at their clasped hands.

"Right behind you." Nickels kept a firm grip on Grace when she would've pulled away and led her to her seat.

"Now I'm not pressuring you two," Carl said. "But it's clear which way the wind blows, if you catch my meaning."

"I've wondered when you'd say something," Grace admitted.

"I'm no interfering busybody, but now's not the time to prance around the issue. What's needed here is a united front."

"Agreed." Nickels nodded at Carl.

"Grace, you need his support, and we both know he has a stake in all this. If that weren't the case, I would've had you take Lizzie and Jake upstairs, Nickels, instead of my doing it."

"I appreciate that." Carl was the patriarch of the Willards—his approval was a step in the right direction. "We need to work together for Lizzie and Jake."

"I worry about keeping the problem from them," Grace said. "Just telling them Max and Celine love them and want to make sure they're taken care of sidesteps the issue."

"It's still the truth, albeit a softer version." Carl planted his chair more firmly. "Frightening Lizzie and Jake by telling them two strangers are trying to steal them from us would only do harm."

"Especially"—Nickels hurried to point out—"when we've only spoken to them once. If it progresses to a legal battle, Lizzie and Jake will need their own representation. Lizzie, at least, is old enough to have a say in the matter."

"And we all know who she'll choose." Carl reached across the table to pat Grace's hand. "I'll stand beside you, too, for whatever it's worth."

"It's worth a lot." Grace smiled at him.

"Good. Now I have an old buddy whose son is a family court lawyer," Carl explained as headlights flashed through the front windows. "That'll be him coming now."

"You called a lawyer already?" Grace seemed astounded.

Her uncle smiled and nodded. "The minute I heard what they were up to."

"They did, too," Nickels reminded her as Carl went to open the door. "It's

229

good sense to be as prepared as possible." He stood up as Carl ushered in a tall, dignified man with smile lines at the corners of his eyes and a sprinkling of silver at his temples.

"Richard Woodbury." He extended his hand to Nickels and then Grace and took a seat.

"Before we take up your time"—Grace lifted her chin—"I'd like to know what your rates are."

Nickels had barely opened his mouth to tell her he'd help with the cost when Carl waved the question away.

"Already taken care of." He gestured for them to sit down.

"Carl saved my father's life back in the war," Richard Woodbury said. "I'm just glad to have the opportunity to repay him. I'm doubly blessed to have such a good cause."

"Thank you," Grace managed. "So where do we start?"

"According to Carl"—Richard took out a pad of paper and read aloud—"Lisa and Jim Willard passed away just under six months ago. Elizabeth and Jacob Willard have been in your care for approximately twelve weeks now. Is that correct?" He waited for confirmation before continuing. "You would have claimed the children more promptly but were teaching English to Guatemalan orphans over the summer?"

"Yes. There were no phones in the village," Grace added. "I was unreachable for the first ten weeks."

Nickels heard the catch in her voice and grasped her hand under the table and squeezed it.

"I can't think of a better reason." Richard smiled at her. "On your first day home, I'm to understand you contacted their caseworker and removed the children from the Lawton Group Home?"

"Of course." Grace squared her shoulders. "They needed to come home."

"Your relation to the children is what exactly?" He peered at his notepad, pen poised.

"First cousin once removed."

"Hmm." The lawyer looked up. "And Celine Rockheart is their aunt?"

"I'm afraid so," Grace admitted.

"Not quite," Carl broke in. "She was Lisa's half sister."

"It's still a valid blood tie. Some would say a stronger one than Grace claims." Richard tapped the pen on his paper. "What was her reason for not coming forward until now?"

"A European cruise," Nickels put in.

"A six-month European cruise?" Their counsel raised his eyebrows. "And they had no way of knowing about Lizzie and Jake during all that time?"

"So they say." Grace leaned forward. "And when I told them I wouldn't simply hand the children over, they swept out of here."

"Didn't even ask to talk to Lizzie and Jake," Nickels said. "I ask you, is that the behavior of a couple desperate to care for the children?"

"No," Richard replied. "Forgive the assumption, but I guess their financial status is somewhat above your own, Miss Willard?"

"No contest." She took a deep breath.

"But her heart's bigger than all their bank accounts combined," Nickels said.

"And that should count. Carl tells me you arranged for new living quarters so he'd be an integral part of the children's lives?"

"Yes," Grace said. "They love seeing him."

"It seems to me the Rockhearts have two advantages in this situation. First, their money. And, second, they offer a two-parent household." He looked intently from Grace to Nickels.

"We can—" Nickels began.

Grace cut in. "So what are our chances if they take this to court?"

"Even with your child-care background and all you've done so far for Lizzie and Jake"—Richard looked solemnly around the table—"you're in for a fight."

Chapter 24

"Hello?" Grace rubbed her eyes as she answered the phone. Who would call at 3:30 in the morning? Not that it mattered—she'd been tossing and turning all night.

"Hey." Eric's voice rumbled over the phone line. "I kind of figured you wouldn't be able to sleep."

"You, too?" She leaned against the headboard.

"Listen—what if I came over so we could hash things out?"

"We already went over everything with Richard," Grace pointed out.

"I've been thinking—there are other things to consider."

"Like what?"

"Like character witnesses. Like hiring an investigator to check into these people." His voice rose with each word until Grace had to hold the receiver farther away from her ear.

"Is there any reason why we can't discuss this in the morning?" She yawned.

"It is morning." He paused. "And I'm already in the driveway."

"Planned it all out, did you?" She pulled back the covers.

"I did indeed." He chuckled. "I brought hot chocolate. Meet me on the porch, okay?"

"You had me at 'chocolate.'" Grace hung up the phone, ran a brush through her tousled hair, slipped into her jeans and knit top, then checked on Jake and Lizzie before stepping outside.

"Morning." He handed her a mug and poured the steamy treat from his thermos.

"A new day." Grace wrapped her hands around the warmth of the mug.

"The first of many with you, me, Lizzie, and Jake." He clinked his cup with hers in a toast. He slid his arm around her shoulders, and she leaned into the crook of his arm, tucking her feet beneath her as he swung them slowly back and forth.

It was the closest she'd felt to sleeping all night. His very presence calmed her.

"I hope that goes from your lips to God's ears," she said quietly.

"God hears us, Grace." Eric rubbed his hand up and down her arm. "And now I need you to hear me."

"I'm listening." She nestled still closer.

"Before the Rockhearts showed up today, I made it clear that I would be with you through the long haul." When he paused, Grace nodded.

"I told you I'd had to face some things before being able to commit to you and the kids like that."

"And you did, right?" Grace pulled back a bit. He hadn't called her up in the middle of the night to say good-bye, so where was this heading?

"Yes." His single syllable reassured her. "But before we can move forward, you need to know what those things were."

"Not now." She tried to slide away from him, but he held her close. "I can't deal with anything more today," she begged him.

"We've made it this far." Nickels held her gaze. "But to face what lies ahead, we need to be honest with each other."

"I trust you." She pushed an errant lock of hair from his forehead. "Isn't that enough?" *Lord, please let it be enough,* she prayed. *If something could cause me to lose him, too, I don't think I could bear it. Was it only yesterday he kissed me for the first time? Was it mere hours ago that I brought Lizzie and Jake back home? Can't my love for the children, and for this wonderful man, keep us all together?*

"No, Grace." He caught her hand and held it to his heart. "You need to know I trust you in return. With my heart, with my mind, and with the secrets of my past."

At that, Grace sighed and put her hot chocolate down. "You have my full attention."

⟶⟶∙⟵⟵

He could see the walls rising in her eyes, as she guarded her heart against what he was about to tell her. *Lord, let her see the truth in what I say. Help my love break through the barriers between us. Give me the strength to go through with this.*

He kept his arm around her, trying to maintain as much closeness between them as possible.

"Six years ago, before I came to Christ, I worked at a major corporation in Oklahoma City. I knew it was against company policy, but I cultivated a relationship with one of the secretaries."

"You loved her?" Hurt clouded her expressive eyes, darkening them.

"As much as one selfish person can care for another." He wouldn't soften this with half-truths.

"What happened?" She swallowed.

"We moved in together." He could feel her pulling away, distancing herself emotionally. A small voice inside urged him to stop, but he pushed onward.

"She became pregnant." He hesitated. "And I asked her to marry me."

"I don't want to hear this." Grace turned away from him, but not before he saw the tears sparkling on her lashes.

"All or nothing, Grace," he reminded her, willing her to stay.

She didn't respond, but she didn't leave him on the porch either. He continued.

"She refused. She wanted to be an actress—said she didn't have the time to waste. She. . .she wanted to have an abortion." The word tasted sour.

"And you agreed?" Horror resounded in her words.

"Never." He fisted his hand on his knee. "I bargained with her. I'd raise our child and buy her a home in California so she could pursue her dream—as long as she didn't abort my baby."

"Where is she now?" Grace choked out the words.

"She died three years ago."

"And your child?" She wiped her eyes with the back of her hand.

"After I bought the house, she went ahead with the abortion." He closed his eyes as he relived the moment she had told him.

"No!" The rage and sorrow in her exclamation were mirrored in her eyes as she stared at him. "No," she repeated in a whisper.

"Yes." He hung his head, the old pain throbbing to life.

"I'm so sorry." Grace embraced him. Her acceptance made him want to cry out in gratitude. Instead he held her tight, refusing to let go.

"I forgave her long ago." Nickels felt the need to finish it. "But I carried the blame with me all this time."

"You're forgiven, Eric." She stroked his jaw.

"It wasn't until God brought you into my life that I realized I hadn't laid that burden down. I had to let go of my self-hatred before being able to love you freely."

Grace looked at him for a long time in silence, tears tracing silvery lines down her face. Nickels waited—he'd said all he could.

"I love you, too." Her words soothed his soul. "I loved you before, Eric, and I love you even more, now that I know how hard you've worked to become the man I admire."

"You understand?" He scarcely dared hope.

"I understand what you lost so long ago." Grace curled up next to him once more. "And I appreciate the strength it took to overcome that and share your pain."

"Then you understand that I've had one child snatched away from me and that I will do anything in my power to help Lizzie and Jake." He kissed the top of her head.

"I never expected less of you, Eric."

"Then we're in agreement?" He felt as though a huge weight had been lifted from his shoulders.

"About what?" She tilted her head back to look at him.

"You heard what Richard said. We stand a better chance at keeping Lizzie and Jake if there are two adults in the home." He slid off the porch swing and bent down on his knee in front of her. "We're not living together as man and wife, but there's something we can do about that, Grace." He gestured with his empty hands. "I don't have a ring yet, but will you marry me and keep our family whole?" He smiled up at her. He longed to show her the depth of his love and dedication.

When she stood, the smile slipped from his face.

"Thank you, Eric—but no." She tugged on his arm until he stood beside her.

"But—"

"Shh." She put her finger to his lips. "I know you mean well, but marriage is sacred. I won't enter into the holy state of matrimony just to give me an edge in court."

"It's not just for the judge," he protested.

"I know it's because you genuinely care for us, Eric, but marriage isn't something to rush into." She raised up on tiptoe and kissed him on the cheek. "I'll see you tomorrow."

With that she went inside, leaving him to pick himself—and his heart—from her porch floor.

Chapter 25

"A re you ready?" Nickels asked her on the big day.

"No." She bit her lip. "I can't believe their fancy-schmancy lawyer arranged for a court date so soon!"

"We knew it was coming." He curled his arm around her to pull her close. "And we've been praying nonstop. God will be with us in that courtroom."

"We're all here for you." Sondra spoke for all her friends congregated on the courthouse steps.

"Let's go." Grace strode into the courthouse, her head held high.

A half hour later, they were called to order as the honorable Judge Benson took his seat.

"I've reviewed the files regarding this case," he began without precedent. "It seems fairly clear-cut. Both the Rockhearts and Miss Willard are petitioning for legal guardianship of Elizabeth and Jacob Willard." He glanced at the children.

"I understand the living situations of both parties and their relation to the children. No need to repeat any of that. Before I speak with"—he peered over his glasses at a document—"Lizzie and Jake, there are a few questions I'd like to ask each party. First, the Rockhearts."

"Yes, Your Honor," Celine almost whined. "We'll do all we can to oil the wheels of justice."

"Do not speak unless answering a question, please." Judge Benson didn't seem to be showing the Rockhearts any favor, which gave Grace hope.

"I understand you live in Maine. How often did you see the children before the deaths of their parents?"

"Oh." Celine looked at Max. "We flew out shortly after Lizzie was born."

"And Jake?"

"We happened to be in Tahiti at the time," Max explained.

"We send cards and presents for every birthday and Christmas," Celine added.

"It seems as though you are quite well traveled." The judge didn't sound enthusiastic about this, but Celine didn't appear to notice.

"We love to travel. Max and I are working our way through every country in the world."

"And how often are you home?" Judge Benson queried.

"It varies," Celine said.

"And how would you be raising two young children when you're out of the country more often than not?"

Grace refrained from cheering at the judge's furrowed brows.

"We could cut back a bit," Max offered.

"And they'd have a nanny, of course." Celine rallied. "The best money could buy!"

"I see." Judge Benson turned to Grace. "Miss Willard, a few questions for you."

Please, Lord, let me have better answers than the Rockhearts. So much is riding on this. Give me Your peace and strength.

She prayed so fervently she almost missed the judge's first question of how long she had been taking care of the children.

"Yes, Your Honor." She resisted the urge to curtsy. "Jake and Lizzie have been living with me for the past three and a half months."

"And during that time, what have you done to see to their welfare?" Judge Benson's steely gaze brooked no nonsense.

"I've arranged for them to go to school, conferred with their instructors, taken them to doctors' visits, furnished our home, bought them a pet, and helped relocate their grandfather—who is welcome at our home anytime—so he'd be closer to the children."

"Very good," Judge Benson grunted before tapping a sheet of paper. "The Rockhearts contest that, as a single woman, you are unable to bear the responsibility of caring for the children. There is also some mention of your being sickly?" He looked her up and down as though searching for visible signs of illness.

"I recently had an emergency appendectomy," Grace admitted. "But to call me sickly would be an insult to the many people who bravely live with chronic health problems. As far as my single status, I have a strong community support system in Lasso and Lawton, as evidenced by the character witness statements on record."

"And you are aware that the children are entitled only to Social Security benefits since their parents passed on without a will?"

"I've known that from the start." She shrugged. "It's not important."

"Thank you, Miss Willard." Judge Benson gave a small smile before addressing the children. "I've only one more question for each of you. Lizzie, who would you like to live with?"

"Auntie Grace." Lizzie didn't hesitate for an instant, though she held Jake's hand in a viselike grip. She beamed at Grace before glancing at the Rockhearts and frowning.

Grace heard a murmured "Well!" from Celine and bit back a smile.

"Jake—" Judge Benson didn't even get a chance to repeat the question before Jake burst out.

"Auntie Grace!" He, too, frowned at the Rockhearts.

"This is where I'd normally adjourn for deliberation, but in this case, I see no need to." Judge Benson looked around the courtroom. "Some of the finest parents I know raise their children alone. Elizabeth and Jacob Willard may not be the daughter and son of Grace Willard, but it is apparent she is raising them as such. It is the opinion of this court that a professional nanny is a poor substitute for that kind of familial love and support. In addition, it does not please the court to move the children from yet another home. It is my ruling that Grace Willard be named legal guardian to both Elizabeth and Jacob Willard." He banged his gavel. "Court is adjourned."

Cheers erupted in the courtroom as Uncle Carl, Eric, Mary, Dylan, Sondra, and the entire crew of the Curly Q clapped and hugged each other. Lizzie and Jake broke away from their court-appointed representative to give Grace a huge hug, which she returned wholeheartedly.

Thank You, Lord, for giving me my family. Her prayer was short on words but filled with emotion. Everyone had left before them, giving them a moment's privacy.

"Are you ready to get out of here?" she finally asked them.

"Yeah." Jake beamed.

"Let's go home." Lizzie swung her arm around her brother's shoulders.

As they exited the building, the crowd parted to show Eric, down on one knee, with a ring box in his hand. Grace froze, overwhelmed.

"Get goin'." Carl gave her a nudge after disentangling Lizzie and Jake.

"Eric?" Grace walked the few steps to meet him.

"Grace." He looked up at her with adoration in his brown eyes. "Now that you can be certain it isn't to win the court case, that I'm proposing because I love you and can't spend another day without you, I want to know one thing." He flipped open the lid of the box to reveal a sparkling engagement ring. "Grace Willard, will you do me the honor of becoming my wife?"

"Yes!" She didn't wait for him to put the ring on her finger, instead kneeling down to embrace the love of her life. He kissed her deeply before slipping the ring on her finger.

"You've made me the happiest man on earth," he whispered.

"It's not me." Grace smiled as Lizzie and Jake broke free from Uncle Carl's grasp to join their hug. "God brought our family together."

"And I'll be forever thankful."

Epilogue

Two weeks later, Nickels stood at the altar of the church as the wedding party made its way slowly down the aisle.

Dylan walked beside Sondra, the two smiling at each other as if they were remembering their own wedding. Lizzie followed, resplendent in her dark green dress, carrying a small basket of roses. Walking beside her, obviously counting his steps, Jake balanced the ring-bearer's pillow. When they reached the front, Nickels grinned at them, and they grinned back. Lizzie pointed to her basket, and he saw Nibbles poking his head out of the flower arrangement. She took her place near Sondra, whose dress couldn't quite disguise the fact that she was very pregnant now.

Nickels barely had time to wonder whether the hamster had been freshly bathed for the occasion before the organ music swelled, heralding his bride.

The doors of the sanctuary opened to reveal his Grace walking toward him on the arm of her uncle Carl. Her white gown moved with her in fluid folds, her thin veil offering only glimpses of her features. The crowd oohed and aahed as she passed by their pews, but she looked straight ahead—at him.

When Carl placed her hand in his with a benevolent smile, Nickels felt as if he'd come home. Together they turned to face the pastor and exchange the vows that would bind them for all eternity.

"Dearly beloved," the preacher began, "we are gathered here today to witness the union of this man and this woman in holy matrimony. If there be any reason why they should not be wed, speak now. . . ."

No reason here. Not anymore. Looking into his bride's radiant face, Nickels knew he had come full circle.

Years ago I entered this church looking for salvation. Now I know God has granted me so much more. Although I'm unworthy, He's blessed me beyond measure through His grace.

KELLY EILEEN HAKE

Life doesn't wait, and neither does Kelly Eileen Hake. Kelly received her first writing contract at the tender age of seventeen and arranged to wait three months until she was able to legally sign it. Since that first contract five years ago, she's reached several life goals. Aside from fulfilling fourteen contracts ranging from short stories to novels, she's also attained her BA in English Literature and Composition and earned her credential to teach English in secondary schools. Currently, she is working toward her MA in Writing Popular Fiction.

By His Hand

Dedication

This story is dedicated to my husband, Albert.
You've been my Prince Charming for nearly two decades.
My heart still pitter-patters when I see you.
I still care about what you think and feel. I still want your very best.
After all this time, you still hang the moon.
Through thick and thin, we've learned what love truly is—
a First Corinthians 13 kind of love. Wow, how I praise God for you.
With that said, how could I keep from thanking and praising my Abba?
Praise You, Jesus. Your mercies never end, and they never fail. I love You.

Prologue

There is a time for everything,
and a season for every activity under heaven.
ECCLESIASTES 3:1

Disinfectant couldn't mask the stench of iodine mingled with other un-identifiable odors. The mixture stung Victoria Thankful's nostrils and brought tears to her eyes. She looked at the hospital bed. She had never seen anyone like this, but this was her brother.

Kenny's practically lifeless body lay still. Stitches raced from the left side of his forehead over his nose and finished at the right corner of his lips. Both eyes were black and swollen from the impact to the windshield.

"Hey, Bubby," she crooned his pet name since childhood and patted his arm. "I'm waiting for you to open those eyes and look at me."

Heavily drugged, Kenny had only spoken a few times over the last three days. He needed rest, but the doctors still wanted him to talk to her every few hours in an effort to keep up his spirits.

"I sent Grams home. She was needing a shower." She swatted her hand before her nose and laughed at her own joke, hoping it would conjure a smile from her brother.

He didn't move. *I'm sure he's sleeping.* She glanced at her watch. It had been two hours since he'd spoken to her. In that time, she'd swallowed down a day-old deli sandwich and finished an Algebra II test one of her friends had brought by the hospital.

A nurse opened the door. "Your parents are on the way."

"Thank you." Victoria sighed in relief and looked back at Kenny. "Mother and Daddy have come back from Europe early. I know they're anxious to see that you're all right."

Victoria glanced down at her clothes. Her mother would disapprove of the sweatshirt and jeans. She walked to the sink and peeked in the mirror. *She's not going to like my hair all pulled back in a ponytail either.*

Walking back to her brother, she wasn't worried about outfits and hairstyles. She only cared about Kenny and seeing him healed and healthy.

"Sis?" His weak voice pushed past barely open lips. He opened his eyes slowly and turned his palm up, inviting her to grab his hand.

Bubble gum stuck to the roof of her mouth. The raspy weakness of his voice still struck her hard. Pushing her hand past tubes and wires, she tried to ignore the machines' protesting beeps at having been jostled. She forced a smile.

"Do we know"—he swallowed—"how bad it is?"

"Let's not worry." She winked and sat in the chair beside his bed. "It's going to be okay."

It wasn't okay. She knew medicine and doctors could fix a ton of ailments and injuries, and she believed anything was possible with God. Still, it didn't appear it was going to be all right at all.

"So tired." Kenny closed his eyes.

She squeezed his hand. "I'm here for you, Kenny. We'll get through." Fear lurked around her, waiting for her to succumb to it. *Give me strength, Lord.*

"Doctor," her father's voice boomed from outside the door. "I'll pay whatever it takes. You make him perfect."

"Your son is in guarded condition. We are doing the best we can. His accident was serious."

Victoria jumped up. *There's no telling what Daddy will say.* She wiggled her hand past the tubes and wires then made a beeline for the door.

"I'm sure you know the Thankful name," her father continued. "I want only the best—everyone, everything. No cost spared. Make him perfect."

"Money isn't the answer to everything. This is a back injury. No amount of money. . ."

"It would have been better if he had died," her mother whispered.

Victoria forced the door shut. She looked at her brother. His eyes were closed, and she prayed he hadn't heard her mother's response. Victoria made her way back to him. She touched his leg and remembered he couldn't feel it. She walked back to the top of the bed, leaned over, and kissed the top of his head. "You're going to be all right."

Chapter 1

Eight Years Later

After twelve hours of chugging java to stay awake, Victoria finally spotted the specific road sign she'd been looking for. She gasped. "Forty more miles on this road! I'm never going to get to Lasso, Oklahoma."

Resting against the leather seat of her Suburban, she glanced at the photograph taped to her dashboard. The boy's shining eyes and chubby cheeks made her smile. "You look so much like your daddy." She ran her finger over his brown ringlets, remembering the last time she'd seen her brother before his fatal accident. His hair had been in desperate need of a trim, and Victoria had teased him mercilessly about it. "Kenny would have been so proud of you, Matthew."

At midmorning, the flat, green land stretched as far as she could see. An occasional farmhouse, barn, or silo dotted the expanse. Cattle clustered inside the never-ending barbed wire. *I'm definitely not in Houston anymore.* Oklahoma was full and alive in a different way, and its serenity beckoned her.

She yawned and started to roll down the window to allow wisps of fresh air to wake her up. Bubble gum and fast-food wrappers swirled through the cab. Grabbing for her directions and the photograph, she popped the window back up. *What was I thinking?*

She pushed the disheveled papers off the passenger seat and laid the directions in their place. *No way am I getting lost. I'll fall asleep for sure if I have to drive one moment longer than necessary.*

Course, I'd fit just fine if I needed to take a nap in this horse of a car. Daddy would never see to reason on allowing her to get a smaller, more economical car. Ever since Kenny's accidents, one paralyzing him and the other taking his life, Daddy had bought only the biggest and best of every model. "He never considered what gas would cost, though, did he?"

She gripped the steering wheel. *I don't even have the means to get back to Texas if I need to.* She cringed when she thought of the penthouse, finely decorated in the sleekest of styles, that she'd left behind. It had been Daddy's idea to fit her in the best of everything while she finished her degree. She couldn't afford any of it now.

God has not equipped me with a spirit of fear. She lifted her chin. She would not be afraid. Money was not the answer to everything. God was.

245

She braked at a stoplight. She smiled as she read the wooden road sign aloud. "Welcome to Lawton."

"One more turn, then sixty miles to the small town of Lasso. . .and to Matthew." She opened her visor mirror. "Ugh. These freckles." She hated them. They made her look much younger than her age. She grabbed her compact from her Gucci bag and powdered her nose and cheeks. "There."

She turned on the radio, hoping she could pick up a Christian radio signal out here in the middle of nowhere. "Yep. That's where I'm at." She patted her steering wheel. "My whole life is in the middle of nowhere." She looked up at the boundless, blue sky above her. "I'm a clean slate, Lord. Whatever You want. Wherever You wish." The reality of it made her smile. . .and tremble.

"That little sister of mine is determined to put me six feet under," growled Chris Ratliff as he finished buffing the candy-apple red hood of his pride and joy, a restored 1973 Corvette. After grabbing a clean, white cloth from his back coveralls pocket, he wiped off the rearview mirror. "You, my Mary Ann, will never make me crazy."

As a boy, he and his dad spent many an afternoon watching reruns of *Gilligan's Island*. Both agreed Mary Ann to be their favorite character. She had been the true beauty with her natural good looks and sweet, giving nature. When his dad gave him the beat-up car for a graduation present eight years ago, he knew she could be named nothing but Mary Ann.

"I said I was sorry. Promise, I didn't mean to."

Chris glared at his sister, Abby. She shoved both hands in her jeans pockets. The plaid button-down shirt she wore hung much too big on her—which made sense. It belonged to him. With her mousy brown hair pulled up in some sort of funky knot with pieces sticking out around her head, she looked like she'd stuck her finger in a light socket. For the life of him, he wasn't sure if she meant to look that way or if she just didn't have a clue about how to brush hair. He didn't know the first thing about it.

Seventeen, hardheaded, difficult, and an overall nuisance, Abby was his to raise. Even after she'd slammed into the mailbox with his work truck, he still loved her and wouldn't want her anywhere else except with him.

Well, maybe not at the moment. "Abby, you get back in that house."

"Brudder." She stuck out her bottom lip.

Oh, brother. Abby always pulled out her childhood name for him when she knew she was in trouble. Admittedly it usually worked. This time he needed to be firm. "You know you didn't have permission to drive it. Go on back in there until I decide your punishment."

"Fine, Chris." She spat out his name, emphasizing the *s*. "Just remember I was goin' to the store to get some milk for breakfast." She strode back to the house and slammed the door.

Chris knew he should go after her and make her apologize, but it was hard. Growing up, he and his sister bickered back and forth. Mom and Dad had been the ones to separate, scold, or paddle them for misbehavior. Less than two years had passed since their dad had died and only a year since their mom left. *I don't know how to be her guardian, Lord. I'm her brother.*

He sulked to the garden, grabbed a bucket from beside the scarecrow, and picked tomatoes from the vine. Most of them were still green; nothing had ripened for picking, but he had to do something. Had to think.

No, he needed advice. He needed to talk to someone who would know what to do. Someone he could trust. He smacked his thigh. *I know. I'll run out to the Wards' ranch.* Snapping off a few more tomatoes, he threw them in the bucket figuring Sondra could make fried green tomatoes or whatnot with them.

He walked back to the house and stepped inside the mudroom. Grabbing his keys off the counter, he hollered, "Abby, I'll be right back. You get lunch going and don't leave this house."

"Fine!"

Fury pulsed through his veins. He shouldn't let her talk to him like that. *If I say something now, I'm sure I'll regret it later.*

He stalked to his car, jumped into Mary Ann's driver's seat, and revved the engine. The growling *purr* sent a calm through this veins. *Now here's a girl a guy can relate to.* He pulled out of the driveway and headed to Dylan and Sondra's ranch.

Extra cautious with his prized treasure, he stopped at the first intersection as the light turned yellow. *I just can't seem to do it, Lord. I don't know what to do with Abby.* Flipping the radio on, one of his favorite country gospel songs sounded from the speakers. The words of God's faithfulness were a soothing balm to the anger and frustration lit in his heart, reminding him he was not alone. *Thank You, Lord.*

Mentally he processed the chords and notes playing from the guitar. This song was perfect for his church's worship team. He'd already ordered the sheet music and could hardly wait until it arrived at Lawton's Christian Bookstore.

He glanced in his rearview mirror. A Suburban bounded toward him. His heart began to pound. "No!" He gripped the steering wheel. "Please, oh, please, no!"

Metal crunched against metal.

Chapter 2

Victoria pushed the air bag away from her chest and face. Fanning the dust particles away with one hand, she coughed and opened the door. She scampered out and looked at the smaller car in front of her.

Please, God, don't let the driver be hurt. Memories of Kenny's beaten body lying in the hospital bed replayed in her mind. She froze. *Please, God, make the driver come out.*

Nothing.

She inched closer to the little car. Her heart pounded. *Move, Victoria. The person may need help.* Tears welled in her eyes. She'd nearly passed out when she'd seen Kenny the first time. She couldn't handle blood. She hated pain.

The door flew open, and a man stepped out with no apparent injury. *Thank You, Jesus.* She let out her breath and swiped at her eyes with the back of her hands.

"No!" The man blazed past her and stared at the back of his car.

"Oh, my." She cupped her hands across her mouth. The impact had broken off the bumper and smashed the whole rear end of the little red Corvette. She didn't know much about cars, but she knew Corvettes were a good kind. Her daddy had one, once upon a time, and Thomas Thankful owned only the best of everything.

She looked at the front of her Suburban. The silver-rack-thingy had dented a bit, but that was the extent of her damage.

"I'm sorry, sir." She peeked down at the overgrown, spitting image of the blond guy from *The Dukes of Hazzard.* Only this man's hair had a red tint to it. He even dressed the part with his mechanic getup covered in grease stains. She wrung her hands together. "I'm glad you're all right. I can't believe I was so careless."

The man stood to his full height, and she nearly swallowed her gum. He towered over her like a daddy to his toddler. Pointing to his chest, he growled, "I'm fine." His jaw set, and he looked anything but willing to accept her apology. He pointed to the Corvette. "Look at my car."

Victoria coughed back the need to duck her head, hide under the asphalt, and enjoy a good cry. She straightened her shoulders. The fault belonged to her, but she didn't need to fall apart. "I'm sorry."

He glowered at her, his eyes big as silver dollars. Disdain covered his face as he scanned her up and down.

Victoria's confident stance faltered. She shifted her weight from one foot to the other. "My insurance will cover it, I'm sure."

By now a crowd had formed. Heat rose up her back. *Stay calm.* Once her embarrassment reached her shoulder blades, it was all over; her neck and cheeks would be a blotchy mess.

"Mary Ann," the man whispered.

"I didn't hear you, sir." She leaned closer to him; then she noticed one of the men on the sidewalk pointed at her and the car as he whispered into a young girl's ear. Two women stood to the left of them whispering at each other and shaking their heads.

The driver walked away and stood, shoulders slumped, next to the other side of the Corvette. He shoved both hands into his coverall pockets, and she took a few steps toward him. He knelt and picked the bumper off the ground. "Mary Ann."

"Sir, my name is not Mary Ann."

He glared at Victoria as if she'd grown an extra pair of eyeballs, a nose, and an additional head. "Mary Ann is my car." The words spat from his lips much like Daddy's elaborate sprinkler system shot water all over their plush lawn at midmorning and early evening.

"Oh." She stared at her hands. She'd heard of men naming their cars but never understood the notion. "I *am* sorry."

"Do you have any idea how many years I've worked on this car?"

His words were a whisper. Surprisingly, they didn't hold anger. It was pain, and she felt them with more force than a slap to the face. Her heart beat faster. *Help me, Lord. What do I do? What do I say?*

People chattered around her. She could hear them asking who she was and where she was from. "I'm sorry." She couldn't look at the man. The tone in his voice, the slump of his shoulders, everything about him made her feel as though she'd committed a terrible crime. "I know my insurance will pay. . . ."

The screeching of a siren drowned her out. The car stopped, and a sheriff stepped out. "What's goin' on here?" The man hefted his gun belt higher onto his waist.

"She hit Mary Ann."

"I can see that." The sheriff scraped his jaw and shook his head. "She was lookin' mighty good, too."

"I've been standing here trying to convince myself she was just a car."

"And I'm sure the lady didn't aim to hit ya."

The driver shook his head and exhaled a long breath. "All that work."

That was it. She couldn't handle any more. *The Dukes of Hazzard* fellow looked as if he planned to give the eulogy at his mother's funeral. It was a car.

It was an accident. There had been no injuries. Her insurance would, without a doubt, pay for the repairs.

"Mister, Sheriff, I'm truly sorry. Can we please hurry on with the report?" She glanced at the still-whispering crowd. "I'd like to get to my sister-in-law's house before lunch."

The sheriff pushed back his hat. "Oh sure. I just need your license, registration, and proof of insurance." He addressed the other man. "Yours, too, Chris."

She walked back to her Suburban, leaned through the passenger window, and popped open the glove compartment. She dug through paper after paper looking for her registration and proof of insurance. "Where are they?" She grabbed the whole pile and laid it on the passenger's seat. Going through one piece at a time, Victoria felt heat rising up her back once again.

"Having a bit of trouble?"

The sheriff stepped next to her. Her shoulder blades burned, and her stomach turned. "I'm just trying to find. . . Here it is." She picked up the registration and handed it to him.

"Yep." The sheriff grinned. He already held the man's papers in his hands. "Now all I need is your license and insurance."

"I know." Victoria shuffled through manuals, maintenance lists, and other papers. The murmurs of what had to be the entire town made her hands shake. Placing the last piece of paper in the glove compartment, she exhaled and smacked the side of her hip. "I can't find my insurance."

The sheriff smiled. "Don't worry 'bout it. Just give me your license. I will have to cite you for no insurance, but just as soon as you provide proof to the judge, everything'll be fine."

"Judge?" The vein in Victoria's right temple throbbed.

"Just a formality. Don't worry 'bout it one bit."

Victoria opened the passenger's door. "Do you mind if I sit down a minute?"

"Course not."

She climbed inside then closed her eyes and leaned back in the seat. What did a real judge look like? The only ones she'd ever seen were the ones on television, and they were often angry and exasperated with the people before them.

Just don't think about that right now. All she had to do was sit a few moments and wait for the sheriff to fix up the paperwork. The leather rested cool against her neck, easing her discomfort a bit.

"I still need your license, ma'am."

Victoria sat up. "I'm sorry." She scooped her purse off the floorboard and rummaged through it. "It's right here in my wallet." She pulled the fuchsia accessory from her bag and snapped it open. Her ID wasn't where it should have been.

"Oh no." Dread filled her as she remembered not being able to find it when the grocery store's cashier asked for it a few weeks before. She thumbed through each card, willing, praying for the card to reveal itself.

"What's the matter?"

The driver had obviously grown tired of waiting. Victoria begged to be awakened from this nightmare as she went through each card in her wallet.

"She can't find her license," the sheriff responded, "or proof of insurance."

Giving in, she leaned back against the seat. "I lost it a couple of weeks ago."

"Then why were you looking for it?" The sheriff folded his arms in front of his chest. His expression transformed to one not so forgiving.

"I—I just hoped maybe I had overlooked it."

"I'm sorry, ma'am. You're driving without a license or proof of insurance. You've caused a wreck." He shook his head. "I'm going to have to take you down to the jail until I can figure out your identity."

"No! Please, my name is Victoria Allison Thankful. I'll tell you anything you want to know. I've lived in. . ."

"You any relation to Sondra Ward? Her name used to be Thankful."

"Yes, yes. She used to be my sister-in-law. I'm here to visit."

"Well, now"—the sheriff smacked his lips together and winked—"we can just give her a call, verify that you're who you say you are, and we'll get you on your way."

"Thank you."

"I hate to do it, but I'll still have to cite you and impound your vehicle."

"What? But how will I get to Sondra's farm?"

"How will I get Mary Ann fixed?"   —

She glared at the man the sheriff had called Chris. How could he think about that car at this moment? Her life had already collapsed into pieces; now the pieces were shattering.

She dug the cell phone from her jeans pocket and grabbed the stationery from the seat. Dialing Sondra's number, all she could think of was getting away from the crowd and this man. The phone rang. It rang again. *Please pick up. Lord, please let Sondra be there.*

"Hello." Sondra's voice sounded through the phone, and Victoria sighed in relief.

"It's Victoria." She swallowed, realizing anew how little she and Sondra knew of each other. "I rear-ended a car."

"What? Victoria, are you all right? Was anyone hurt?"

"We're all fine, but I can't find my license or proof of insurance." Perspiration beaded on her forehead. In any other circumstance, Victoria would have never called Sondra for help. They barely knew each other. "The sheriff is taking my Suburban."

Victoria swallowed the golf ball that had formed in her throat. She couldn't begin to fathom what her one-time sister-in-law must think. Why would Sondra want to help a Thankful anyway? The family had been nothing but cruel to her.

"Oh, honey." Sondra's voice sounded smooth as silk and filled with compassion.

"He wanted me to call you to prove who I am."

"Whas madder, Mommy?" Victoria could hear the concern in her nephew's voice. She wanted so much to scoop him up and squeeze him in a big hug. She needed a hug, too.

"Everything's fine, PeeWee. Go check on your sister. Victoria, let me talk to Troy."

"Who's Troy?"

"The sheriff."

"Okay." Victoria handed him the phone. She waited as Troy smiled and talked to Sondra as if nothing had happened.

He gave it back to her. "She cleared you. I'm sorry, but you still can't have your vehicle."

Focusing on staying calm, she put the phone back to her ear. "Sondra, I'm embarrassed to ask, but is there any way you can pick me up?"

"I don't have a vehicle, Victoria. My van's in the shop, and Dylan took the truck to check on some cattle."

"Oh."

"Who's there besides Troy?"

"Uh, everyone who lives in this town is gathered on the sidewalk, and the man I hit—I think Troy said his name was Chris."

"You hit Chris's car?"

"Yeah."

"Mary Ann?"

What is up with this car? "Yeah."

"Let me talk to him."

"What?"

"Just let me talk to him. Everything will be fine."

Victoria walked toward the man who still knelt at the rear end of his car. "I'm sorry, but my sister-in-law would like to talk to you."

He stood and took the phone. "Yeah. . .yeah. . .okay. . . okay." He handed the phone back to her. "She'd like to speak to you now."

Victoria grabbed the phone with one hand and twirled her diamond stud earring with the other. The whole ordeal had set her head to pounding in what Victoria felt sure could be considered a migraine, or at least the beginning of one. "Sondra?"

"Chris will bring you to the ranch."

"What?" She looked at the overgrown man who had turned toward Troy. Victoria watched as the sheriff nodded his head to whatever Chris had said to him.

"I can't ride with him."

"Yes, you can. Trust me. He's a great guy. I'd come and get you in a heartbeat, but I can't."

"But. . ."

"Trust me. You'll be fine."

"But he hates me."

"Chris Ratliff hates no one." A crash followed by crying sounded over the phone. "Gotta go."

Victoria pushed the OFF button on her cell phone and glanced toward her ride. Chris stood with both hands shoved in his pockets. His eyes glazed and his jaw set in a hard line when he looked at her. Lifting one side of her mouth in an attempted smile, Victoria gave up the notion, walked to her Suburban, grabbed her purse, and popped open a bottle of pain reliever. She swallowed two tablets, struggling to push them down her seemingly swollen throat. Begging God to keep her from getting sick, she noted the scowling expression on Chris's face. Victoria felt confident that Sondra had no idea what she was talking about.

⁓⁓⁓

"Buckle up." Chris tried to sound nonchalant as he clicked his seat belt. He'd had to put his bumper in the back of Troy's cruiser as there wasn't enough room in Mary Ann for it and that gal's suitcase. Two more gigantic pieces of luggage remained in the back of her Suburban. The same two pieces he had offered to pick up and take to the ranch after he dropped off the young woman.

Is this some kind of test, Lord? His frustration with Abby had not even minimally subsided when this lady slammed into his car. Now he was chauffeuring the Mary Ann Mangler and a third of her belongings to the Wards' ranch. It didn't help matters that they were a good half hour away. He turned onto the one-lane road that could be named the longest driveway in the history of driveways. *I don't have the patience of Job.*

A glob of bird dropping hit his windshield. *Perfect. The day can't get much better.* He pulled Mary Ann to the side, opened the door, yanked his handkerchief from his back pocket, and wiped off the mess. Folding the remains into the center of the handkerchief, he carefully shoved it back into his pocket. He slid into the driver's seat and looked at his passenger peering over the suitcase resting in her lap. Her jaw had dropped, and her eyebrows had risen. Chris shrugged. "Just habit. I've been cleaning and shining this girl for eight long years." He patted the freshly oiled dashboard.

"You've fixed this car up for eight years?"

"Yep. She was a high school graduation present from my pa. It took me awhile to buy all the parts she needed."

"How long have you had it fixed?"

"Couple months."

She gasped. He peeked at her. She had lowered her head. "I'm truly so sorry."

Chris felt as though his heart would split in two. He knew she hadn't purposely caused the accident, and she had been so worked up about not having her license and insurance. Not that he blamed her.

He had to admit she was quite a cutie. Long, dark brown curls were pulled back in a ponytail, even though a few pieces had escaped and touched her cheek. Her profile showed the sweetest, little button nose he had ever seen. She was probably a few years younger than he, and he had to admit under different circumstances he might have taken a second look her way. "It's all right."

"No, it's not. I'll—I'll pay you back. Promise."

"We'll work it out." He started his car. In all honesty, though, he wondered what would happen if she didn't have insurance. His insurance would pay for the repairs if he wanted, but then his rates would probably go up to more than he could afford. Unless she had money.

He glanced at her again. She did seem to wear rather spiffy clothes. She smelled awfully good, too. If his memory served him right, Sondra's deceased husband had at one time been fairly wealthy. It seemed like his parents had disinherited him when he married Sondra. If that were true, then this lady probably did have some avenues with which to pay him back. *Then why wouldn't she have insurance?*

Of course she'd have insurance. Lots of people couldn't find the proof when they needed it. Chris shook his head. He sneaked another peek. Her head was down, her eyes closed. She seemed to be praying. Something inside him stirred, compelling him to make her feel better. "Don't worry about that citation of yours."

She looked at him; fearful innocence wrapped her face. "I've never even seen a judge."

"Henry's soft as a new puppy. You've got nothing to worry about. Show him your license and insurance, and he'll thank you and send you on your way."

"With a fine?"

Chris shrugged. "I don't know. Probably."

"That's what I thought."

She wasn't going to have insurance or cash flow. Chris could feel it. Eight years. After eight long years of fixing up Mary Ann, he'd have to stick her back in the shop and work on her a little at a time. He didn't want to think about it. Didn't need to think about it. More than anything, he just wanted to get home, eat some supper, take a hot shower, and go to bed. The sooner this day ended, the better.

Chapter 3

Victoria smiled as the trees cleared and Sondra's ranch came into full view. The country home screamed of serenity and coziness. "I'm so excited to meet my nephew." She twisted her purse handle around.

"You haven't met PeeWee?"

"Mother and Daddy wouldn't have any. . . Well, it's a long story."

The front door burst open. A small boy toddled out followed by Sondra holding a baby girl on her hip. Matt clapped his hands and danced around the porch. Before Chris had time to turn off the car, Victoria hopped out and ran for her nephew. She scooped him in her arms and twirled around. He squealed in delight.

"He's not afraid of me!" Victoria exclaimed as she nestled him closer to her chest.

"PeeWee isn't afraid of anyone"—Sondra laughed—"but he's been waiting for you to come. I've been showing him your picture on the refrigerator."

Happiness filled Victoria's spirit, and she hugged Sondra with her free arm. "Thank you." She turned back to her nephew and tickled his belly. "It's so good to see you"—she gazed at Sondra, willing her to fully forgive her for the years of silence—"all of you."

"You stay as long as you like. I'm glad you've come."

"Aunt Vic." Matt poked Victoria's shoulder.

"He knows my name?"

"Oh yes." Sondra tickled Matt's belly. "PeeWee's a smart boy, aren't you, PeeWee?"

"Boy." Matt pointed at himself.

"Yes, you are." Victoria ran her fingers through his small locks of brown hair. "You look just like your daddy."

"Daddy!" Matt squealed and leaned away from Victoria. She turned and saw a tall cowboy walking onto the porch.

"There's my little man." The cowboy took Matt from Victoria's embrace.

"Victoria, this is Dylan." Sondra pointed to the man Matt had called Daddy. A twinge of pain pricked Victoria's heart. Kenny was Matt's daddy, not this man. She tried to push the thought aside. Kenny would want Matt to be raised by a man who would love him. According to Sondra, Dylan was a wonderful Christian man.

"Here's your bag."

Victoria turned to find Chris standing on the front lawn holding her suit-case. "I'm sorry, Chris. I'll get it."

"No, I'll take it." Dylan grabbed the bag before she could. "Swap." He handed Matt to her. Victoria hopped back onto the porch before her nephew had time to protest.

Sondra chuckled. "Come on, everyone; let's have a glass of iced tea."

"I can't stay." Chris jingled his keys and nodded toward Victoria. "I'm going to get her other two bags and bring 'em to the ranch. Then I oughta get back to Abby."

"No need to," said Dylan. "I'm going to put this suitcase in Victoria's room and then head right into town and pick up the others."

Victoria held Matt a little tighter as heat rushed up her spine. "I'm sorry for all this inconvenience."

Sondra shook her head. "Don't you worry. I needed Dylan to run to the store anyway." She turned to Chris. "Tell Abby I said to be good."

Chris grunted then nodded. "I sure will."

Victoria wondered at the odd tightness in her chest when Sondra mentioned the woman's name. She watched as Chris walked back to his car, slid inside, and then drove away. "Abby's Chris's wife?"

Dylan's boots clanked against the porch, and the door slammed as he went into the house with her suitcase. Victoria felt Sondra staring at her. Her question had come out a little more inquisitive than she had meant it to sound, so she adjusted Matt's shirt and avoided Sondra's gaze. She didn't care if Chris was married. Why would she?

"No, Abby's Chris's seventeen-year-old sister. He takes care of her."

Victoria gawked at Sondra. "Really?"

"Yeah. The girl's a little rough around the edges. Not a bad kid, really, but she gives Chris fits most of the time."

Victoria laughed. "I bet being raised by him gives Abby fits, as well."

Sondra seemed to ponder the notion. "I guess you're right. She probably needs a woman's influence." Sondra winked and walked through the front door.

Victoria didn't know if Sondra tried to imply anything, and she didn't want to think about it either. The last thing she needed was to worry about a rough-around-the-edges teenage girl.

Snuggling Matt closer, she kissed his cheek and walked into the house. It looked nothing like Victoria had imagined. Rustic femininity. Aside from the sippy cup and toy horses on the floor, Victoria felt as if she'd walked into a *Country Living* magazine. It felt so nostalgic, so homey.

"Not a four-story mansion, huh?"

Victoria jumped at Sondra's voice. "No. It's wonderful."

Cocking her head, Sondra seemed to study her. Finally she smiled. "Would you like a glass of iced tea, or do you want to unpack first?"

"I think I'd like to go ahead and unpack."

"Sure thing." Sondra pointed down the hall. "Your room is the first one on the left. Dylan's already put your luggage in there."

"Thanks." Victoria put her precious nephew on the floor next to his horses. "I'll be back to play with you in just a minute." She caressed his chin. *I wish I had seen him as a newborn, held him, kissed him, spoiled him.* She sighed and then stood. "Thank you, Sondra, for letting me come. I wish..." Victoria's voice cracked, and she knew at any moment she'd have to allow herself a good, long cry.

"Get yourself on to your room. I'll get the tea, plus a batch of cookies I just made up. Unpack a bit, and then we'll talk."

Victoria nodded and headed down the hall. *Sondra is a wonderful person. Mother and Daddy were wrong. So wrong.*

✦

"Tell me that you did not burn lunch." The stench of burned eggs filled the room. Chris waved his hand through the layer of smoke above the stove. He peered into the living area connected to their kitchen and saw Abby lounging in the recliner with her back to one of its arms and her legs draped over the other. She wore her fluffy house shoes that were caked with mud from tromping back and forth to the garden. Instead of stomping the mess off outside or even in the mudroom, clumps of earth had fallen on the floor beneath her feet.

"Hang on a sec." Abby covered the phone with her hand. "I didn't aim to, Chris. The phone rang, and well, I've been cleaning it up."

Chris glared at the partly scraped skillet sitting in the sink. Abby hadn't even put soapy water in it. She'd just left it there. He supposed she thought animated farm animals came in and cleaned up irresponsible teenagers' messes. "Get off that phone."

"But..."

"Now." The fact that she had the audacity to be talking on the phone after driving the truck without asking, smashing the mailbox, and burning lunch made Chris's blood boil.

"I gotta go. My brother's about to flip out on me."

Chris gritted his teeth. He had every right to be angry with her, yet she continued to be openly disrespectful and didn't seem to care a bit.

"One year, and I'm gone." Abby clicked off the phone and folded her arms in front of her chest. "Go ahead. Lay it on, *big brother*. It ain't like I meant to burn the eggs."

That was it. He'd had it. "Abby, you are grounded for a month. No TV. No phone. No friends. Nothing."

"But, brudder..."

"No buts."

"You're going to ground me the summer before my senior year?" Her voice resonated calm, controlled. Chris had learned this tone, the let's-talk-reasonably one that somehow always seemed to land Abby with whatever she wanted.

"Yes, I am."

"Now, brother, let's be reasonable." She spoke softly as she turned on the kitchen faucet. "I will clean this up a bit, and then we'll talk."

Chris did not miss the sarcasm that dripped from her lips. She intended to manipulate the situation in such a way that he became the bad guy. He pressed his car key against his lips, allowing its coolness to keep his temper in check. "You will clean this up, but you are still grounded."

"Now, Chris. . ."

He shook his head. "I'm not changing my mind, Abby."

She huffed, and her lips formed a straight line. He could see she was about to lose her composure when she smacked the countertop. "You're just. . .just an overgrown meanie."

"And you're still grounded." He walked out of the house and slammed the door. He wasn't even hungry anymore. Stalking to the garage, he pulled a paper and pen from his coveralls. He'd just assess the damage to Mary Ann. If he never saw another female in his life, that would be too soon.

❧

"I'm too tired to unpack." Victoria flopped on top of the bed. She stared at the stucco, flower-looking pattern on the ceiling. Exhaustion claimed every inch of her being. The very thought of putting her clothes and accessories away seemed incomprehensible.

She willed herself to sit up on the bed. *I don't have to do everything today. Talk to Sondra, yes, but unpacking can wait until tomorrow.* She opened her suitcase to freshen up her makeup and brush her hair before going to the kitchen. Her license fell onto the bed. "I can't believe it."

Picking it up, she remembered Ms. Ginny had found it underneath the microwave when she was cleaning. She had given it to Victoria just before she left for her new job. Upset about losing the woman who'd been working for the Thankful family since before Kenny's birth, Victoria simply pitched it in the suitcase and hugged the dear, older woman one last time.

"If I don't get my head on straight, I'll never be able to take care of myself." She peered in the mirror above her new dresser. Curly wisps had escaped her ponytail. Most of her makeup had worn off from the long drive. She looked like she was about sixteen. Grabbing her hairbrush, she pulled the elastic band out of her hair and brushed out her curls. She covered her freckles with powder again. "That's a little better."

Straightening her shoulders, she lifted her chin and stared at her reflection. "You can do this." The knot tightened in her belly as she opened the bedroom door and walked down the hall. She had a lot to talk about, and she had no idea how her sister-in-law would react. "Sondra?"

"In here," Sondra called from Victoria's left.

"Hey." Victoria felt shy as she joined her sister-in-law at the massive wooden table in the kitchen/dining area. True to her word, Sondra had cookies and iced tea waiting for her.

"I went ahead and laid the kids down for a nap. I wanted us to have a chance to talk."

"Okay." Victoria's heart sank. She wanted so much to play with Matt, yet she knew they needed to have this time.

Sondra pointed to the plate. "Have one. Is chocolate chip your favorite just like your brother?"

"Yeah. Grams used to make them for us." She took a small bite and gasped. "Sondra, these taste just like Grams's."

Sondra smiled. "I know. They're her recipe. She taught me how to make them for Kenny while we were dating." She looked Victoria in the eye. "I loved your brother very much."

Victoria gawked at the woman sitting across the table from her. Tears welled in Victoria's eyes. Why had she waited so long to come here? She knew why. Fear. Fear of her daddy disowning her just as he had Kenny. Fear of not being able to make it on her own.

And what did all that fear get me? The last weeks of Kenny's life—missed. The first two years of Matt's life—missed. A real relationship with her sister-in-law—missed. *Forgive me, Lord. I should have trusted in You. Bless my relationship with Sondra and Matt now.*

Victoria wiped the tears from her eyes. "I'm sorry I missed all this time with you."

Sondra touched the top of Victoria's hand. "It's all right. We can start now. I'm glad you're here." She leaned back in her chair. "Seeing you brings a wave of sweet memories to my mind. I still miss Kenny at times."

"What about Dylan?"

"I love Dylan completely. Kenny was a part of my life. He still is, in the form of his son. My life and heart are committed to Dylan, but I still remember and love your brother." Sondra stopped. "Kenny would approve of Dylan."

Victoria nodded. "I believe you're right. He seems to be a wonderful man."

Sondra smiled. "Okay, now that that's cleared, how long are you going to visit? Victoria, we want you to stay as long as you can. . . ." She touched the top of Victoria's hand. "But I don't want to make things hard on you. If your dad wants you home, don't worry about hurting my feelings. I understand. . . ."

"You don't have to worry about that."

Sondra's eyebrows furrowed. "I don't?"

Victoria shook her head and tried to conjure the courage to tell Sondra the truth. *Just spit it out.* "Sondra. . .well. . .it appears I can stay as long as you'll have me, or at least until I can get a job and an apartment."

"What?"

Victoria twisted her napkin between her fingers. The stunned expression on Sondra's face did not make telling the truth any easier. Victoria had lived her entire existence in an abundance of wealth. Admitting her state of destitution proved far more difficult than she had imagined. *Get on with it.* "It seems my daddy hasn't always managed his affairs in completely legal ways."

Victoria's tongue stuck to the roof of her mouth. She took a long drink of tea. She couldn't taste it; she only felt the cool liquid flow down the back of her throat. No matter how many gulps she took, she still felt parched.

"Just tell me. You'll feel better once it's out."

Victoria set the glass on the table. "You're right." She swallowed. "It seems Daddy embezzled a good deal of money from his company. He claims to be innocent, yet he and Mom flew to who-knows-where to get away from the law."

She closed her eyes. She couldn't look at Sondra. "Everything belongs to the government until Daddy goes to court. What I have with me is all I own in the world." Her bottom lip quivered. "I have to make it alone. I don't have any money. Now I've hit a man's special car. I pray my insurance will take care of it."

Victoria felt Sondra's arms wrap around her. "I want you to stay with us for as long as you need. I don't want you to even think of going anywhere else. You are welcome here."

Fresh tears streamed down Victoria's face. The day had been entirely too emotional. The long drive only aided her exhaustion and feelings of helplessness. Victoria hugged her sister-in-law in return. "Thank you, Sondra. I wish I had come years ago. I wish I could turn back time."

"The past has passed. We have today and all of the tomorrows the Lord gives us."

"That's true. . ."

A man cleared his throat behind her. Victoria wiped her eyes with a napkin as Sondra looked around her and said, "Hi, Chris. Back so soon?"

Knowing her face was a blotchy mess, Victoria prayed he would leave quickly so she wouldn't have to acknowledge him.

Metal jingled in his pocket. "Dylan called. Seems Jeff needed some help on the ranch right away. He asked me to go and get Victoria's other suitcases for him."

Victoria closed her eyes and exhaled. She would have to turn around and talk to him. He would see the red blotches she knew covered her eyes like a raccoon. He'd see the freckles that splattered her face. If her guess was right, he'd also see mascara streaming down her cheeks. *Why did I have to start crying?*

Knowing etiquette demanded she thank the person who had just made a special trip to bring her luggage, she turned and stood slowly to face Chris. Looking up at the towering figure, she nodded and said, "Thank you, Chris. I'll show you where to put them."

He followed her to the bedroom. She stood in the door as he placed both suitcases on the floor. Her heart beat faster when their gazes locked through the mirror above the dresser. He didn't turn to face her but continued to stare in the mirror.

"Did I scare you?" His voice was barely audible.

"What?"

"Earlier today. Did I scare you?"

"No." She frowned. "Why would you think that?"

"I'm big, and I can come across as gruff; I can see you've been. . ."

"Crying." Victoria finished his sentence. "No. That has nothing to do with you." Embarrassment washed over her, but she couldn't take her gaze from his. Something about the overgrown, grease-covered man drew her. She wanted to tell him all that had happened. Wanted to hear him say that everything would be okay.

She peered out the window. *What is wrong with me?* She didn't know this man, not the first thing about him. For all she knew, he was a horrible criminal. *No, Sondra wouldn't have let him bring me to her house if that were true.*

She glanced back at the mirror. He still stood looking at her. She lifted her chin and pushed away from the door. "Well, thank you, Chris."

He moved closer until he loomed more than a foot over her. "You're welcome."

Her chest tightened, and Victoria felt she'd soon be gasping for air. She lifted her shoulders and took long, slow breaths, willing herself not to come undone in front of this stranger. "Be sure to let me know how much I'll owe you for the damages."

"Oh, I will."

Victoria stepped away from the intensity of his gaze. He walked down the hall, nodded toward Sondra, and then went out the door. Victoria grabbed her chest, watching as he took long strides toward his truck. She had no idea what had just happened, but she felt fairly confident that whatever it was it wasn't good.

Chapter 4

A hint of sunlight streamed through Victoria's window. Glancing at the alarm clock beside her bed, she gasped at the early hour. She slipped out from under her covers and slinked into her robe and slippers. Stretching her arms above her head, Victoria yawned and then rubbed sleep from her eyes. She stumbled to the window just in time to see the sun finish its ascent into the expansive heavens. *Oh, Lord, Your handiwork is amazing.*

Deep green pastures extended as far as she could see. The sky lifted bright and full above her. It reminded her of the enclosure and privacy she felt as a small girl when she would make a fort with extra blankets from her closet, and yet the sky was not in any way private. It was vast and clear and awesome.

The bedroom door creaked open. Sondra stuck her head inside and smiled. "You're up. Great! I came to see if you wanted to gather eggs with me."

Victoria smiled and tried to imagine what gathering eggs could possibly be like. Would she have to touch the chickens? Victoria had always heard they were quite disgusting creatures, but then most animals were a bit on the yucky side. "Sure, but what does a gal wear to gather eggs?"

Sondra giggled quietly. "On a warm day like today, a gal wears a pair of shorts and a T-shirt." She wrinkled her nose. "Course, the chickens just might be offended if you don't match."

Feigning hurt, Victoria rested her hands on her hips. "Are you making fun of me?"

"Yes. Now hurry before the kids wake up, and I'll show you around the ranch."

Victoria grinned and shut the door. She unzipped her suitcase and rummaged for a pair of casual shorts. "Note to self," she murmured as she tossed one article after the other onto the bed, "I must unpack first thing after breakfast." She picked up a silk shirt and wrinkled her nose. "And find some ranch-appropriate items." Sighing, she decided on a pair of jean shorts and a designer button-down shirt. *At least I have some old tennis shoes.* After scooping them up from the closet floor, she put them on, tied her shoelaces, and hopped off the bed.

The thought of being around live, squawking chickens made her stomach churn, but she had determined to make the best of it. In truth, part of her was excited about learning the life of a country girl. Walking to the window, she glanced once more at the chunk of nature that lay all around her. She spotted the pigsty and its enormous inhabitants and snarled. *It's a small part of me, that's for sure.*

Victoria walked out of her bedroom and down the hall. Too tempted to just pass by, she peeked into Matt's room. Her precious nephew lay in his toddler bed holding a small, flannel-squared blanket close to his face. *Kenny had a favorite shirt that color.* She touched the corner of her mouth. *I wonder. . .*

Tiptoeing closer to Matt, she noted how his small blanket had been hand-stitched and not store-bought. Softly brushing his cheek, she whispered, "I'll have to ask your mommy." She sighed at how peaceful he appeared. Quietly closing the door, Victoria tiptoed down the hall and out the front door.

A warm breeze whipped her hair, escorting with it the strong odor of cattle grazing nearby. Victoria frowned and covered her nose.

"The smell actually starts to grow on you." Sondra came from behind her.

"You scared the life out of me." Victoria placed her hand on her chest to calm her now fast-beating heart.

"Sorry." Sondra handed Victoria an empty basket and then hefted her own higher onto her forearm. "I hated the smell out here at first. Believe it or not, now I actually look forward to it when I'm coming home from town or wherever."

Victoria wrinkled her nose. "Really?"

Sondra nodded. "Yeah. It's a funny thing what living in the country will do for you after a while."

Victoria didn't respond, and Sondra turned and headed toward what Victoria assumed was a chicken coop. In actuality it looked like a rather fun, oversized playhouse. Sporting a door and latticed windows in the front, the entire building was painted white and trimmed in country blue. Sondra walked around the back and pointed to the wire-fenced "yard" for the chickens. A small ramp connected the ground and the opening of the building. Several chickens squawked around the yard.

"We have a lot of chickens." Sondra said. "I love to take the baby chicks to the Lawton Group Home to let the children hold them."

"That's wonderful." Victoria tried to count the chickens but soon had to give up due to their scurrying around. Walking back around the building, Sondra opened the door and went inside. Victoria braced herself for an attack of white-feathered beasts. To her surprise, nothing happened.

"Come on in. There's plenty of room," Sondra called.

"Actually, I have a question about Matt." Victoria grasped her basket. There was no way she intended to go inside that little building with all those creatures. Visions of chickens pecking her feet and pulling at her shoelaces filled her mind. *Can chickens fly?* Victoria shuddered as she imagined them flying around her and plucking at her hair.

Sondra opened the door wide. "What are you waiting for?" She motioned for Victoria to join her. "So what's your question?"

"Well, I noticed. . ." Victoria stopped when she saw several squares sitting three by three against the wall. Fencing seemed to separate the chickens from the humans. Slowly Victoria stepped inside. She watched as her sister-in-law unlatched and opened a section behind one of the squares.

Sondra scooped an egg from the nest. "See, not as bad as you thought." Sondra showed the egg to Victoria and then placed it in her basket. "You get the next one. Nothing's going to get you."

Determined not to act like a spoiled rich girl, Victoria swallowed and opened a second square. Pulling the egg from the nest, she held it up. "I did it." She placed the egg in her basket and commenced to collect more eggs.

"You'll be just fine." Sondra grabbed a bag of feed from beside her. Victoria watched as she filled a large can that had an opening on the other side of the fence. In a matter of moments, the chickens' feed spilled out in front of them. "So what did you notice about PeeWee?"

Victoria turned toward Sondra. "His blanket."

Sondra exhaled. "It's made from Kenny's shirts."

"I thought so."

"It's a little piece of Kenny that Matt can hold on to. When he grows older, I plan to put it away and give it to him when he's grown."

Victoria's chin quivered as her emotions threatened to get the best of her once more. "I'm so grateful for you."

Sondra furrowed her eyebrows. "What?"

"Kenny was blessed to have you, even though your time together was short. I know you made his last months wonderful."

"I hope so. I want PeeWee to know who his father was and that Kenny loved him." She looked at Victoria. "Dylan and I both want that."

"I'm glad."

Sondra hooked her arm with Victoria's. "Before we continue our tour, why don't we head to the house and get breakfast started?"

Victoria's stomach grumbled. "Sounds good to me."

Feeling as inept in the kitchen as she had in the chicken coop, Victoria did little more than watch as Sondra rolled biscuits, fried bacon, scrambled eggs, and mixed gravy. Being given the seemingly simple task of cracking eggs, Victoria had even botched that by dropping as much shell as egg into the skillet.

"You'll learn." Sondra had tried to encourage her. "Just takes time."

Victoria didn't feel encouraged. She felt like a poor excuse for a person. The things she was good at, like shopping, cosmetology, and hairstyles, were not practical for everyday, real-world living. She could hold her own at movie and television trivia, as well, but that didn't help here on the farm either.

Matt woke up, scampered into the kitchen, and wrapped his arms around Sondra's leg. "I tirsy, Mommy."

Victoria smiled at the patch of curls that fell into his eyes. He shook his head and swiped them away.

"I bet Aunt Victoria will get you a drink of juice." Sondra unwrapped his arms from her leg and pushed him toward Victoria.

"Come on, little buddy." She extended his arms, and he scampered into them. Lifting him to her chest, Victoria nestled her nose against his soft cheek. *How could I have spent so long away from you?*

"Juice, Aunt Vic, juice!" Matt grabbed a handful of hair and pulled.

"No, Matt." Sondra turned and scolded him. "Do not pull hair. Say please."

Matt frowned and stuck out his little bottom lip. Victoria thought she would melt. The child could have her hair, the whole head full. She didn't want to be the cause of his tears first thing in the morning. Victoria tickled his chin, and he smiled. "Pwease."

"A gal can't resist that." She grabbed the sippy cup Sondra had set on the counter, opened the refrigerator, and, with one arm still holding Matt, managed to pour the juice and attach the lid.

"Pretty good for a first timer." Dylan walked into the room, and Matt squealed and practically launched himself toward the man he called *Daddy*.

"Come here, PeeWee." Dylan grabbed him out of Victoria's arms and then tossed him in the air like a play toy. "You gonna help Daddy feed the horses?"

Matt giggled and nodded his head. A needle still pricked Victoria's heart that Kenny wasn't the one taking Matt to feed the horses. Logically, she was happy Matt would have a father to take care of him, but emotionally, Victoria longed to see Kenny with his son. *God, Kenny would have been such a good dad.*

"Dylan's a great dad." Sondra's words interrupted Victoria's thoughts.

"I can see that."

Sondra scooped the scrambled eggs into a serving bowl. "Did you know Dylan was with me when PeeWee was born?"

"No." Victoria transferred the fresh-from-the-oven biscuits from the baking sheet to a plate.

"He was. Dylan took care of me when Kenny couldn't. It's probably hard for you to see Dylan and Matt together, but he's proof of God's mercy and blessings to me and Matt. Even to Kenny."

Victoria gazed at Sondra. She couldn't imagine how it could possibly be a blessing to Kenny.

"Kenny wouldn't have wanted me to struggle alone."

Victoria sighed. She gazed out the kitchen window and saw Matt scampering as quickly as he could behind Dylan. He struggled to carry a sack, a smaller version of the one Dylan held. No doubt it was the feed for the horses. Even from a distance, Victoria could see Matt's happiness at getting to help his daddy.

In that instant, Victoria felt a peace, a *real* peace. Sondra was right. God had been merciful. He had blessed Sondra, Matt, and even Kenny. Matt was under the tutelage of a man who helped bring him into the world. Kenny would be happy.

"I need to tell you something, Victoria."

Victoria looked at Sondra who was wringing water viciously out of a dishrag and into the sink. "What?"

Sondra pointed to a chair. "You may want to have a seat."

"I'm okay." Bile rose in Victoria's throat. Something was about to happen. Something monumental. Again. Victoria didn't know if she could take many more surprises in her life.

"A friend of mine is in the insurance business." Sondra sighed. "I called her last night and asked her if there was any way she could find out who your dad had his insurance with."

Victoria slunk down into a chair and plastered a fake smile to her lips. "Yes?"

"My friend had already heard about your dad's, uh, situation. He's fairly well-known. Many people vied for his services." Sondra wiped splattered milk and egg drippings from the counter. She turned and eyed Victoria. "I might as well just say it. Your dad's insurance policies weren't paid up when he left the country."

"What are you saying?"

Sondra placed her hand on Victoria's shoulder. "What I'm saying is, you don't have any insurance."

⁓

Chris unscrewed the top to his truck's gas tank. After selecting the cheaper unleaded gas, he shoved the nozzle into the tank and started to fill up the truck.

"How's your car?"

Chris turned and saw Mandy Reynolds filling up at the pump beside him. "Needin' some work."

"I heard." Mandy smacked her free hand to her hip. Her two young sons in the backseat began to squabble over a toy. "Roland came home from the vet's office last night. Said he saw the whole thing and that the girl wasn't paying a bit of attention."

Chris cringed. He tried to keep a low profile in this "Mayberry" town. He hated being the topic of conversation, especially after the rumors that had gone around when his ma had up and decided to leave. He and Abby still dealt with the hurt that resulted from the townsfolk's talk.

"Virginia called me last night, too. Said the gal was just a hoity-toity, young thing. Came running through the town like she owned the place. Virginia said that girl wasn't the least bit sorry for ruining that wonderful car you spent all that time fixing up." Mandy turned toward her sons whose squabble had escalated to an all-out, fist-flinging war. "Give me that toy. Neither one of you gets it."

Chris released the handle to the pump and pulled it away from the tank. Glad he'd used his debit card, all he had to do was screw on the cap and he could go.

"I don't know who these young gals think they are these days," Mandy continued, "thinking they can go around slamming into people's cars. . . ."

"It was an accident, Mandy," Chris interrupted her. "She was sorry. It could happen to anyone." With a nod of his head, he jumped in the truck and added, "Have a good day." He started the engine and drove toward the ranch. He hoped Victoria didn't plan on staying too long. If he was having a conversation like that this early in the morning, then Victoria would have a hard way to go around here.

He glanced at the paper on the passenger's seat beside him. He'd figured a very fair—actually quite low—price. Her insurance company shouldn't have a problem with it, especially once they saw the pictures he had taken last night. The fact that he would do the labor for free should also help keep her rates down a bit.

Pulling into the ranch, he couldn't seem to get a handle on the sinking feeling that seemed to plague his gut. *Probably just the burned biscuits and undercooked eggs from breakfast this morning.* Abby had awakened still miffed over her one-month grounding, but Chris had stuck to his guns. He had spoken nicely to her but hadn't budged on the punishment.

Chris shut off the engine, grabbed the paper, and opened the truck door just as Victoria opened the screen with a coffee cup in her hand.

"Chris?" Her eyes widened in surprise. "We just finished the breakfast dishes, but I'm sure Sondra won't mind if I find you something to eat. . . ."

"I'm fine. Already eaten." Chris smiled. Either country hospitality had already begun to rub off on her, or she genuinely had a sweet turn. Taking in the truth and sincerity radiating from her light eyes and remembering her silent prayer in his car the day before, Chris decided to believe the latter assumption. "I just came to pick up the eggs for the food bank. Brought some milk, too."

Victoria frowned. "Food bank? Milk?"

"Yeah, we swap. I bring Sondra milk, and she donates her extra eggs to families in the county who need them."

"That doesn't surprise me at all. You take them for her?"

"A few years back when my pa was still living, he came up with a ministry to take the eggs to the bank, as well as distributing them to those who couldn't get out."

Victoria wrapped both hands around the coffee cup and peered into the sky. "Sounds like your dad was as giving a person as Sondra."

"Yep, true about both of them."

She glanced back at him. "But why does your truck say By His Hand on the side?"

"My sister was so excited about Pa's ministry that she wanted to give it a name. Once we decided on one, she and I painted the letters on Pa's older work truck."

The memory of his sister and him working all day one Saturday to paint the letters drifted into his mind. They'd gotten into a paint fight, and by the time they'd finished, they were covered in blue and red splotches from the tops of their heads to their toes. Abby'd had blue paint splatters in her hair for weeks afterward.

Victoria sighed, forcing Chris from his memories. "I don't know what I'd do without Sondra right now."

Unsure of where this conversation was headed and confused by the winsome tone in her voice, Chris cleared his throat and scuffed his shoes along the dirt. "Yes, well. . ."

"Anyway." Victoria placed the cup on the porch railing and wiped her hand on her shorts. Her neck and cheeks blazed red. "Can I help you load them or anything?"

"No, she always has them boxed and ready by the coop." He pointed toward the building.

"Oh." Victoria furrowed her brow. "I helped her with that this morning and didn't even realize what we were doing."

Her sincerity struck Chris as funny, and he laughed. "It's all new to you, huh?"

Victoria shrugged and smiled, exposing straight teeth, whiter than he'd ever seen. "Yep, but I'm enjoying it." Her light eyes danced as she scanned the land around him. "I think I could get used to all this. I've never seen so much green and blue in all my life."

Chris followed her gaze and wondered if he took nature's beauty for granted. Looking back at Victoria and the childlike awe in her expression, he knew he did.

"Do you think God likes blue and green the best?"

"I'm not sure."

"Have you ever noticed how so much of nature is colored in some shade of the two? I'd never realized it before."

"Can't say that I've paid much attention either." Chris smiled and stepped closer to the porch, feeling drawn to her innocence. For a moment, he wanted to see things from her eyes. He wanted to get to know her more, to find out what she was thinking and what made her think that way. He wanted to ask how her heart felt about the God he served. Could she be as sold out as he wanted to be?

She blushed again and backed up toward the door. "I'm sorry. Sometimes I say the silliest things. I better go and see if Sondra needs any help."

Knocked back into reality, Chris shook his head and looked down at the figures he held. "I also wanted to give you the estimate for fixing my car."

Her expression fell, and her eyes clouded. "O–kay."

The weight lodged in his gut again, seeming to hold his breath beneath it. Something strong and fierce told him that she would not be able to pay to fix Mary Ann, and he would spend the next two or three years raising the money to do it himself.

Sondra walked out onto the porch. "Chris, how nice to see you. Come on inside."

Chris shook his head. "I just came to bring you some milk and pick up the eggs for the food bank. Give Victoria my figures, as well." He handed the paper to Victoria. "They're low. I only put the cost of parts on there since I'll do the labor myself. Your insurance company shouldn't have a problem."

"O–kay." Victoria took the paper from him. Her eyes widened as she scanned the page.

Sondra nudged her shoulder. "You need to tell him."

Chris looked from Sondra to Victoria. Victoria's eyes welled with emotion for a moment, but she quickly blinked it away. Something in him longed to touch her cheek and tell her everything would be all right. He shook his head. He didn't even know the woman, except that she was a disaster waiting to happen. And he could sense the wait was about to end. . .again.

❧

Victoria glanced at her sister-in-law.

"Just be honest with him. He's a great guy," Sondra whispered. She turned to Chris. "I've gotta check on the kids. I'll let you two talk."

Victoria glanced at Chris. The snarl on his face compared to that of a bulldog. She just couldn't quite see the "great guy" Sondra kept talking about. Every time Victoria spoke with him, it was under a large amount of tension. Admittedly, tension caused by her, but it made her nervous nonetheless.

"So what's going on?" Chris said the words with what could only be described as vehement dread.

Victoria inhaled and straightened her shoulders. She would not feel inferior to this man. The accident was her fault. Her circumstances were not. She would do what she could, in whatever way she could, to make things right. After all, she had the Creator of the universe to turn to for guidance, and He never failed her. She smiled. "Would you like to have a seat?" She pointed to one of the rocking chairs on the porch. Lifting her cup, she added, "Maybe a cup of coffee?"

Chris frowned, and the snarl deepened. *The Dukes of Hazzard* hunk had transformed into a red-eyed bull whose gaze targeted on her. Victoria looked down to see what she'd chosen to wear this morning. Noting the crimson color, she wished she'd chosen more calming attire.

"No, thank you. Just tell me what you have to say."

He did add a "thank-you" to the "no," which encouraged her. Maybe he would take her news better than she'd anticipated. *Just spit it out and get it over with.* "It seems I don't have insurance. My daddy didn't renew our policy, and I didn't know it."

Chris lowered himself into one of the rocking chairs. He closed his eyes and exhaled. She watched as his Adam's apple bobbed up and down in an effort to control what he must be feeling.

Okay, so maybe he's taking it exactly as I expected. She sat in the chair beside him.

"All those years. All that saving," Chris mumbled.

"I am sorry. I'll do whatever I can. . . ."

"Are you?" Chris's eyes opened, and he sat up straight. "Well, that's wonderful. You come storming into town, smashing my car with no insurance, but you're nice and sorry." He stood and stomped off the porch. "I'm *so* glad you're sorry."

Victoria jumped out of the chair and walked to him. She stood to her full height even though he still towered over her. Lifting her chin, she glared at him. "I will still pay for your *precious* Mary Ann."

"That's good. It's the least you could do. After all, it's your mess. . ." He pointed at his chest. "And I'm fixing it."

"Go on home, Mr. Ratliff." Victoria stomped away from him. Reaching the porch, she turned to face him. She touched her finger to her other palm. "The money is as good as in your hand."

Chris jumped in his truck, growled with the engine, and drove away.

She bit the inside of her lip. "Now how am I going to go about doing that?"

Chapter 5

Victoria looked away from the pawnshop owner and down at the ring one last time. It had been a priceless treasure to her grandmother. Her grandfather had died before Victoria was born, and Grams had often told her stories of their courtship.

"My daddy used to chase your grandpa off the porch each time he came around." Victoria could hear Grams's voice and her tongue clicking as if she were in the room with her.

"But your grandpa would come back the next day anyway." She had laughed. "Used to drive my daddy crazy."

Victoria would nestle into her grandmother's lap and close her eyes as Grams combed her fingers through Victoria's hair. "But your grandpa and I were crazy in love."

Victoria touched the small, round diamond resting in a square setting. Smaller diamonds made their home on each side. In truth, the ring wasn't much to look at, but it had always been precious, first to her grandmother, and since her death, to Victoria.

"You know, I really don't mind loaning you a little money to help get you started," Dylan leaned over and whispered in her ear.

Victoria flashed a smile at the oversized cowboy. He'd really grown on her in the last few days. "I can't let you do that."

"Pride isn't always a good thing, Vic."

Victoria sighed, gazing back at the ring. "It's really not about pride. I've never had to work for anything. Never had to lose anything." She peered up at Dylan. "I'm spoiled. I always have been. I don't know if I can fully explain it to you, but I have to do this on my own."

Dylan wrapped his arm around her shoulder and gave her a quick squeeze. "You're all right, Vic. You're gonna be just fine."

With that, Victoria quickly handed the ring to the pawnshop owner and grabbed the offered money off the counter. "You'll keep my ring for one month, before anyone can buy it?"

"Yes, ma'am." The man smiled, exposing a missing front tooth. He didn't appear like someone to be trusted, according to every television program Victoria had ever seen, but Dylan promised that the man ran a legitimate business.

"Are we ready?" Victoria forced a smile.

271

"Whenever you are."

"Let's go." Victoria turned toward the door and bumped into an even larger figure. "Oh, excuse me." She glanced at her feet and tried to walk around.

"Victoria, what are you doing here?" She looked up at the sound of the familiar voice and watched as Chris extended his hand to Dylan. "Well, hello, Dylan."

Victoria exhaled and crossed her arms in front of her chest. *This is just great.*

<hr>

"Dylan, I don't reckon I've ever seen you in here before." Chris shook hands with his friend. "You don't play any instruments on the sly, do you?"

Dylan shook his head and waved his hands. "Oh no."

"Buying some jewelry for Sondra?" Chris glanced at Victoria. Her eyes had doubled their size, and she appeared as if she might keel over. "You okay?"

"Just running some errands," answered Dylan. "So what are you doing here?"

"Looking at guitars." The color in Victoria's face returned. He wondered if he'd scared her when he stormed off the other morning. He probably needed to apologize. Never would he want a woman, or anyone for that matter, to be afraid of him. "Victoria, I'm sorry if I scared you the other day."

"Vic's all right. She's a tough ol' gal," added Dylan.

Chris frowned at Dylan. He was acting mighty strangely. Glancing at Victoria, Chris smiled. "You go by Vic?"

She shrugged and half smiled. "PeeWee gave me the name."

"I'm not sure if you look like a Vic. You're young. Innocent. With a bit of fire." Her eyes widened, and Chris laughed. "Yeah. I guess it suits you just fine."

Victoria lifted her chin. "So what was it you said you were doing here, Chris?"

He gazed down at his guitar and the music papers in his hand. "I love to sing worship at church, but my guitar has just about given out. It'd still be good for someone who likes to fiddle around a little bit, but it won't make it much longer being used three times a week and then whenever I feel a drawing to her in the evenings."

"Does your guitar have a name, as well?"

Chris laughed out loud. "As a matter of fact, she does." He lifted the guitar toward Victoria. "Vic, this is Belle. Belle, this is Vic. I'm sorry you won't get to know each other much as I'm getting ready to trade in Belle, but you've been introduced just the same."

"Do you trade in your girls often?"

"Not the ones worth keeping." Victoria's neck and cheeks turned crimson as she looked away. He hadn't meant anything by his words. Did she think he spoke of her? Chris drank in her whole image, as well as considered her fiery spirit that mingled with sincerity and truth. If Victoria Thankful was anything, she was definitely worth keeping. "I don't think that came out. . ."

"Well, there you have it." Dylan interrupted. He grabbed Victoria's arm. "We best get going. Sondra's expecting us back soon."

"Okay." Chris waved, feeling confident he'd made a total fool of himself. "I'll see you at church on Sunday. Hope to see you there, Vic."

Dylan and Victoria walked toward the door. She leaned closer to him and whispered, "What did he mean by that?"

Dylan shook his head. "Not a thing, darlin'. Don't go overanalyzing the things men say. Sondra makes me crazy when she does that."

Chris closed his eyes at the overheard conversation. He had hurt her feelings, but there was nothing he could do about it now. Frustrated, he turned and walked to the counter. "Hey, Vern. My guitar needs a bit of updating. Think we can make up a deal?"

"I'd reckon." The man pointed to the guitars hanging on the wall. "Pick out what you want, and we'll see what we can do."

Chris selected the one that would suit his need but wouldn't be too expensive. He set it on the counter and counted out the amount Vern wanted for the trade. "I was wondering. . . ." He handed the money to Vern. "Did that man and woman who were just in here buy anything?"

Vern shook his head. "Nah. She just wanted to pawn a ring." He sighed. "She had a hard time parting with it." He handed the change to Chris. "If people would learn to pay with cash instead of credit, they wouldn't have to give up the treasures they love." The man clicked his tongue. "Course, then I wouldn't be in business."

Chris placed the change in his billfold and put it in his back pocket. "Could I see the ring she brought in?"

"Sure." Vern grabbed a tray from underneath the counter.

Chris picked up the ring. It was actually kind of small, not something he would have expected Victoria to wear. *Why would she want to pawn this small ring?*

"That little ring there is actually worth a nice piece of money. It's a perfect diamond, and they don't make settings like that anymore. Sure, someone could try, but there's detailing to it that proves the ring's age."

Chris put the ring on the tip of his pinky finger.

"Said it was her grandma's," Vern added.

So it was important to her. Chris didn't understand his need to help the woman who had banged into his life and turned it upside down, but he couldn't deny the desire was there. Each time he peered into her honest eyes, he wanted to confess a million feelings, though he still couldn't quite put his finger on what they were. "How much do you want for it?"

The man shook his head. "I promised her I'd keep it a month, and you know I'm a man of my word."

Chris picked up his guitar. "Yep, you are, and I'm glad of it."

"Tell you what I can do." Vern slid a piece of paper and a pencil in front of Chris. "Give me your number, and I'll give you a call if she doesn't get here in a month."

Chris grinned. "I'd appreciate that."

⌒⌒⌒

Victoria walked through the door and scooped her excited nephew off the floor. "I miss you, Vic."

"I missed you, too, PeeWee."

She hugged him close, inhaling the sweet baby-shampoo scent that lingered in his soft brown curls. "Where's your mama?"

Matt struggled for her to put him down. She did, and he grabbed her hand, pulling her toward the kitchen. "Come. I sew you."

"So how'd it go?" Sondra sat Emily in her high chair and belted her in. She popped open a jar of bananas and grabbed a baby spoon from the drawer. "Oh, I forgot her bib. Will you get one for me?"

Victoria took one from the drawer and fastened it around Emily's neck. Leaning over, she gave her a kiss on her cheek before the child's face became a World War II battle zone covered in mushy bananas.

"I think I got enough to get my Suburban back, pay for three months of insurance, and even cover the court expense. Hopefully it will be small."

"That's wonderful." Sondra opened her mouth to coax Emily to do so, as well. When she did, Sondra shoved a spoonful inside. Emily laughed as she blew it back out. "The little stink. She thinks this is a game."

Victoria laughed. "It is." She sobered and sat in a chair beside her sister-in-law.

Sondra wiped Emily's mouth. "What's wrong, Vic?"

"I can't pay Chris."

"Dylan and I will be happy to loan you the money."

"You know I can't take it." She folded her arm over the back of the chair and gazed out the kitchen window above the sink. "I thought God wouldn't give us more than we can handle, and, Sondra, I just don't think I can handle any more."

"Nope." Sondra popped a glob of bananas in Emily's mouth and smacked her lips together in an effort to get her little one to do the same. Instead Emily giggled and allowed the mush to run down her chin. Sondra groaned. "That's not what the Bible says."

"What?" Victoria turned and gawked at her sister-in-law. "Yes, it does. I remember reading it." She watched as Sondra made the spoon into a mock airplane and zoomed it around Emily's face until it landed in her mouth.

"Nope. The Bible says that no temptation will be greater than what we can bear because God is faithful." Sondra scraped the bottom of the jar and popped the last bite of banana into Emily's mouth. "It's in First Corinthians."

"Are you saying Chris is a temptation?"

Sondra laughed. "Not exactly. Chris is a wonderful Christian man. Just talk to him. You two can work something out."

Victoria stood and walked to the kitchen window. She believed with all her heart that God was faithful, and as far as Chris being a temptation went. . .well, she was tempted to run away from the Dukes of Hazzard look-alike and never acknowledge him again. But she couldn't do that. She had to face him, even if he sure seemed bent on loathing her. She peered outside and watched a hog wallow in the mud. She huffed. *Sure, Chris and I will work this out, when that pig grows wings and flies.*

Chapter 6

Come here, Victoria. There's someone I'd like you to meet." Victoria scanned the crowded church lobby in the direction of Dylan's voice. She found him standing beside another man.

"Great," she mumbled between clenched teeth as she made her way toward them. "I hope he's not playing matchmaker."

"Victoria, this is Zack Bradshaw. He's one of the loan officers at our bank."

Victoria sucked in her breath. She needed to find a way to pay back Chris, but she wasn't ready to take out any loans. At this point, she didn't even have a job. Forcing a smile, she extended her hand. "It's a pleasure to meet you."

"The pleasure is mine. I hope this doesn't seem too forward. . . ."

Oh boy, here goes.

"Dylan was telling me that you're looking for a job. One of our tellers is going on permanent maternity leave." He laughed. "She'll *need* to stay home since she's having twins. But, anyway, I'd like to invite you to come by the bank and fill out an application."

Victoria could hardly believe what he said. A *job*. He was offering her a job.

"I have it on good authority"—the banker leaned closer—"that you'd have a good chance of getting the position, seeing as I do the hiring and Dylan's given you a gleaming recommendation."

Victoria stared up at Dylan, appreciating him more each moment she knew him. "Thanks, Dylan."

Glancing back at Zack, she took in his light blond hair sporting just the right length in a trendy hairstyle. His tailored gray suit spoke of the time he'd spent in the gym as well as being proof of his professional status. He wasn't an overly big man like Chris and Dylan. In truth, he was just the right size for her to drink in the light gray flecks shimmering in his pale blue eyes. Maybe a little matchmaking wouldn't be all that bad. She swallowed the excitement bubbling inside her and nodded. "I'll be by first thing in the morning."

"I'll be watching for you." He winked, and Victoria thought her heart would melt. The man couldn't have been much older than thirty, and who cared about an eight- or ten-year age difference anyway. She surely didn't. It had to mean something that his size and coloring fit the faceless groom she'd dreamed of so many times after watching her favorite fairy-tale shows as a young girl. She could almost hear birds chirping their approval in the background. Biting the inside of her lip to squelch a giggle, she shook her head. *I have got to get a grip.*

Maybe God had brought her to this small Oklahoma town. After all, He worked all things together for good for those who love Him. He could turn the bleakest situations into something beautiful. Maybe He wanted her to meet Zack Bradshaw. *And what a nice, solid name.*

She lowered her gaze. "Well, I'd better find Sondra and tell her the good news." She nodded and walked away on shaky legs toward the hall she hoped led to the nursery where she and Sondra had dropped off the children before Sunday school.

Looking down at her light blue slacks and matching slip-on, heeled shoes, she smirked. "My wardrobe is definitely more fitting for a woman who works at a bank instead of a ranch." Excitement mounted within her as she thought of what Sondra said about God giving her what *He* could handle. Victoria knew that God was handling everything.

⌒∞⌒

"Abby"—Chris motioned for his sister to follow him down the church hall—"we need to have a talk." He stopped a little ways before the nursery and turned to face her. I-don't-care-what-you-want reeked from her posture and expression, and Chris squelched the desire to put her over his knee and paddle her. "You whispered with your friend all through church."

She huffed and crossed her arms in front of her chest. "Did not."

"I watched you, Abby. You did." He glowered at her old jeans with a hole in one knee and her long-sleeved, green T-shirt that she had cut holes in the bottom of each arm for her thumbs to fit through. A dark blue, tighter T-shirt had been pasted over that. Her hair, pulled back in that same weird band, had pointy brown wisps sticking straight up and out all around her head. She looked more like a person going to a rock concert or just stepping out of bed than someone who'd just come from God's sanctuary to worship. "Abby, I know you're already grounded for a month."

She snorted. "Yeah, big brother, so whatcha gonna do now?"

He thought for a moment. What could he do now? He didn't have any experience raising children. Abby was only nine years younger than he, and they'd spent their lives bickering like siblings. He'd never been a caregiver type to her. Until last year. "Next week, you're sitting with me."

Her mouth dropped open. "You're kidding, right?"

Chris shook his head, feeling pretty good about the discipline he'd just thought up. The punishment should fit the crime. You talk in church; you don't get to sit by the person you talked with in church. Maybe he could do this parenting thing after all. "Not kidding. Next week you can sit with me, and if it goes well, I'll let you sit with your friend the week after that."

Abby smacked her hand to her hip. "This is a big joke. I can't wait until I'm eighteen, *Dad!*" She popped her hand up to cover her lips. "Oops, I forgot. My dad died. You're just my *brother!*" She stomped away from him.

Okay, so maybe I'm not going to be writing any child-rearing books at this point. He raked his hand through his hair and then scratched his jaw. "Abby, come back here."

She waved him off. "I'll be in the truck. Silent. Like a good little girl."

"Having some trouble?"

Chris looked behind him and found Sondra holding PeeWee's hand with Emily firmly planted on her hip. Her purse and a baby bag hung haphazardly off her shoulder. "I think you're the one having some trouble. Let me take something." He reached for the bags, but instead she handed him the live, wiggling bundle. Emily cooed and grabbed at his hair.

"That kid loves to pull hair." Sondra flipped several wisps behind her shoulder. "I'm going to have to cut mine short if I don't get her broke of that and quick."

"It's just fascinating to her, that's all." Chris tickled under her chin. She giggled and blew slobber bubbles at him. He wrinkled his nose and wiped her mouth with her bib.

Sondra laughed. "She's already insolent, a complete handful. Must be the way of women, even from the very beginning."

Chris caught the teasing tone in Sondra's voice and looked at her. "Abby's going to be the death of me. I don't know how to parent her."

"I can see that." Sondra pushed Emily's slipping shoe back up onto her foot. Emily protested and tried to kick it off again but failed. "Abby needs a woman in her life."

Chris thought back to a time somewhere around ten years ago when Abby had sat on the floor in front of the couch while their mom brushed her hair. She would count each stroke and say that Abby's locks grew softer with every one. "The woman who should be doing this ran off a year ago."

"I know that's hard on you both." Sondra grabbed a pacifier from the baby bag when Emily started to fuss. Popping it into the baby's mouth, she asked, "Have you heard from your mom?"

"Not a word. Not even an idea if she's still alive."

"I am sorry, but maybe there is someone who could help Abby grow into a young lady. She's a good kid down deep. We both know she loves the Lord."

"Do we? Most times I don't see any proof of the Lord in Abby's life."

Sondra picked up Matt who had begun to get fidgety standing in the hall. "Think of what she's like when she's helped me at the group home. She loves to play with the children and the baby chicks." She hefted Matt higher on her hip. "Remember how good she was with Lizzie and Jake before Grace came home from her mission trip and took custody of them. Abby's just struggling right now."

Chris remembered a week before when he'd seen Abby reading her Bible late in the evening. She'd had the purity book her Sunday school teacher had purchased for the teenagers, as well. Later he'd noticed she'd scribbled several notes along the sides of one of the pages. Not wanting to invade her private thoughts, he closed the book and put it on the dresser in her room. Chris sighed. "I don't know who would be good for Abby. I don't even know who has the time. Sweet Mrs. Nielson has tried to reach out to her, but Abby wouldn't really open up."

"She doesn't seem to open up to me either." Sondra chuckled when Emily started to whine and rub her eyes. "It may have something to do with my constant interruptions." She set Matt back on the floor and took Emily from Chris's arms.

"Maybe we should pray about it."

"That's a wonderful idea." Chris watched as Sondra's eyes widened, and she nodded her head. "Or maybe God has already answered our prayers."

❧

"Victoria."

Victoria looked up just before colliding into Chris. He grabbed her arm when her heel slipped from beneath her. Once steady on her feet, she glanced up at Chris. "Sorry." Looking to her side, she saw Sondra standing beside her.

"How was church?" asked Sondra.

Victoria smiled. "It was terrific. The music was wonderful." She peeked up at Chris.

"Thanks," he said. "I've been waiting for weeks for Lawton's bookstore to get that sheet music in. It's one of my favorite songs on the radio."

"I could tell. It was as if angels sang directly from your lips. My spirit wanted to rise up and fly with the eagles in the song." She bit her lip. *What am I saying? I sound like a complete fool.* Heat warmed Victoria's cheeks, and she knew blotches would soon follow on her face and neck. She looked back at Sondra. "I mean. . ."

Sondra raised her eyebrows and grinned. "Well, how was Sunday school?"

Bless you, sweet sister-in-law, for the change in subject. "I felt an instant connection with the people in my class."

"We were glad to have you," said Chris.

Victoria forced herself to look up at him. "Thanks."

"We don't often have newcomers. Usually people leave us singles and join the marrieds." Chris laughed. "I'd be happy to introduce you to more people in the group."

"It would be wonderful for you to make more friends," added Sondra.

Chris crossed his arms in front of his chest. "That's right. One thing I've learned from Abby, girls love to chat with friends."

"Well, I did meet one new person today."

"You did?" Chris's eyebrows lifted in surprise. Something about his tone seemed to mock her. *What does he think, that I'm inept at meeting people in any way but crashing into their bumpers?* She brushed the thought away. *I'm just imagining things.*

"I think I have a job."

"A job?" Sondra and Chris asked in unison.

"Yep."

"That's great," said Sondra.

"Dylan introduced me to a man who works at your bank. Zack Bradshaw." Chris's eyebrows furrowed. "Hmph."

Victoria scowled at him. Why the man, out of nowhere, determined to set her fury wheels to spinning was beyond her. She'd never met a person who infuriated her so completely. "He asked me to come by tomorrow and fill out an application." She smiled and looked back at Sondra.

Sondra hugged her with her free hand. "That's wonderful news. You've got to tell me all about it"—she bounced Emily as the child started to fuss—"as soon as we get home. I think I'm going to have to get these kids home. Nap time is calling."

"I'll help." Victoria reached for the bags.

"No, you stay here with Chris. He needs to talk to you, too."

Victoria frowned. She didn't know what Sondra was thinking. Victoria didn't need to stay with Chris. She needed to help Sondra, to be away from Chris.

"I think God may have answered our prayers before we had time to actually mouth them." Sondra winked and walked down the hall. Before she could take two steps, Dylan had appeared and scooped PeeWee into his arms.

"Makes sense."

Victoria peered at Chris, noting the sarcasm that dripped from his words. She shifted her weight, anxious to get to the van and head back to the ranch. Something about the oversized mechanic made her uncomfortable. Not that he hadn't always treated her as a respectable man should, he just made her feel different. And it had nothing to do with the car accident. "What makes sense? What are you talking about?"

"Zack Bradshaw."

"Zack?"

"He's definitely your type."

Victoria lifted her purse higher on her shoulder and straightened to her full height. "And how, Chris Ratliff, would you know my type?"

He huffed. "It's obvious."

"I don't know why Sondra wanted me to speak with you, but I'm sure it wasn't so we could argue. Because I have no desire—"

He lifted his hand to stop her. "I'm sorry. I had no right. Zack's a great guy." He leaned his head back and glanced at the ceiling. "I'm just tired, overwhelmed really. I can't seem to get a handle on her."

Chris stared down at Victoria whose expression exposed nothing short of confusion. Why he had felt the sudden yank of jealousy at her mention of Zack Bradshaw was a mystery to him. He liked and respected Zack, and Chris definitely didn't have any interest in Victoria.

Taking in her matching blue pants and jacket, the way her hair fell curly and full at her shoulders, and the sweet, soft scent that washed over him when she was near, Chris wondered if maybe he did. He shook his head, needing to remember the purpose of this conversation, and in truth, he felt confident Sondra had a good idea. *Now to convince Victoria.*

"What are you saying?" Victoria placed a manicured hand on her hip. She seemed none too happy to have been left with him.

Chris motioned for her to walk ahead of him. "Could we talk a minute?"

"Sure." She didn't budge.

"We could sit in the sanctuary." She still didn't move. He grinned. "Or we could stand right here and talk."

Victoria exhaled. "Look, if it's about the money for your car. I know I should have gotten with you before. I need to be honest. . . ."

He lifted his hand to stop her. "I wasn't going to ask you about the money for my car."

"You weren't?"

"You said you'd give it to me." He motioned to his hand. "As good as in my hand, remember?"

Her mouth twitched. "Okay, so what are we supposed to talk about?"

Chris cleared his throat. "Well, I have a younger sister. She's a teenager. . . and our mother has been gone for over a year." He loosened his tie. "She's gotten difficult for me to handle."

Victoria furrowed her brow. "Okay, I've heard as much. What are you asking?"

"Actually, Sondra was saying that she needs a female influence. Someone who could teach her manners, how to be a lady." Chris shoved both hands in his pants pockets and studied the floor. "She must think you'd be good for her."

Silence permeated the hall. Most of the congregation had left the building. Anxious for some kind of sound, Chris jingled the change in his pocket. The cool metal had a calming effect on him, feeling good between his fingers.

"What do you think?" Her gaze bore into him with intensity.

The clear sincerity reflected in Victoria's eyes attracted him in the most basic of ways. He couldn't deny his attraction for her. Any man with a pulse would be drawn to her. "I think you'd be a perfect influence."

Victoria smiled. "Then why don't you introduce me to her?"

"Let's go. She's in the truck."

Calm down. Victoria scurried to keep up with Chris's much wider stride. *I have no reason to be nervous. The man whose car I trashed just wants me to be a good influence on his wayward sister.* Victoria exhaled, blowing stray curls away from her eyes. *How did I get myself into this?*

Scanning the parking lot, she noticed few vehicles remained. Sondra and Dylan stood on each side of the van leaning into it, probably buckling both children into their car seats. She knew the kids had to be on the verge of a complete exhaustion meltdown, so she'd have to make this introduction quick. Looking ahead of her, she noticed the aged, dark green truck occupied by an obviously disgruntled teenager.

Chris gently touched her elbow in a way that felt protective. His breath kissed her ear as he whispered, "I apologize ahead of time for anything Abby may say to you."

"Don't worry." Victoria, swatted the air as a knot formed and tightened in her gut. The attraction she felt for Chris made no sense, and she had to fight it. She focused on the truck, and as they drew closer, Victoria noted Abby's arms were crossed in front of her chest. The teen's clamped lips formed a straight line, and her squinted eyes glared out the windshield and past them, as if she were staring at the church.

Somewhere inside Victoria a giggle formed. She coughed and willed herself to squelch it, but it wouldn't go away. Feeling it wiggle its way up to her lips, Victoria couldn't shake Abby's resemblance to a younger version of Granny from *The Beverly Hillbillies* and the sour expressions she constantly wore.

"Are you okay?" Chris stopped just before the truck and peered at her.

Victoria nodded and then covered her mouth with her bulletin as another giggle escaped. She walked to Abby's door to avoid looking at Chris for fear she might burst into full-blown laughter. Victoria sneaked a peek at Abby, whose eyes squinted in defiance. The teen bit her bottom lip, and Victoria wondered if Abby had trouble holding her own giggles at bay. The expression proved too much, and Victoria laughed. Offering her hand through the rolled-down window, Victoria said, "I'm Victoria. You must be Abby."

Abby half smiled and nodded.

Victoria coughed and tried to clear her throat to settle down but couldn't shake the smile from her lips. "Look, I'll just be honest. I'm new here. In fact, I'm the gal who hit your brother's car."

"You're the Mary Ann Mangler?"

Victoria raised her eyebrows and glanced at Chris, who looked away from her but not before she noticed his face had turned bright crimson. "Yes, that's me. Well, your brother mentioned that you—"

"Dylan, did you say you need some help? I'm coming!" Chris yelled toward the Wards' van. Dylan looked up, an expression of confusion on his face. He eyed Sondra and shrugged. Chris glanced back at Victoria. "I'll be right back."

That dirty rascal. Victoria shook her head. *He just ditched me.*

"Chris can't take the heat," said Abby.

Victoria glanced back at the teenager who smiled, exposing perfect, white teeth and eyes that sparkled in merriment. "Abby, you're a beautiful girl."

"Huh?" Abby's eyes widened, and she leaned back in her seat.

Victoria pulled down the visor. "Look at yourself. You're a natural beauty. When you smile, your whole face lights up."

Abby sneaked a quick peek. "You think so?"

Victoria nodded. "Definitely."

Abby exhaled and tapped her fingers on the dash. "Okay, fine. I'll be your project."

"What?" Victoria stepped back in surprise.

"But only if you promise not to boss me around. I hate it when Chris does that. I'm seventeen years old. I'm not a baby."

"No, you're not a baby."

Victoria thought for a moment, unsure how to respond. She didn't have any experience mentoring a teenager.

"That is why Chris brought you over here to meet me, right?" Abby's tone took on a sarcastic flare. "Because I need a good female role model."

The truth shall set you free. The scripture sang in Victoria's heart. If she intended to mentor Abby, she planned to be as honest and genuine as she could be. They'd have to learn from each other.

Victoria grinned. "Yes, you're right. Beautiful and smart."

Abby nodded, and Victoria realized the teen needed her to be honest and upfront with her. "Okay. You want to come over tomorrow evening? I'm grounded, so I'll be there."

For the first time since she'd arrived in Lasso, Victoria felt needed in a way that had nothing to do with herself. Sure, she'd felt needed by PeeWee and even Emily, which was something Victoria had always yearned for. But helping Abby gave Victoria a purpose. She could shower the teen with all she knew about makeup, clothes, manners, boys. . . . Okay, maybe Victoria could use a little help in that area, as her experience had been little to none. It didn't matter. Victoria could feel that God had given her a project. . .and a friend. "Absolutely."

Chapter 7

Sitting straight and proper as she had been taught in etiquette class, Victoria clasped her hands, resting them on top of her crossed legs. The white, tiny-flower print skirt and matching bright green summer top she wore spoke of a mixture of professionalism and femininity. She had been careful to apply extra foundation to ensure coverage of the freckles that made her appear young. Taking additional precaution, she swept her long curls into a tight clip allowing only a few ringlets to escape and frame her face.

Lord, please let me get this job. And let me get my Suburban back. She thought of Sondra taking a sleeping Emily from her bed and buckling her into the car seat. PeeWee had been happy to make the trip to Lawton, but Victoria knew it to be an unplanned excursion and interruption in a busy day for Sondra. *Hopefully I'll get my vehicle back soon.*

A middle-aged lady with a beehive hairdo approached Victoria. She held a stack of folders in her hand. Her frazzled expression bespoke that the last thing the woman wanted to do was take care of a job applicant. "Mr. Bradshaw will see you now."

"Thank you." Victoria rose and gripped her bag. She glided with ease in her nude-colored heels across the carpeted floor. If Victoria knew nothing else, she knew how to conduct herself as a lady in a public setting. She could thank her mother's determination that Victoria attend every one of her etiquette classes for that. Today she hoped the training would pay off.

Walking through the mahogany door, Victoria noted the soft contemporary Christian music playing from somewhere in the room. She smiled at Zack's greeting. His entire face seemed to shine, and his eyes smiled with his lips when he saw her. As a woman, Victoria sensed his approval of her appearance. Flutters of excitement and pleasure coursed through her at the realization.

"Have a seat." He motioned to the leather chair that sat across from his oversized, mahogany desk. Scanning the room, Victoria noticed wall-to-wall bookshelves, some adorned with popular Christian books she recognized as her own favorites.

Squeaks momentarily overpowered the music as he sat in the large matching leather chair behind the desk. Glancing at her potential employer, a paneled window streamed light from behind him, giving Zack an innocent, angelic appearance. His light, masculine scent filled her senses, and Victoria couldn't deny her attraction to him.

She lowered her lashes as she obeyed his bidding to sit. "Thank you."

"Victoria, you are more than qualified for this position." He glanced at her application. "You majored in business in college and seemed to do well. Did you have any positions in mind before coming to Lawton?"

"Not really."

"Your lack of an employment history probably does hurt your job search." He furrowed his brows. "You never had any part-time employment through school?"

She shook her head, realizing Zack must not know her history. *He must be fairly new to the community.* Everyone she spoke with, everywhere she went, seemed to know her as Sondra's sister-in-law. As she thought about it, that probably wasn't accurate. Most people recognized her as the Mary Ann Mangler, as Abby put it.

She smiled at the thought. The mishap had given the townsfolk something to talk about, keeping them from thinking about her background. Maybe the wreck had been a blessing in disguise. She needed a fresh, new start. The last thing she wanted was for people to learn she was the daughter of an oil magnate who'd embezzled a large sum of money.

She remembered Chris's stunned expression when he saw the damage to his car. She thought of him jumping out of it to wipe bird droppings from the windshield, proof of how much the car meant to him. Chris would never think of the wreck as a blessing.

"What about transportation?" asked Zack. "Lasso's a bit of a drive from here."

"I should be fine. I hope to have my Suburban back very soon."

"Well, Dylan's recommendation covers any lack of experience you have, and I'm sure they'll help get you here until you get your vehicle." The young banker stood and extended his hand to her. "I'd be glad to offer you the position."

Victoria stood as well, almost wavering against the inviting scent of his cologne. She grabbed his hand, soft as her own, and realized Zack Bradshaw might just very well be the man she was looking for. "Thanks so much. When do I start?"

"Can you start training now?"

"Absolutely." Relief flooded over her. Finally, things were starting to look up.

∽∾∽

Chris touched the back of his neck. Having just gotten a haircut, he could almost feel the hot shaving cream the barber lathered on the back of his neck before taking a straight razor to it. That was his favorite part. His neck felt soft as a peach with no fuzz.

He walked over to his truck and hopped inside. Scooping up his work ledger, he made sure he had recorded his business expenses and payments correctly. He'd been busier than usual this week and planned to spend some of the extra income on parts needed to fix Mary Ann.

Of course, Abby needed a few more pairs of jeans and a few long-sleeved shirts before school started in a little over a month, so he'd have to set a bit aside for that. He tallied a second time to be sure he'd made as much as he thought. Once finished, he leaned back against the seat and looked through the windshield up to the heavens. *God, You are so good. You promised to provide what we need, but already You have provided enough for me to get some of the parts I need to fix Mary Ann.*

Smiling, Chris grabbed the checks he needed to deposit and jumped out of the truck. He whistled "Amazing Grace" as he strode along the downtown sidewalk toward the bank. A contemporary version to the old hymn popped into his mind, and he shifted his tune, mentally playing the notes on his guitar. *I'll have to try it like that when I get home tonight.*

He opened the front door to the bank. An older lady who supported herself with a cane walked through. He nodded to her and waited for her to get through before he let the door shut behind him.

Looking up, he saw Victoria and Zack behind one of the teller booths. Victoria was sitting on a high-seated stool. Zack leaned over her shoulder and pointed to something on her desk. Something stirred inside Chris.

He watched as Victoria nodded, picked up a pen, and wrote something down. A sweet expression wrapped her face as she looked back up at Zack. A knot formed in Chris's throat, and his temperature rose when Zack smiled down at Victoria.

Chris could see the words "Good job" drip from Zack's lips, and then Victoria lowered her eyelashes and gazed back down at the paper. The muscles in Chris's arms began to twitch as anger raced down them. *What is the matter with me?* Chris glanced at the painting on his left and then shook his head and shoved his fists in his jeans pockets.

I'm full-blown jealous. He glanced at Victoria, who now sat alone in her booth. She seemed busy writing something on a notepad. The green shirt complemented her dark curls and light complexion. She looked like a breath of fresh summer air. But he couldn't be jealous over Victoria. The notion was ridiculous on too many levels.

Just get your deposit done and get on out of here. It's been a long week. He walked toward her and placed his checks and deposit slip on the counter. "Hi, Victoria."

She jumped. "Chris, I didn't hear anyone come in."

"I see you got the job."

"I did." She clasped her hands, and Chris couldn't help but notice how perfect her nails seemed, how soft her hands looked. He also noted her fingers were bare of any jewelry except a small silver band on her right-hand ring finger.

She added, "And I love it already."

"That's great." All thoughts and words seemed to escape Chris. He stood looking at her, taking in that he'd never before noticed her lips actually had a kind of pouty shape to them. They were appealing and seemed to be more enticing with each blink.

She cleared her throat. "Did you want to make a deposit?"

"Yes." Chris pushed the checks and deposit slip closer to her.

"It may take me a minute." She smiled. "I'm new at this, you know."

"Take your time. I took the day off to run errands, get my hair cut, stuff like that."

She glanced up at him before turning back to her computer. "Your hair looks nice."

He felt his ears burn at her compliment. "Thanks."

She finished the transaction and handed him the receipt. "You were my first bank customer."

Chris noted the slip with the correct amount and account numbers typed on it. "Well, you did a great job."

"You know, I'm supposed to come by and spend time with Abby today, but I don't know if I will be able to."

"She'll understand that you had to work."

"It's not that. I get off at four, but I hate to ask Sondra to come pick me up, take me to your house, and then have to pick me up again." She sighed. "I'll be glad when I get my Suburban back."

"I'll be in town. Why don't you let me pick you up at four, and then I'll take you home whenever you're ready?"

Victoria peered at him. "Do you really want to do all that for the Mary Ann Mangler?"

"I'm beginning to see that the Mary Ann Mangler is a very nice woman who doesn't deserve that nickname."

Victoria's eyebrows rose. "Oh? And what nickname does she deserve?"

Chris felt his stomach knot and his chest tighten. He had to admit he was falling for her. Falling for her hard. Now he had to decide if he wanted to ignore his feelings or if he wanted to go after this girl. He cocked his head as nicknames of endearment and love filled his mind. "Fresh air," he whispered.

"What?"

He shook his head and willed his attraction to take a backseat in his brain. "Never mind. So will you come? Can I pick you up at four?"

"Sure. I'll call Sondra and tell her she doesn't have to worry about me." Victoria placed her hand on Chris's. His heart sped up with the touch, and he feared she could feel his racing heartbeat through his veins. "Thanks for trusting me with Abby."

Abby? Trusting her with Abby wasn't anything. It was the fact that she seemed to be taking hold of his heart that had him worried. "Think nothing of it."

Victoria pulled her favorite pink-grapefruit lipstick from her purse. She applied it to her lips and then smacked them together. Four o'clock had arrived quicker than she would have imagined. She rearranged the curls she'd allowed to frame her face. The clip in her hair had held tight, but she couldn't deny her longing to let her hair fall to her shoulders. She didn't know when she'd kept it up for so many hours.

After placing the lipstick back in her purse, she pouted at her reflection in the bathroom mirror. Zack had already left work for some type of meeting at another bank. Victoria had hoped to be able to talk with him more. She'd even come up with a few questions she could ask him intermittently through the day. She sighed. Her plan had been a sneaky one, and deep down she knew that wasn't pleasing to God.

I'm sorry, Lord. I don't know what to say to a man, especially one like Zack. But I don't want to be sinful or manipulative either.

Determined not to ask Zack a single phony question when she saw him the following day, Victoria walked out of the restroom and bank to see if Chris had arrived. She spied him waiting in the parking lot in his green truck. Walking over to him, she poked her head in the passenger's window. "Hey, thanks for picking me up."

"It's all right." He patted the seat. "Hop in."

She had to yank hard before the heavy door squeaked its willingness to let her do just that. Lifting one foot up to the floorboard, she grabbed the sides of her skirt and giggled. "I didn't know it was such a leap to get into this thing."

"There's a handle above your head."

"You're kidding." She looked up, and sure enough there it was. Victoria grabbed it with one hand and held her skirt with the other. With a quick hop, she pulled herself inside and slammed the protesting door.

"I didn't think about you needing a change of clothes," said Chris.

"What?"

"There's no telling what Abby will want you to do."

Victoria frowned. "Aren't I supposed to be the one influencing her?"

Chris laughed. "Yeah, and I hope you can do it. Just the same, you'd be more comfortable in jeans or shorts. Abby will probably have some you can wear."

"Okay." An uneasiness gnawed at Victoria. Surely she hadn't gotten in over her head with Abby. She leaned over and grabbed the handle to roll up the window. Having never seen one before except on television, Victoria wasn't sure exactly how to work it. The handle was stiff, but she turned it both ways until she managed to get the window to rise.

"No air-conditioning."

"What?" She gawked at Chris whose mouth split in a full grin.

"The truck doesn't have air-conditioning. You'll have to leave it down."

"Well, this should be an adventure."

"I'd reckon it will be." Chris turned the key in the ignition. It grumbled and then roared its willingness to start.

Bluegrass gospel music pealed from the radio as the inside of the cab shook like they were in the middle of an earthquake. Victoria felt as if she'd stepped out onto some newly remade *Twilight Zone* program. She grabbed for her seat belt only to have it fight her for several moments to stretch long enough to fasten into its lock.

Chris put the truck into DRIVE and pulled out into the street. Heat from the engine seemed to wrap around her feet making her start to perspire. She could feel wisps of hair slip away from her clip. Her shirt blew hard against her skin as the wind whipped all around her.

The cab jerked and bumped over every dip in the road. Her purse fell onto the floorboard, and she bent over to pick it up. As she sat up, Chris must have hit a pothole because she was popped high in the air. She gasped when her bottom reconnected with the torn, vinyl seat.

"You okay?" asked Chris.

Victoria had never felt like this. She'd never been in anything so primitive, so rustic, so nostalgic. *Okay, Victoria, you're being a little dramatic.* But she didn't care. She felt so country. . .so free. She loved it.

Grabbing her clip from her hair, she shook her curls loose and kicked off her heels. She glanced at Chris whose expression bespoke nothing short of complete awe. "This is great."

"Um. . .okay." Chris peered back out the windshield. Victoria couldn't help but notice his chiseled chin and how stubble, a much deeper red than his hair, covered it. Strong arms gripped the steering wheel, and she realized how protected she felt in Chris's presence.

She shook her head and glanced out the passenger window. The wind blew the blanket of flat, golden wheat in ripples before her. She shouldn't think about Chris and his chin or arms or anything else for that matter. A country boy/mechanic obsessed with naming his inanimate treasures after women—no, Chris Ratliff could not be the man for her. He was nothing like Zack. And Zack was perfect.

Chapter 8

What have I gotten myself into? Chris watched as Victoria hopped out of the truck and held open the door. She giggled as she ran her fingers through the tousled curly mass that sat atop her head. Her wind-kissed cheeks matched the nail polish he'd inadvertently noticed covering her toenails.

Abby threw open the screen door. "Hey, Victoria." His little sister waved at the woman who'd stolen his breath the entire trip home to come inside. "What's so funny?" Abby asked as a smile split her much-too-dark-painted lips. The first smile he'd seen in days.

Victoria glanced back at Chris. "Your brother's truck."

Abby furrowed her brows. "What?"

"That truck is great." She scooped her heels from the floorboard and slammed the door shut.

"What's so great about it?"

"It's like an amusement park ride. It bounces and turns, jerks and twirls."

Chris shook his head as he stepped out of the cab. "The lady spent a long time stuck inside a bank today." He looked at Abby and circled his finger beside his temple. "Too many hours counting greenbacks, I guess."

With her heels dangling from her fingers, Victoria stomped around the truck toward him. She lifted her shoulders and peered up at him. "I'll have you know I had a great time on my first day of work."

A long strand of hair fell in front of one of her eyes while the mass of it hung down her back. Her tiny nostrils flared in a pitiful attempt at anger. Her eyes betrayed her as they sparkled with merriment.

He cleared his throat. "I'm glad you had a good day."

"You"—she poked the middle of his chest—"were my first customer." She smiled, and her face lit up brighter than the sun peeking through a batch of rain clouds.

He brushed the wayward strand away from her eye. His fingers caressed her soft cheek. "I'm glad I was your first customer."

Her face flushed, and she touched her cheek. Chris gripped the door handle as he fought a primitive urge to scoop her lithe body into his arms and carry her off to a cave somewhere far away from civilization.

Instead he turned and grabbed his keys and the papers from his day's errands out of the truck. He shrugged at Abby as he walked toward the house. He looked

290

back at the two. "Victoria doesn't have a change of clothes. Would you mind her borrowing something of yours that's a little more comfortable?"

"Sure." She glanced at Victoria. "You're a little taller than me, but I'll see what I can find."

"Let's go then." Victoria walked to the door. When she stood beside Abby, Victoria lightly bumped the teen with her hip. Abby giggled and grabbed Victoria's hand, dragging her fully into the house.

Chris shook his head and grinned. Sondra Ward had to be the most intelligent person he knew. Victoria would be the perfect person to influence Abby.

Victoria squelched the gasp that threatened to escape when she stepped past the mudroom and into Chris's kitchen. The furniture seemed to be in good condition, but the house was a wreck. Dishes, covered in every imaginable food, overflowed on one side of the double sink. Clean dishes had been stacked just as high on the other side. *Do they even have any dishes in the cabinets?* The stove had some sort of grime coating the top. Papers and notebooks, a purse, a pile of clothes, and even a lone tennis shoe sat on the counters and kitchen table.

"Sorry 'bout the mess," Abby said as she guided Victoria past the kitchen. "I have a bad habit of dropping everything at the door." Her teen friend looked back at her, and a glimmer of pain shot through Abby's expression. "Used to drive Mama crazy."

"Oh, I don't mind a bit."

And in truth, what did it matter that the kitchen was a little disheveled? That's what she had come for anyway. . .to show Abby how to be a lady. And Victoria knew that part of being a lady was learning how to pick up after yourself. In fact, she hadn't spent too many hours of her life cleaning dishes and clearing counters—okay, she had never done any kind of manual labor in the home. Still, she always picked up after herself, and she knew *how* to clean dishes and whatnot. Surely Victoria could help Abby get on the right track.

They walked through a surprisingly clean living area. At a quick glance, Victoria marveled at how comfortable the room felt. Dark furniture circled an oversized wood fireplace. Various pictures of Chris and Abby adorned the walls. Victoria wanted to stop and look at their childhood memories, but she hurried after her protégée instead.

"Here we go," Abby said as she opened her bedroom door.

"Wow!" Victoria raised her eyebrows in surprise. Never in her life had she seen such a disaster. Tornadoes couldn't do so much damage. Clothes, wrappers, CDs, books, more items than Victoria could take in, were strewed all over the room.

Victoria shrieked, and her blood drained from her head and pooled in her feet when a small, yapping object leaped from atop a pile of clothes. Placing her hand on her chest, she willed her heart to slow down as Abby scooped the li fur ball into her arms and allowed the creature to lick her face.

"This is Sassy-Girl." She buried her face in the ball of hair. "She's my bestest buddy in the whole world." Turning to the animal, Abby's voice took on a high, childlike pitch. "Ain't you, baby? You're my precious wittle girl, ain't ya?"

The copper-colored animal yelped and wagged her tail wildly.

Swallowing, Victoria hesitantly reached toward the animal. Yaps sounded from the dog in continual succession, so Victoria gingerly lowered her hand, palm up, under the animal's nose. Sassy-Girl sniffed for several moments before her tail began to wag. She licked Victoria's palm, and Victoria had to conjure up all the effort she'd ever known not to hurl on the floor.

"She likes you." Abby squealed.

Victoria shrugged. "I guess so."

"No, you don't understand." Abby placed her hand on Victoria's shoulder. "Sassy-Girl doesn't like anyone. All my friends tease about her being the grumpiest dog they've ever seen. She doesn't even like Chris half the time."

"Hmm." Victoria cautiously reached for the dog. Sassy-Girl wagged her tail feverishly and practically leaped into Victoria's arms. "I've never had a dog, but I always wanted one." She held the animal in the crook of one arm and petted her with her free hand. "What kind of dog is she?"

"She's a Pomeranian. You can love on her any time you come over." Abby grabbed Sassy-Girl from Victoria's grasp and placed her back atop the pile of clothes on her floor. "But let's get you out of that snazzy outfit before she gets hair all over you." Abby shifted her weight from one side to the other and then crossed her arms in front of her chest. She bit the inside of her lip and twitched her mouth. "I don't think I have anything that will fit you."

Victoria took in the tiny frame of the teenager. The girl was a good four or five inches shorter than she, and though Victoria's size was on the slim side, Abby couldn't be considered anything bigger than petite.

"Hmm." Abby twirled a piece of her hair that was pulled up in a knot.

Victoria noticed how thick and lush the strand appeared. Her hair was long and dark and had potential to be stunningly beautiful. Why Abby had it tied in a ragged knot, Victoria didn't have a clue. That style, if worn too often, would do nothing but break her hair off in uneven pieces.

The makeup Abby wore was worse. The lipstick plastered on her lips smeared dark, too dark for Abby's light skin. Sure, dark-haired women often wore more bold lipsticks, but they were usually older and going to late-night events. On Abby, the color gave the impression of a girl who a law-abiding citizen wouldn't want to meet on the street when the sun went down. Her eyes were just as bad, covered in various shades of green. *Note to self: Be sure to explain to Abby that a gal should never wear eye shadow the same color as her eyes. It makes others focus on her makeup and not her natural beauty.*

Abby walked toward the bedroom door. "I'll be right back."

Victoria inhaled as she watched her young friend disappear down the hall. *And those jeans are atrocious. They do nothing to complement Abby's slim figure.* Yes, she had a lot of work ahead of her, but first things first. The two of them would need to go through the house and learn the fine art of picking up after oneself. Abby might just find she owned treasures she'd long forgotten about.

Abby walked back into the room holding a pair of sweatpants and a ragged Oklahoma State T-shirt. She lifted them up. "These are my brother's from years ago. They're too small for him now, so they may not be too awful big for you."

Victoria widened her eyes and pointed to her chest then toward the clothes. "You want me to wear those?"

Abby frowned. "If you don't mind."

Victoria forced her lips to smile. "Of course I don't mind."

Chapter 9

Ready to go?" Chris handed Victoria her purse from the cleared table. The entire kitchen had undergone an amazing transformation since Victoria arrived some four hours before. The sun had finished its descent into the earth, and Chris knew Victoria had to be exhausted.

"Ready as ever." She held her heels in her hands. "Mind if I keep these off?"

"Would it matter?"

She shook her head and flashed him a smile that nearly knocked him out of his socks.

"Then I don't mind." He walked her to the truck and opened the door for her. Shutting it behind her, he went around the front and jumped into the cab. "I wondered if we could talk a bit?"

She gazed over at him. "About what?"

He shrugged. "About you. I figure if you're going to be spending a lot of time with Abby I oughta get to know you."

Her expression lit like a match. "You don't trust me?"

"I didn't say that."

"Not in so many words, but you implied it."

"No, I didn't."

"Yes, you did."

"Are you always this angry?"

"You make me angry."

Chris sighed. "Okay, I didn't mean to insult you."

"Then what did you mean?"

"I'd just like to get to know you, that's all."

"Make sure I'm not some kind of a masked murderer in disguise? You're the one who asked me to work with Abby."

He patted the top of the steering wheel and peered out at the star-filled sky. "Look, I didn't mean it the way it sounded. I'll tell you about myself. I've lived here all my life. Always wanted to work with cars. Always. Always loved to pick my guitar and sing for Jesus, too. I get to do that every Sunday at church. I'm pretty much doing what I always wanted."

He shifted his weight in the seat. "I didn't expect to finish raising Abby. Truth is, I'm not very good at it. I pray every day God will show me what to say, what to do, how to respond. Most days I end up flat on my face begging God to show me what to do with her."

Chris cleared his throat, fearing he'd been too honest with his shortcomings. He slowed down as a small rabbit jumped across the road and into the swaying wheat.

"It's great you've always known what you wanted." Victoria's voice was almost a whisper. "I graduated college and still didn't have a clue. No reason to. Daddy had lots of. . ." She laid her heels on the seat between them. "Well, anyway, I haven't really had any life goals. I accepted Jesus several years back, and since then I've just been trying to live each day for Him."

"Sounds like a good plan."

"It always has been, until. . ." She peered at him and smiled. "It still is a good plan. I really enjoyed spending time with your sister today. She's a great girl."

"I hope you're right."

"I am." She touched the top of his hand. "Thank you for trusting me."

Chapter 10

Placing her hand in the small of her back, Victoria sat up and leaned as far back as her body would allow. The sun had risen to its peak and beat down heavier on her and the garden. She wiped beads of sweat from her brow. *I don't think I've ever worked this hard in my life.*

Since it was a Saturday, Victoria had gotten off work at noon, and Sondra had dropped her off at Chris's so she could spend more time with Abby. She couldn't deny that cleaning the kitchen and Abby's room on her previous visit had been nothing short of a blast. Abby had a wonderful, sweet spirit and a quick sense of humor. Victoria didn't understand why Abby and Chris had so many battles.

"Uh, I think that was a plant." Abby pointed at the leafy object in Victoria's gloved hand.

Victoria furrowed her eyebrows. "I thought it was poison ivy."

Abby covered her mouth with a dirt-caked hand. The black gunk had found a home beneath each of her fingernails as well as staining the creases of her fingers. Victoria frowned and wondered why the teen had insisted on attacking the garden bare-handed.

Abby giggled. "That's a green pepper plant."

"What?"

"You know. You can eat them raw or cut them up and cook them in meat loaf or chili. Some people even make stuffed green peppers."

Victoria swatted the air. "I know what they are. I just thought this looked like a poison ivy plant. Don't poison ivy stems have three pointy leaves?"

Abby nodded. "Yes, but that looks nothing like poison ivy. It's a green pepper plant." Abby smiled and pointed to the cushy-looking plant that Victoria had been unsure of what to do with. "You pulled the green pepper plant and left that?"

"I didn't know what to do with that. It looks so soft and fluffy. I thought it might be some sort of vegetation."

"It's a sticker weed."

"A sticker weed?"

"Yeah, at least that's what I call 'em. You know, it's real prickly like a porcupine."

"I suppose I should pull it."

Abby giggled again and nodded her head.

Embarrassed, Victoria grabbed the weed with all her strength and pulled.

It didn't move. She was supposed to be the one teaching Abby about becoming a lady, and yet she was humiliating herself with her total ineptness at gardening. She yanked on the weed again. The thing seemed determined to stay in the ground, so Victoria pulled a little harder. It still didn't budge. *This thing has a mind of its own.* Grabbing one piece of it, Victoria yanked until some of it came up. She'd just have to get it a little at a time.

"I kept my room clean. Kitchen, too."

Victoria looked up. A strand of hair fell into her eyes, and she swiped it away with the back of her wrist. "That's great."

"Chris was real happy about it. Said if I could keep it up he'd give me more privileges."

"That's wonderful."

"Yeah." Abby pulled a small weed and threw it away from the garden. "But it's kinda weird, ya know. Chris and I have always acted like brother and sister, not like he's my dad. Sure, he's a lot older than me, but we used to play house together. He was the dad, and I was the mom."

"Really?" Victoria raised her eyebrows in surprise.

Abby sat back on her bottom and chuckled. "I'd make him hold my babies and feed them and burp them."

Victoria laughed. "I can't imagine your big, burly brother so domesticated."

"Chris would do it until a friend came over or until he couldn't take it no more. Then we'd fight." She grinned at Victoria. "I mean, we'd really fight. We'd punch each other and roll around on the floor until Mama came and made us split up and go to our rooms."

"But he's so much bigger than you. He could have really hurt you."

"Well, that's the really funny thing. Chris was a scrawny little thing all through high school. It wasn't until after he graduated that he started growing."

"How interesting."

"Yeah, I could take him back then." Abby smiled. "Course, I don't think he ever put his real might into fighting me."

"I think he really cares a lot about you, Abby."

Abby grabbed up another weed and cast it away from the garden. "I don't know. He acts like my dad. But he ain't my dad."

"I know. He knows that, too."

"My dad was wonderful. He was perfect." Abby twirled a blade of grass between her fingers. "He used to come home from work and help Mama cook dinner. She would try to have it ready for him, but she never could quite get it done."

"Did your mom work, as well?"

"No. She had diabetes really bad, and she was always tired. She slept a lot." She paused. "After dinner, Dad, Chris, and I would do dishes. Every night. Chris washed. I dried. Dad put them away."

"Where was your mom?"

Abby looked at the grass in her hand. "Resting."

"Oh."

"Then Dad read Chris and me a Bible story. Every night." Abby paused. "I miss him so much."

"Abby, what happened to your mom?"

"She left."

"I'm. . .sorry."

Abby looked at Victoria. Her eyes filled with tears. "I don't know why she left us." She shrugged her shoulders. "I was angry for a long time, but now I just don't understand why she wouldn't listen to reason."

Victoria listened as Abby told her more stories about her parents and arguments she had with Chris. Abby needed consistency, but she also yearned for compassion and patience in her life. Though her situation was different, Victoria understood all too well the teen's feelings of abandonment and confusion.

From what Victoria had seen of Chris, she could well imagine why the girl felt exasperated by her older brother. She herself had been a recipient of Chris's frustrated words or, at the very least, words said in such a way they came across as offensive. The man also formed unusual attachments to inanimate objects.

And yet she thought about him all the time.

She plucked another weed from the garden. How did Chris feel when all this happened? He must have struggled. Surely he needed to talk to someone. Maybe he had spoken with their pastor.

Still, Abby is his responsibility. He's already admitted the trouble he has relating to her. He has to see to more than just her physical needs.

Abby leaned over and wrapped her arms around Victoria. "Thank you for listening."

Victoria squeezed and then released Abby. "You're a wonderful young lady, Abby. You can talk to me anytime."

"Let's get this garden done so we can order some pizza."

"Sounds good to me." Victoria grabbed what she hoped to be a weed and pulled it out of the ground. *I think Chris and I need to have a little talk.*

Chris tapped the steering wheel to the tune of the music he planned to play at church the following morning. His day couldn't have been any longer—or any worse. Everything had gone wrong. He'd lost his favorite wrench, hit his head on the hood of a car, spilled a tub of old, nasty oil all over the garage floor, not to mention he never could determine what pained Mrs. Mitchell's car. He was booked full on Monday besides trying to squeeze in figuring out that car's ailment.

Inhaling, he pulled into his drive and looked over to find Victoria and Abby sitting in the garden pulling weeds. The memory of seeing Victoria just a few days before wearing his clothes filled his mind. Something in him had stirred in a way he had been unprepared for when he saw her small frame swallowed in his old shirt and pants.

He had pushed the unwelcome feeling away until that evening when he found the clothes folded on the corner of his bed. He picked them up to find her sweet scent had lingered, which forced his thoughts of her to whirl in his head like a tornado.

A tornado proved a perfect description for her. She'd come into his life, wrecked his pride and joy, and knocked him off his feet each time she came near. He couldn't eat without wondering what foods she liked. He couldn't receive money from his clients without seeing her behind the desk at the bank. He couldn't sleep without envisioning her long lashes against her cheek as he'd seen them that first day when she had prayed on the way to Sondra's farm. His whole life had gone topsy-turvy since Victoria Thankful slammed into it.

And there she was again with the sun shining down on her dark hair, setting reddish pieces in it afire with beauty. Abby adored her. Even Sassy-Girl loved her, which proved to be some weird miracle unto itself. That dog didn't even like him most of the time, and he usually fed her.

God, I don't know why she makes me feel this way. We both know she's not right for me. Rich versus poor—well, okay, working income. Beauty versus beast—well, okay, average.

What about Christian versus Christian, his heart seemed to ask. He shook the thought away, parked the car, and got out. It didn't matter that they shared the same faith. They were direct opposites, and he'd like to spend his days with a wife with whom he had something in common. *Wife? Who said anything about a wife?*

In desperate need of getting the woman out of his mind, Chris was grateful when the time finally came to take her home. After opening the door for Victoria, Chris hopped into the front seat of his truck. "I appreciate all you're doing for Abby."

"She's a wonderful girl. I'm loving every minute of it."

"Good."

"Thanks for taking me home. I have court on Monday afternoon. Hopefully, after that, I'll have my Suburban back."

"That's great."

"I think on Tuesday, Abby and I are going to start working on how to wear hair and makeup."

Chris knew Abby needed all the help she could get in that area. "That would be wonderful."

Silence wrapped around them. Chris started to envision Mrs. Mitchell's car's engine. There had to be something he had missed, something he couldn't quite get a grasp of. Everything he'd checked looked good, seemed good. Mentally he removed each plug, trying to remember what he'd missed.

"Would it be all right if I took her to get her hair cut?"

Chris could hear Victoria's voice tense. He looked at her and frowned at the frustrated expression that overtook her face. Maybe he was just imagining things. It had probably been a pretty long day for her, as well. "That would be fine."

"She needs to feel accepted, Chris."

He glanced at her again. This time he could tell she was mad. "I agree."

"By you."

The words spit from her lips with what he was sure was vehemence. He tried to think of a time he may have made Victoria believe he didn't accept Abby and couldn't think of one. Abby seemed to enjoy making his life more difficult, but he loved and accepted her completely. "I do accept Abby."

"No, Chris, I don't think you do. This has been a very hard couple of years for her. She needs compassion and tenderness from you, not constant criticism and punishment."

"I don't think you know what you're talking about."

"Oh yes, I do. Abby told me you do little more than berate her. She said you are always looking for things to be upset with her about." She smacked her hand against her leg. "I have no trouble with Abby. She does everything I ask."

"You haven't asked her to do something she doesn't want to do."

"Oh yes, I have. Do you think she *wanted* to clean her room and the kitchen? And yet she did it, and she's kept both clean." She paused. "She's not used to you being her parent. She's used to you being her brother."

How dare Victoria criticize him for the way he treated Abby! How dare she be so condescending, so know-it-all with him! He did the best he could with his sister. Abby was the one who wouldn't give him a chance, who wouldn't listen to reason or a single thing he had to say.

Chris stopped the car in front of Dylan and Sondra's house. He willed the mounting fury to stay put in his gut as he turned to look Victoria in the face. Pointing to his chest, he said, "That's what I'm used to, as well."

Victoria flung the truck door open and jumped out. She leaned forward into the cab. "Then quit acting like such a jerk." Slamming the door, she walked up the porch steps and into the house.

What was I thinking? I should have known Victoria Thankful would pull something like this. The woman lives to make me crazy.

He yanked the truck into gear and skidded out of the drive. Did Victoria take the time to ask him about anything Abby said? Did she give him the chance to tell his side? No! He was the bad guy. He was always the bad guy. Nothing he could do would ever be good, or even okay, in Victoria Thankful's eyes.

Well, what do I care anyway! I haven't liked that woman from the moment I saw her. He huffed and turned onto the road leading to his house. *And yet I can't seem to get her out of my mind.*

Chapter 11

C hris shut the hood of the car. Three vehicles behind on his schedule, but he had finally figured out what was wrong with Mrs. Mitchell's car. Walking over to the front desk, he called and left a message that she could stop by and pick it up at any time. He flipped through his appointment book and growled. If he wanted to get through all of them today, he'd have to stay until well after dinner. Noting his filled calendar for the rest of the week, he decided he'd order a pizza and just go ahead and stay.

Dialing the number to his house, he listened to rings and waited for the answering machine to pick up. Abby had gone to the group home with Sondra to visit the kids, so he needed to leave a message for her so she wouldn't wonder where he was this evening.

Abby's recorded voice sounded over the phone. She sounded so young, so sweet. It had been more than a year since Chris had thought of Abby and sweet at the same time. He remembered all Victoria had told him two days before. Did Abby really feel he didn't accept her? It had been hard for him to switch from brother to guardian. He still struggled with the reality, the truth of it. Of course Abby would struggle, as well.

He thought of Abby sitting beside Victoria during church. Both had smiled and clapped their hands while he played his new song. When the chorus came and he invited the congregation to join him, both seemed happy and ready to join in. In truth, he hadn't seen Abby that worshipful in over a year.

His mind replayed the rainy day that sent his already faltering world into a tailspin. "I can't take it anymore." His mother's voice sounded as plain as if she stood beside him.

He closed his eyes and saw her standing in the kitchen. Her eyelids were swollen over her dark eyes. Wrinkles spread across her much-too-quickly aging forehead. Graying hair pulled into a haphazard bun, she took a shaky hand and pushed stray strands behind her ear.

"I need some time." She grabbed Chris's arms with both her hands. She squeezed him tight, and he looked down and saw the suitcase at her feet. "I don't have the strength, the energy," she continued. Sobs wrenched her body, and she released him and shook violently. "I miss him so much."

"It's okay, Mama." Chris gazed past his mother and saw Abby standing in the kitchen door. Her eyes were swollen from crying, as well. "Chris and I will do whatever you need. We'll keep the house up and cook and whatever," she simpered.

"No!" His mother squealed back at Abby. She looked at Chris and shook her head. "No." Wiping her eyes with the back of her hand and sniffing, she leaned over and picked up the suitcase. She stood up straight and set her jaw. "I have to go."

Then she was gone.

Chris peered out the window of his shop. She'd said no good-bye. No "I love you." No "I'll come back soon." She'd simply walked out the door, and they hadn't heard from her since.

Abby had cried for days, but she didn't talk about it. He'd been thankful. He didn't think he could talk about it either. What could he say anyway? He had no answers, nothing that made sense. After his dad died, Chris had worked double the hours to make sure he provided for his mom and sister. Abby helped around the house, as she never had before. There were no logical reasons for his mom to walk out on them.

And yet she had.

Maybe he should have talked to Abby about it. Maybe both of them should have talked. Maybe he came down too hard on her. And the truth was, Victoria seemed to be filling a spot in Abby's life that had needed filling for quite some time. He never tried to be Abby's mom or dad, but maybe he hadn't been as open with her as he should have been.

God, show me how to reach my sister. Show me how to be a better brother. He thought of Victoria and the angry expression on her face when she slammed his truck door. He took a deep breath as he realized how much it hurt to have Victoria upset with him. *Show me how to make amends with Victoria, too.*

Victoria gazed up at the cold, stone structure. The courthouse's aged exterior didn't make her think of justice; it scared her. And why did every courthouse she'd ever seen look like some smaller version of the White House? She had probably read or heard the reason at some point in school, but she couldn't recall it. At the moment, she didn't care much about past history lessons. She wanted to get her vehicle back.

She opened her handbag and checked for the hundredth time to be sure proof of the six-month insurance plan was still inside. Sondra had already found out what Victoria's court cost would be, so she checked again to be sure she had enough for it. Looking through her wallet, she found her driver's license in its correct place, as well.

I'm as ready as I'm going to be. She inhaled and walked up the steps. After opening the heavy half-glass, half-wood door, she walked inside. Her heels clicked against the concrete floor, making the empty, enormous hall seem all the more overwhelming.

A door on her left had a sign that read CIRCUIT CLERK. To her right, she saw doors that read VEHICLE REGISTRATION and DRIVER'S LICENSE. *I don't think I'm supposed to go to any of those.* She grabbed the ticket Sheriff Troy had given her out of her bag. She was supposed to go to district court.

Scanning her left and right, she didn't see any doors that mentioned anything about a district court. Wishing she hadn't been so adamant with Sondra about not coming to allow PeeWee and Emily to take their naps, Victoria walked back to the front of the building where she spied a staircase with a sign that announced district and circuit courts were held upstairs. She sighed in relief, gripped the handrail, and willed herself to scale the flight of stairs.

A few months ago, I would have never dreamed I'd be doing this. At that time, she'd been shopping in malls, spending any amount of money she chose on a pair of shoes or a perfect purse. She might have been out to lunch with her mother at the most expensive restaurants. Never would she have been going to court to get her Suburban back. She'd never even stepped foot in a courthouse.

God, I am absolutely terrified. Please let this go well. Let the judge be kind to me. Please let it be over quick.

It had been humiliating to have to take half a day off work for this when she'd been employed less than two months. Of course, Zack had been kind about it. In fact, he was kind about everything. Victoria still found herself drawn to him, and she felt certain he had almost asked her out on a couple of occasions; however, their conversations had been interrupted by an employee or a customer.

It was a mystery she didn't understand, but somehow she didn't quite feel a romantic connection with Zack. At first, she would have given anything to have him ask her out. Zack had everything she'd ever dreamed of in a partner, and yet there didn't seem to be a spark between them. Yes, that was what she missed—the spark, that yearning-all-day-to-see-you-again feeling. Though she loved to see Zack, loved to talk with him, she just didn't seem to have the happily-ever-after feelings.

But then I've always been known to be a bit dramatic. Didn't Mother always say I lived in my own fairy-tale land all my life? She smiled at the remembrance of playing dress-up in her princess outfit as a girl. Kenny would begrudgingly pretend to be her prince.

I probably wouldn't know real love anyway. And doesn't the Bible tell us not to trust our emotions? Zack is perfect for me. A picture of Chris popped into her mind, and she shook her head. *I need to focus on getting my Suburban back.*

Reaching the top of the stairs, Victoria found the district courtroom and walked in. More people than she had anticipated sat in wooden benches facing the mound of wood the judge sat behind. Sliding into a pew beside an older woman and a small boy, Victoria looked around, surprised at the ornate features in the room. Flowers and loops and fancy shapes had been sculpted into the stone along the walls and ceiling. Three enormous, antique chandeliers hung in a row from the middle of the ceiling. The room screamed of history, and Victoria found herself wondering about the people who had sat in her very seat years and years before her.

She gazed up at the man seated at the front, the judge she'd dreaded for several weeks. He did seem to be as gentle as a puppy. His face hung in wrinkles, reminding her of a bassett hound. Not a single hair topped his head, except the gray circle that wrapped around just above his ears. He looked like a grandpa, a cuddly, friendly grandpa.

"Betty, Bobby," the judge spoke to a young couple in a slow, soft voice, "I can't give you your van back."

"But Judge Henry, I haven't been able to get to work," the man responded.

The judge shook his head. "Bobby, I spoke with your pa last night. He said he'd been offering you rides and you wouldn't take them."

"But..."

"No buts. You can't have your vehicle back until you have insurance. That's the law."

"Judge..."

"Now listen, son." Judge Henry leaned forward. Concern wrapped his features. "You two have yourselves a little one now. It's time to grow up, Bobby."

"I am grown." Bobby puffed out his chest.

"Then take care of your family. It's time, Bobby." The judge leaned back. "Tell you what I'll do. Seeing how I've known you since you were toddling around the courthouse steps, you come back in two weeks. If you've gone to work every day, I'll even sport you half of what you need for three months' worth of insurance."

"Thank you, Judge Henry." Betty smiled. "I'll see he gets to work every day."

Bobby grumbled but didn't say anything else as he followed Betty out of the courtroom. Victoria leaned back in the pew. *I think Chris was right. The judge seems like a very kind man.* She watched as Judge Henry dealt with a few more cases before hers. Finally, her name was called.

Standing, she felt the ease slip from her body as her stomach twisted with nervousness. Her heels clicked louder than ever as she made her way toward the front. The judge peered down at his paper and then at her. "Victoria Thankful, I presume."

Her voice squeaked. "Yes, sir."

A slow smile formed on his lips. "No need to be nervous, dear. I'm Judge Henry. It's a pleasure to meet you."

She nodded and willed her hands and legs not to shake.

The judge leaned back in his chair. "So you're the Mary Ann Mutilator."

"I thought it was Mangler."

Judge Henry laughed and smacked the top of the podium. "I think I've heard it both ways. So have you made arrangements with Chris yet?"

Dread filled her stomach. "Not yet, sir."

"No need to worry. He didn't press any charges, and he's a good man. He'll give you time."

She nodded, praying the judge would hurry. She felt the stares of everyone in the courtroom. Swallowing, she feared she might lose her breakfast at any moment.

"Do you have your license and proof of insurance?"

"Yes, sir." She took the papers from her purse and handed them to him.

He read through her insurance papers and frowned. "You didn't have insurance at the time of the accident."

"No, sir. My"—she cleared her throat—"my insurance policy had run out, and I wasn't aware of it."

"Hmm." He shuffled through the papers again and then glanced up at her. "Technically, I can cite you for not having insurance at the time of the wreck, but since Chris didn't press charges and you made arrangements to get insurance so quickly, I'll let it go."

Relief flooded her heart. "Thank you so much, sir."

"You will have court fees."

"Yes, I know."

He handed the papers back to her. "Well, young lady, I think I'll send you on your way. You can pay your fees downstairs and walk next door to the sheriff's office to get the keys to your vehicle."

"Thank you, sir."

"You have a good day, Ms. Victoria Thankful."

"Victoria Thankful?" A male voice sounded from the back of the room. "Are you Victoria Thankful, the daughter of Thomas Thankful?"

Victoria peered at the back of the room. Her feet seemed to freeze beneath her as she didn't recognize the man.

"Well," he continued, "are you the daughter of the man whose business name was Marcus George?" He walked toward her. "The man who was an oil magnate caught embezzling money?"

"Young fellow, what are you talking about?" asked Judge Henry.

"Your Honor, I'm just wondering if Thomas Thankful is her father."

Victoria's heels nearly fell out from beneath her. She grabbed the nearest pew and looked away from her accuser. The gazes of more than twenty people glowered at her. Most seemed confused. A few had already recognized the name and seemed downright angry.

"Well, I. . ."

"Are you?" The black-haired man's face would have been handsome except for the expression of contempt that wrapped his features. "My cousin was supporting his wife and four children on the income he made from working at a Thomas Thankful's oil company. When the man was found to be embezzling money and decided to evade the law and run off to who-knows-where, my cousin lost his job. And now he's about to lose his home."

Judge Henry hit the podium with his gavel. "That's enough. Victoria is not on trial about her father, in any way, shape, or form."

Tears filled Victoria's eyes. She had been devastated by her father's actions and so consumed with her own dilemmas because of them that she hadn't really considered the families who had been affected by her father's misdeeds.

"He has a daughter." The man had reached her side. He whispered, "Are you her?"

A tear spilled down Victoria's cheek, and she peered at the ground. "I am."

With all the energy she could muster, she fled amid the murmurings of everyone in the room. Running down the stairs, she composed herself and made her way to the correct office to pay her fee. No one followed her. *They're probably all discussing the many ways Daddy hurt families they knew. God, how could I have been so selfish not to think of the pain he'd caused others?*

Swallowing back her imminent spilling of emotion, she made her way to the sheriff's office, got her keys, and found her Suburban. With the turn of the ignition, the dam of her heart broke and tears spilled from her eyes. How much devastation had her father caused? Pain for that family, pain for other families, and pain for her own life seemed to stab at her insides. *Why, God? Why did Daddy do this?*

Chapter 12

"Hi, Abby." Chris walked into the kitchen to find Abby sitting at the kitchen table peeling potatoes. His sister's transformation had been amazing since Victoria started visiting. She hadn't gotten her hair cut as yet, but Victoria had taught Abby how to wear her face paint a coat or two lighter. Chris had forgotten that his little sister's lips were actually pink in color and not some funky dark shade of purple.

"Hey, big brother." Abby half smiled, but her voice sounded distraught. "Have you seen the paper?"

He shook his head and opened the refrigerator. After grabbing a water bottle and an apple, he sat down at the table across from his sister and picked up the weekly newspaper. "Anything happen this week?"

Abby huffed. "You could say that."

Chris frowned. It must have been pretty big news to capture Abby's attention. The girl only flipped through the pages to find the TV guide. He started to skim the front page. *An accident on the other side of town with injuries. Another water advisory notice and some town council suggestions on what to do about its continual reoccurrences.*

"Look at the bottom," said Abby.

Chris opened the page to its full length. He almost choked on his apple when he saw a picture of Victoria leaving the courthouse. The caption above it read, "Embezzler Among Us?"

"It's Victoria," said Abby. Chris looked up to see his sister's eyes pooled with tears. She placed the potato peeler on the table and swiped her eyes with the back of her hand. "You and I both know she's not an embezzler."

Chris tried to skim through the article, but as tears raced down Abby's cheeks, he lowered the paper and touched the top of her hand.

"She doesn't even have the money to pay you for Mary Ann. She's not a criminal." Abby pulled a tissue from her jeans pocket and wiped her nose.

"What does it say exactly?"

"Remember that guy they showed on all the stations who'd taken money from his oil companies?"

Chris thought back to the news stories a few months ago about an oil magnate who had embezzled money from his company, but that guy's name wasn't Thankful. *What was that guy's name? It was George, somebody George.* "But that's

308

not her dad," said Chris. "That man's last name was George."

Abby shook her head. "No, George was his business name." She stood and walked toward the bathroom. "I don't know what's going to happen. I'm afraid Victoria will want to leave." She covered her face with her hands. "I need her here." She ran into the bathroom, slamming the door behind her.

Chris's heart pounded with uncertainty. Maybe he should try to talk to Abby. But what would he say? He didn't even know what was going on. Besides, he didn't know how to talk to Abby. That had been their problem since long before Mom left. He glanced at the bathroom door where Sassy-Girl had already made her appearance. She pawed at the door just as Chris heard the water running in the shower.

Sighing, he picked up the paper and read through the article. *This can't be right.* He scratched his chin and read through it once more. He rolled up the paper and stuck it under his arm. *There's only one way to find out the truth of all this.* Grabbing his keys, he walked to the bathroom door. "I'll be back, Abby. Go ahead and fix supper. I'll find out what's going on."

The door opened. A towel was wrapped around Abby's head, and a much-too-big robe hung from her small frame. Her face had been scrubbed clean and shiny, but her eyes were still red and swollen. She didn't say anything; she just sighed deeply and then looked up at him. Her expression begged him to make it all better.

An urge he hadn't had in months filled him. Without thinking, he grabbed Abby into a tight hug. Sobs overtook her, and she cried into his shoulder. He combed her hair with his fingers and held her tight. She drove him crazy, but God had blessed him with his little sister. God had also given him the job of taking care of her. With Victoria's help, he now realized that meant providing more than food and clothes. Sometimes it meant a hug, a compliment, a promise. "It's going to be all right. I'm not letting her go anywhere."

Abby peered up at him. "Promise?"

He closed his eyes, overwhelmed with a mixture of feelings. Loss for his dad. Loss for his mom. A real need not to lose Victoria. Suddenly he understood how much all of it felt to Abby, too. "I'll do my best."

His mind spun in a whirl as he drove to the Wards' ranch. Was Victoria a fraud like her father? The reports about Mr. George's dealings with employees and business partners had been appalling. He thought of how upset Victoria had been when he'd given her his estimates to fix Mary Ann. In his gut, he knew she had been genuine in her want to make amends for the accident.

After pulling into the driveway, he yanked the keys out of the ignition and scaled the steps up the porch. Before he had time to knock, Sondra opened the door. Her lips parted in a smile that didn't quite make it to her eyes.

"Where is she?" Chris asked.

"At the bank." Sondra motioned for Chris to come inside. "I just laid the kids down. We can talk."

Chris followed her into the house. The sweet smell of fresh-cut roses filled his nostrils as he walked into her kitchen and saw a vase full sitting on her table. Dylan leaned against the counter taking a swig from his coffee mug. Upon seeing Chris, Dylan put the cup down and offered his hand. "Good to see you."

Chris barely shook it before he took the paper from under his arm and opened it. "What's this about? Is it true?"

"It's true."

"But Victoria. What does that mean about Victoria? Is she a fraud? Has she been lying to us since she got here?"

Dylan crossed his arms in front of his chest while Sondra sat at the table. She looked up at Chris. He could tell her gaze searched him at the depths of his being. "What do you think, Chris? You've been around Victoria. Do you think she's a fraud?"

Chris frowned. Sondra's words were not said in accusation or malice. They were formed—stated exactly and perfectly. She was asking him to decide within himself what he knew to be true.

His mind played reels of moments he'd spent with Victoria. He drifted to the day he found Abby and Victoria working in the garden. He thought of the time she had deposited his money at the bank. He saw her with PeeWee in her arms the first time she'd met the little guy. "No. She's not a fraud." With the words spoken aloud, Chris knew without reservation they were true. "What did happen?"

"Mama, I no feel good."

Chris glanced toward the hall just as PeeWee vomited all over the floor. Sondra hopped up and ran to him as Dylan grabbed paper towels from the cabinet. Scooping up the boy, Sondra raced to the sink as another bout of sickness came. Chris looked over to find Dylan gagging as he wiped up the mess from the floor.

Emily started to cry from her bedroom just as Chris's cell phone began to vibrate in his coveralls pocket. Dylan picked up the drenched paper towels and carried them to the trash. The smell must have overwhelmed him, because once he reached the can, he was sick. Ignoring his phone, Chris turned toward Sondra who had already stripped PeeWee down to his birthday suit. "You want me to check on Emily?"

Hacking sounded from the baby's bedroom, and Sondra looked at Chris, her eyes big as the headlights of his car. "No. You better run. We must have the stomach virus that's going around." Sondra exhaled and grabbed a two-liter bottle of lemon-lime soda from the cabinet.

Chris's cell phone began to vibrate once more. "You sure? I can stay and help."

What do I do?" His stomach clenched at the idea of cleaning vomit, but he'd do it to help.

Dylan tore a clean paper towel off the roll and wiped his mouth. "Sondra's right. You get on out of here so you don't get sick, as well."

Chris grabbed his cell phone from his pocket as he walked toward the front door. He looked back at Dylan. "If it gets to be too much, you call me."

"Vic." Sondra turned from washing her hands at the kitchen sink. "Can you pick up Vic? Wouldn't you know the poor woman gets her Suburban back, and my van breaks down! I dropped her off at work."

"Not a problem. I'll get her. Do you need me to look at your van?"

"I think it's something I can fix." Dylan smiled as PeeWee streaked buck naked across the floor yelling for his mom to help his sissy. "You run on out of here. Your day's a'coming."

"I don't know about that." Chris laughed as he opened and then shut the front door behind him. He flipped open his still vibrating phone. "Hello."

"Mr. Ratliff?"

"Yes."

"This is Vern from the pawnshop."

"Yes?"

The man cleared his throat. "Well, it's been well over a month since that gal brought that pretty little ring to my shop. I tried giving her a bit of extra time, but I'm planning on putting that little beauty on my shelf today. I promised you I'd call first."

Chris's mind churned with a sudden idea. The more he thought about it, the more he liked it. "Yes, I'd like to purchase it. How much do you want?"

The man quoted the price he had told Victoria she'd have to pay to get it back. Chris's heart sank. It would take every penny he'd tried to save to get the right bumper for Mary Ann. A slow smile formed on his lips. *Vic's worth every penny.* "I'll be there in half an hour."

❦

"Victoria, I'm going to be honest with you. I'm in a bit of a quandary."

She looked at the man standing behind his desk. Once again the light streaming from the window behind him wrapped his frame, giving him an almost angelic appearance. This time his expression held anything but pleasure.

Zack gripped the back of his oversized leather chair. "I've spent the entire morning on the phone with my boss, as well as several presidents from our sister banks."

Victoria leaned her head back and closed her eyes. Overwhelming anger and frustration filled her to her core. She'd had nothing to do with her father's embezzlement; she'd barely even been to his office. Sadness washed over her with urgency. People would always associate her with "the embezzler." She choked back her yearning to scream, to cry at the unfairness of it all. *God, give me the patience and self-control to make it through this meeting with Zack without outbursts of any kind.*

She looked around the room. How many times had she dreamed of being back in this office with Zack gently touching her hand and asking her to accompany him on a romantic evening of a candlelit dinner and a quiet walk in the park? Or maybe he would ask her to a movie and an ice cream afterward.

She gazed at the man who fit her every dream for the perfect mate. Not this. Never in her daydreams of Zack Bradshaw had she imagined this.

"I want you to know I believe in you, Victoria." He moved from behind his desk until he stood just inches from her. "You and your father are not the same person."

Victoria glanced at her shoes. Her perfect, pointy-toed, brand-name, crème-colored shoes. "No. No, we're not."

"My hands are tied, though." Zack squeezed her shoulder as if to reassure her. "I have to put you on suspension until your father's investigation is over."

Gazing into his eyes, Victoria could see it pained Zack to do this. He had fought for her. He didn't have to say it. She could see the truth in his eyes. "I understand."

And she did. How could she blame a company—a bank, to be exact—for feeling uncomfortable letting the daughter of a multimillion-dollar embezzler work there until she had been cleared of any wrongdoing? "It's okay, Zack."

She turned to leave his office. Her mind swirled with problems. She had planned to buy back her grandma's ring. Now she couldn't. She had insurance to cover her Suburban for a few months, but now she wouldn't have gas money to drive it around. And Chris. How would she ever pay him to fix his Corvette?

"Victoria." Zack grabbed her hand. She turned and looked at him. His gaze held a yearning she had longed for weeks to see. "I really care about you. I've been praying and pondering how to ask you. . . . I mean, it's a little awkward because you're an employee. . . . I mean, there aren't any rules or anything; I just haven't been sure how to approach you. . . ."

Victoria watched as Zack fumbled with his words. Words she had waited for. Words she had played and replayed in many different ways in her mind. His beautiful, blond hair lay in a perfect style crowning his head. His eyes glimmered with a mixture of regret and want. His clothes had been pressed to perfection and hung perfectly on his formed frame. His hand, soft as her own, covered hers.

And she felt nothing.

How could she feel nothing? Zack Bradshaw was the epitome of the man she wanted, the man she needed. But she didn't want him. She didn't need him. The truth of it hit her with such force she couldn't deny it. "Zack, you're my friend."

He tightened his hold on her hand. "Please, Victoria. If it's about your job, believe me, I know you're an honest person. I trust you with every account in this bank."

She shook her head. "I believe you, Zack. And I believe you're my friend, as well." She smiled when the words left her lips.

He let go of her hand and nodded. Exhaling, he said, "I'm glad we're friends."

"I'll see you at church on Sunday," she said as she walked out the office door.

"Yes, Sunday."

Walking out the front door of the bank, Victoria saw Chris's truck parked across the street. "Hey." She recognized the voice and the large figure that loomed beside her.

Glancing up at Chris, her heart flipped, and she was surprised at how glad she felt to see him. "Let me guess. You're here to pick me up."

Chris laughed. "Seems the kids start puking their guts out when I come around."

"You do have that effect on people."

"Thanks."

"Seriously, are they okay?"

"Yeah, Dylan and Sondra have it under control." Chris shoved his hands in his pockets. "But I'd like to talk to you if you wouldn't mind."

"About the paper?"

He nodded.

"Sure, why not? It's not like I haven't talked about it enough today." Victoria smacked her hand to her thigh and then gazed up at Chris and realized he was exactly who she wanted to talk to.

Chapter 13

D o you mind if we run by my shop a sec?" Chris jingled the keys in his hand. "I'm supposed to deliver eggs tomorrow, and the truck I use for my By His Hand ministry is in desperate need of some new plugs."

Victoria watched as a slight breeze danced through his hair. His need of another trim belied subtle hints of the wavy thickness that rested upon Chris's head. Being late in the day, stubble covered his jaw and chin, and Victoria wanted to feel the contrast between the two. "Without a ride, I'm at your mercy."

Chris frowned. "My truck can wait. I wanted to talk to you, too."

"I was just kidding. I didn't mean to sound snippy."

"Been a long day at work, huh?"

"You could say that." She lifted her purse higher on her shoulder and started toward Chris's truck. "But it's the last one, for a while anyway."

"What do you mean by that?" Chris came up beside her.

"It seems I'm on suspension until my dad's case is decided." She turned and looked at him. "I'm assuming you've read the paper."

He nodded. "That's why I want to talk, remember?"

"Yeah."

"But I don't understand why Zack would suspend you. It's hardly your fault."

Victoria noticed the anger that laced his words and realized that Chris had taken her side. Not that there really were sides to take, but it felt nice to know he didn't believe her to be a thief. She touched Chris's rough hand, so unlike any she had ever touched. It felt strong and stable, a blue-collar worker's hand, and she liked it. "It wasn't Zack's fault either. His boss made him, and I'm really okay with it." She released his hand and grabbed the handle to the truck door. "Except that I don't know how I'll pay you. . .or get back my grandma's ring," she mumbled as she hopped into the truck's cab.

Chris pushed the door shut behind her. "Don't you worry about paying me. I should be paying you for all the time you've spent putting up with Abby."

Victoria peered down at her manicured fingernails, the very ones she'd spent hours scrubbing garden dirt out from under after Abby convinced her to feel the earth between her fingers. She thought of how humiliated Abby must be to know the woman who's teaching her to be a lady has a criminal for a daddy. "I love your sister."

"She loves you, too."

"Has she read the paper?"

"Yes."

"What does she think of me now?"

"She made me promise to make you stay in Lasso."

Victoria looked into Chris's eyes. "She did?"

The honesty in his gaze nearly took her breath away as he nodded. His Adam's apple bobbed as he swallowed slowly. The yearning in his expression made her afraid to ask if he wanted her to stay, as well.

Her emotions consumed her. Maybe it was just plain exhaustion. Tears filled her eyes and spilled down her cheeks in such a race she had no chance to make them stop.

As she tried to swallow back her cries, Chris scooted over in the seat and wrapped his arms around her. She leaned into the crook of his neck, inhaling the deep scent of him. Without realizing it, her senses had come to recognize the smell of Chris Ratliff—his smell, the one that made up the man. She loved the scent and found comfort in it. She nestled her face into his shoulder. He tightened his hold, and she'd never felt so safe, so secure.

"It's all right, honey," he crooned and gently raked his fingers through the length of her hair.

"I don't want to be embarrassed anymore. Why doesn't God rescue me? What purpose is there in torturing me?"

"Oh, Victoria." Chris loosened his hold and lifted her chin toward him. "You listen to me. God loves you. He has a plan for every season of your life. He'll take care of you during this time." He caressed the side of her cheek. "Maybe He'll use me to help."

Victoria gazed at Chris's lips. She felt his desire to kiss her. Closing her eyes, she admitted how much she wanted it, too. She leaned toward him and allowed their lips to meet. His stubble scratched around her mouth, but she didn't care.

He tightened his embrace. "Promise you'll stay." He gazed into her eyes, and she knew he sought permission to kiss her again. Without reservation, she closed her eyes and found his lips once more. Without a doubt, God had sent her to Chris.

⌒⌒⌒⌒⌒

I love her, Lord. Chris peered out the windshield at the buildings lining Main Street. He flipped his turn signal on and turned toward his shop. Glancing at Victoria, he tried to read her silence. Was she angry with him? Maybe he should apologize for kissing her, and yet not even a morsel of remorse filled him over those kisses. Everything in him longed to kiss her again.

He turned off the truck and opened the door. Before he could get to her side, she had already hopped out. He looked down at her, and she smiled and blushed. *I don't think she's angry with me.*

"I'll try to fix it as quickly as I can." Chris guided her inside. He showed her the refrigerator, the snacks, and the magazines, and then he escaped to the back of the shop. He popped the hood of the truck and removed and replaced the old plugs as quickly as possible.

He stood to his full height, glanced at the clock on the wall, and realized Sondra and Dylan might be worried about Victoria's whereabouts. Leaning over the truck, he made sure all the caps were tight. "You might want to call Sondra and tell her where you are," he hollered so that she could hear him in the other room.

"I already called her."

Chris bumped his head on the hood when her voice sounded from right behind him. "Ouch." He rubbed the top of his head.

She placed her hand over her mouth and giggled. "Sorry about that."

"How long have you been standing there?"

"Awhile." She leaned against one of his tables. "Did you know you hum church hymns while you work?"

He felt the heat rush up his face. "Guess I hadn't thought about it."

"It's nice."

Chris walked over to the sink and washed his hands with detergent to get the grease off. He turned and looked at Victoria. She was more than he'd ever dreamed of, in every way. After drying his hands, he walked to her and touched her cheek. "You're beautiful, Victoria."

She smiled and walked toward the door. "I'll wait for you in your truck."

⌒◦∞◦⌒

Victoria laid her Bible and prayer journal on her bed and her cookies and milk on the nightstand. She flipped on the lamp and then nestled into her covers. She thought of Chris standing next to the truck in his shop, in his element. Grease stains covered his legs and hips, not to mention his hands and arms. He even had the cutest smudge across his forehead. *And the kiss.* Victoria had never felt such a connection in her life. Even now she tingled all the way to her toes with the memory of it.

God, guide my feelings for him. They're so strong. Please tell me if they're from You. She took a bite of a cookie and then opened her Bible to Ecclesiastes. Since she'd accepted the Lord into her life, she'd been reading a chapter of the Bible each day. God never ceased to amaze her at how He spoke to her through His Word no matter where in the Bible she was reading.

She started at chapter three, her heart open and ready to accept whatever God showed her, especially concerning Chris Ratliff. After taking a drink of milk, she almost choked when she read verse one. She read it again. "There is a time for everything, and a season for every activity under heaven."

"God,"—she peered up at the ceiling—"what was it that Chris said to me today?" She thought about when she'd cried into Chris's neck and shoulder. She'd asked him why God would allow all this to happen to her. *What did Chris say? It was something about You being in control of every season of my life.*

She shut her Bible and closed her eyes. "God, what Daddy did has been so hard, but You are in charge of everything in my life. You can use anything for Your glory. Anything."

She thought of Chris saying that maybe God would use him to help her. A shiver of excitement ran through her at the remembrance of his words. "God, I would have never asked this when I first came to Lasso, Oklahoma." She bit her lip and grinned as she mentally looked up at the overgrown mechanic. "But if You want to use Chris to help me, I'm okay with that."

Chapter 14

I s that what it's supposed to look like?" Chris cupped his jaw, willing himself not to cover his eyes at the exposure of his sister.

He had agreed to take her shopping for a dress for her advanced chorus concert. Mrs. Smith had given the girls two requirements for attire. The dress needed to be semiformal, and it had to be black.

"I think most of the girls will wear one like it." She lifted one of the spaghetti straps higher onto her shoulder. The straps continued down her back in crisscross fashion, exposing skin to her waistline. Cut off in a flair at her knees, the length wasn't too bad, and the front of the dress appeared modest enough. But the back. . . He shook his head. "I don't know if I like this one, Abby."

"Oh, come on, Chris." Abby pouted.

God, Abby and I are having a good day, but I can't let her wear that to the concert. Chris cleared his throat and sat back in the chair. "Hmm. Well, how do you feel about it? Does it feel a little more revealing than you'd have wanted?"

She twisted and touched her waistline as she gazed into the three-way mirror. "Maybe a little." She spun around, allowing the bottom to twirl. "But I love the skirt part."

The clerk tapped her index finger to her lips. "I think we have another one that's similar but isn't backless."

Abby smiled, and Chris exhaled. "Let's see it," they said in unison, and Abby giggled.

An hour later, they left the department store with a much more modest dress and matching heels. He watched as Abby hopped into the cab of the truck. Her eyes shone like a freshly polished grill on a new car. Thankfulness filled his spirit. He hopped into the driver's seat. "I'm glad we found something you like."

She clasped her hands. "Me, too. I had so much fun with you today."

"I had a pretty good time myself."

Abby half smiled. "You're not so bad after all."

Chris grunted. "Thanks." He started the truck and then sneaked a peek at Abby. She opened the shoe box to look at her purchase once more. "How 'bout we go to that Mexican restaurant you love for dinner?"

Abby shut the lid. "You mean it?"

"Sure."

"I say this day can't get much better."

Chris knocked on the screen door at the Wards' ranch. "I brought your milk." He smiled when Victoria opened the door holding a sleeping Emily against her chest.

"You want to come in?"

"I probably should get the eggs and go."

PeeWee ran to the door with a cape tied around his neck. "Hi, Cis. I'm Sup–Man."

He raced away with his arms spread like an airplane.

"Where's Sondra and Dylan?" asked Chris.

"I told them to go for an afternoon picnic. They don't get much alone time."

Chris peeked inside and watched as PeeWee jumped from his toy chest to the floor then zoomed down the hall. "Better get the big one."

Victoria groaned. "Come on in." She walked over to PeeWee. "You can be Superman as long as you stay on the ground."

PeeWee nodded. "O–tay, Aunt Vic."

Victoria shook her head and looked at the ceiling. She glanced at Chris. "I'm going to lay her down, and then we can visit."

"Can I watch?" *Where did that come from?* He'd never been interested in babies and children. Sure, he liked them just fine, figured he'd even have one or two some-day, but he didn't go out of his way to hang around them. Still, something stirred inside him when he saw Victoria holding baby Emily to her chest.

"Sure."

He followed her to the baby's room and watched as Victoria laid Emily in her bed. She petted Emily's hair and smiled. "She looks so peaceful."

Chris gazed at Victoria's profile. He drank his fill of her flowing curls, her light skin, her smooth neck. "You'll make a great mother."

Victoria looked up at him. "I hope so. I never thought about it before I came here. I've always been a fairy-tale kind of girl, dreaming of my Prince Charming."

"Prince Charming?"

Victoria looked up at him and smiled. "Yeah."

"You'd make a beautiful princess, Victoria, inside and out." He moved to-ward her, yearning to kiss her once more.

A crash sounded from the living room, and Victoria raced from the room. Chris grunted and walked out, as well. *If only the little guy could have waited ten seconds longer.*

Victoria's hands grew moist as she walked toward the familiar building. It had been two weeks since the newspaper article, and she needed to pick up her last check from the bank. Trying to avoid as many coworkers as possible, Victoria had decided to go on Saturday. *Lord, please don't let Zack be here.*

Guilt filled her heart. Zack had been nothing but kind to her when they saw each other at church services. He hadn't done anything to make her feel as though he didn't trust her, and yet the thought of seeing him at the bank made her stomach queasy.

Her hand slipped from perspiration when she grabbed the long, metal door handle. *How embarrassing. Mom would die to know I'd let my nervousness show so much on the outside.* Grabbing the handle more firmly, she straightened her shoulders and pulled open the door.

"Hi, Victoria." Zack's smiling face greeted her from just inside the door. "Here to pick up your check?"

A thud landed in her gut, and she swallowed the pride mixed with embarrassment that threatened to heat up her cheeks. She forced herself to smile. "Yes."

"I'll get it for you." He escaped to the back office and then returned with her check in his hand.

"Can I go ahead and cash it?"

"Absolutely." Zack walked behind the counter. He grabbed a pen from beside the computer and handed it to Victoria.

Willing her hand not to shake, Victoria focused on writing her signature. She pushed the check toward him. "Thank you."

Zack opened a drawer and counted out her earnings. He then repeated the procedure as he placed the crisp bills in her hand. When he placed the last bill on top, he looked up at her. "Victoria, I'll be so glad when that case is over. Everyone is anxious to get you back."

Victoria looked up and into his eyes. He obviously meant every word he said. She gazed around the office. One of her coworkers waved from behind her desk. Victoria smiled and waved back. Putting aside her pride, she admitted how much she had enjoyed working at the bank, and it wasn't because of Zack at all. She liked all her coworkers, and she loved handing customers the cash from their well-earned checks and crunching numbers to be sure her drawer balanced correctly. She did want to return to her job. "I'll be glad, as well."

He touched the side of her hand. "Would you like to go to lunch today?" She looked back at Zack. "As a friend," he added, but his gaze told her he wanted to go as more than that.

She smiled. "Maybe another time. I'm heading out to Chris's house."

"Chris's?"

She felt her cheeks warm. "Well, I go out there to spend time with Abby."

Zack's eyebrows lifted, and he nodded slowly. "Abby's a wonderful girl." He exhaled a long breath and then winked. "Chris is a pretty nice guy, as well."

⌒⌒⌒

"Hey, Sassy-Girl." Victoria bent down and scooped the dog off the floor. Though she'd never had animals while growing up, she'd found them to be real treasures. Abby's dog always made her feel welcome and didn't care a whit about who her dad was and what he'd done. She lifted Sassy-Girl to her chest and allowed her to lick her cheek once. Petting the dog's head, she walked through the mudroom and into the kitchen. "Abby, you home?"

"In here."

Abby's muffled voice sounded from the back of the house, probably Abby's room. When a sniff sounded, Victoria knew Abby had been crying. Victoria swallowed the lump in her throat. Though she and Abby had talked about Victoria's dad and the article in the paper, Victoria carried a deep fear that kids at school would make fun of Abby for associating with the "embezzler's daughter." Especially since the article came out just a few weeks after Abby had started her senior year.

Most of the townspeople received Victoria as they had before, probably because of Victoria's relation to Sondra as well as her consistent attendance at church, but still a few would yell cruel things to her from the grocery parking lot or mumble ugly comments under their breath at the gas station. Victoria remained determined not to let those people make her feel bad; she also knew the town had come to associate her with the Wards and the Ratliffs, and she surely didn't want to make things hard for any of them.

Victoria peeked into Abby's room to find her young friend sitting on her bed hugging her pillow to her chest. She sniffed and wiped the back of her hand across her eyes. Victoria set Sassy-Girl on the floor, and the dog hopped onto the bed and curled up beside Abby. Victoria's heart constricted. "What's the matter?"

Abby shrugged.

"Not ready to talk about it?" Victoria sat on the edge of the bed, allowing a little space between them.

Abby clutched her pillow to her chest. "It's Austin."

"Austin?" Victoria's mind raced through the people she and Abby had talked about since Abby had gone back to school. "Is that the boy in your advanced chorus class?"

Abby nodded.

If Victoria remembered correctly, he was the one with the striking blue eyes and sleek black hair who also played tight end for the football team. Victoria also thought he'd sounded a little too flirty and quite a bit too pushy for her liking. "What about him?"

"He asked me to the chorus dinner." Abby broke out into fresh sobs.

Victoria's mind raced. *What is a chorus dinner?* She'd been a bit of an introvert in school, but she had always known the usual teenage outings. A chorus dinner she'd never heard of. "That's okay. You don't have to go with him."

Abby smacked the pillow to the bed. "I want to go with him."

Victoria frowned and tried to think of where the pain in this scenario was for Abby. "Okay then, I don't know what you're supposed to wear exactly, but it sounds fancy, so we'll find a gorgeous dress, and we'll fix your hair and makeup."

Abby shook her head. "I already have a dress. Chris and I went shopping, and he already agreed to let me get my hair and makeup fixed. My friends and I were going to go to Cut and Dried together the day of the concert."

Victoria felt a bit confused and had to admit the prick of hurt that stabbed her heart as to why Abby hadn't told her about the dinner. She would have loved to help Abby pick out dresses and hairstyles; however, this new piece of information was something to ponder. Abby had shared this special occasion with her brother, the very one who had known precious little of what to do with Abby when Victoria met him, who carried a handkerchief in his pocket and wiped bird droppings off his windshield with it, who often carried a wrench in his side pocket. And he, Chris Ratliff, had taken Abby shopping for a dinner dress.

A smile formed on Victoria's lips when she thought of the tough, burly man sitting in front of the dressing room's three-way mirror waiting for Abby to show him yet one more fancy gown.

"We were going to surprise you," Abby interrupted Victoria's thoughts.

"Huh?"

"Yeah. Chris and I wanted to show you how well we had done together." Abby shrugged. "Kinda show you how much you'd taught me."

"Oh, Abby." Victoria's heart felt it would burst with love for the young lady sitting beside her. She wrapped her arms around Abby and hugged her tight. "I am so proud of you. . .and Chris. It sounds like you're going to have a great time."

Abby pushed away and shook her head. "Nope. He dumped me."

"What?"

"Two weeks before the dinner, and Austin up and decides he wants to take Mallory instead."

"Oh, honey." Victoria grabbed Abby into a hug. "I'm so sorry."

"I don't even know why. He didn't give me a reason. Just broke off the date."

Victoria lifted Abby's chin. "I know just what we need. Go wash your face and get your shoes on."

Abby gasped. "I'm not going anywhere like this."

Victoria swatted her hand. "This is no time to think about appearances. We have to do some seriously productive mourning."

Abby wrinkled her nose. "What?"

"We're heading to the store to splurge on every flavor ice cream we can find, and then we're going to stop by the video store and rent every funny movie we walk past. Then you and I will come back here and drown ourselves in icy sugar and ridiculous laughter."

One side of Abby's lips tilted up slightly.

"Come on now." Victoria stood and helped Abby up, as well. "We'll even share with Sassy-Girl."

The dog barked and wagged her tail. Abby wiped her eyes and headed toward the bathroom. "Okay."

Victoria counted the money in her purse. *Good thing I cashed my check.* Victoria sighed, knowing she should be cautious with the last of her income. She had planned to seek God in how to best spend and save what little bit she had for this indefinite amount of time. Splurging on ice cream and movie rentals probably was not the wisest choice.

Water spewed from the faucet in the bathroom, and then a cabinet shut. "Victoria." Abby peeked around the side of the door.

"Yeah."

"I'm so glad you came by today."

Victoria smiled as her whole being filled with a true sense of belonging. *Thank You, Lord. You never fail to guide me, even when it comes to how to spend the last bit of my earnings.*

Chapter 15

A flash of thrill filled Chris as he pulled up to the house and saw Victoria's Suburban in the drive. It had been a productive day at the shop; he'd even squeezed in an hour to work on Mary Ann between his afternoon appointments. But it had been a long one, as well, and seeing Victoria's beautiful smile and sparkling eyes would be the perfect reprieve from his work. He turned off the truck and hopped out.

Whistling, he bounded up the steps and opened the door. "Hello, Vic and Abby," he called as he kicked off his boots in the mudroom. The only greeting was laughter sounding from the living area. Turning the corner, he walked into the kitchen and found steaks marinating in some kind of good-smelling sauce. Toothpicks stuck out from every angle of the steaks—he assumed to hold in place the bacon that wrapped around each of them.

A squeal of laughter sounded again from the living room. He smiled as he walked toward them. "Sounds like we're having a good. . ."

He stopped when he reached the room. No less than ten partially eaten cartons of ice cream sat on the coffee table, the end tables, and the cushions of the couch. Abby sat on the floor with her legs crossed and three cartons sitting around her. Victoria sat on the couch with her knees under her chin and her arms wrapped around her calves. He couldn't tell if she was comfortable or possibly willing away a stomachache.

Once again Victoria sported an old pair of his sweats and shirt while Abby wore an old pair of pajamas. Both of them had their hair pulled up in a knot with strands sticking out from every angle. Chris wondered if the plan had backfired and Abby had taken the lady out of Victoria.

A noise sounded from the television, and both Abby and Victoria broke out into new peals of laughter. Chris glanced at the screen then back at the girls. Victoria stuck her spoon in a carton of chocolate-looking ice cream then licked the spoon. She glanced toward Chris. As her eyes bulged and her cheeks flushed crimson, he knew she'd just realized he'd gotten home.

He lifted his eyebrows. "Having fun?"

She uncurled her legs and hopped off the couch. "I didn't know you were here." She gawked at her watch. "Wow, it's later than I thought."

Abby looked up at him and waved. "Hey, Chris. We're in mourning."

"What?" Chris furrowed his eyebrows.

Victoria grabbed his hand and guided him into the kitchen. A stirring whipped through him as he followed the ruffled woman wearing his clothes. Maybe it was the softness of her skin or the light tickling of her fingernails when she touched him. Or maybe it was the wisps of hair that clung to the back of her neck from beneath her knot.

Whatever it was, he wanted to twirl Victoria around and grab her in his arms. He wanted to pull the knot from her hair and let the length fall down her back. He shook his head to clear his mind.

The time was coming when he planned to tell Victoria exactly how he felt, but it wouldn't be tonight in front of his little sister. Victoria stopped and whirled around. She rested her finger over her lips, telling him to be quiet. Leaning closer to him, her soft perfume filled the air. "Austin broke off their dinner date."

"What?"

"She's been really upset because he broke off their date, so we spent the. . ."

Chris walked away, opened the cabinet, and grabbed the church directory. "I'll take care of this. No boy is going to treat my little sister with such disrespect. He knows better than to do a girl like that." He flipped open the book.

Victoria put her hand on top of it. "Chris, don't. It will only make things harder for Abby."

Chris shook his head. "Austin knows better."

Victoria nodded. "Yes, he does, but if you call and his parents make him take her, Abby will be miserable. She'll resent you all over again." Victoria nudged him with her shoulder and grinned like a Cheshire cat. "I heard you took her shopping for her dress. I'm so impressed."

Chris bit his lip. Victoria's playfulness was about to undo him. If she wasn't careful, he'd be wrapping his arms around her and planting a firm kiss on her inviting lips. He looked into her eyes and shrugged. "It wasn't *too* bad."

Victoria stood on tiptoes and kissed his lips. "I'm really proud of you."

She didn't know what had come over her. Chris just seemed so rugged, so manly with the blots of grease on his forehead and cheek. When his work-worn hands grabbed the directory with an urgency to right the wrong that had been done to his sister, Victoria nearly came unglued. She wanted him to care for her in such a protective way.

Actually, she wanted to talk to Chris about her feelings for him. They hadn't spoken of their kiss in the truck, and Victoria wondered if Chris had felt as much a connection as she had. She opened the refrigerator door and grabbed the ingredients for the salad. Shutting the door with her hip, she looked around the kitchen. Was she willing to live in this small country home?

The thought struck her hard as she placed the lettuce in the sink to wash it off. When Victoria insisted that Abby watch the rest of the movie, Chris had offered to help her cook dinner as soon as he cleaned up. The shower turned off, and Victoria knew it would be a matter of moments before he returned.

Her heart pounded as she considered a life of cooking every day. Sure, she had loved her time at the ranch. She had enjoyed collecting eggs, feeding chickens, cooking, and doing chores, but was she ready for the permanence of it? Maybe she had to be. Daddy had taken the only life she'd ever known. She knew when he and Mother ran off her life would be different forever, so why did she suddenly feel burdened standing in Chris's kitchen?

"It smells wonderful in here." Chris walked up beside her. "What are you cooking?"

"It's my old cook's version of filet mignon. It's a little different than what you'd get in a restaurant. She used a light marinating sauce that softens the meat."

Chris rubbed his stomach. "Sounds good to me. I've never tried it, so I wouldn't know the difference anyway."

Never had filet mignon? Hadn't everyone had filet mignon? In Victoria's opinion, it was the best cut of steak. Additional proof their lives had been so different.

"What can I do?" Chris interrupted her thoughts.

"You can chop up the cucumber for the salad." She placed the knife and washed vegetable into his work-worn palm. She loved the strength in his hands. Surely she'd never resent their roughness or that they were permanently darkened from his work.

She gazed up at him. He towered over her even when he slumped to cut the vegetable that seemed so small in his grip. She loved his height, the mass of his shoulders and arms. His blond, reddish hair curled slightly at the nape of his neck. She wanted to touch the curl.

"All done. What now? The pepper?" He pushed the cucumbers to the side of the cutting board and grabbed the bell pepper beside the sink.

"Sure." She watched as he focused on his new task. No man who had ever been in her daddy's acquaintance would have stood beside her at the kitchen counter cutting vegetables for a salad.

She opened the oven to take out the potatoes. As she reached for the oven mitt, Chris grabbed it first. She contemplated him, and he smiled. "I'll get that for you." She watched as he lifted them out of the oven.

Remembering him standing before the church with his guitar in hand, flutters filled her heart. His love for the Lord proved undeniable. His kindness for her and his sister also attracted her in ways that every woman wanted. An inner excitement filled her as she admitted that if she got to spend every day for the rest of her life in this kitchen with this man, she'd savor every one of them.

Chapter 16

Chris lifted his guitar from its case and stood before the church to lead the congregation in praise songs. Looking out into the crowd, he saw Victoria seated in the second row beside Abby and one of her friends. He had already experienced enough pain in life to know how to praise God in the valleys. A smile tugged at his lips. Now he was learning to praise God on the mountaintops.

He raised his hands. "Stand up and praise the Lord with me." The people stood, and he started to pluck his guitar and lead them in worship.

His heart filled with awe for the Lord as words of love and adoration spilled from the lips of his brothers and sisters in Christ. He looked out and saw Grace and Eric Nichols who had married less than a year before and were taking care of Lizzie and Jake. Unknown to their congregation for several years, Eric had struggled with his past, but God had overcome all their trials.

He glanced at Sondra and Dylan, holding hands as they sang. God had given Sondra a second chance at love and Dylan a wonderful wife. He almost chuckled aloud at the thought of the many Wards he presumed he'd see running around the church building in a few years' time. He saw Mr. and Mrs. Nielson who still attended church every Sunday despite Mr. Nielson's battle with cancer and Mrs. Nielson's arthritis. Even when they had to prematurely turn the furniture business they loved over to their young son, the couple still remained faithful to the Lord.

His gaze traveled to Victoria. With her eyes closed and her face uplifted, he could tell she sang the praises from the depths of her spirit. His heart tightened. A few months ago, he had begged God to rid him of women. *I praise You, Lord, for answering that prayer with a No.*

⚜

"Victoria."

Victoria turned at the sound of Zack's call from behind her. He motioned for her to wait, so she moved away from the exiting congregation and toward a wall. Once he reached her, she smiled. "Hey, Zack."

"Hi. How have you been?"

"Good. And you?"

"Good. We're still missing you at the bank."

Victoria stared at her feet. "Yeah, I miss it, too. I hope my dad's case is settled soon. I'd really like to come back."

"Do you think it will be much longer?"

Victoria shrugged. "As far as I know, no one has heard from my parents. I don't even know where they are."

"I'm sorry about that." Zack shoved one hand in his pants pocket and adjusted his tie with the other. "Victoria, we are friends, right?"

Victoria gazed at him. "Yes. I think so. What's wrong?"

"Well, I have a favor to ask you." He pulled at his collar. Victoria noticed a spot of perspiration on his forehead.

"Zack, what is it?"

He leaned closer to her. "I really don't want anyone to know."

Her curiosity piqued and a giggle formed in her throat at the secretive expression on his face. "Okay."

"I'm trying out for Lawton's community play."

"I didn't know you liked to act." Victoria studied Zack, feeling perplexed at the crush she'd had on him when she'd really known nothing about him.

"Well, it's kind of a closet passion. I've always been interested but too shy to try out."

"Why now?"

Zack stared past her, and Victoria turned to see what he was looking at. A young redhead came out of the ladies' restroom. Her short, springy curls bounced when she walked. She gazed at Zack with ice-blue eyes and then smiled for the briefest of moments.

Victoria chuckled. "Rosa?"

"Shh." Zack put his fingers to her lips. "She's trying out, as well. Look, I've got the script, and I just don't want to fall on my face. I hoped you might rehearse with me."

"You know it's a musical."

"Yes. It's a production of *Oklahoma*."

"That means singing."

"I know."

Victoria lightly punched his arm. "Zack, I didn't know you sang."

"Well, I can't sing as well as Chris, if that's what you're getting at, but hopefully, I'll be able to carry a tune well enough. So will you help me or not?"

Victoria covered her mouth to squelch her laughter. "Of course I will. I'm so happy for you." She gave Zack a quick hug. "So when do you want to meet?"

Chris felt as if someone had punched him in the gut. He had been sure Victoria felt the connection he did. Preparing dinner with her the week before had only confirmed his feelings. Now she was hugging Zack and promising to meet him. *What a fool you are, Ratliff.*

He grabbed the keys from his pocket. Clutching his Bible tighter in his hand, he determined to walk past them without their noticing. Abby came up beside him and touched his arm. "So did you ask her?"

"No." He walked toward the door, willing Abby to take his lead.

"Don't be nervous, Chris. I know she'll say yes."

"I don't intend to ask. . ."

"Victoria!" Abby yelled as she grabbed Chris's arm tighter. With her free hand, she motioned for Victoria to come to them.

Great. Now what do I do? Victoria's whole face lit up with a smile as she walked toward them. "No, Abby. Don't say anything."

Abby grabbed her hands when Victoria reached them. "Guess what? I'm going to the chorus dinner with Tyler."

Victoria's eyes widened, and Chris couldn't help but smile at Victoria's genuine interest in his sister. "You didn't tell me before church."

"I thought Chris was going to tell you."

"Chris?" Victoria frowned and peered over at him.

"Yeah. The school needs chaperones for the dinner, and they asked Chris, and he was going to ask you to go with him." Abby jumped up and down and clapped her hands. "It'll be so much fun."

Victoria gazed up at him. The intensity in her eyes nearly took his breath away. "You were going to ask me to her dinner?"

"Well. . ."

"I think he thought you'd say no, but I told him you wouldn't. I don't know what these guys worry about."

Chris wanted the floor to open up and suck him down into the center of the earth. Humiliation washed over him until he felt sure his entire body had turned the deepest crimson possible.

He exhaled and watched Victoria. She bit her bottom lip, and he could see she was about to laugh. She nodded. "I'd love to go."

Chapter 17

Chris knocked on the Wards' front door. Sondra opened it and smiled. "Hey, Chris."

"Hey. Here's your milk." He handed her two quarts. "I came by to pick up the eggs for By His Hand."

"They were beside the barn, weren't they?"

"Yeah." Chris shoved his hands in his pockets. "I wanted to remind Vic about the dinner tonight, also."

Sondra smiled. "I think she remembers. She had the most beautiful dress dry-cleaned."

Heat warmed his cheeks. He felt like a young high school kid standing on his girl's porch waiting for approval from her parents to come inside. "Well, I was going to make sure she knew I'd be by at six."

Sondra bit her bottom lip, but not before a little giggle escaped. She placed her hand on her hip. "You want to talk to her yourself?"

Chris wanted to growl. He didn't know why Sondra seemed bent on making this so hard. Yes, he wanted to talk with Victoria. The last time he'd spoken with her, she'd been talking about meeting up with Zack.

He wanted to mention the dinner and then gauge her response to see if she just felt sorry for him on behalf of Abby. He could have put his little sister over his knee for the way she practically shamed Victoria into going to the dinner with him, like he was some kind of pity case. Well, he had news for the both of them: He could get a date if he wanted one. He wasn't sure whom he'd get a date with, but he knew he could find one.

"She's around back." Sondra chuckled and then bit her bottom lip a second time. "I'm sure she'd love to see you."

Chris mumbled a thanks under his breath and then strode around the house. He didn't know what Sondra found so funny. Maybe it was the thought of Victoria and him as a couple. Who was he kidding? Sondra was right. They were as opposite as night and day, as oil and water, as Ford and Chevy.

He rounded the corner and saw Victoria leaning all the way over in a patio chair painting her toenails. A blue robe swallowed her, and numerous small curlers stuck out all over her head. She sat up, and her eyes bulged, surrounded by a goopy green mess of gunk that covered her face and neck. "Chris!"

"Hey." A slow smile lifted his lips.

"What are you doing here?" She dropped the nail polish, tightened the robe around her chest, and turned away from him, all in one swift movement.

He laughed then. "I came by to pick up eggs and thought I'd remind you that I'd be here at six tonight for Abby's dinner."

She didn't look at him. "I remembered."

"Good." He eyed her toes and realized the nail polish had fallen and spilled on the patio. "Oops. The nail polish fell." He bent down to pick it up.

Victoria turned and leaned over, as well. His head met hers, and some of the goopy green stuff smashed into his forehead. "Sorry," she squealed and sat up and away from him.

"What is this stuff anyway?" He wiped some off his forehead and smelled it. It had a clean, yet medicinal kind of odor.

"Chris, you're not supposed to see a lady like this."

"Like what?"

Victoria huffed and turned back toward him. She waved her hands up and down. "Like this. I'm getting ready for the dinner." She crossed her arms in front of her chest. "You're not supposed to know it takes"—she crossed her legs—"it takes this much effort to get fixed up."

She turned away from him again. Chris held back his chuckle at her exaggerated dramatics. He didn't want her to be embarrassed. "Okay. I'll leave, but I'll be back at six."

"Okay." She didn't look at him. Chris could hear the uncertainty in her tone.

"Victoria."

"Yes?"

"Look at me."

He waited as she sighed and then slowly turned toward him. Taking her hand in his, he rubbed his coarse thumb against its softness. "You could go in a potato sack, and you'd still be the most beautiful person there."

She contemplated him for a brief moment, and then she smiled. "Thank you, Chris. I'll see you tonight."

⟡

Victoria clasped the strand of pearls around her wrist. Her grandmother's ring would have been a beautiful accent to the matching necklace and bracelet set that Sondra had loaned her. She looked at her naked finger. But she'd never have the opportunity to wear the ring again. When she'd called the pawnshop owner a little over a month after the due date, he'd told her someone else had bought it.

Sighing, she peered into her makeup mirror. *Grams would have loved Chris.* Picking up her coral lipstick, she applied a fresh coat to her lips. She fluffed the curls at the nape of her neck and then lightly sprayed them once more.

The doorbell rang. Glancing at the clock, she knew it was Chris. Allowing

Dylan or Sondra to answer it so that she didn't seem too anxious, she stood and walked in front of the full-length mirror. Her gaze scanned the simple, knee-length, aqua dress that rested perfectly against her shape. The spiked heels that she'd never before had the courage to wear made her legs look long and sleek, and she had to admit she'd never felt so appealing.

A rush of heat flushed her cheeks. *I wish Chris hadn't seen me in a face mask and curlers earlier.* She remembered his sweet words just before he left. Looking in the mirror, she whispered, "Well, I'm definitely not wearing a potato sack." She twirled, allowing the hem of the dress to dance in the air. "I think he'll prefer this."

A soft knock sounded. "Chris is here," said Sondra. "Can I come in?"

"Yeah."

Sondra opened the door. She gasped. "Victoria, you look amazing!"

"Thank you."

"You better get out here before Chris paces a hole into my floor." She hooked her arm with Victoria's. "I've never seen him so nervous."

"That makes two of us."

Victoria walked down the hall and into the living room. Chris looked like the perfect gentleman in a navy blue suit and red silk tie. He looked up. Victoria sucked in her breath as his gaze scanned her briefly. "Hi, Chris. You look nice."

He nodded, and she watched his Adam's apple bop up and down. He stepped toward her. His height and breadth seemed to wrap around her. Touching her chin, he lifted her face until their gazes met. "You look amazing. You're absolutely beautiful, Vic."

She felt her cheeks warm at his sincere compliment and looked away to find Sondra and Dylan watching them. Sondra touched Dylan's arm and then dabbed her eyes as if she were Victoria's mother sending her daughter on her first date. Though much too close to Victoria's age, in a way Sondra had been a maternal figure for Victoria. She'd taught Victoria to cook, to clean, to care for herself. She glanced at PeeWee who had toddled into the room holding his sippy cup in one hand and a toy horse in the other. Sondra had also taught her how to care for others.

"We'd better get going. I'd say the chorus director would like for his chaperones to be on time." Chris touched her arm in a way that made her feel as though she belonged to him, as if he would protect her from anything that could ever happen. She loved the feeling.

"Okay." Allowing Chris to help her wrap her shawl around her shoulders, she then waved good-bye to her family and followed Chris to the front door.

"Close your eyes."

"What?" Victoria turned to find Chris mere inches from her cheek. His gaze seemed to grip hers, and she couldn't help noticing how easy it would be to lightly kiss his lips.

"I have a surprise." His breath raced against her ear, sending a shiver down her back. "Trust me. Just close your eyes."

Trust him. Trust him? She couldn't believe how much she trusted him. If he asked to drive her to an altar this night, she felt confident she would pledge her life to him. She closed her eyes, and he took her hand. The cool October air kissed her face and whipped through her hair. She gripped her shawl tighter with her free hand. Feeling the porch steps beneath her, she held tight to Chris's hand. Once the ground was beneath her feet, she asked, "Can I open them now?"

"Not yet." He stepped beside her, still holding her hand, only now his free hand touched the crook of her back. If only he would take her in his arms and declare his love for her. Surely Prince Charming would have claimed his princess by now, and she wanted so much to live happily ever after with Chris.

She listened as a car door opened. "Okay. You can look."

She opened her eyes. "Oh, Chris." Victoria covered her mouth with her hands. She gazed up at him and touched his arm. "It's Mary Ann."

"Yep." He smiled, and his eyes danced with merriment. "She's fixed. You don't have to worry about her anymore."

She slid inside the Corvette, inhaling the scent of newly cleaned leather. Chris walked around and hopped inside. His frame barely fit inside the small car, but he beamed with excitement as he started the ignition. Buckling her seat belt, Victoria grinned. "I guess I didn't ruin her forever."

Chris gazed at her, his expression honest as a hard day's work. "You didn't ruin anything, my Mary Ann Mangler." He touched her hand, and a wave of pleasure wrapped around her. "You helped me restore a ruined relationship with my sister. That was worth every moment, every cent that went into repairing this old girl's bumper. If anything, I'd say I owe you."

"I'd say we're even. All those rides back and forth from town to the ranch. Getting to spend time with your sister. Feeling a part of a family." She felt her cheeks warm with the slip of the last statement. She looked at Chris, who simply smiled.

Once seated in the auditorium, Chris tapped the inside of his coat. Victoria's grandmother's ring was still nestled safe inside his pocket. He'd decided to follow his heart and ask Victoria to be his wife. Sure, he wanted to date her, but they'd spent so much time together over the last several months that he wanted to date her and plan their wedding at the same time.

He stared at her sitting beside him. The strands of curls that fell softly over her shoulders beckoned him. With every ounce of strength, he gripped the program and willed his fingers to keep to themselves. His gaze followed the slight curve of her jaw, tempting him to kiss his way to her lips.

He squelched a growl and looked away from her. *Besides, I'm not getting any younger.* He smiled as he thought of his twenty-seventh birthday in just a few weeks. In truth, he had plenty of time to date her, but he wanted any excuse he could conjure to make Victoria Thankful become Victoria *Ratliff.*

The concert ended, and a wisp of Victoria's perfume washed over him. He glanced over and found her leaning close. "I'm going to run to the ladies' room," she whispered.

Chris swallowed to keep from grabbing her, pulling her into his lap, and keeping her there for all time. He nodded and watched as she walked away.

"Abby is improving by leaps and bounds." A voice sounded from behind him.

Chris turned to find Mrs. Smith, Abby's music teacher, addressing him. "Yes, she is doing better."

"May I sit for a moment?" The older woman motioned toward Victoria's chair.

"Sure."

Mrs. Smith sat and clasped her hands in her lap. "I had been very worried about Abigail."

Chris bit back a chuckle. He hadn't heard anyone call her that in several years. In fact, the last time he recalled anyone calling her Abigail was when she'd sneaked a snake in the kitchen, nearly scaring their mother to death. Dad had come home and called for her using her full given name in order to come downstairs and receive her discipline.

"Since our father died and our mother left, I didn't know how to handle Abby. Victoria, the lady who's with me tonight, has done a world of good with her."

"Yes, since that lady crashed into your life"—the older woman snorted at her own joke—"she has made quite a difference for both of you. I noticed your car in the parking lot."

"Yep, she's all fixed up."

"That's good. I heard you took Abigail to buy her dress, as well." She smiled. "That was mighty brave of you. I've never been able to get my Bruce into a women's clothing store."

"Victoria made me see how much Abby needed me. How she needed to feel a part of a family. That she had someone she could count on."

Mrs. Smith patted his hand. "You're a good man, Chris Ratliff, with a heart of gold. Any lady would be lucky to have you."

Chapter 18

Any lady would be lucky to have you." Victoria snarled, mimicking the woman's words into her makeup mirror only moments after he had dropped her off after the concert. How dare Chris Ratliff pity her! His comments about her needing to feel part of a family echoed in her mind. She cringed at what she must have missed hearing him say when the waitress dropped and broke a plate beside her while Mrs. Smith and Chris were talking.

"How could I have been so foolish?" She took off her bracelet and placed it on the dresser. Victoria had actually believed she wanted to spend the rest of her life with that man. She snorted. *Yeah, here I've felt as though I've been on trial every day of my life for my daddy's mistakes, but I've always been honest. Mr. Ratliff, however, deserves an award for his ability to completely fool a crowd.* She gazed into her makeup mirror, watching as tears filled her eyes. "All this time, he's just been pitying me."

She thought of the kiss they'd shared in his truck. Goose bumps covered her skin, and she shivered. The connection she'd felt had been so real. Anger erupted inside her at her foolishness.

"What is it that scripture says?" She yanked off a high heel and threw it in the closet. "The heart is deceitful above all things." Pulling off the other, she tossed it in, as well. "And my heart has definitely deceived my mind. To think that I had even considered. . ." she fumed and turned away from the closet.

After taking off the pearl necklace, she slipped out of her dress and into her nightgown. She nestled into her sheets and pulled her Bible and prayer journal from the nightstand drawer. Not feeling completely ready to start her daily reading, she flipped through pages in her journal. Hardly a day had passed since she'd moved into the Wards' ranch that she didn't pray for Chris and Abby. They had become part of her family, in her heart at least.

"Why, God?" She glared at her ceiling. "Why was Chris just playing me? How could he have ever imagined that pretending to care for me would in any way make things better?"

A soft tap sounded on her door. "Vic?" Sondra's voice whispered.

"Yeah. Come on in."

The door opened, and Sondra handed her the phone. "You have a phone call."

"Who is it?"

"I don't know, but I'm going to put Emily to bed, so can you hang it up when you finish?"

"Sure." Victoria took the phone. Assuming it was Chris, she exhaled and braced herself for whatever lie he had to say. "Hello."

"Sugar!"

"Daddy?"

"I'm so glad you're there! Your mother and I just got home. My lawyer's about to prove me innocent. I'm going to be cleared."

"You're. . .what?"

"Yes, and I can hardly wait to see you. When can you come home?"

"But I thought. . ."

"You thought I was guilty, didn't you?"

"I guess I did." Victoria felt a sudden wave of guilt that she hadn't believed in her dad, followed by questions that pummeled her mind. "But you ran off."

"My lawyer's advice."

"And I had a wreck and no insurance."

"I just heard about that today. My policy was about to be renewed right before the charges were filed. Somehow it didn't get paid." He exhaled into the phone. "Oh, honey, I'm so sorry about that. I'm glad you're okay. We'll clear everything up when I get to see you. When can you come home?"

Victoria's mind raced. "I don't know." She thought of her chance to get her job back now that her dad was about to be found innocent. She thought of PeeWee and Emily. If she left, she didn't know when she'd see them again. And Abby. "Let me figure some stuff out, and I'll call you tomorrow."

"It's so good to hear your voice, sugar. I hated leaving like that." He exhaled again. "There's just so much to explain. . .in person." Her dad's tone was softer than she'd ever heard it. "And new things I want to share, as well."

"Yes, we do need to talk." Her heart burned with renewed feelings of the desertion she had experienced when she had awakened that morning several months before to find her parents gone.

A remembrance of trepidation washed over her and mixed with the twinge of excitement she felt at seeing her nephew and starting a new life on her own. Her head started to throb at the decisions she'd have to make, questions she needed answered. Her eyelid on one side began to twitch, a telltale sign of an oncoming stress migraine. She needed to go to bed, to not think for the moment. Chris. . .Abby. . .Daddy—it was too much. "I'll call you in the morning?"

"I love you."

Victoria was taken aback by her father's declaration. She hadn't heard those words from him in years. "I love you, too, Daddy."

She hung up the phone and looked down at her prayer journal. She'd come to the day when she'd read about how God has a time for everything. Closing her eyes, she begged God for guidance. Maybe the time had come for her to go home. . .to her parents. She could hear the tenderness in her father's voice.

Maybe he had softened in other ways, as well. Maybe he would finally listen to her about his need for the Lord.

Her eyelid twitched more steadily, and heaviness rested on the top of her head. *I'm going to be sick if I don't go to sleep.*

She turned off the light, closed her eyes, and nestled into her covers. "God, it seems You've taken care of my life once again. The time has come for me to go home, to be a witness to Mother and Daddy."

Chris took the box from his inside jacket pocket. He had planned to give Victoria the ring, but the evening just didn't seem to finish as he had hoped. When she'd returned from the restroom, Victoria seemed frustrated. She said something she ate must have disagreed with her, which he believed because his stomach had been in knots the whole night, as well.

"Didn't get to pop the question, huh, big brother?"

Chris turned to find Abby leaning against his bedroom door. She was a beautiful sight, all dressed up in her black gown with her hair all wrapped up on the top of her head and little curls hanging down all around. Makeup, no longer caked on her face, seemed to bring out the brightness in her eyes. Thanks to the patience and persistence and advice from Victoria, his little sister had grown up.

He shoved the box into his dresser drawer. "What are you talking about?"

Abby crossed her arms in front of her chest and grinned. "Come on, Chris. You are *way* too obvious. I knew you were getting ready to pop the question."

He smiled and leaned against the dresser. "Smart girl. You're right." He sighed and loosened his tie. "Didn't happen as I'd hoped."

"She'll say yes."

"You think so?"

Abby nodded. "Oh yeah. She loves you. She just doesn't fully realize it yet."

Chris took off his jacket. "I guess we'll have to wait and see." He turned back toward Abby. "But enough of that. How was your night?"

Abby giggled. "Wonderful. I think I really like Tyler."

"You do?"

"Yeah. He, like, pulled out my chair and everything. Really made me feel special." She shrugged. "I thought I liked Austin, but I don't know if he would have been as worried about me and what I was needing as Tyler was. In fact, did you see Austin?"

Chris shook his head. He wasn't sure if he'd seen anyone but Victoria tonight.

"He was flirting with Kelly the whole time Mallory was in the bathroom. I felt so bad for Mallory. I would have died if he'd done that to me. I'm glad he broke off our date."

Chris nodded. "Me, too."

Abby cocked her head and smiled. "I'm really glad we're friends again."

Chris walked over to her and wrapped her in a hug. "Me, too, little sis."

"How 'bout a game of Monopoly?" she mumbled into his chest.

Chris remembered the times he and Abby had set the game up on the dinner table and played for hours. He had always let her beat him.

"This time I'll beat you on my own," she added.

He released her. "What?"

"That's right." She smiled. "I knew you let me win, but I'm a big girl now. I'll whip you all by myself."

Chris chuckled. "You're on."

<hr/>

"Daddy, Mother, what are you doing here?" Victoria opened the front door wide.

Her father grabbed her in a hug and twirled her around. "I could hardly wait to get here." He put her back on her feet. "We just had to get up here to see our grandson."

"Grandson?"

Sondra walked up to them holding PeeWee on her hip. He buried his face in her cheek and clung to her neck. A slow, somewhat hesitant smile split her lips. "Hello, Thomas and Ethel. It's good to formally meet you."

Victoria raised her eyebrows and looked from her sister-in-law to her parents. "Sondra, did you know they were coming?"

"We knew." Dylan's deep voice resounded from the hall. He walked toward them, holding Emily in one arm. He smiled and nodded his head toward her parents. "We're happy to have you in our home."

Victoria watched as her parents greeted Sondra and Dylan. Daddy seemed downright giddy to get to know them. He sneaked little tickles at PeeWee's sides and talked about cattle and ranching with Dylan. He even asked Sondra about her chick ministry. Mother proved much more hesitant. Polite. Proper. But hesitant. She held PeeWee for a moment, but when he started to play with the diamond pendant around her neck, she handed him back to Sondra.

"I can't believe you're here." Victoria took PeeWee in her arms when Sondra and Dylan announced they would get some refreshments for the family.

"Yes, well, it seems your father's had a change of heart these days," her mother murmured as she opened her purse and took out her compact.

Curiosity sped through Victoria's veins. Her father had changed. She could see it in his eyes, in his smile. It was in his countenance, in the way he spoke and carried himself. *Oh, precious Jesus, could it be?*

"It seems your father has found the Lord." Her mother rolled her eyes and stared into her small mirror.

"Daddy?" Victoria gawked at her father, praying he would say what she hoped.

He smiled. "Your mother's right. I've found the Lord."

"Oh, Daddy!" Victoria stood and hugged her father again. "I'm so happy for you! How? When? What happened?"

He leaned forward in his chair. "When my lawyer called and said I needed to leave the country because I was being accused of embezzlement, I was stunned. I couldn't even move from my desk for several moments. My world was crumbling around me, and I could feel it. Every thought, every action I'd had in my life seemed to pass before me."

He clasped his hands. "All I could think about was his suggestion to leave you, my only living child. He said if I took you with me, people would believe you were guilty. I couldn't bear the thought of it."

"I'd already lost your brother." He stood and paced the floor. "How could I leave my baby girl, as well?" He stepped in front of her and touched a strand of her hair. "Then, for some reason, my childhood invaded my mind. Over and over again, I was in church with your grandma. The preacher's sermons about God's love, His grace, His mercy, His restoration kept running through my mind."

"Oh, Daddy." Victoria touched his hand.

He squeezed it tight. "When I got to the Cayman Islands, I sought out the first preacher I could find. Your mom thought I was nuts...."

"Still think you're nuts," her mother murmured as she applied a fresh coat of lipstick to her mouth.

He chuckled. "But I had to know. Had to find out. Had to experience God's love. He showed me, honey. That preacher opened his Bible and showed me scriptures I'd long forgotten." Her daddy raked his fingers through his thinning hair and then swiped his hand over his tear-filled eyes.

"God was faithful and merciful to this old man. I got down on my knees and begged Jesus for forgiveness. I never embezzled money, but I sure did steal time from my wife, my son, and my little girl. And I lost all this time with my little grandson."

He nodded toward the kitchen. "I'm just thankful that Sondra and Dylan are willing to allow us to get to know him now."

Victoria wiped her own tear-filled eyes. She would have never imagined God would work things out so perfectly. "Daddy, I'm so happy, and I'm so glad you came."

"Me, too, sugar. And after we stay and visit a day or two, we'll all go home together."

Chris shut the door and kicked off his work boots. He'd been at the shop since before dawn, and the sun had descended into the ground some two hours before he made it home. He rubbed the back of his neck while he moved his head from side to side in an attempt to work out some of the crick that seemed to linger from the day before. The way he felt, he might have to bypass dinner and simply hit the sack.

"Chris, we have a guest." Abby's voice sounded quiet, winsome.

"A guest?" Chris walked into the kitchen and saw Abby holding Sassy-Girl close to her chest. An older, gray-haired woman sat across from her. With some difficulty, the woman placed her hand on the table and tried to stand.

"Please, you can sit." Chris walked over to her and offered his hand. "I'm Chris Ratliff. I don't think we've met."

She shook his hand. "I'm Junie Osborne. I'm glad to meet you."

"She was one of Mama's teachers when she was a girl," said Abby.

Chris frowned. "I'm sorry, Ms. Osborne. We haven't seen our mother..."

"Mama was living with Ms. Osborne."

"What?" Chris fell into the chair beside the aged woman. "Where is Mama?"

The woman took off her oversized glasses and placed them on the table. A small tear traced her cheek. She wiped it away. "I'm so sorry. I had to come and tell you in person." She paused. "I'm afraid your mother has passed away."

Chris felt as if he'd been struck. He leaned back in his chair and swallowed the knot in his throat. He looked at Abby, who'd covered her face with a tissue. He pulled her, chair and all, over to him and wrapped his arms around her.

"You may not have known, but your mother had diabetes."

"We knew." Chris fought the eruption within him. Anger. Hurt. Sadness.

"About a year ago, Winnie showed up at my house. She was such a fragile thing, mourning her husband's death. I was happy to have her stay with me." The woman sighed. "I had a time getting your mother to take all her medication. I tried to convince her she'd feel better if she would take her depression medicine."

"Mama took medicine for depression?" Abby looked up at Chris.

"Yeah. Sometimes it's a symptom of diabetes, and Mama always struggled." Chris looked at Ms. Osborne. "Daddy used to have to coax her to take it. She'd feel better sometimes and wouldn't want it."

The woman nodded. "Yes, I'm sure that's true. Once I couldn't get her to take the depression medicine anymore, she gave up on eating right. Her diabetes was beginning to really affect her sight and her feet. She had another appointment to see my doctor the day..." The woman's voice caught. She stopped and took a tissue from her purse. "I'm sorry. I wanted so much to be strong for you, to make it easier to tell you."

"Go ahead." Chris held tightly to Abby. He'd allowed her to hurt alone once, but he wouldn't do it again.

"She slipped into a diabetic coma. The paramedics rushed her to the hospital, but she never woke from it." Ms. Osborne shook her head and touched Chris's hand. "I'm sorry I didn't contact you sooner. I didn't know..."

"She didn't tell you about us." *How could she? How could she care so little about us that in a year she never mentioned her own children?*

"She told me you were her relations. She had pictures of you all over her room. She kissed you good night every day. Without her medicine, she couldn't fight her depression."

"But how could she not tell you about us?" cried Abby.

"Listen, honey." Ms. Osborne leaned forward. "Your mama talked about you both constantly. She loved you. She just couldn't see clearly."

A knock sounded on the door. Chris stood.

"It's my cab."

"Your cab?" Chris looked at Ms. Osborne. She stood slowly and grabbed the cane that rested against the table.

"Here's my address." She handed Chris a slip of paper. "You come and get your mother's things whenever you and your sister are ready."

"Ma'am, you don't need a cab. I will be happy to take you—"

She touched his arm. "Stay with your sister. She needs you." Patting him, she added, "In the best way she knew how, your mother loved you both."

Chris nodded and helped her to the door. He watched as she and the driver walked to the cab and got inside. She was the only link he'd had to his mother in over a year. He'd never met the woman before, and she told him he'd never see his mother again.

"Deep down, I think I always knew Mama was depressed."

He nodded and allowed his heart to tender, to hurt, if for nothing else, for his sister. "Her diabetes was really bad, Abby."

"I know. But how could she not call us? How could she just up and die like that?" Abby cried. The finality of his mother's life began to sink into his heart. "Do you think she loved us?" whispered Abby.

Chris remembered Mama fixing cupcakes for them each year on their birthdays. He thought about how she always had one item that each member of the family liked for supper every single night. He remembered how she planted a specific flower for each of them in the garden each year. There were several things she did special for her family. "Yes, I think Ms. Osborne is right. She loved us."

Abby chuckled. "Remember how she used to sing 'Jesus Loves Me' at the top of her lungs in the shower?"

"I remember."

Abby wrapped her arms around his waist. "Mama had a beautiful voice."

"Yes, she did."

"I'm going to miss her." She tightened her hold. "But at least we know where she is."

Chris exhaled. *Thank You, God, for telling us. Now we can heal, and Mama has been made whole with You.* "Yes, we do."

Chapter 19

Victoria pulled her Suburban into the street parking space. She grabbed her purse and the picnic basket and walked toward Lawton's community park. The warmer-than-usual November air whipped through her hair. Despite the higher temperature, Victoria could feel the oncoming of cooler weather. The leaves, a mixture of red and golden hues, were also proof of it.

Three days had passed since the chorus concert, and she hadn't spoken to Chris. She had decided to go home with her parents the following day. Dylan, Sondra, and even Zack had tried to talk her into staying, but she knew she couldn't. Her heart belonged to Chris, and she had to get over him.

Abby. She dreaded telling her young friend of her plan to leave. Victoria's love for Abby was every bit as strong as if the girl had been born into her own family. Hoping Chris would still be at the shop, Victoria planned to drive by their house and talk to Abby before going back to the ranch. *God, You'll have to walk me through that conversation.*

Shaking her head, she determined to ponder that later in the day. For now, she needed to find Zack. Peering around the park, she spied him already sitting on the bench with his script and a cooler of drinks. He waved, and she picked up her pace.

She had been surprised at what a wonderful actor and singer Zack proved to be. He had really taken the community play seriously, and she had a feeling, come this weekend when he was able to try out, that Zack would have the lead male part in Lawton's version of *Oklahoma*.

"Hi, Zack." She lifted the picnic basket a little higher. "Do you want to eat first or practice first?"

"I'm starving. How 'bout we eat first?"

She opened the basket and pulled out some paper plates and napkins. "Sounds like a plan to me. I brought homemade chicken salad sandwiches, compliments of Sondra, a bag of chips, carrot sticks, and some yummy brownies, made especially for us by PeeWee and yours truly."

"Mmm. Delicious. And I brought some drinks." He opened the cooler. "I think I got the easy end of this deal."

"Don't you worry about that. PeeWee and I had a blast putting this basket together. Emily even joined in and threw a few carrot sticks at us."

Zack sobered. "It's going to be hard to leave them, huh?"

"Unbelievably. I don't know how I will do it." Victoria placed the sandwiches on the plates and then opened the bag of chips. She grabbed one and popped it into her mouth, willing herself not to envision driving away from her new family. "My parents and I are leaving tomorrow. I've already packed."

"I haven't heard anything about your dad's case on the TV."

"It's not been finalized in court. But soon."

"It all happened so fast. Their coming back. Your dad's change of heart. Your leaving."

Fast didn't even begin to describe it. Victoria felt as if she'd been caught up in a whirlwind. She'd been praying for God's guidance, but everything seemed to be coming at her quicker than she could be sure of His answers.

"I know. I could hardly believe it. And he and Mother are finally getting the chance to meet their grandson. Once they saw PeeWee, they couldn't deny he was Kenny's." She bit into her sandwich and then took a drink. "And Dylan has been amazing about letting them stay. He's a truly wonderful man." She smacked her leg. "But enough about me. How is Rosa?"

He smiled. "Beautiful."

Victoria giggled. "Have you talked to her yet?"

"No."

"When do you plan on it?"

"I don't know that I'll ever get up the nerve."

"Sure you will. Tryouts are this weekend. Talk to her then."

Zack dipped his head and played with his napkin. "I'll try."

"You'd better, because I'm coming back for the play, and you'd better be dating Rosa by then."

Zack smiled again. "I hope so."

Victoria stood up. "Ya ready to practice?"

"Ready as ever."

Chris splashed some cologne on his chest. It had been three full days since he'd seen or talked to Victoria. Every vehicle in Lawton had decided to break down in some form or fashion. He'd been working sixteen-hour days, but all he could think of was when he could see her again.

He grabbed his tie and put it around his neck. He'd called the ranch to see if Victoria would spend the day with him. Sondra had told him she'd gone to the park to rehearse for Lawton's community play. *I didn't even know Victoria acted.* There was still so much to learn about each other, and he longed to spend every single day of the rest of his life learning every facet of Victoria Thankful's personality.

Opening his dresser drawer, he picked up the small black box tucked away inside. He popped the top and gazed at the small ring. Knowing it had meant so much to Victoria, he couldn't wait to see her face when he presented it to her. He shut it and placed it in his pants pocket. Sliding into his coat jacket, he grabbed his keys.

"Today's the day?"

Chris peered back at his sister. "Yep."

She walked over to him and adjusted his tie. "You look very nice."

"Thanks."

"I can't wait to have a big sister."

Chris smiled. "I can't wait for you to have one either." He leaned down and kissed Abby on the cheek and then walked out the door.

The park will be a beautiful place to propose, and it's such a nice day. He stopped at the florist's shop and picked up a dozen red roses. He envisioned her sitting on the park bench reading the lines of the play. Her long hair whipping in the wind. He could almost smell her sweet scent and feel the softness of her cheek. He would take her hand in his, get down on one knee, and declare his love for her.

Turning onto the park's street, he saw her Suburban, and his heart raced. He experienced a mixture of excitement and nerves. Pulling Mary Ann into the space behind her vehicle, he closed his eyes and offered a quick prayer to the Lord for courage. As he reached for the roses, he realized his hands had grown clammy, so he wiped them on his pants legs. Exhaling a slow breath to calm his nerves, he grabbed the flowers and opened the door.

A smile split his lips as a song of praise filled his mind. He'd never been so excited, so sure of a decision in his life. He could hardly wait to make her his wife, to take her into his arms, to kiss her as a man kisses his wife. With purpose, he walked into the park.

He saw her.

He gasped.

Zack Bradshaw knelt before her. He held one of her hands in his.

Chris's heart dropped as Victoria nodded.

Chapter 20

Disillusioned, Chris turned away. *I don't think they saw me.* He couldn't bear the thought of speaking to either one of them. How could he have been so wrong, so stupid? He didn't even know Zack and Victoria had spent any real time together. *Well, she had hugged him at church, agreeing to meet him somewhere.*

His heart thudded against his chest. Then why had she gone with him to the chorus dinner? To appease Abby, he supposed. But why had she kissed him in his truck? Why? *God, I love her. I was so sure she was the right one for me.*

A sudden fury filled his gut as he envisioned Zack holding Victoria in his arms. He couldn't bear the thought of it. He wouldn't bear the thought of it. He loved Victoria, and he was willing to fight for her. Turning on his heels, he bounded back up the sidewalk toward the woman he had every intention of spending the rest of his life with. "Victoria," he called.

She turned toward him. "Chris?"

Chris closed the last few steps between them, threw the roses to the ground, and took her hands into his. He looked at Zack. "I like you, Zack, but I have to do this." He gazed back at Victoria. "I can't stand by and let this happen. You cannot marry Zack." He pointed to his chest. "I love you. I want you to be my wife."

"What?"

"And I won't take no for an answer. I don't know what has happened here. I didn't even know you and Zack were spending time together, but I'm willing to do whatever I need to, to show you that I am the right man for you."

Zack started to laugh. Chris glared at him. "This is not funny."

He covered his mouth and hunkered down. "I'm sorry," he mumbled. Grabbing the cooler, he added, "I think I'll leave now."

Chris snorted and peered back at Victoria. "See there. The slightest bit of opposition comes his way, and Zack is hitting the high road."

Victoria crossed her arms in front of her chest and stomped her foot. "You are making no sense. What are you talking about, Chris Ratliff?"

He grabbed her arms. "I'm saying I won't let you marry Zack. I love you. I want you to be my wife."

Victoria frowned. "Why would you think I'm marrying Zack? I'm not marrying Zack. We're friends."

"But. . ." Chris released her arms. "But he just asked you to marry him, and you nodded yes."

Victoria shook her head. "No, he didn't."

"Yes, he did. I saw it."

Victoria's mouth opened in a perfect O, and she covered her lips with her hand. A small giggle escaped. "We were practicing the play."

"The play?"

"The community play. Zack is trying out and asked me to help with his lines."

"I thought you were trying out."

Victoria shook her head. "No, I was helping him. Where would you ever get the notion that I was trying out?"

Heat raced up Chris's spine into his neck and to his cheeks. "So you didn't just accept a proposal from Zack?"

"Nope. In fact, Zack's got a bit of a crush on Rosa from church."

"He does?"

She nodded.

"I guess I've made a big ol' fool of myself then."

Victoria nodded again, and Chris bent down and picked up the roses. He tried to straighten them out a bit and then extended them toward Victoria. "Can I try again?"

Sighing, Victoria stepped away from him. "I don't want your pity, Chris."

"My pity?"

"Yes. I heard what you said to Abby's teacher."

He scratched his head. "Now *I* don't have a clue what *you* are talking about."

"I heard you the night of the chorus dinner." She crossed her arms in front of her chest. "I heard you say that I just needed to feel a part of a family." She opened her arms wide. "Well, you know what, Chris Ratliff? I did feel a part of your family. I wanted to be a part of your family, but not out of pity." She turned away from him. "Never out of pity."

Chris tried to recall what Victoria was talking about. Then he remembered Mrs. Smith talking to him about Abby. He smiled and touched Victoria's arm. She flinched. "Vic, I wasn't talking about you. Mrs. Smith and I were talking about Abby. I said that Abby needed to feel a part of a family." He walked around her so that he could face her. "I told her you had made us like a family again."

Victoria peeked up at him. "You did?"

He nodded and touched her cheek. "I think we're both a little goofy." He caressed her skin with his thumb. "Victoria, I love you."

"Promise?"

The sincerity, the sweet honesty that shone through her eyes never ceased to nearly unravel him. He could read her wants and her desires so perfectly in her gaze. "Oh, Vic." He ran the back of his hand down her cheek and jaw. When she closed her eyes, he traced her lips with his index finger. "I promise."

She opened her eyes and wrapped her arms around him. She kissed his lips quickly. "Oh, Chris, I love you, too. I've been miserable these last few days. So much has happened that I want to share with you."

"I've been so busy, and I have so much to tell, as well." He stuck his hand in his pocket and pulled out the black box. Getting on one knee, he took her hand in his. "But I want to spend every day of the rest of my life hearing everything you want to share with me."

He opened the box, and Victoria gasped and placed her hand on her chest. "My grandma's ring. I thought it was gone forever."

"I made a deal with the pawnshop owner. If you weren't able to purchase it before the time was up, I'd buy it. I did, and I hoped, knowing how much it meant to you, that you would want to wear it as my wife."

Joy surged through her as if she'd been struck by lightning. "I had always hoped to wear it. Oh, Chris." She jumped into his lap, almost knocking him to the ground. "Of course I'll marry you."

<hr style="width:15%" />

Victoria took a quick bite of the cream cheese–covered bagel Sondra had brought from the ranch. If she didn't stop eating, she'd never be able to squeeze into the bodice-fitted dress she and her mother had picked out. "I think I'm weird."

Sondra furrowed her eyebrows. "Weird?"

Victoria nodded. "How many brides do you know who can't *stop* eating on their wedding day?"

Sondra laughed and rubbed her blossoming belly. "Weirder things have happened. Try having three kids in a little over three years!"

Emily toddled toward her mother and wrapped her arms around Sondra's leg. Her little bit of light brown hair had been coaxed up into the tiniest pony-tail Victoria had ever seen. Victoria bent down and tightened the satin bow at Emily's tummy. "You look like a little princess."

"Well, what do you think, sis?"

Victoria turned at the sound of Abby's voice behind her. She gasped and stood to her full height. Drinking in her soon-to-be sister-in-law's long, dark curls swooped up and away from her face but down her back, Victoria could hardly believe the perfect fit of the light green satin gown that streamed down her shape. "You're the most beautiful maid of honor I've ever seen."

"I agree." Ethel tousled a few of Abby's curls.

Victoria bit back the spilling of emotion that threatened at the tenderness between her mother and Abby. Though her mother hadn't made a commitment to Christ yet, the embezzlement scare had frightened her enough that she was valuing her time with Victoria as well as taking Abby under her wing as a second daughter. Victoria was sure it was just a matter of time before her mother also recognized her own need for a Savior.

"Lizzie's ready, as well." Grace walked into their makeshift dressing room that was actually one of the Sunday school classes. She placed her hand in the small of her back and stretched. "I wouldn't mind if this baby decided to come right this minute." Her cell phone started to ring. Pulling it out of her purse, she looked at the caller ID and shook her head. "Eric Nichols is the biggest mother hen I know. I better get on out there before he comes looking for me."

Emily released her mom and ran for Lizzie. She grabbed the older girl's hand and swung it back and forth. Victoria smiled. "You two are the prettiest flower girls ever."

"Definitely. Now I think we'd better be getting you into your dress," said Ethel.

Abby agreed. "Yep. My brother will be beating down this door if you're not down at that altar when you're supposed to be."

Victoria bit back a chuckle, as she believed Abby to be exactly right. Slipping into her dress, she inhaled, wishing she'd eaten one less bagel as her mom fastened each clasp. With a final once-over, her mother hugged her and then left to go to her place at the back of the church to await one of the ushers to escort her to her seat.

"You ready?" Her daddy's voice sounded from outside the door.

"Yes." She opened it and watched as her father's eyes glazed.

"Oh, honey, you're beautiful."

Victoria felt her own eyes mist, and she swatted her hands in front of her face. "Daddy, don't make me cry. My makeup will smear, and my freckles will pop out."

He placed her hand into the crook of his arm. "Your freckles are beautiful."

She allowed him to guide her to the back of the church. She tried to see Chris through the crack of the door but couldn't. Instead she sneaked peeks of Abby, Sondra, Lizzie, and Emily as they started their descents down the aisle. Finally, it was her turn. The doors were opened wide, and she saw the altar. . .and Chris!

His eyes widened, and a smile split his lips. Her heart fluttered, and even from a distance, he made her feel as if she were the most special woman in the world. The aisle seemed too long. Her dad moved too slowly. She wanted to be beside the man she loved. She could hardly wait to say her vows and have Chris take her into his arms as his one and only.

"Aunt Vic's pretty."

Her sweet nephew's voice echoed through the church. Among the laughter, Victoria skimmed the crowd and saw Zack and Rosa holding hands in a middle row. She grinned and then gazed at PeeWee. He stood tall and proud beside the only daddy he'd ever known.

His face lit up with pure happiness, and Victoria had never been so thankful that God had allowed a tragedy to be the biggest blessing He had ever bestowed. Not only had she become a part of a family in Lasso but one with her own parents, as well.

Closing the distance between them, Chris took her hand in his. The coarseness of his palm scratched hers, and she relished the feel of it. Her man worked hard, completely, and with integrity. He loved the same way.

She gazed up at him and noted her burly fellow's eyes glistened with the threat of tears. He leaned over and whispered, "You're beautiful, my Mary Ann Mangler."

She smiled. "I love you."

"I love you." His gaze spoke of his commitment and yearning.

They turned and faced the pastor. *There is a time for everything*, God's Word spoke to her heart, *and a season for every activity....* Victoria thought of all the seasons of life she'd weathered this year—the alleged embezzlement, the wreck, her first job, PeeWee, Abby...and Chris. *Maybe God will use me to help.* Chris's words from the night of their first kiss ran through her mind.

And He had. Chris had shown her patience when precious treasures were damaged, he'd shown her strength when people in their lives were tough, and he'd shown her love, even when he thought it wouldn't be returned. God had used Chris, and Victoria longed to see what God would show them for the rest of their lives together.

They turned to face each other to recite their vows. Chris leaned over and whispered, "I've never felt so blessed."

Victoria gazed up at him. "By His hand...neither have I."

JENNIFER JOHNSON

Jennifer and her unbelievably supportive husband, Albert, are happily married and raising Brooke, Hayley, and Allie, the three cutest young ladies on the planet. Besides being a middle school teacher, Jennifer loves to read, write, and chauffeur her girls. She is a member of American Christian Fiction Writers. Blessed beyond measure, Jennifer hopes to always think like a child—bigger than imaginable and with complete faith. Send her a note at jenwrites4god@bellsouth.net.

A Letter to Our Readers

Dear Readers:

In order that we might better contribute to your reading enjoyment, we would appreciate your taking a few minutes to respond to the following questions. When completed, please return to the following: Fiction Editor, Barbour Publishing, Inc., P.O. Box 719, Uhrichsville, OH 44683.

1. Did you enjoy reading *Oklahoma Weddings*?
   ❑ Very much—I would like to see more books like this.
   ❑ Moderately—I would have enjoyed it more if _____

   _____

   _____

2. What influenced your decision to purchase this book?
   (Check those that apply.)
   ❑ Cover   ❑ Back cover copy   ❑ Title   ❑ Price
   ❑ Friends   ❑ Publicity   ❑ Other

3. Which story was your favorite?
   ❑ *In His Will*   ❑ *By His Hand*
   ❑ *Through His Grace*

4. Please check your age range:
   ❑ Under 18   ❑ 18–24   ❑ 25–34
   ❑ 35–45   ❑ 46–55   ❑ Over 55

5. How many hours per week do you read? _____

Name _____

Occupation _____

Address _____

City_____ State _____ Zip _____

E-mail_____